The years of Oraeyn's short rule have been peaceful, but now ominous nightmares plague his sleep and cling to him during his waking hours. When two of his most trusted advisors disappear without a trace and not even the power of dragons can locate them, the fell promise of the king's nightmares becomes reality.

From the furthest reaches of the world, an ancient enemy stirs. Stretching beyond his crumbling prison walls, this foe seeks to bring life to the darkest of shadows. His army marches towards Aom-igh with deadly intent, threatening all Oraeyn holds dear.

Aided by dragons, and with the warrior Brant and Princess Kamarie at his side, Oraeyn must journey into the wilds of a forgotten realm. Trusting in the wisdom and skill of the enigmatic minstrel, Kiernan Kane, the companions race against time in search of Yorien's Hand, a relic that may hold the power to save them all.

The Minstrel's Song

YORIEN'S HAND

BOOK THREE OF
"THE MINSTREL'S SONG"

JENELLE LEANNE SCHMIDT

Published by Stormcave
www.jenelleschmidt.com

YORIEN'S HAND

Printed in the United States of America

ISBN-13: 978-1517076368

Book design by Jenelle Schmidt

Cover art by Angelina Walker

For everyone who asked for more.

ACKNOWLEDGMENTS

Writing a book is not an endeavor I ever complete in isolation. I could not bring any of these stories to completion without the fantastic family and team that surrounds me on a daily basis. As such, there are a few people I would like to thank personally:

Derek, my amazing and supportive husband. Thank you for everything you do to encourage my authoring aspirations. Thank you for the web-designing, mapmaking, brainstorming sessions, and all the ideas you so freely give. One of these days, I really should give you the co-writing credit you deserve!

James and Nancy, my fantastic editors. Thank you for all the hard work and effort you put into this book. I am so grateful for editors who not only love my writing, but also see the potential in the rough drafts and are committed to making sure my stories shine as brightly as they are able.

Angelina, my incredibly talented cover artist. Thank you for the beautiful cover and for persevering in the face of some bumps in the road. I love this painting and I love your artwork. This cover may be my favorite so far (though I love them all very dearly). Thank you.

Ally and DJ, my awesome beta readers. For your thoroughness and attention to detail. Really, you two put so much effort into your notes that you deserve to be credited more as editors than beta readers. I cannot thank you enough for all your comments, critiques, and encouragement. I know this story is better because of your suggestions.

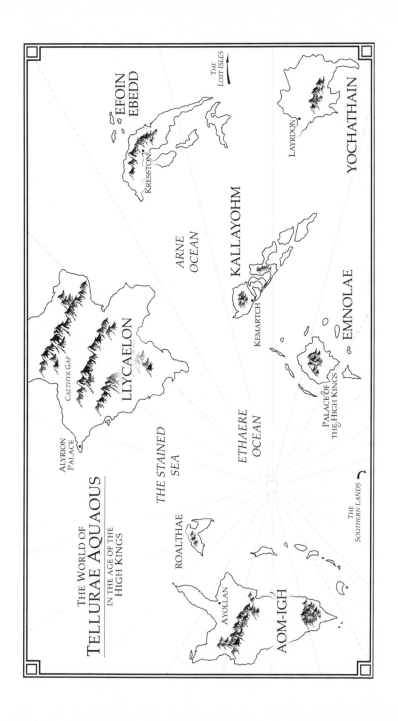

THE WORLD OF
TELLURAE AQUAOUS
IN THE AGE OF THE
HIGH KINGS

THE LOST ISLES

EFOIN EBEDD

KRESSTON

YOCHATHAIN

LAYRDON

ARNE OCEAN

KALLAYOHM

KEMARTCH

EMNOLAE

CAETHYR GAP

LLYCAELON

ALYRION PALACE

THE STAINED SEA

ETHAERE OCEAN

PALACE OF THE HIGH KINGS

ROALTHAE

THE SOUTHERN LANDS

AYOLLAN

AOM-IGH

PROLOGUE

Oraeyn sat on the shore and gazed up at the stars. The heat of the day had long since fled though the air and the sand beneath him still held a certain warmth. A cool breeze wafted pleasantly across his face, whispering promises of adventure and rest in equal strength. The gentle rustle of the waves washed up to meet the shore in a steady rhythm. On the horizon, the Toreth rose: a large, silver disc that hovered over the water like a glimmering beacon. It beckoned him though he knew not where it might lead. His head ached, though he had removed his crown before leaving the palace to wander along the shores of his kingdom.

His kingdom. Ayollan. It still felt surreal. The oaths he had sworn that morning before many of his countrymen weighed heavily upon him; they wrapped him in their solemnity and the responsibility for which he was now solely accountable. It was the weight of those oaths he now bore, not the remembered insignificant pressure of the crown he was as yet unaccustomed to wearing.

It had been nearly a year since King Arnaud announced his intent to abdicate the throne and proclaimed Oraeyn as his chosen successor. In that time, Oraeyn went from an orphaned squire, toiling towards knighthood in relative obscurity, to a direct descendant of one of the greatest kings Aom-igh had ever known. Since learning all this, Oraeyn had followed King Arnaud constantly: observing how to run a kingdom, how to interact with the members of his staff, who his greatest supporters would be, and who might try to cause trouble. The work was grueling, but it satisfied the deepest corners of his soul.

There were moments when Oraeyn was not sure he believed any of it. But the proof hung at his side. The Fang Blade, a weapon from an ancient era, passed down to him as though King Llian himself had reached a hand through time and bequeathed him the sword. Though the weapon could be wielded by any who grasped its hilt, it had lain for centuries in its hiding place, protected from falling into the wrong hands. The wizard Scelwhyn secreted the sword deep in the heart of the Mountains of Dusk and woven an enchantment around it that could only be broken by one of Llian's direct descendants.

Oraeyn's hand rested lightly on the hilt of the sword. He had found it by accident. He could have lived his entire life and never gone close enough to its resting place to hear the call. It was unfathomable how such a small event could change the course of his life forever. And now, today, he was king. It was a position he never would have sought, a responsibility he never desired to shoulder.

Thankfully, he was blessed with excellent mentors. Arnaud, former king of Aom-igh, had become like a father to him. And then there was Brant. Former King's Warrior and champion of Aom-igh, he was the man Oraeyn looked up to the most. One year ago, in the same journey which brought Oraeyn to claim the Fang Blade, he had also met Brant. He and Princess Kamarie had been sent to find the man and request his aid against the invasion from the Dark Country: Llycaelon.

At the end of that encounter, it was revealed that Brant originally came from Llycaelon, and was by rights a prince. Though the throne was rightfully his, Brant declined to rule, instead making certain that the crown passed to his young nephew, Jemson. Jemson's youth was a concern to many of his people. At twenty-three years, he was the same age as Oraeyn, but people in Llycaelon aged differently than people in the rest of the world, and so Jemson was considered in many ways to still be a child. Because of this, Brant's time was now divided between both countries as he traveled back and forth acting as counselor to both young kings, and liaison for the newly formed and fragile alliance between these two great nations.

Heaving a deep, heavy sigh, Oraeyn lay down in the sand and stared up at the stars. It had been a long, long day, and more long days stretched out before him without end. He only hoped he was up to the challenge.

Far away, deep beneath the earth in his prison, an ancient power shuddered. For centuries had he lain in wait, biding his time, conserving his strength. At long last, his patience had paid off; there were cracks in his prison once more. He would be more careful this time, he would reserve his strength. But he would also have to be wary. His enemy was vigilant.

Stretching out through one of the fractures in his prison, he sought a new host. He had done this before, many times. Subtly, quietly, he offered his power to the mere mortal, and promised greatness he did not intend to ever bestow.

A jolt of triumph surged through him as he wove his own power into his new host's body. This time, it would be different. This time, he would find a way to break free from his cell, and then he would never be chained again. He would be king, lord, and master, as he was always meant to be, and not even his ancient enemy could stop him from achieving his goal. Not this time.

CHAPTER
ONE

On the other side of the world from where Oraeyn sat contemplating his life, an army of were-folk marched out from the Eastern Isles upon its long campaign. They swarmed onto the beaches of Yochathain. Delicate Yochathain, jewel of the world, untouched for centuries by conflict or war, was overwhelmed by the flood of monstrous creatures that invaded its pristine borders. The country writhed in anguish as the relentless army swept over her virescent hills and tranquil forests, marching over her plains and leaving death and sorrow in their wake. Their feet churned up the mud and their shrieks and hideous cacophony turned the hearts of her countrymen to ice.

The invasion came with little warning. The sea to the southeast churned and tossed, and then the creatures emerged. Tens of thousands of them, they tore into everything, and left devastation behind. The creatures that ravaged the countryside were hideous beyond belief, nightmarish in appearance and immune to reason. They were the were-folk: creatures out of nightmare and legend. Whyvrens, seheowks, wulfbana, dracors, and spidryns, they struck terror into the hearts of all who saw them. They crept and flew and slithered, bits of darkness that combined and twisted all manners of beasts into forms ghastly beyond imagination. And high above them all soared the silver-winged werehawk.

A giant beast of icy blackness, the werehawk's approach froze its enemies with terror. The fierce, bird-like creature screeched in fury and wheeled, its body flashing through the air with powerful speed. It snapped its long, razor-sharp beak closed, cutting off its own cry and diving out of the sky towards its unwitting prey far below. The werehawk plummeted in dread silence, striking at the last moment with strong claws. The creature it hunted never had a chance.

Ghrendourak, master of the greatest army the world had ever seen, watched as the werehawk hunted. Clad in armor, he was a massive figure. A cape swirled about his shoulders, lending him an air of mystery. The were-folk shrank from him, for he was their leader, their master, and they bowed before the power within him, for it was the same power used in their own creation. He allowed the werehawk to gulp down its prey, and then he called it to him. The creature came, its beak snapping and a wild look in its eye, but it came. Ghrendourak stepped onto its back and together they rose up into the heavens.

The massive beast never tired. It was the fiercest and most powerful of the were-creatures; the first of these mystical creations, and it had survived with its creator for thousands of years.

Despite his exterior calm, Ghrendourak quailed every time he called the steed to himself. The werehawk was the only creature Ghrendourak himself feared, for he was not its master. He lived in terror that its power was greater than his own, for he knew it was fed by the same master who supplied him with strength. The werehawk tested him constantly, always searching for a weakness in its shackles. Ghrendourak laughed outwardly at the creature's efforts, but silently he worried that one day the beast might find that weakness. Without their common master, Ghrendourak was just a man, and secretly he worried that one day his master might deem him unworthy and strip away the strength he had provided. He strove to align his goals with that of his master, to prove himself worthy of the strength and power that had been bestowed upon him. Two separate entities, they worked together as one.

Ghrendourak sneered as he looked down upon his army. His victory drew near and he could already savor its sweetness. His lip curled with contempt at the thought of how easy it had all been. From the back of his werehawk it was as if he could see all of Tellurae Aquaous spread out before him, ready to be conquered and annihilated.

"Soon, soon it will all be mine, and there is no one to stop me this time!" He whispered the words to himself. Or perhaps it was the power controlling him that whispered. It was more difficult every day for Ghrendourak to discern between his own thoughts and words and those of his master. "None will stand before me this time." He leaned forward and patted his werehawk on the neck with an almost gentle fondness. "Can you taste their dread my beauty? Can you smell it? It tastes like freedom. This time we will not be stopped, we will not be driven back, our prison will be destroyed and I shall never be caged there again. Soon I shall reclaim my true form, and then I will rule forever as the king I was meant to be!"

The werehawk lifted its head and loosed a shrill scream of defiance into the night. Ghrendourak felt grim pleasure at the sound. He stretched his hand up into the night sky, straining to touch one of the stars that dangled there. He looked up at Yorien and laughed.

"You will not stop me this time," he snarled. "You are powerless without someone to wield your pathetic *gift*. And I have already found him. I have touched his nightmares, he will not be able to stand before me. Not this time."

The constellation was unmoved by his comments. The stars glittered in the night sky, aglow with calm defiance. Ghrendourak hissed in rage and dug his heels into the sides of the werehawk, taking his hatred out on the closest thing to him. The werehawk screamed again and its pain soothed his anger.

In desperation, the people of Yochathain fled to the cities, burning everything behind them, for fire was the only thing the were-creatures regarded with any amount of consternation. And so, beautiful Yochathain burned, and the hostile enemy laid siege to the cities.

Layrdon, the capital of Yochathain, held strong against the enemy for eighteen months. Despite being unprepared for a siege, Layrdon was well-stocked with food and water. In addition to a secret, underground river that ran below the city there were also tunnels and caverns upon which the foundations had been built. It was through these tunnels that messengers were sent and some inhabitants of the city were able to be smuggled away to safety. Supplies could also be funneled into the city through these tunnels, but it was not comfortable. There was no easy way to supply an entire, overcrowded city's needs through a few tunnels. The inhabitants huddled within Layrdon's walls suffered. Many died once Cold-Term arrived. And then the food began to run out.

King Drebune stared down at his once-beautiful city, his hopeless, starving people, and knew defeat had found them all. The ravening army outside his walls had issued no demands; no surrender could stop their advance. But survival might still be possible, for though these creatures slew many, they did not appear to be bent on killing everyone. But even if he and his people did not survive, word must be sent; he must attempt to warn others before they suffered the same fate as Yochathain.

Making the most of what might be his last hours as king, Drebune called his most trusted and courageous messengers and gave them their assignments.

"Though we have sent for help, no help has come. We can only guess that our messengers never made it to their destinations. But we must try once more. We have enough left within us to make one last stand, which must buy you the needed time to bring word to the people of Kallayohm, Efoin-Ebedd, Llycaelon, Aom-igh, Endalia, and Emnolae. You must warn them, because when we fall, they will be next."

"The Dragon's Eye shines brightly on Aom-igh, but thunder rolls across the rest of the world," Kiernan Kane mused to himself.

The gangly minstrel perched precariously on his windowsill and stared out at the bright blue sky; his eyes mirrored the tranquility of the morning. His face held a somber expression. A bird chirped at the minstrel cheerily, laughing at his apprehension. Kiernan Kane jumped and almost tumbled backwards off his ledge.

"He rises once more," the minstrel insisted, glaring at the saucy creature on the tree branch outside his window. "The Ancient Enemy stirs. I can feel it. He has begun his latest bid for freedom, and perhaps this will be the final confrontation. He is powerful, more powerful than he has ever been before."

Clouds drew across the sky like ominous curtains. Kiernan Kane shivered, and wrapped his long arms around himself. The bird hunched down on its branch warily. A chill wind rustled the leaves of the tree.

Softly, the minstrel began to sing. The tune was low and haunting, and the words were grim, but his face was light, almost cheerful.

> *"Only two can stand before him*
> *Only one can hope to fell him."*

He shook himself. "Ah!" he exclaimed. "When that enemy rises again, shall the fool be the wild card then? Only the minstrel remembers; does the enemy remember too? He must, he must! Does he tremble? Does he know of the strength that may well be his undoing? Shall the fool lead the king when all other bonds fail? Perhaps, perhaps." His face took on that strangely cunning look that belied its innocent appearance, and the room dimmed.

Kiernan Kane sprang from the window and landed neatly on his hands. His agility was surprising, given his accustomed gawkiness. He chirped cheerily at the bird and flipped to his feet with cat-like grace.

"Cruithaor Elchiyl watches us all, and he would not have us

fail, even when faced with an impossible task," he whispered. Then he squared his shoulders. "Neither would he have his servant filled with doubts."

Humming, he descended the stairs from his tower to the rooms below. As he neared the end of the hallway, he did a little dance that almost landed him in a heap at the bottom of the stairs. Pulling himself upright, he stopped humming and managed to get himself safely through the door.

"I do wonder what's for breakfast this morning?" Kiernan Kane mused aloud. He tapped a finger to his nose, adopting his tranquil and unassuming expression once more.

The eerie, discordant song that the minstrel had been humming, however, lingered about the stairwell long after he left. One by one, the candles in the room flickered and went out, and still the memory of the song remained, portending some evil. A chill wind swept across the land, but none noticed it. None, that is, except the minstrel, but he was too busy downing pancakes to be bothered by a breeze.

"The border patrol cannot hold much longer," the aethalon captain reported in a matter-of-fact tone.

"What is going on?" Jemson asked, his eyes narrowed. "The seheowks have always been a nuisance, yes, but they have never attacked in such force and numbers before."

"There is a change in these beasts," the captain replied. "Even Lord Brant has commented on the difference in these attacks over the past few months."

At the mention of his uncle's name, Jemson's thoughts drifted. Brant had left for Aom-igh early that morning. It was a week earlier than he had planned, but Brant had his reasons. Jemson suspected that one of those reasons was the Lady Dylanna. Brant might not even realize it himself, but Jemson saw the way his face lightened whenever her name came up. It was the same look Jemson's father used to get when he looked at his wife. At the thought of his mother, a pang of sorrow shot through Jemson's heart.

"Your Majesty," the captain shifted and paused. His next words came with awkwardness, as if he was reluctant to speak them, "Is there any way your uncle might lend us aid in this battle with the vile creatures?"

"He has recently returned to Aom-igh, part of his purpose for traveling there is to discuss this very concern with King Oraeyn. His heart is divided with the concerns of both Llycaelon and Aom-igh."

"Could he not be persuaded to remain here permanently as your counselor until you come of age and take your rite of passage through the Corridor? You will be a great king for Llycaelon, but you are also the youngest to ever take the throne. Could Sir Brant..."

Jemson raised his head, his hand curling into a fist. "It won't happen."

"But, Sire…"

"No," Jemson said, his voice quiet, but firm. "Brant's heart is in Aom-igh. There is no way he would be willing to remain in Llycaelon for seventeen years waiting for me to grow up. I begged him to take my father's place on the throne, but he refused. He told me that if he took the throne for any amount of time there was no guarantee that the people would let him step down when I came of age. He said he had never tasted the power of kingship and he did not want to start.

"No, it is up to me. All I can ask Brant for is his advice, but I can't even make him stay here for a week at a time. If the dragons had not consented to fly him back and forth I might be able to keep him here for longer periods of time, but his heart would never be here. He cares about Llycaelon because it is where he was born and because he has happy childhood memories of this place. But his home is in Aom-igh." *And the son he would have chosen is Oraeyn, not I,* Jemson did not say the words out loud. There was no bitterness in the thought, only a deep sadness.

"It is still hard to believe that Brant had no desire for the crown at all," the captain said. "I am old enough to remember the rumors, the whispers of the prophecy. Everyone was intent upon giving the throne to Brant."

Jemson shook his head. "Brant is the most loyal man there is. He never had any wish to take what he saw as his brother's right."

The captain nodded, his expression filled with respect. "I understand. What shall we do about the seheowks, Sire?"

"We fight, as we always have," Jemson said, as he set his chin with a determination that belied his twenty-three years. "Take as many men as needed. Every king before has held our borders safe against the vile creatures and I am sworn to do so as well. I will not fail in this charge. My own sword is committed to this fight if need be."

The captain nodded sharply and saluted with the customary fist over heart that was reserved only for the king. The warrior turned on his heel and strode from the War Room. Jemson took a deep breath and then turned to other weighty matters that required his immediate attention. He was a king, trapped in his palace, while his warrior's heart longed for the freedom of the battlefield. His thoughts were never far from his aethalons, though his many duties kept him from them, for now.

CHAPTER
TWO

Again and again the aethalons beat the seheowks back into the sea, and again and again the evil creatures surged forward. The men were exhausted and the seheowks could sense it. They uttered chilling shrieks of triumph as their tireless ranks renewed their attacks once more. The aethalons met these enemies with equal ferocity, but theirs was a battle of desperation. The men knew how precarious their position was and were aware that the seheowks, with steady deliberation, had forced their ranks to retreat to this specific location.

Llycaelon had a natural defense from sea attacks with its sheer, rock-faced cliffs which bordered much of the nation's perimeter. The cliffs often ended in sandy beaches or dunes that sloped down to the sea. The cliffs themselves were unassailable, but there were breaks in this mountain wall, and it was towards Caethyr Gap, the largest of these breaks on the Northern border, that the battle now raged. No longer were the cliff walls at their back, but rather the open fields, homes, and towns of their countrymen. The aethalons knew their strength would soon fail, and they understood the consequences of this defeat.

The seheowks had been a recurring problem for centuries

though their presence had always before been a mere nuisance. They were predators, with blueish-black scales and long, wiry limbs that ended in clawed hands and feet, perfect for ripping into their prey. They were shorter than most humans, but much stronger and swifter. Their faces were elongated like a lizard's, but they had long, sharp teeth like a wolf or a bear. It was a rare occurrence for seheowks to slip past the Border Patrol, but when they did, they killed everything in their path: sheep, cows, dogs, birds, bears, and people. They were most eager to kill humans.

They were not pack animals and usually did not appear in companies larger than three or four. The Border Patrol had been created to keep on the lookout for the creatures and deal with them. But in the past few months, the seheowks had begun to work like an army. Their attacks were coordinated, cunning, and precise, and their numbers were staggering. The Border Patrol members were no longer fighting a senseless creature for ownership of a beach. They were fighting a purposeful, organized enemy for dominion of their country and their future.

"We're losing ground, Sir!" one of the Aetoli warriors screamed to his captain over the roar of the seheowks. The shouts of men could be heard on every side amidst the clash of battle, and the ever rolling, thundering waves of the sea created a steady, deafening rumble. The sand churned beneath the hooves of horses and the clawed feet of the seheowks. "We cannot hold this ground!"

"We must!" the captain yelled back. "If defeated here, we lose our country."

"Sir, this is a senseless sacrifice of good men," the warrior called out.

"You are an aethalon. You knew the perils when you chose to serve here!" the captain's commanding voice rang out above the clamor of the battle. "We defend the border at all costs!"

"At the expense of our lives?" the warrior yelled, gesturing at the troops as he fended off another beast who had leapt onto his horse's flank. "Would the king truly order such a sacrifice? You know as well as I that we cannot hold our position, and when we are dead, the seheowks will march over our lifeless bodies to complete their invasion. Our people will have no warning and our deaths will serve no purpose."

"You are dismissed," the captain shouted over the body of the seheowk he had just slain.

"What?" The warrior stared at his captain in open amazement and disbelief. His sword faltered. A seheowk jumped on what it thought was an opportunity, leaping through the air with a powerful bound. The Aetoli's presence of mind was the sole thing that saved him, he thrust his weapon up and his sword pierced through the creature's neck just in time.

"What is your name?" the captain demanded in harsh tones as he pulled his horse back a little from the fray.

"Devrin of House Merle."

"Courageous hawk?" the captain shouted in disbelief. "You were ill-named, lad, I have no place for a coward in my command, you are dismissed."

"Sir, you don't understand, if you would only listen…"

"Not one more word, you are dismissed."

Devrin glared at the captain and then shook his head in disgust. He turned his roan charger and kicked the horse into a gallop. A haze of red fell across his vision as he rode away from the battle.

"Dismissed as a coward," he muttered to himself wrathfully. "If the captain would have listened, this task could have been made easier. Well, it's just you and me, old boy," the warrior patted his horse's neck. "Come on, they can't hold that gap much longer. Yah!"

Clapping his heels to the red horse's sides Devrin leaned low over his steed's neck and raced up the hill to where the warriors had pitched their camp. A plan was already formed in his mind, and he meant to put it into action, with or without permission. He knew how to keep the seheowks from crossing through the gap. The Border Patrol needed a better weapon, and Devrin planned to provide it.

"And when this is over I shall call our boy-king to account for every man dead in this fight," he growled to himself. "Too long has the fate of Llycaelon been ruled by the pride of kings.

Too long have good men felt the sting of dishonor because of the House of Arne!"

The camp was set back from the gap, but in clear view of it. Tents and carts were scattered throughout, with small cooking fires dotting the area. Devrin dismounted and raced over to the largest tent. He quickly dismantled it and dragged it to his mount where he tossed it over the horse's hindquarters in a heap, then he clambered back up into his saddle. The roan danced a little but settled quickly and accepted his master's odd behavior and the additional burden with long-suffering stoicism. Next Devrin rode over and grabbed one of the long torches that was stuck in the ground and used to light the camp after nightfall. He thrust the end of it into a nearby cooking fire until it burst to life.

Holding the torch high and balancing the mounds of canvas behind him, Devrin raced his horse back down the beach towards the gap and the fighting.

The drums of the seheowks were pounding as he neared the battleground and he knew he must hurry. He tugged on his horse's bridle, urging the beast to greater speed. The tent flapped and wobbled as they raced towards the battle. Every moment was precious, and Devrin could sense his time running out.

The aethalons were all but defeated when Devrin reached the battleground. The seheowks surged forward, and the aethalons fought and fell where they stood. The great warriors battled desperately, but with a sense of resignation. All hope had been drained hours ago, and the seheowks reveled in this hopelessness. There was an arrogant disdain for their enemy in the seheowk's every move, as if they knew that victory was near.

Devrin rode up to a weary aethalon and shouted at him. "I need your help!"

"We all need help," the weary young man whispered back through cracked lips.

"I have a plan!" Devrin shouted, ignoring the man's comment. "But I can't do it alone. Come on! I'll show you what needs to be done."

"Must... keep the seheowks... from getting through," the warrior mumbled back mechanically, making no move to follow

Devrin's lead.

Devrin seized on the warrior's words. "Yes! We must keep them from getting through. I have a plan that will keep them from getting through! Help me with this."

The man stared at Devrin in confusion. "What?"

"Fire," Devrin said grimly, "the seheowks are terrified of it. With fire we can force them back into the sea where they belong. But I cannot do it on my own."

The young warrior's face lit with sudden hope. "If we can build a pyre big enough…"

"And keep it burning long enough…" Devrin encouraged.

"We might yet win this day!" the warrior finished Devrin's thought. His eyes lit with excitement and renewed hope. He burst into action as Devrin indicated the mound of oiled canvas, seizing upon the small hope that was proffered.

Together they rode through the battle, each of them holding onto an end of the bulky tent, trampling seheowks as they went until they had reached the front line. The gap was thirty or forty paces wide, and the tent would not fill even a quarter of it, but it was a start. Devrin thrust the torch into the tent. Flames darted towards the sky and the seheowks nearest to it screamed and tumbled away from the sudden heat and light.

The aethalons paused to stare and Devrin seized on the opportunity.

"Get the tents! Get the carts! Get everything that will burn!" Devrin shouted. "Burn the camp, fill the gap with fire!"

A full score of aethalons wheeled their horses away from the fighting and raced across the sand. The wait was interminable. As he swung his sword again and again, Devrin could see their chances slipping away with every second that passed. But the men returned shortly, carrying torches and tents. Behind them came more men wheeling carts. The flames grew as more pieces of the camp were added to the fire, and the seheowks retreated, recoiling from the hated blaze.

Devrin directed the men as they created the wall. He sent several men into the nearby forest with a travois and instructed them to return with as much wood as possible.

As he gave them their instructions, he reminded them, "Our hope lives only so long as we can keep this fire stoked. With this fire we *will* hold the gap until the king sends reinforcements."

To himself, Devrin thought, *If the king even knows that we need reinforcements.*

The aethalons grasped Devrin's words like starving men grasping for a loaf of bread and threw themselves into their work with an energy restored and a purpose renewed. They raced onto the battlefield brandishing fiery weapons. When the seheowks saw their enemy rushing towards them with flaming branches, they fell back in dismay. Sensing alarm and seeing their enemies' hesitation, the aethalons surged forward and now it was the seheowks who were bewildered and overwhelmed by a sudden attack from a foe that had been defeated mere moments before. The monsters retreated as the aethalons attacked, wielding weapons that struck terror into whatever passed for a seheowk's heart. With a loud roar, the men fell towards their enemies, brandishing swords and torches. The great pyre grew larger, and the fire burned hotter with every passing moment as the warriors worked feverishly to build a wall of flame that would keep their border safe for yet another day.

At long last the pyre stretched across the width of the gap and the fire sprang brightly into the darkening sky. The aethalons backed through the tiny gap that was left and then threw more wood on the fire, completing the wall of flame. The seheowks were contained between the fire and the sea and the aethalons raised a cheer at their success. More warriors returned with wood and they were immediately set to work keeping the wall of fire in place. It was a temporary solution, but it would hold for now.

Devrin felt a thrill surge through him as the final pieces of the wall were put in place and the seheowks were cut off completely. It was a good work, he thought. Even if it was his last work as an aethalon.

"Devrin," a warrior came rushing up to him, "are you Devrin?"

Devrin turned. "Yes?"

"The captain, he's asking for you."

Devrin's shoulders slumped. "Take me to him." He rode behind the other man, wondering if he would be allowed to keep his rank. He had worked hard to attain the coveted Aetoli title. There was no escaping the dishonor of being dismissed, but he hated the thought of giving up his rank.

The other warrior led Devrin to the back of the line where the captain was waiting. But it was not the reception Devrin had expected. The captain was lying on the ground, his face pale. He had a blanket draped over him, but Devrin spied the bloody rags in the hands of the man sitting next to him and knew the captain had been wounded.

He dismounted and knelt on the ground next to the man. "Sir?" Devrin asked. "You wanted me?"

"I was wrong," the captain whispered, his voice rasping with the effort. "You are no coward. I saw what you did. That was... brilliant."

"Thank you, sir," Devrin said.

"Forgive my harsh words about your name. They were spoken in haste and despair."

"I've heard words like them before. They don't matter."

"I thought the name House Merle sounded familiar. Did you serve in the King's Helm? You seem young for it."

"My older brother, sir. He died in Aom-igh."

"I am sorry to hear that. We could use more good men like you."

The captain's breath caught and grew ragged. Devrin leaned forward in concern.

"Sir?"

The captain waved a hand. "I do not think I am long for this world. I wanted to ask you... have you held a command?"

"Yes, sir," Devrin affirmed. "In the palace guard, before I asked to be reassigned to the Border Patrol."

"Not much experience leading men in battle, then?"

"No, sir."

"But you acquired the Aetoli rank, I see," the captain gestured at the pin on Devrin's collar.

"Yes, sir, a few months ago."

"And you've got a good head on your shoulders. That fire was quick thinking, and the men followed your orders," the captain gasped and coughed, spitting out blood.

"With all due respect, sir, you should be resting," the attending warrior said quietly.

"I'll rest in a moment," the captain growled then paused as he was seized by yet another fit of coughing. When he had recovered he lay back, panting. "Devrin of House Merle, I hereby leave you my command."

Devrin felt a shock course through him. "Sir?"

"Son, some leaders are born, and some are made. The way you handled yourself tonight, anyone can see that you were born to lead. I have no doubt that you can do this. Besides, you must have talent, they don't bestow Aetoli ranks upon just anyone."

"I am too young to command an entire patrol!"

"New rank or not, you earned the title of Aetoli. Do you know that is one of the highest honors you could have been given?"

Devrin nodded, feeling suddenly much younger than his fifty years. "Aye sir, I know it well."

"No one will question your capability. No one, that is, but yourself."

Devrin bit his lip, and then he nodded reluctantly. "Yes, sir."

"Good." The older man fumbled with the pin on his own collar and then made a frustrated sound. "Stephran," he said weakly. The warrior who had been attending him looked anguished, but he bowed his head and helped the captain remove his pin.

"There is no uniform for this position," the captain said, his voice growing weaker, "just a small token that most will never notice, but you will find the respect of your men to be worth much more than any uniform. You have surely earned that today. You will need to earn it every day." He placed the pin in Devrin's hand. The captain made a fist and clapped it over his heart in a salute.

Devrin saluted back, overwhelmed as the other man breathed his last.

CHAPTER THREE

Dylanna strained against her bonds and struggled to keep herself from screaming; she was not certain she could even utter a sound. She could not see, hear, or feel anything. Worse than that, she could not reach her magic. It was there, tantalizingly close, but she could not take hold of it or use it. When she reached for it, instead of the surge of warmth and calm she was accustomed to, she came up against a net that prevented her from reaching it. She could feel it, almost see it, but she could not use it.

Dylanna had not the faintest idea where she was. Darkness wrapped around her and she was suspended in nothingness. There were no chains or ropes, no floor, no walls, no anything. There was no sound, only absolute, desolate silence.

After her initial terror upon waking, she found the strength to compose herself. She was not about to succumb to despair. Not without a fight. Dylanna set her mind to work. She was the logical one. Of Scelwhyn's daughters, Dylanna was the planner, the one who always maintained a cool-headed logical perspective. She would worry a problem from every angle, thinking through every possible circumstance, no matter how unlikely; then she would act, based on the most logical solution.

At least, that was how she usually worked. However, since Brant entered the picture Dylanna found herself acting much more impetuously, almost rashly. She would berate herself for hours over the fact that she could not get his dark eyes and quiet smile out of her head. She recalled a moment beside the fire, when Brant had taken hold of her arm with a lightning quick grab: reflecting both steel and a tenderness, telling her they needed her strength. Had he said they... or he... needed her strength? Dylanna ground her teeth in impatience with herself, now was not the time to be thinking about Brant. First she must figure out how to escape, she would sort through her emotions about the wanderer from Llycaelon later.

She told herself that every cage had a keyhole, and every lock could be picked, *if* one possessed the right tools and the patience and skill to use them. Taking a deep breath, the wizardess set to work exploring her prison as well as she was able in her limited position. She tightened each muscle individually, trying to discover exactly how much movement she was allowed. She was not sure how this knowledge would help her, but she knew that if this prison had a flaw, it was likely to be infinitesimally small.

Her mind wandered again as she wondered briefly what had happened to Leila. She shook the thought away, forcing herself to focus on the task before her. If Leila was also a prisoner, there was nothing Dylanna could do until she herself was free. And if Leila were free, she would be searching for Dylanna right now. She tried to think. How long might it be before anyone discovered she was missing? If Leila was also trapped, it might be days. They had sent a message to Oraeyn shortly before trying Leila's experiment, so it would be two days at the very least before Oraeyn became aware of their absence, and that was being generous and assuming he would send a reply immediately. But how long had she been gone, a minute or a day?

Devrin felt alone and insignificant. The camp buzzed with activity, but he had nowhere to turn. Entrusted with command of the Border Patrol, he was at a loss as to what his next move should be.

Kelan, Devrin let his thoughts wander to his brother. *You were the leader, not me. What should I do next? I don't know how to lead these men. I wish you were here.*

"Sir?" a voice broke Devrin out of his thoughts.

He turned and saw the man who had been tending to the captain. Devrin suddenly realized he knew the man from his training days. He could not remember his name, but he recognized the face.

Devrin nodded. "Yes?"

"I am the captain's chief of staff. As you are now the captain, it is my job to assist you in taking on your new orders. My name is Stephran. We were Gyrfalcons together, I believe."

"Yes, I believe you are right. It is good to see you again, Stephran. And I am grateful for any assistance you can provide."

"Begging your pardon, Sir, but you look a little confused."

"Well, I am a little at a loss for what to do now," Devrin admitted.

"The first thing is to present you to your commanders and later to the entire camp. Everyone will want to meet the man who pulled us out of the fire by throwing everything else into it." Stephran's lips twitched and his eyes twinkled in merriment. Devrin was relieved to see that his chief of staff apparently had a sense of humor.

He followed Stephran to his new campsite. As they walked, Stephran kept up a steady stream of conversation, helping Devrin feel a little less lost and alone.

"Are you new to the Border Patrol?" Stephran asked at one point.

Devrin shook his head, feeling a bit numb. "I've been in the Border Patrol for just under three years now, but I was only transferred to this regiment a week ago."

"Well done, sir. Been here a week and already in command. No wonder you looked a little at loose ends when I found you. No worries though. Not very long ago the entire Border Patrol was lost, and you set that to rights. I think you'll find your way around this command, sir. Not a doubt in my mind."

After a warm welcome from his commanders and men, Devrin gave his first orders, sending every man who could be spared into the Iron Wood, the nearby forest, to retrieve timber to keep the wall of flame alive.

Once that was done, Devrin plied his commanders with questions about the structure of the Border Patrol, and requested recommendations for young men of promise. Then he asked for their opinions on strategy and results: what had worked, and what had failed in the past, and what had yet to be tried. The wall of flame flickered in his peripheral vision the entire time he spoke with them, a constant reminder that his solution was a temporary one. He had ended the battle and bought them a reprieve, not a victory.

After many hours late into the evening, Devrin adjourned the council. "Thank you, men, for your hard work, your thoughtful consideration, and your long hours. Get some rest and be back here at first light. We have much to do."

As they departed, Devrin found within himself a deep and abiding contentment. He was well-pleased with his commanders. They were thoughtful, creative, and insightful.

"If you need anything, sir," Stephran offered kindly, "my duties are to assist you in yours."

Devrin nodded. "Thank you."

"Unfortunately, some young hero burned the captain's tent earlier today, so you'll have to make do with sleeping under the stars," Stephran's voice held a hint of laughter.

Devrin chuckled in spite of the urgency of their situation and the threatening enemy camped just beyond the fiery barrier. "I should give that young hero a stern talking to," he replied.

Much later that night, when the Toreth was even higher overhead, Devrin sat a short distance outside the camp. He stared into the wall of flame that danced between him and the enemy and he wondered how much time he had bought and if his actions would even matter. It was strange to think that only hours ago he had felt like a man with nothing to lose. His family's honor already bore a stain, what did it matter if he defied orders? He could do nothing more to mar the good name of Merle that hadn't already been done, not that it was Kelan's fault, though there were those who blamed him anyway. Now he sat in command of an entire patrol, and the weight of that responsibility lay upon him like plated mail. For one wild moment he let himself believe that he might redeem his family's honor. The men here did not appear to know or care about Devrin's shame. They greeted him as a brother and not a one blinked when he mentioned his family name.

He gazed into the night. On one side of the fire, silhouettes of his men moved with lithe purpose as they tended the wall of flame and built it higher. Through the wall he also discerned the shapes of seheowks as they milled about in frustration. In his hand he held the small pin the captain had given him. He rolled it about between his fingers, lost in thought.

The pin was fashioned in the shape of a dragon. Dragons disappeared from Llycaelon hundreds of years ago, another reason the land was often dubbed the "dark country." But they had returned in recent days. Devrin had even seen them. He still remembered the first time: the great beast landed on the palace lawn and a man swung down off its back.

Devrin's reaction to the sudden appearance had startled even him. He was not afraid, he merely felt a deep longing when he saw the dragon, and he instantly knew what the creature was, no one had to tell him. When he saw the man dismount, Devrin found himself consumed with a wave of envy so strong that for a moment all his senses were blocked by it.

A sudden, sharp pain in his hand pulled him out of his musings and made Devrin glance down. He watched in quiet fascination as his blood rolled down the back of the pin. Blood blossomed like a tiny flower on the tip of his finger where he had accidentally stabbed it, but his thoughts were too far away to be bothered by such a small thing. His mind danced across the clouds on the back of a dragon, free to conquer the open skies and fly up to the starlight, impervious to the trivial concerns of name or house or even honor. With a monumental effort, Devrin brought himself back to the ground with a rueful laugh; such fancies were foolish and perhaps even dangerous, but the longing was still there.

The next morning, Devrin woke up early and greeted his men personally. He was quick to use the authority of his new position, and he sensed that the men were beginning to respect him even in the first few hours of his command. The words of the old captain echoed in the back of his mind always, and he now understood their meaning: the respect of these men was reward enough. Devrin was not convinced that he was any more capable of commanding the Border Patrol to victory over the seheowks than anyone else, but the command was his and he did have ideas.

"I need two divisions of archers atop the cliff wall. The seheowks will realize soon enough that they cannot get through this gap. I do not know if they can scale these cliffs, but I am determined that nothing they do will surprise us.

"Build fires on top of the cliff faces and see what you can do with your longbows. Rotate the men so we have constant energy on the fire above and fresh perspective on the enemy below. Make sure your men know where they should be and what they should do at all times. If they have any questions, report to me. Any questions?" Devrin asked.

None were offered, so Devrin continued, "The Border Patrol has guarded this country from the attacks of the seheowks for hundreds of years, and we will continue that tradition with pride and skill."

The men broke apart as he finished, each with new purpose and determination, each with a wary glance at the wall of fire to make certain it was still there. Maintaining those flames was foremost in every man's concern.

I mean to do more than that, too, Devrin thought to himself quietly. He had several goals, lofty perhaps, but he meant to see them through. In addition to restoring his family's name, Devrin wanted to get the Border Patrol recognized for their effort, and he meant to beat the seheowks back for good. He meant to defend the borders so well that the Patrol would no longer be needed. Perhaps others older and wiser than he would have told him that such a dream was pleasant, but impossible. But the men did not care that their captain dreamed of things unattainable. For them, for now, it was good to have a leader with such energy and vision.

And someday, Devrin added to his list of dreams, *I'll fight the seheowks from the back of a dragon.* He let out a pent up breath and berated himself for being childish. Even he would admit that such a dream was foolish. He was not even sure why the idea of riding a dragon fascinated him so much. Ever since he had seen the dragon near the palace, a part of him yearned to see another one, to get close enough to touch the scales. He longed to sit upon the great, spiked back and rise up to the clouds to meet the dawn. He shook his head, now was not the time for dreams of dragons. There was work before him, and it was up to him to make sure that it got done.

Devrin looked around the camp with sober mien as he watched his plans spring to life. The Border Patrol was about to make history, and Devrin was fiercely proud that he would be there to see it.

CHAPTER
FOUR

It was dark. So dark that Oraeyn blinked several times just to reassure himself that his eyes were, in fact, open. For a moment, he panicked, wondering if he had gone blind. Then a pinprick of light appeared on the horizon, and the air began to grow brighter. Fear raced in his heart as he caught a glimpse of his surroundings. He was inside an enormous cavern of some kind. The ground below him was made of packed earth and it rumbled and quaked restlessly.

Oraeyn became aware of a pressure on his left hand. Something was squeezing his fingers together. It was painful. He turned to look and saw that Kamarie was with him. He had almost forgotten she was there. Her face was pale in the dim glow. As he turned to her to ask what was happening, her lips parted to speak, and then the ground quaked again and the cavern floor ruptured below Kamarie's feet. As she fell, her grip on his hand tightened. The sudden, unexpected weight on his arm pulled Oraeyn to the ground. He slid to the edge of the chasm, grasping Kamarie's hand with all his strength.

She stared up at him, her face filled with terror. "Oraeyn!" she gasped. "Please! Don't let go!"

Oraeyn sat up in bed with a shout that brought his servants running to his side. He blinked blearily and reached up to rub his hands across his face, nearly beheading Anya with the sword that was clutched in his right fist. The faithful servant ducked and flinched away, his face whitening in consternation.

"Sire," Emyth gasped from the other side of the room, "surely you don't sleep with your sword unsheathed!"

"I don't sleep with it at all." Oraeyn stared at the Fang Blade, with bleary perplexity. The golden blade glinted with brilliant innocence in the full light of day that poured in through his window. He shook his head. "I haven't even taken it out since the coronation. I keep it hanging on the wall, you know that. Forgive me, Anya." While the ancient sword was like a piece of his own history, Oraeyn felt uncomfortable wearing it, and much preferred his old, plain one for everyday use.

"No harm done, Sire," Anya's wrinkled face was a portrait of deep concern and his voice was shaky.

"Ah," Emyth pursed his lips dubiously. The two servants shared a meaningful look across the bed. "Yes, well, very well. I shall warn the others about waking you too suddenly in the future."

"I mean it, Emyth," Oraeyn protested, "I have no idea how the Fang Blade ended up in my hand just now."

"I see," Emyth's tone was less than convinced. "In any case, it is time for you to get up, that messenger you are expecting should arrive soon."

Oraeyn decided it was no good trying to argue his point any longer and submitted himself to the ministrations of his staff. At length, he was released. Almost as an afterthought, Oraeyn buckled the Fang Blade to his waist. Despite his reluctance to carry it, the sword hung at his side comfortably. He wasn't sure why he had decided to wear it today, but something about its presence felt right.

The castle sparkled white against the brilliant blue sky like a picture out of a book of fairy tales. The beauty of the day contrasted starkly with Oraeyn's nightmares, banishing them from his memory. All that was left was a troubling memory that would soon fade. Rays of light glistened on the water of the moat and warmed the iridescent fish flitting about beneath the surface. Just beyond the palace walls lay the ocean. The waves thundered against the rocks and lapped lazily across the sandy beach.

High in the azure sky, a red-gold dragon circled. Huge, leathery wings kept the great beast aloft. Its scales sparkled in the bright daylight, creating the illusion of fire in the air. The creature might have been hunting, or perhaps merely enjoying the freedom of the open sky. Across the meadow behind the palace at the edge of the Aura Wood a pearl-white unicorn grazed, unconcerned by the monstrous dragon that dipped and wheeled overhead; myth-folk did not hunt each other. Unicorns were timid, but sightings were not as rare as in days past. If one was courageous enough to venture deep into the wilderness, even the mighty gryphon could be found nowadays. The winged horses kept to the great plains beyond the Mountains of Dusk, but those who saw the noble beasts never forgot them.

Oraeyn stood on the high wall of the palace, waiting expectantly. He watched the dragon and the unicorn and breathed a deep sigh of contentment. It was good to see them in the light of day again. Most of these powerful beings had departed to an underground realm called Krayghentaliss centuries ago, shielding themselves from humankind who hated and reviled them. Oraeyn himself had journeyed in that realm, and he still remembered the awe its massive tunnels had inspired within him. But the myth-folk belonged in the world above, not cooped up in the cold realm underground. They had been dying out down there, away from the open air. When Arnaud welcomed them back above-realm the myth-folk had accepted with deep gratitude.

The kingdom of Aom-igh had known peace for the past three years, ever since the battle against Llycaelon had ended. Oraeyn had been king for the past two years. He still found himself surprised at the ease with which he had taken over the kingship. Of course, he reminded himself, he was not without help. Brant was there, ready to advise and aid him in the formation and retention of good relations with several other countries, namely Llycaelon. And Arnaud was still nearby to offer advice when Oraeyn needed it.

Brant's travels took him back and forth between Aom-igh

and Llycaelon more frequently of late, though. With the help of his young friend Yole, the dragon, the trip took but a day, rather than the weeks it would take by ship. Oraeyn understood Brant's desire to spend as much time as he could in Llycaelon. The warrior's young nephew, Jemson, was seated on the throne there, and Brant wanted to make sure that the boy was learning to rule with compassion, courage, and kindness. Oraeyn chuckled ruefully. Brant wanted to make sure that Oraeyn possessed these same traits.

The two wizardesses, Dylanna and Leila, Kamarie's aunts, were keeping busy as well. They were currently in the midst of an attempt to devise rapid and secure communications with their allies. Oraeyn hoped to receive a message from them today containing good news with regard to their endeavors. He was sure their idea would facilitate the great effort towards peace in new and different ways.

A bird alighted on Oraeyn's arm, startling him out of his thoughts with a rude screech.

"Right on time, little friend." Oraeyn set the bird down and untied the note with one hand while offering a berry with the other.

"What does Aunt Leila have to say today? Something good, I hope," Kamarie said as she joined him on the wall. She waved at the bird. "Safe travels, sweet Redcrest."

Oraeyn caught her around the waist and drew her close for a kiss. "Of course you would name all the birds in the kingdom. I haven't had a chance to open this missive yet, and... let's elope!"

Kamarie laughed and kissed him back. "I don't think your royal subjects would appreciate that very much. And think of Leila and Dylanna and Mother, they would be crushed if we didn't let them decorate. Yole and King Rhendak want to come as well, and everyone expects a big party to celebrate... so many people would be disappointed." She nudged him with her shoulder to let him know she was only half-joking.

Although their relationship had gotten off to a rather rocky start, Oraeyn and Kamarie had learned to respect one another, and that respect eventually turned into a deep friendship. Oraeyn was still not sure when their friendship had deepened and turned to love, but Kamarie had been his constant support. He was certain he would have drowned trying to navigate the waters of ruling a kingdom if she had not been by his side through it all. Six months ago, he had found himself asking her to be his wife, and to his delight she said "yes" without hesitation.

Oraeyn sighed in mock despair. "All right," he said, opening the note. "The dragons have decided to return to the Harshlands," he said after scanning the note.

"That's wonderful news," Kamarie said. "Aunt Leila never thought the Mountains of Dusk would be big enough for all of them. Especially since the gryphons prefer the mountains to the forests. I'm surprised at how quickly the myth-folk have re-entered the upper realm, though—they were so cautious about accepting Father's invitation."

"They were growing desperate," Oraeyn replied. "Your father's invitation was their only hope. I'm glad that our people have welcomed them back so graciously."

"The agreement to leave livestock alone is what did it," Kamarie agreed. "It creates trust among all parties."

Oraeyn nodded absently, reading the note for more details. "Dylanna says their previous attempts have been disappointing, but Leila has a new idea for a way to allow instantaneous communication between non-magical beings. They're going to try again today."

"That would be incredible," Kamarie's face glowed. "Imagine being able to talk to King Jemson without anyone having to travel anywhere!"

Oraeyn folded up the note and stared out to sea lost in thought. A sense of ill-defined vulnerability that had been resting in the back of his mind all morning loomed to the forefront of his thoughts with an intensity that caused him to wince and double over in pain. A dread foreboding crept over him like a frigid wind and he shivered.

"Oraeyn?" Kamarie asked. "Are you all right?"

Oraeyn remained silent.

"Oraeyn?"

"Something is coming. Something evil."

"What?"

"I don't know. I don't know!" Oraeyn put his hands over his face. "I can't remember."

"Then how do you know something bad is coming?"

"Look at the Fang Blade."

"What? You never carry the Fang Blade," Kamarie began, but then stopped, for Oraeyn drew the great sword and held it up. The blade glowed even brighter than usual, casting a strange, golden light on Oraeyn's face.

"What is it doing?" Kamarie asked, mystified.

"Something important is going to happen," Oraeyn said, he felt absolutely certain about this. "I can feel it. I don't know how I know, but I do know it isn't good."

"I don't understand," Kamarie shook her head and stared up at Oraeyn, worry etched in every line of her face.

"I don't either." The sword's glow faded, and Oraeyn shuddered as though waking from a trance. He flashed a brilliant smile at Kamarie, like nothing strange had happened. "How are your warriors coming along?" he asked, abruptly changing the subject.

Kamarie's brow furrowed, but then she shrugged and let the matter drop. "The Order is really coming together," she said, her voice growing excited. She always grew animated whenever talking about her Lady Knights. "We have new women arriving every day to take up the shield. The knights have been so helpful and have taught us so much. I'm so glad that they support our work. It has certainly enhanced our appreciation of theirs."

Oraeyn felt his heart swell with pride at Kamarie's enthusiasm. Before King Arnaud abdicated the throne and handed the crown to Oraeyn, he granted his daughter the honor of training a new class of knights: a class which Kamarie christened The Order of the Shield, emphasizing its role as one of defensive battle. The king charged her with creating a revised code for this new class of knights, and then gave Kamarie the authority to oversee and implement the recruitment, training, and outfitting of this new force for full readiness in three years' time.

Arnaud knew this was a huge undertaking: precisely the kind of challenge his daughter was best suited for.

As expected, Kamarie poured herself into the challenge and began planning at once. The law of the kingdom stated that no woman should be trained as a knight or allowed to enter into combat. Princess Kamarie, however, had ignored those rules, convincing one of the older knights to train her as his squire. After witnessing first-hand the recent war with Llycaelon, Kamarie understood that the battlefield was not the place of glory she had dreamed. When Kamarie was offered the honor of becoming the first woman to attain knighthood, therefore, she declined, preferring instead to become the first female warrior of the Order of the Shield. Instead of calling themselves "knights," Kamarie had spoken at length with Brant about names and had settled on Aela, an archaic word in Llycaelon's history that meant "rampart." In Kamarie's mind, the name stood for the idea that their role in a battle was to defend, to buy time, to protect their people in order to survive another day, another dawn. The women who joined were first called Shield-Guardians and could rise through the ranks to become full-fledged Aelan.

Kamarie was selective and demanding. Age or class distinction did not matter, but courage, character, and love for Aom-igh were paramount requirements. Induction into the Order of the Shield was only possible after a minimum of two years of intense training. Then the women were required to claim their oath: that they would follow the rules of the Shield which included upholding the king and defending the weak, that they would conduct themselves with honor, and that they would never take a life except in defense of themselves or someone else.

Kamarie's main concern had been that the Knights of the Realm would be opposed to her work. Her worries were quickly relieved. Upon learning of the rules of the new order, the knights became the most ardent defenders of the idea; they even offered to help train the first group of women until there were enough full members of the Order that their aid would no longer be needed. It did not hurt that they bore the king's approval, nor did it hurt that Kamarie was respected and beloved by everyone.

"Forgive the interruption, Sire," the servant's tone contained the faintest hint of exasperation; Oraeyn was starting to believe it was a requirement for servants to always sound just a bit irked with the world at large.

"Yes?"

"Lord Brant has just arrived. He awaits your presence in the Grand Hall."

Oraeyn's spirits lifted. "He's not supposed to be back for another week."

Together Oraeyn and Kamarie made their way to the Grand Hall. Brant was leaning against the doorway as they entered the room.

"Brant!" Oraeyn cried. "What are you doing here?"

The warrior's hair was a bit longer than usual, and windblown from riding a dragon all day. His square jaw was set in a grim expression, even as he stepped forward to clasp Oraeyn's hand.

"I come with urgent news from Llycaelon," Brant's words were quiet, but they carried a great weight. "The seheowk annoyance has grown in the past months to a sizable threat. They attack in great numbers and with a coordination and intent we have never before seen. I must speak with you about the possibility of sending reinforcements."

Oraeyn's joy at seeing his friend and mentor dimmed. "Of course, whatever Jemson needs."

"I may need to meet with King Rhendak, as well," Brant continued. "Warriors would be welcome, but dragons could really make the difference. Jemson had just received a report from the Border Patrol when I left; it sounds as if the situation out there is growing desperate."

"Do we need to worry about seheowks here?" Kamarie asked, her voice worried.

"I do not know," Brant replied. "They don't usually venture this far east, though it has been known to happen a time or two." He raised his eyebrows at Kamarie. "I once stood with your father and beat them back from your shores many years ago."

"My father fought seheowks?" Kamarie's voice was filled

with wonder.

"Your father was quite a warrior when he was younger," Brant replied with a quirk of amusement about his mouth.

"You must be weary from your travels. Won't you sit down?" Oraeyn gestured to a smaller room off the Grand Hall.

Brant and Kamarie followed Oraeyn's lead. As they settled themselves, Oraeyn pulled on a cord that rang a bell in another part of the castle.

"Is it simply dragons the seheowks are scared of?" Oraeyn asked. "It must have been something else all these years protecting Aom-igh, the dragons have only recently come back to the upper realm."

"I believe Calyssia was partly responsible as well," Brant said after a moment of thoughtful silence. "She took her duties as Gatekeeper very seriously."

"Calyssia did a lot more than most people realize," Oraeyn's voice was thoughtful.

"That she did," Brant agreed. "She was the most powerful being I have ever met. I am convinced she was a mage."

"I thought she was a wizardess?" Kamarie said.

"Yes, that was her race. I was speaking to her magical ability. In the hierarchy of power human wizards are near the bottom though unicorns are considered lower due to the fact that their power is confined mainly to healing. Mixed through the middle are gryphons, mer-folk, and pegasi. At the top, of course, are dragons."

A servant entered the room with a tray that held a plate of fruit tarts and tumblers of spiced wine. The three friends partook of the refreshments.

"Is there anything else I can do for you, my lords, lady?" the servant asked.

"That will be all for now. But if you could ask the cook to prepare lunch and have it ready in the small dining room, I would appreciate it," Oraeyn replied. The servant bowed and left the room.

"You can see through illusions," Kamarie said to Brant after taking a delicate bite of her tart. "What does that make you?"

"I believe there must be some wizard's blood in my ancestry," Brant shrugged and took a sip from his cup. "And there is the Oath of my country, which is old and powerful. I believe it grants us strength beyond our normal capabilities."

"But what is a mage?" Oraeyn asked returning to Brant's earlier comment and taking a sip from his own cup.

"It is a being who can wield even more powerful magic than a dragon," Brant replied. "They are very rare, but incredibly strong."

"And you think Aunt Calyssia was one?" Kamarie queried, fascinated by this explanation. She had never heard it put so neatly before.

"I don't know for sure," Brant admitted. "I'm convinced Scelwhyn himself was a mage, or near it. Calyssia was part wizardess, part mer-folk, and a dragon ward besides. She held Pearl Cove under a protective shell for over twenty years, and she maintained wards of protection around the entire border of Aom-igh. All I know for sure, however, is that she was the most powerful being I ever had the privilege of knowing."

Oraeyn put his tumbler down and let his hand fall to the hilt of the Fang Blade, his fingers brushing the steel pommel. Ever since he came to possess the great sword magic had intrigued him. In that same adventure that had given him the weapon, Oraeyn had also had a strange encounter with a wood nymph that had shaken him to the core.

"You have other abilities besides seeing through illusions," Oraeyn commented.

Brant's face took on a thoughtful expression. "True. I learn languages easily and can hear what most people cannot. For instance, I understand tree-speech," he chuckled at the incredulous looks that he received from both Oraeyn and Kamarie. "Yes, even the forests have a language of their own." He stared at Oraeyn through narrowed eyes. "Are you still trying to solve the riddle of the Fang Blade?"

Oraeyn sighed. "Besides the wood nymph, no one else can tell me if I actually have my own magic. To tell the truth, I kind of hope it was all the Fang Blade."

"That sword is an extraordinary weapon," Brant said, "but only a living creature can hold and retain magic. A sword, ring, or other device is merely a catalyst. However, I have long thought that perhaps the Fang Blade responds more to the goodness in the heart of the one who wields it than it does to magic. Llian was never attributed with any extraordinary powers, but all accounts agree that the Fang Blade blazed brightly for him and helped him protect his country in the face of overwhelming odds. That is power of a kind though not the sort that wizards and dragons wield."

Oraeyn made a face, but accepted Brant's words. He brushed a few crumbs from his lap. "Dylanna said much the same," he replied, his voice wry. "You are right. Mostly I'm just curious; I don't like thinking there are things about myself that even I don't know."

"I can understand that," Brant replied.

"Yes, yes, breakfast was most delicious," Kiernan Kane's cheerful voice rang out as he entered the Grand Hall with a servant. "Oh! Our hero has returned early, welcome, welcome!" Kiernan bowed to Brant as he neared the three friends. The act of bowing nearly landed the gangly minstrel on his ear, but he managed to catch himself in time.

"Breakfast?" Oraeyn asked. "It's time for lunch."

"Oh, hurrah!" Kiernan jigged a step. "I'm starved."

Oraeyn laughed. "But you just finished breakfast."

Kiernan's face took on a pained look. "Majesty," he complained, "look at how thin I am! I have many years of starvation on the road to make up for, this is the first job I have held in a very long time that has provided me with three good meals a day." The minstrel's face was a perfect mask of sorrow, but his tone held a hint of laughter.

The servant bowed. "Lunch is ready as requested, Sire."

Kiernan unslung his mandolin and began to pluck a cheerful tune, ostensibly in celebration of lunch being served.

Brant shook his head in amused silence. The initial enmity between the warrior and the minstrel had long since been placed by the wayside, especially since Oraeyn had offered Kiernan

Kane a full-time position as Court Minstrel. Now the two men tolerated each other. Kiernan often made a point to poke fun at Brant, and Brant more often than not ignored the minstrel. The two men were not friends, but each was content to respect the other's perspective, and stay out of one another's way as much as possible. When their paths did cross, they were as friendly as could be expected.

Brant cleared his throat. "Oraeyn, I still want to discuss your offer of sending men to help in Llycaelon's battle with the seheowks."

Kiernan clapped. "Bravo, bravo! This is what we need, a united front for all the right reasons. Excellent, my boy... er... Sire..."

Brant shook his head in exasperation, but he refrained from comment.

"We can talk about relations between Llycaelon and Aom-igh after we eat," Kamarie offered. She held Oraeyn's hand as they walked towards the smaller dining room. "Come along, Kiernan, let's see if Cook can't help you out with that starvation problem of yours."

Kiernan Kane nodded enthusiastically and capered after the trio, making inane comments about how hard it was to maintain one's health when one's diet consisted of the roots and berries that could be found along the side of any road.

CHAPTER
FIVE

$\mathcal{D}$ylanna could feel her mind slipping. She was so tired, but she was afraid to sleep, fearful that if she slipped out of consciousness she might never wake again. She fought against the weariness, struggling to focus her thoughts on something, anything besides how tired she was. Her thoughts found Brant, and she clutched at his memory with what little strength she still possessed. She pictured his face, and tried to hold on to the image, forcing herself to stay awake.

Colors escaped her. She could not remember what they looked like. She forgot what it was to see, and the image in her mind of Brant's face grew fuzzy. In desperation Dylanna bit the inside of her lip, hard. Her teeth sank into her own flesh and covered her tongue with a warm, metallic flavor. The sharp pain brought her wide-awake again. She winced, but made herself face it, clinging to the one sense left to her. The pain helped her focus, but it served another purpose as well, it helped her know she was awake, and thus, still alive.

Upon waking from yet another disturbing nightmare, Oraeyn retired to his study. Dawn had not yet broken over Aom-igh, but he could no longer sleep. Yawning and stretching, he decided that if sleep was going to continue to evade him, he might as well be productive.

Emyth had mentioned that a few strange missives had come in over the past few days, but Oraeyn had been too busy to even peek at them. He sat down at his writing desk and stared at the pile of messages in weary dismay. They had doubled in number since the last time he looked at them two days ago. His steward had continued to collect them and place them together. Each one was marked with a different crest, and none of the crests were immediately familiar. As he scrutinized the wax seals, the realization grew in his mind that he did know them, but had seen them so rarely they were not easily identifiable. These were messages from other nations: Yochathain, Kallayohm, Efoin-Ebedd, and Endalia. Why would they be sending him messages?

He unrolled the first parchment and scanned its contents. As he read the hastily scrawled words his stomach clenched and he came fully awake.

Yochathain... burning... Oraeyn had never been to Yochathain, but Brant and Kiernan both spoke of it. Their descriptions of its beauty always transported Oraeyn's imagination. Surely this message could not be correct. The entire country burning?

With trembling hands, he opened the rest of the missives and studied their contents in depth, reading and re-reading every line. Each was the same.

Dark creatures attacking... master riding a giant werehawk with silver wings... none left alive. Could it be true? Could such evil and destruction exist in the world without him knowing even a hint of it?

His nightmares from the past several nights surged to the front of his thoughts. Always, upon waking, the nightmares faded from his memory. He was unable to recall any details, all that lingered was the unsettling sensation that his dreams had been unpleasant. But now, reading the information contained in the scrolls, every detail returned to haunt him in perfect clarity. The sickening sensation that all was not well rose up to overwhelm him.

He rested his head in his hands, the messages and papers

crumpled under his elbows. His fear, his most secret worries, sprang to life, and he had no idea what to do next.

After a moment, Oraeyn sat up, ready to act. He would send a message to Leila and Dylanna. He would speak to Brant and Arnaud, they would guide and counsel him on what must be done. They would give him advice on how to prepare for what was described in these messages.

He grabbed a quill and scrawled a note to Leila. Then, attaching one of the messages he had just read to his own note, he called Emyth, who arrived looking a bit disheveled and bleary.

"Send this to the Lady Leila," he instructed, handing the parchment to his steward.

"At once, Sire."

After he left, Oraeyn sat for a long while in his study. He would wait to hear back from the wizardesses before he did anything rash like announcing that a giant invading army might be on its way. He did not wish to cause panic. His birds were swift, Leila or Dylanna would return his message by tomorrow. Would one day cause too much delay? Perhaps he should speak with Brant now. No, he would follow the course of action he had chosen. But he would not be idle. There were defenses and escape routes he had yet to explore or investigate. Kamarie knew the palace and the surrounding area better than anyone, perhaps she could help him in his study of Aom-igh's natural defenses. But he did not wish to cause her undue worry. Perhaps he could recruit her help without telling her what he was doing.

Jemson furrowed his brow as he listened to the daily report from his chief scribe, little of which held any interest at all for the young king. Financial reports and legal matters were important, of course, but the desperate concern on Jemson's mind was the Border Patrol. He feigned interest and nodded patiently, willing this conscientious man to conclusion. After what felt like an age, the scribe stopped talking and asked if the young king had any questions or notes to add to the report. Jemson looked up and rubbed his chin, then dropped his hand, embarrassed. It was becoming a bad habit, checking for signs of stubble whenever he was overwhelmed by his duties as king.

"What about the Border Patrol? Has there been any official word from them yet? I was hoping to hear an update."

The scribe shook his head. "Sire, we sent two divisions to help them as requested, but we've not heard from them for several days. The information I have is merely hearsay."

"Well, what have you heard?"

"Apparently the captain of the patrol stationed near Caethyr gap was killed in battle. Before he died, he passed his command over to a young Aetoli named Devrin of House Merle. The lack of communication may be due to this change in command. But according to what I've heard, the seheowks are contained for the moment."

Jemson frowned and rubbed his chin absently. Devrin. That name sounded so familiar, but he could not recall exactly why. He forced his hand away from his face and resisted the urge to pick at the embroidery on his tunic.

"For the moment," he repeated, "but for how long? How are they contained? What is going on out there? Why have the seheowks suddenly become such an enormous threat? In the past they've only been a nuisance. You say they are 'contained.' What does that even mean? We don't 'contain' the seheowks. We defeat them. We destroy them. We remove them from our borders and drive them back into the sea whence they came. Now I'm told they have been merely contained? Contained for how long? Contained by what? Something has changed out there, and I need to know what."

The scribe looked down at the crumpled papers in his hands. "Sire, my sources have reported that the seheowks have been trapped behind a wall of fire."

The young king growled with impatience. "That cannot last long. Not now that the rainy season has begun."

"No, Sire."

"Why have they not been driven back into the sea?"

"I do not know, Sire."

Jemson dropped his shoulders as weariness overcame him,

and put his head down in his hands with a sigh. He wondered for a moment why his father had ever wanted this responsibility. Jemson himself was not sure he wanted it, most days. What he really desired was to be a part of the Border Patrol and defend his country as an aethalon. His greatest desire was to pass through the Corridor, earn a rank, and then travel a bit like his uncle. He wanted so much more than to sit in this castle and give all the interesting and exciting assignments to someone else. He hated being the last to know, especially when his heart longed to be the first to lead.

"Very well," Jemson said, a firm note of decision in his tone, "the borders are my first priority. Hearsay is no foundation for creating a plan of defense. I will ride out there myself, find this young captain, and learn exactly what is going on."

"Your Majesty! You cannot do that!" The scribe sounded properly shocked.

"I most certainly can," Jemson replied, "and I most certainly will."

The scribe's face paled. "But, Sire! Deliberately putting yourself in harm's way... you have a responsibility to your country and your people to remain here."

"There you are wrong. I do indeed have a responsibility, and that is to ensure the safety of our people. If that safety is threatened no worthy man, let alone king of Llycaelon, hides behind the last line of defense. I may be king, but that does not rob me of my honor or my duty as a man to fight side-by-side with my brothers in this battle. How can I provision and reinforce this defense based on idle talk? I need to be there. I need to see it. I must add my sword to theirs."

"When do you mean to leave?"

"Now," Jemson replied. He looked thoughtful for a moment, and then he nodded in satisfaction. "Yes, I will leave now. Put everything on hold until I return. I must go meet this young captain and see this wall of fire."

"As you please, my lord."

"Ready my horse," Jemson said. "I will leave within the hour. Inform my grandmother of my plans."

Lady Fiora had recovered some since Brant had returned home. She was still frail, and her mind was not as steady as it once had been, but Brant's return had driven away her madness. Jemson had never really known her as he grew up, she kept to herself, lost in her own sorrow. However, the healing process that had begun in her had given him back a piece of his family, and the two of them had become quite close. Jemson felt rather shy of her at first, and perhaps she had been a bit shy of him, as well. But the past three years saw a bond between them grow and deepen.

After the scribe left, Jemson felt the bars around his heart spring open. Perhaps he would get to experience true leadership after all. Excitement swept over him; for a few hours at least, he would escape this prison of a palace and do the real work of leading his country with honor.

Kamarie stepped through the door of the cottage into the already warm air of the morning. Upon departing the throne, Arnaud and Zara had wanted nothing more than a simple home with good land to farm. They chose a property near the castle so they could remain as counselors to Oraeyn, and so Kamarie could remain close to her beloved. The cottage and farm needed work, but it was precisely the sort of work Arnaud had missed for too many years.

Kamarie was glad her father could enjoy the quiet life he had always longed for. Arnaud's step was lighter without the weight of the crown, and the worry lines departed from his face. There was something rich about his life as he worked and built this humble farm that had never been present in his life and duties as king.

"There's something about doing real *work*," Arnaud often commented. "Being king is harder than anyone realizes—it's the kind of work that drains you, sucks the life out of you. Real labor with your hands doesn't do that, it rejuvenates a person and makes him feel alive again."

Kamarie could not deny that it had given her father back his youth. Their life now was simple, peaceful. She had never seen her parents happier. She was delighted that they had the ability to live their lives together without the weight of the kingdom pressing down on their shoulders. Kamarie herself still spent most of her days in the palace. It felt strange to her that she no longer lived in the place that had been her home for twenty years. When she entered the castle grounds it was often with the wistful sense that she had lost something precious and dear to her heart. Its walls were no longer her home, and she had no claim to any of the rooms. Every once in a while she would walk down a hallway and be struck again by how familiar it felt, and yet how foreign, as well. Sometimes she was hit with a wave of homesickness and she would lean against a wall and just let the memories of her childhood wash over her.

Of course, she thought, *I will live there again once Oraeyn and I are married, and yet, somehow it will never be quite the same.*

Her homesickness eased as she thought of her betrothed. She remembered the first few days they had spent together: she, a willful princess, convinced he was going to prevent her from having the adventure she craved, and he, an unwilling escort, certain that she was just a stuck-up noble. Somehow over the course of their adventure they had become friends. Kamarie shook her head in amazement and then yelped in alarm as someone grabbed her by the arm.

"Kamarie! Kamarie, it's okay, it's just me!" Oraeyn's voice, full of suppressed laughter, broke through Kamarie's fright.

"Oraeyn!" Kamarie's tone was exasperated, and a twinge of embarrassment at her extreme reaction surged through her.

"I wondered if you would like to go on a picnic?" Oraeyn asked, feigning innocence as he held up a basket for her to see.

"You scare me half to death just to ask me to go on a picnic with you?" Kamarie demanded, her heart still racing a bit faster than she would have liked.

"Did I scare you?" Oraeyn asked.

"No!" Kamarie retorted, her cheeks growing warm. "Well, yes," she admitted. "What was I supposed to think with you sneaking up on me and grabbing my arm? Don't you have a kingdom to rule or some papers to sign or an ambassador to meet today?"

"I cleared my schedule," Oraeyn's voice was light, but something about his tone sounded preoccupied. "I wanted to spend the day with you."

The thought of a pleasant afternoon away from Oraeyn's duties at the palace filled Kamarie with delight, but she hesitated. "You don't get to take a day off from being king, *they* might not like it," she teased.

"Well, this king takes a day off now and then," Oraeyn said cheerfully. "And if *they* don't like it, *they* can give the crown to somebody else."

"You don't take your duties *that* lightly," Kamarie retorted.

Oraeyn sobered. "No, I don't," he admitted. "But the palace staff is overly concerned that I make time to eat, and even kings ought to get a day off every now and then. That's advice I got from both Brant *and* your parents, so I don't think anyone will complain. I happen to think it's excellent advice."

"You're right, I can't argue with that; where are we going?"

"I thought we'd explore the caves up by the coast," Oraeyn said. "Brant says they're worth taking a look at, which probably means they're more than just caves, but Brant's so close about everything I couldn't get any more information out of him."

"That's our Brant," Kamarie agreed, "although, he is better about it than he used to be, you have to admit."

"Agreed," Oraeyn conceded, "but sometimes I think he's even more close-mouthed than ever. Anyway, let's go, even if the caves aren't exciting or spectacular, the beach is still the perfect place for a picnic."

The basket was filled with delicious food, all Kamarie's favorites. She sat on the ground and dug her bare toes into warm, wet sand, enjoying the freedom of it. Oraeyn was unusually quiet as they ate, but she did not pester him about his thoughts. She attributed his silence to a simple enjoyment of being away from the tangible reminders of his duties. However, when they finished their meal, she looked up and saw him staring out at the ocean. His lips were pressed together as if holding back a tide of words. She cocked her head to one side, puzzled, and opened her mouth to ask him what he was thinking about.

Just then, Oraeyn glanced over at her and an impish expression filled his face. He leaped to his feet and raced out into the waves. Kamarie shrieked with laughter as a rain of cold water showered down over her head. The water ran down her face and dripped off the end of her nose.

"Oraeyn!" she shouted. "I'll get you for that! This dress is ruined now!"

Oraeyn might have felt sorrier about the dress if Kamarie had not been laughing so hard. He was already dripping wet himself anyway. He darted back as Kamarie leaped after him, dancing just out of her reach. Kamarie made a careless lunge but tripped and nearly fell face-first into the water, but Oraeyn skipped off to one side and deftly caught her. He helped Kamarie find her balance, and then, holding her hand, he turned and began walking along the shoreline.

"Come on, let's go see those caves," Oraeyn said.

Kamarie tugged at her hand, but after a moment she gave up with a merry chuckle. "Didn't Brant say the caves reminded him of a place where he used to play as a child, when he still lived in the Dark… I mean, Llycaelon."

"He told me that, too."

"Do you think they lead anywhere?"

"I don't know, I've never paid much attention to them before," Oraeyn's voice held a grim note that Kamarie wondered at, but did not comment on. Instead she shrugged and followed his lead.

They approached the great rock formations and paused, admiring the twists and turns of the rocks that had been created by the sweeping waves of the ocean. The entrances to the caves were massive, yawning caverns that led to a myriad of tunnels and chambers. Some were no more than shallow imprints, but others extended far beyond the line of sight.

"They're bigger than I remembered," Kamarie breathed, a little awed.

"I wonder how many were created by the tides," Oraeyn

spoke thoughtfully. "They could be the answer to a siege."

"A siege?" Kamarie asked, feeling as if she had missed something important.

"If we could tunnel into the caves from the palace, they could become a very useful secret passage," Oraeyn continued, heedless of her concern.

"Why would we need to prepare for a siege?" Kamarie asked. She enjoyed secret passageways as much as anyone, but she was not sure she understood the purpose of this new idea. The tunnels would be a great hiding place, but they just ended a person up on the shore with nowhere to go but the ocean.

"Just in case," Oraeyn said nonchalantly.

Kamarie turned to look at Oraeyn. "What are you not telling me?"

Oraeyn shrugged and turned away, hiding his expression from her.

"Oraeyn," Kamarie's tone was filled with warning. Her fingers tightened reflexively around his hand. "What is it? You've been quieter than usual and you're contemplating something you're not sharing with me. What is going on?"

"I don't want you to worry, it could be nothing."

"We said we wouldn't keep secrets, remember? We promised to trust one another. We both agree that it can help to look at a problem from a different perspective. You can't protect me from every difficulty that arises," Kamarie kept her words calm, though her stomach was beginning to turn nervous flips.

Oraeyn sighed and dropped his shoulders. "I have a premonition that our time of peace is coming to an end."

"What makes you say that?"

"I've received messages from other nations."

"Llycaelon?"

"No, although Brant's reports about the seheowk attacks on Llycaelon's borders might be linked to everything else. Yesterday evening there were a handful of urgent messages on my desk from many nations. Yochathain and Kallayohm mostly… they were warnings."

"Warnings about what, exactly?" Kamarie's stomach

continued to dance about.

"It seems they have all come under attack. All the messages are the same: an army of vicious beasts came up out of the sea and overwhelmed them. Creatures of unfathomable ferocity and relentless malice surged across these nations, leaving death and destruction behind them."

Kamarie pursed her lips. "What does Dylanna have to say about all of this?"

Oraeyn opened his mouth to speak and then hesitated. Kamarie's stomach stopped doing flips and clenched into a cold little ball of tightness.

"Oraeyn?" Kamarie asked, trying to read the expression that fell over his face. She forced herself to remain calm, but a prickling sensation crept across the back of her neck.

"Something strange has happened," his voice was so quiet she had to strain to hear. "I sent them a message this morning, before dawn, but it returned before I came to get you. It was unopened."

"Did the bird get lost?" Kamarie let go of Oraeyn's hand and began to pace.

"I don't think so. It's possible, but it's never happened before. The birds are incredibly reliable."

Kamarie whirled to stare at him. "When were you going to tell me this?" she demanded. Two spots of color appeared in her cheeks. "They are my aunts. I ought to be informed if they go missing!" Fury made her speak in cold, choked sentences.

"We don't know they're missing. And I was going to tell you if your mother couldn't find them," Oraeyn reassured her quickly. "She didn't act overly concerned, so I thought she might already have some idea as to what is going on. They were supposed to be in the middle of an experiment after all."

Kamarie calmed down a bit at hearing this. She breathed a deep sigh and tightened her lips, clamping them together to prevent any more angry words from spilling out.

Oraeyn put a hand on her shoulder. "I'm sorry I didn't tell you, your mother did not act worried and I just..."

"Didn't want me to worry, either," Kamarie finished for him.

Oraeyn kicked the toe of his boot into the sand. He squinted warily up at Kamarie and nodded slightly.

"What is so wrong with me worrying?" Kamarie asked, her tone much gentler than before. "You worry about things all the time. Everyone I know worries, even Brant, and it hasn't killed them yet. What's so wrong about me hearing bad news and worrying a little over it?"

"I just feel that you just shouldn't have to, I guess," Oraeyn mumbled. "I'm sorry."

Kamarie looked down, a little ashamed of her reaction. "I'm sorry, too. I just don't like not knowing about important things."

Oraeyn nodded, somewhat abashed. "I wouldn't like it either."

Kamarie's frustration began to dissolve. "Where is my mother now? Is she still looking for Aunt Dylanna and Leila?"

"Yes."

"And you're positive she didn't seem too anxious about their silence?"

"Fairly certain," Oraeyn replied.

"Well, she'll let us know when she's done, I'm assuming you told her where we were going?"

"Yes."

"Then let's explore these caves and see if that secret tunnel idea would work."

"All right," Oraeyn said.

He followed Kamarie into the caves, pondering her words. Even he did not fully understand his overwhelming need to protect her. It was her quick thinking and skills that had gotten them out of many potentially perilous situations in that first journey. The dread brought on by the nightmares that plagued him rose up in his mind, but he banished their memories. They were just dreams, he assured himself. Despite his best efforts, a sensation that something terrible was coming gnawed at Oraeyn's mind, but he hid his worry from Kamarie, letting her words and presence ease his mind, and her spirit of adventure draw him out of his gloomy thoughts.

CHAPTER
SIX

Zara wrinkled her brow in perplexed frustration. Shoulders sagging, she descended from the summit of Fortress Hill. Defeat tasted bitter, but there was nothing more she could do on her own. The better part of the day had been spent attempting to contact her sisters without any results to show for her efforts. Although she had not been particularly perturbed about their silence when Oraeyn first asked for her help, a sliver of apprehension now niggled at the back of her mind.

She reached the palace and sat down in the Cottage Room to wait for Oraeyn and Kamarie to return, settling into her favorite couch: a soft, comfy, overstuffed thing covered in a beautiful, but threadbare, flowered print. The Cottage Room had been a parting gift from Scelwhyn. There was a delicate, beautiful magic woven throughout the chamber to make it feel like a little cottage in the woods, separate from the palace of which it was a part. Upon entering, one always caught a subtle whiff of pine needles and woodsmoke. The air was tinged with orange light. Nearly imperceptible sounds filled the room, and one could just pick them out if one sat very still and listened: the burbling as of a nearby stream, the muted swoosh and murmur of a summer breeze tickling the leaves on tall, old trees, the buzz of insects, and the chirping of birds.

Zara let her mind drift into memory. Scelwhyn had never been a man of grand gestures, but he wanted to bestow something special to show his approval of Arnaud as both a king and soon-to-be son-in-law. He had asked Arnaud to name something he thought he might need to help him rule Aom-igh. Arnaud's expression had grown distant and filled with longing, and he had asked, timidly, for a piece of home inside the palace.

Scelwhyn may not have thought it the most practical thing, but he had agreed, and Arnaud had been asked many times for his input as Scelwhyn worked the enchantment. When it was finished, Arnaud furnished it with simple, comfortable furniture. The tables were plain wood. A woven rug of earthy colors and simple fabric graced the floor. Zara could still remember the first time Arnaud showed the room to her.

"My residence may indeed be a castle," he told her, "but this room, at least, will be our cottage."

Over the years, this room had been their haven, the place where they spent the most time as a family. The walls were sealed to prevent the intrusion of outside sounds upon the peaceful chamber, and Arnaud had made it clear that nothing in the world was important enough to interrupt his family time when they were here. Thankfully, decades of peace had made it easy for the palace staff to obey this mandate.

When they moved out of the palace, Arnaud had brought Oraeyn here and explained its purpose. He gave Oraeyn permission to change the furnishings as he saw fit, but Oraeyn refused to alter a single thing. Understanding the importance of this place to his betrothed and her family, he told the three of them that they had a standing invitation to enter the palace, and specifically this room, whenever they wished.

Zara did not have to wait long. Oraeyn and her daughter burst into the room just a few minutes after she arrived. Kamarie was giggling. A bunch of tiny, light-blue flowers were woven into her hair like a crown above her sparkling eyes and flushed cheeks. Oraeyn was doing a poor imitation of someone who had yelled at them for being too boisterous, not realizing, of course, that it was the king he was reprimanding. When they noticed

Zara though, their laughter died.

"How long have you been waiting?" Kamarie asked in concern.

"Only a moment," Zara said reassuringly, then she looked out the window and started in surprise. "Is it night already?"

Kamarie nodded. "Toreth-rise came about an hour ago."

Zara took a deep breath and let it out slowly. "I suppose I have been waiting longer than a moment then," she made a sound that was halfway between a chuckle and a sigh. "I must have drifted off; I had forgotten how much energy that kind of work takes. And I had forgotten how much I love this room."

"This was the first place Arnaud showed me after he gave me the crown," Oraeyn commented. "It's my favorite part of the palace."

"It was ours, too," Zara said fondly.

"What did you find?" Oraeyn asked.

Zara leaned her head back and rubbed her temples with her fingers. "Nothing."

"Nothing?" Oraeyn sounded startled.

"What do you mean?" Kamarie asked, her voice faltering a little in dismay.

"I don't quite understand it myself, but I'll try to explain what I was doing so that you can better understand the implications. When Oraeyn came to me and told me he was worried about Dylanna and Leila because he had not heard from them, I was not too concerned. You see, I already knew that Dylanna and Leila were planning on attempting a new experiment. It did not surprise or alarm me that a message returned unopened. I thought perhaps they had created a barrier around Leila's house in order to prevent unwanted distractions.

"I went to the top of Fortress Hill. I believed its ancient power might help me focus my search. As sisters, Dylanna, Leila, and I are all linked; if I concentrate, I can sense them when they are nearby. I can even find them when they are farther away. No barrier should prevent that. Even when Calyssia was in Pearl Cove I could still sense her as a distant presence. But when I sent out strands of magic to find Leila and Dylanna today those strands never ended."

Kamarie looked confused. Zara sighed and pressed her palms together in front of her lips. "How to explain? It's like a ball of yarn," she said, struggling to put the concept into more familiar terms. "If you hold onto the loose end of the yarn and roll it against a wall, the ball should bounce off the wall and roll back to you. Well, what if there is no wall? Then the yarn just keeps rolling until it hits something. That's what happened. I threw out my magic, and it never bounced back. It's as if my sisters suddenly ceased to exist."

"How far did you look?" Oraeyn asked. "What if they were picked up by unfriendly dragons and flown to another island? Would you have been able to find them across a distance like that?"

"I thought about that," Zara said. "So I refined my attempt, changing its purpose and strengthening it. Then I sent it out again, this time I sent a strand in every direction and allowed the strands to travel far beyond our borders: same results. I spent the entire day searching, and found nothing. Absolutely nothing." Zara's tone hinted at her frustration and concern and Kamarie picked up on it.

"Maybe their experiment shields them even better than Calyssia's barrier did," she said in a reassuring tone. "Oraeyn said they've only been missing for a day or two at the most. For all we know they're still at Leila's home."

Zara nodded, but her expression was filled with doubt. "Perhaps. If we do not hear from them soon, though, I will try again. I have a few other ideas for finding them. I simply used the easiest method first."

"I'm sure that the dragons would be willing to help," Kamarie said, forcing a cheerful tone.

"Yole would, at the very least," Oraeyn added.

Kamarie nodded in agreement. Yole had grown quite a bit since their first meeting. Then, he was just a bedraggled orphan wandering through the Mountains of Dusk. He was the one who had helped them discover the Fang Blade, but neither Kamarie nor Oraeyn had suspected that the boy was actually a child of the

Lost: dragons who had chosen to remain above-realm in human form when most of their kin had fled to the underground tunnels and caverns of Krayghentaliss. Brant had known, of course. Very little surprised Brant.

When the conflict between Aom-igh and Llycaelon ended, King Rhendak had offered Yole a place with his true people, and Yole accepted. He still visited the palace often, but he loved his true form and the family he had found among the dragons. Kamarie missed her adopted little brother sometimes, but she was happy he had found a place that he could call "home." She believed it was better that Yole had chosen to live with his people; among humans he would always have felt like a stranger.

"That's true. I hadn't yet considered asking the dragons to help," Zara said thoughtfully, "they are indeed more powerful than I, and their aid would be welcome. Perhaps tomorrow…"

"But it is late now," Kamarie interjected, "and father will soon be concerned."

An icy fist clenched around Kamarie's heart. Distress over the disappearance of her aunts consumed her thoughts though she clung to a semblance of composure. Though she tried to hide her worry, she fooled neither her mother nor Oraeyn.

Zara nodded reluctantly. "True, we should be getting home." She rose and glided out of the room with queenly grace and Kamarie moved to follow.

Oraeyn tapped Kamarie on the shoulder lightly as he walked her out of the room. "We will find them," he promised.

She turned and threw her arms about his neck, taking comfort in his strength, and nodded silently against his shoulder, struggling against the tears that wanted to fall. Oraeyn hugged her tightly and then let go as Kamarie stepped back. She nodded again, her heart too full for words.

"Good night," Oraeyn said.

"Good night," Kamarie's voice was barely a whisper, and then she was gone.

Much later that night King Oraeyn again stood atop the great wall of his castle. He liked the feel of the cool night air, the soft breeze filled with a salty scent wafting in from the ocean, and the silence that was not present in the long, echoing halls of the palace. Even late at night, those halls were always full of servants who scurried about on various errands. He was weary, but he did not seek sleep. Vague memories of nightmares made him loath to retire to bed. They were troubling and difficult to shake. Even upon waking, he was never sure whether the visions were real or imagined. They came every night now, rendering useless any sleep he did manage to find.

Oraeyn took a long, deep breath. Above him the stars shone clear and bright, coldly removed from the pain and concerns of the world. Oraeyn's fascination with the night sky had prompted Brant to teach Oraeyn their names and the stories behind the constellations. It amazed Oraeyn that despite all their differences, the stories about the constellations were the same in Llycaelon as they were in Aom-igh. Now, Oraeyn easily found the outline of Yorien.

"You understood only too well the weight of the crown," Oraeyn whispered to the outcast king. "You made the decision I wish I could have made and look at where you ended up. Was your sleep troubled by nightmares? Could you feel the threat coming before it ever reached you?"

There was no answer, but Oraeyn did not expect one. He leaned against the stone railing. The night was breezy, and the wind carried the fine ocean mist on its back. Oraeyn welcomed the tiny droplets of water on his face. He could hear the crash of the waves below him and his thoughts wandered to the caves he and Kamarie had explored earlier that day.

They had ventured inside, marking the turns they took so they would not get lost. The tunnels went much further back than Oraeyn had expected, and he believed there was at least one secret passage leading from the castle to the beach.

His thoughts wandered again, this time to the messages he had perused much earlier that morning, and his concern over the missing wizardesses. He would show the messages to Brant and Arnaud tomorrow, he dared not put it off any longer. He feared that taking even a single day to ponder them might have been a foolish and fatal mistake.

Shifting restlessly, Oraeyn wondered how many kings had stood in this very place. How many of them had been sure of themselves, and how many had been afraid? He shivered, imagining the ghosts of kings long dead huddled around him. He sensed their presence. Strength. Pride. Regret. Always searching. Always preparing. Always hoping. They kept watch with him, ever-sharing his concern for the welfare of Aom-igh.

CHAPTER
SEVEN

It was time. Time for another nightmare. In his prison, he felt only pleasure as he stretched out a bit more of his power and touched the mind of his only obstacle. A surge of annoyance swept through him as he remedied his thoughts: the only obstacle he could reach. The other... the other would have to wait until he could reclaim his true form. But his plans were advancing with perfection. Ghrendourak was carrying out his orders well. He had been an excellent choice. Ghrendourak was using his power and his suggestions exactly as the imprisoned one wished. Yochathain, Endalia, and Kallayohm lay in ruins. Efoin-Ebedd was well on its way to joining their fate. It was a mere matter of a few days, or weeks at the most, before he would have what he needed.

There was the small matter of his enemy, of course. He sneered and shook away the irritating thought. No, he was stronger. He had always been stronger. But he hadn't always been as cautious as he needed to be. This time it would be different. This time, he would make his foe feel the agony of betrayal, as he had felt so many centuries ago. His enemy would beg for mercy, beg for forgiveness, and beg to become his loyal servant before he was through.

This was a pleasant thought, and the prisoner lingered over it with loving fondness for a long while. Then he turned his full attention towards the boy. The boy! What a laughable thought, that he might pose a threat! But he had learned to be careful, to be attentive; his enemy had used such weak-seeming pawns before in their endless game of Karradoc—had used them to devastating effect.

No, he had learned not to ignore any of the Minstrel's pieces on the board, no matter how insignificant they might appear. That was a mistake he had made too often. But not this time.

If he had possessed teeth, he would have gnashed them together. The long imprisonment was wearing him down, and he was still rebuilding his strength from the last failure. It would not do for him to lose his focus like this. His full attention was needed upon every detail if he hoped to win this round and taste the freedom he deserved. But he would not be content with mere escape from his bonds, no, he would ascend much higher and take his rightful place as ruler of this pitiful world the Minstrel loved so much. He would grind it beneath his feet and bend it to his will. He would remake it in his own image.

Reaching out from his prison, he found the boy: he was just drifting off to sleep. With a gleeful snarl, he stretched out a tendril of his power and wove it into the boy's mind. Of all the possible futures, he wove the one that would hurt the lad the most and then spun the images through his dreams. The boy with the golden sword moaned and tossed in his bed, but did not awaken.

Exhilarating in his strength, and full of smug satisfaction, he pulled away. His touch would linger, the nightmares would permeate the boy's dreams, and he would find no rest in sleep. His plans were proceeding, but he must continue to be diligent. He could not see his opponent, could not guess where he would next move. Caution, caution was key above all else, this time.

He was running along the edge of a high cliff. Kamarie ran beside him. The landscape was unfamiliar and wild, and Oraeyn could not remember how they had traveled here. It was impossible to tell if it was day or night.

A wild wind swirled around them, whipping Kamarie's long hair around her shoulders and across her face. Lightning split the sky as large, cold raindrops began to fall. Thunder rumbled endlessly. There was something urgent tingling in the air. Oraeyn's heart raced. Time was running out.

Suddenly Kamarie stopped. When Oraeyn turned to see what was wrong she was standing very still, staring at him in quiet defeat. Although she was only a few feet away, she was unreachable.

"I can't run anymore, Oraeyn," Kamarie shouted above the noise of the wind.

"I know you're tired," Oraeyn shouted back. "But we have to keep going! We're not safe yet!"

Kamarie's shoulders sagged and her expression was one of pain and weariness. Oraeyn grabbed her hand and tugged it sharply.

"Come on! We have to keep going!"

Kamarie allowed herself to be pulled along, stumbling and tripping as she tried to keep up. Without warning the ground at the edge of the cliff gave way, and she fell. Oraeyn threw himself to the ground, holding onto her hand as though it were a lifeline. Her weight dragged him to the edge of the cliff. He held onto her wrist with his left hand, and with his right he clutched wildly for something solid to anchor them both. His hand found a rock or a root and he grasped it desperately.

"Hold on Kamarie!" Oraeyn screamed over the noise of the storm. "I'll pull you up!"

Kamarie stared up at him, accusation written in every line of her expression. Oraeyn strained to lift her, but he could feel his strength failing. Tears blinded him and he screamed in frustration. His right hand slipped and his heart sank with the knowledge that he did not have the strength to do what needed to be done.

"Oraeyn," Kamarie's voice was quiet, but it rang out over the thunder and the wind and the rain. "Oraeyn."

"Kamarie, I can't pull you up, I can't."

"I know," she said softly, calmly. "Let go."

"What?" Oraeyn shouted. "I can't do that! I'll never let you go! I may die here but I won't let go!"

"Oraeyn, you have to go on, you have to find…" her words were drowned out by the storm. Then she screamed at him, her voice rising above the maelstrom, "Let go, you have to go on! Go! If you don't, all will be

lost."

"I don't care!"

Kamarie's face turned sad. "I love you," she said wistfully, and then slipped from his grasp.

"NO!" Oraeyn shouted, reaching, reaching...

"Sire?" the concerned voice cut through the dream, drowning out the noise of the storm. "Sire, are you all right?"

Reaching... and then he reached too far. Oraeyn tumbled over the edge of the cliff. He tried to scream but his voice failed him. He felt himself falling, and he flailed wildly in the air, his hands grappling in an attempt to catch hold of something, anything, but nothing could save him now and he was falling, falling...

Oraeyn woke with a start and a yell as he hit the floor. He had rolled to the edge of the bed in his sleep and the floor was harder than he would have thought. Still caught in the remains of the nightmare he thrashed about, attempting to free himself from the tangle of blankets and sheets that had wrapped themselves around his limbs. After a few moments of struggle he managed to stand up. He gasped for breath like a drowning man and then his head began to clear. He was dry and whole, and he was half surprised and wholly relieved to find that he was not lying amidst the knife-like rocks at the base of the cliffs in his dream.

"A dream," Oraeyn breathed in relief, and he sat down on the edge of his bed. "Just another nightmare."

"Sire?"

Oraeyn blinked at the concerned servant, his head felt fuzzy and gritty from having just woken up. "I'm all right now, Emyth. Thank you for waking me."

"Yes, Sire," the servant backed respectfully out of the room. "I will be nearby if Your Majesty needs me."

"Thank you, Emyth."

The servant disappeared and Oraeyn sat on his bed trying to calm his racing heart. With shaky hands he threw open the window and let the rays of the Dragon's Eye wash over his face, welcoming its warmth. A bird chirped its merriment to the world, and there was not even a hint of clouds in the sky.

Despite finding himself safely in his own room, remnants of the nightmare clung to him.

When he regained a bit of calm, Oraeyn began to lay out his clothes for the day. The normalcy of the chore helped to dispel what remained of the nightmare, but he wondered how much more he could take. He was not sure how long the pattern had existed, but it occurred to him that each night had been the same for many weeks now. Each night he dreamed that he lost someone he cared about. Most of the time they ordered him to go on without them and each one of them firmly believed that he was supposed to do something important. Even more disturbing than the dreams themselves were the words they had all used: "Go! If you don't, all will be lost."

Oraeyn sat down and yawned. He was more exhausted each morning than the previous night. Perhaps not sleeping at all would be preferable to experiencing the nightmares. He determined to talk with Zara. Perhaps she could prevent these dreams and allow him at least one full night of desperately needed sleep. Still yawning, Oraeyn crossed the room and immersed his face and head into the basin of cold water set near his bed. The shock helped clear away the remnants of the dream as he prepared fading energy for a dawning day.

His head felt fuzzy as he began to get dressed, but he shrugged his own discomfort away and pushed through the fog that clouded his mind. He was determined to ignore his weariness as best he could. He was just about to leave the room when someone knocked on his door.

"Yes?" he called out, through the door.

Brant entered the room in several strong, fluid, silent strides. Brant could cross a crowded room before anyone even noticed he had moved. Brant did not walk so much as he seemed to glide. It was the mark of an assassin, but Brant was hardly a hired killer. Anyone born and raised in Llycaelon could move with similar stealth and grace. It was a trait Oraeyn envied and had attempted more than once to emulate. Brant had begun teaching him the warrior art, but Oraeyn knew it was a skill he would never master in the same way. Aethalons began learning the art as soon as they could walk, and people in Llycaelon lived much longer than people in other lands. Brant had seen the passing of seven decades and was still judged to be young. Most people in Aom-igh would guess that Brant was in his mid-to-late thirties.

"Kamarie says Dylanna is missing." Brant had never been one for small talk, and he cut straight at the heart of what he wanted to talk about without preamble.

Oraeyn nodded. "And Leila as well. I have not heard from either of them in several days."

"I spoke with Zara. She is much more worried than she lets on. She's used every tactic she can think of and nothing has worked."

"We're asking the dragons for help in the search," Oraeyn replied. "When my messages returned from the Harshlands unanswered I began to feel troubled. We all know Leila would never let one of my birds return unrested or unfed, no matter what experiment she might be in the middle of."

Brant nodded. "That's a good idea. But that's not all that can be done, you know. You have risen late, for being worried."

Oraeyn bit back the urge he felt to snap at Brant. He refused to let his headache or weariness make him speak rash words. He looked at his friend and took in the disheveled hair and the hint of wildness in Brant's aspect and his irritation melted in a surge of sympathy. He knew how distraught he would be if it were Kamarie who had vanished.

"I'm anxious as well," Oraeyn kept his tone mild. "I did not mean to sleep late."

Brant nodded tersely, accepting the unspoken apology in Oraeyn's tone. "Kamarie and Zara were up with the dawn. They contacted Yole and have been searching for several hours already. So far the search has yielded no results."

Oraeyn could feel his headache growing more intense, with a promise to become much worse in the very near future, but he pushed it away, ignoring it as best he could. "We will find them," he said in a tone that sounded much more confident than he felt.

"Oraeyn, this is more than just a search for a couple of people who are missing," Brant began, his voice sharp. "Kamarie told me about the messages you received. I have received similar reports from my contacts. Why didn't you tell me about them sooner? This threat is not one to be taken lightly."

Oraeyn interrupted, all the while commanding himself to keep his tone even, remembering that it was Brant's feelings for Dylanna speaking, "I know that. You don't think I am aware of Dylanna and Leila's importance to this kingdom? Brant, I rely on them more than anyone."

Brant gave a single, impatient shake of his head. "Listen, you cannot treat this as if it's normal. Don't you think it's strange? Two wizardesses disappear and no magic can find them? Zara says they're not dead, she told me she'd know if that happened. This is not something we can shrug off, something is very wrong."

Oraeyn's tenuous grasp on his self-restraint slipped. "I'm doing all I can, Brant, everything that can be done to find them is being done, I'm sorry you're worried, but your yelling at me is not going to fix this problem," the heated words were out before Oraeyn could stop them, his voice far sharper than he meant it to be.

He regretted the words the moment they were out and he turned away from Brant, taking long strides across the room to calm his anger. He struggled to bring himself away from the edge. He did not want to snap at anyone, least of all Brant. He wished, not for the first time, that Brant would just admit that he felt more than mere affection for Dylanna, instead of trying to hide it from everyone, even himself.

"Oraeyn," Brant's voice was calm, "I am not here because Dylanna is the one who is missing."

Oraeyn concealed a groan, wondering yet again how the man was always able to ascertain what he was thinking. He would have pondered that question longer, but Brant was still talking.

"I'm trying to tell you that this is just the beginning."

"The beginning of what?" Oraeyn was starting to feel exasperated.

"I'm not sure, yet. The reports of invading armies trouble me. The seheowks attacking the borders of my own country are far more organized than they have ever been, and their numbers are increasing. I do not know what has caused the change. I believe they are linked, but I do not yet understand how."

As he finished speaking Kamarie entered through the still-open door with Yole, Arnaud, and Zara trailing close behind her. They all wore expressions filled with varying degrees of unease and frustration. Arnaud's arm was around Zara in a comforting gesture, but Oraeyn thought it looked like Zara needed help standing more than she needed comforting. They all looked weary, and Oraeyn realized just how late he had slept.

"Did everyone rise with the dawn this morning?" Oraeyn snapped, his tone filled with irritation, though it was himself he was vexed with.

Kamarie looked at him in bewilderment and she opened her mouth to respond to his sarcasm, but then thought better of it and closed her mouth. Oraeyn wondered at that, it was not like Kamarie to refrain from speaking her mind.

Instead, her words were directed towards the heart of the matter at hand. "Yole says…" she stopped. "You explain it, Yole."

The boy stepped forward and Oraeyn was struck by how much older he appeared. Even though Yole was still a child by dragon standards, his three years with his people were evident in numerous small ways. His eyes glowed with an inner fire, and their color, which could have once been termed light brown, was now decidedly and indisputably golden. There was a tilt to his head that bespoke confidence, and he held himself taller, always conscious that his small human frame was not his true form. He spoke with more self-assurance, no longer the timid orphan with no place in the world. And there was an air of poise about him that had not been there before. He wore his human form with more comfort than the other dragons, but his true nature was beginning to shine through. Brant had taught Oraeyn how to recognize myth-folk in disguise, and Oraeyn had noticed that dragons were the easiest to spot. There was something ancient, wise, and cunning about them, a power that could not be easily concealed.

"The long and short of it is that I can't find either of them, plain and simple, they don't exist," Yole's words pulled Oraeyn out of his reverie.

Yole had not yet acquired the dragons' formal speech. Though he sometimes sounded a little like Rhendak, most of the time he still spoke like a street urchin.

"What do you mean?" Oraeyn asked.

Yole shrugged helplessly. "I'm not sure. I linked with Zara to try finding them. Together, we should have been more than strong enough, no matter how far away they might be. It should have been enough even if they were shielded by their experiment. But they're just not there. When I was linked to Zara I could sense through her bond with them that they are alive, but it's like they've been cut off from magic itself."

"How is that possible? Who could have done something like this?" Oraeyn felt like someone had punched him in the stomach, driving away his breath.

Everyone gave him blank looks. Zara's face grew pinched and lines that had not been there before deepened, making her look a hundred years older. Kamarie turned her head questioningly, staring at him in disbelief. Yole hissed, a sudden intake of breath as he caught Oraeyn's words and comprehended their meaning.

"Why do you think there might be someone behind this?" Arnaud asked after a meaningful pause.

Oraeyn turned the question over in his mind for a moment and then dropped his shoulders with a sense of surrender. He had not meant to speak aloud his worst fear, but the words had flown from his lips and there was no retrieving them.

"Dylanna and Leila are two of the most powerful allies this kingdom has," Oraeyn began, choosing his words with care. "They disappear without a trace, and no power we possess can locate them. Add to that the messages I have received about an invading force spreading across the world, the recent increase in seheowk activity around Llycaelon, and the nightmares that have been plaguing my sleep for the past several weeks. All are troubling on their own, but together they begin to reveal a truly sinister picture." Oraeyn hesitated, unwilling to reveal his own weakness, but then he plunged on in what felt like a confession, "There is dread in my own heart, and I am anxious about what is coming. I have no idea what it is, but even the ghosts of kings long dead seem to have grown restless. I… I have felt them, walking the halls of the palace. For weeks now I have been plagued with terrible nightmares every night: dreams so real that I wake up exhausted and have to convince myself the horrors did not actually happen. I believe they are a warning, but of what I do not know and cannot guess. Something or someone wielding a great and terrible power is rising up against us, and I fear that whatever or whoever it is has taken Leila and Dylanna captive."

He winced, knowing he sounded insane, but when he gathered his courage to look up, he saw each of his friends gazing at him with trust. Oraeyn was not sure if he should be relieved by that or not. If they had doubted, he could have laughed off the foreboding growing in his own thoughts, but their belief strengthened his certainty. His heart shuddered violently as he recalled his dreams. Were they visions of what *would* happen, or merely specters of what *might* be? He set his jaw; visions or no, he would not let them become reality. He refused to lose these people, this family. They would find and rescue Dylanna and Leila, wherever they were. How that would happen he did not know, but he did know he would not give up until the people he loved were all safely back together again.

"But who? Who could have done this?" Zara sagged against her husband who put his arm around her for support.

Oraeyn and Kamarie looked to Brant, but Brant shook his head and Oraeyn's heart plummeted. He had hoped desperately that Brant, who knew so much of the world, might be able to lay his mind at ease once again, but Brant was as much at a loss to answer this question as any of them. But the answer came suddenly from an unanticipated source.

"An enemy so powerful none can stand against him," Kiernan Kane's voice sounded very loud as he appeared in the doorway. The words rang out against the silence, shattering it into tiny fragments.

Everyone started in surprise at the minstrel's unexpected materialization. No one had heard him arrive and none of them even noticed his presence until he spoke. Oraeyn was honestly surprised the minstrel had not arrived sooner. His obvious devotion to Leila should have made him as frantic as Brant. In fact, Oraeyn amended his thought, the minstrel should be decidedly more dramatic about his heartsickness than the stoic warrior from Llycaelon would ever be. It was strange indeed to see Kiernan acting so calm. Oraeyn wondered how long the minstrel had been standing in the doorway, but before he could ask about it the minstrel's words registered.

"What enemy?" Oraeyn demanded.

"An ancient enemy, one who has slept a long time and gained power while he slept," was Kiernan's enigmatic response, and his usually cheerful voice now sounded soft and menacing. Kamarie shivered as with a sudden chill, and Zara leaned more heavily on Arnaud's arm.

Oraeyn stared hard at the minstrel. The man often acted as if he were nothing but a fool, a court jester who could juggle and tell stories, but little else. He was awkward and oafish, his gangly limbs and gawky height causing him to stumble into trouble more often than not. But despite his tendency to boast about his own skill at minstrelsy, everyone liked him. Kiernan helped them laugh when they forgot they had the ability, and he brought them to tears with heartbreaking melodies and lyrics that summoned beloved memories. His skills and talent more than made up for minor annoyances. Upon taking the throne, Oraeyn had installed Kiernan as his permanent bard. Since then, Kiernan had been a constant presence in the castle, and he had become a dear friend.

As Oraeyn studied him, however, Kiernan's face did not appear so benign. There was a shrewd look in those eyes that could turn vacant in an instant. The man stood in the doorway and Oraeyn found himself wondering how much of the minstrel's awkwardness was a show. There was something deeper to Kiernan Kane, something Oraeyn had never paid much attention to before, but he now took very close notice of it.

"An ancient enemy, and all Tellurae Aquaous trembles at his approach," Kiernan Kane repeated softly.

"What ancient enemy?" Yole asked.

"One that too many have forgotten, his name lost in obscurity," the minstrel said, his tone so quiet that they had to strain to hear him. "Perhaps all have forgotten, except Kiernan Kane."

There was a warm, golden glow about the air. Dylanna stood outside on a pretty little cobblestone walkway that led up to a small, quaint-looking cottage. Where was she?

With a start, she recognized her surroundings. It was the village of Peak's Shadow. Below her in the valley she could just see the roofs of several other cottages, and even farther away was the outline of the tiny town where supplies could be bought and sold.

Mount Theran loomed up over the rolling fields and homes of the village like a massive guardian. Dylanna felt herself relax. Of course she knew where she was, this was her home. She had grown up here and now she was beginning a family of her own. She and Brant had decided to stay in Peak's Shadow after they married. She was glad of the decision, there were so many happy memories for her here in this village.

It was here she had met Brant, he had ridden into town to sell crops he had grown in a town to the south. His village had been going through some hard times, and Brant made the trip to Peak's Shadow in search of better prices. Her father took an interest in the young man and invited him to dinner. By the time dessert was served Brant was working for her father.

She remembered the first time she saw him. She had known instantly that there was something special about him, and mysterious... she shook her head. Where did that thought come from? There was nothing mysterious about Brant.

Bordering the walkway on both sides were gorgeous flowerbeds filled with every color of blossom imaginable. Dylanna had insisted they would add just the right touch, making her little cottage feel brighter and more cheerful. Brant had simply agreed with her in his quiet way though his lips twitched with amusement at how excited she was about flowers. With a sigh of contentment Dylanna turned to go back inside. Supper simmered over the fire and she had to be careful not to leave it too long unattended. Brant would be home from the fields at any moment and she wanted to make sure she was not late getting food on the table.

As she turned to enter the small cottage, Dylanna hesitated. She bit the tip of her tongue, trying to figure out what was wrong. Something was definitely wrong. She should not remember this cottage. She chuckled lightly at herself, feeling silly. Why should she not remember her own home?

But in spite of her laughter she still hesitated. What had she thought when she first came outside? That she recognized where she was? That was an odd thought about a place she knew as well as she knew her own name. No, it was something else, something more ominous. Something darker... darker... dark... something about Dark Warriors? But no, that could not be right, there had been no warriors in Aom-igh for centuries. Her thoughts crashed against a stone wall and she rubbed her arms, trying to dispel the uneasiness growing in her heart.

The day grew gloomy and menacing. Out of nowhere a cool breeze sprang up, causing Dylanna to shiver and pull her cloak tighter around herself. She hurried inside, forgetting whatever she needed to remember.

CHAPTER
EIGHT

Devrin looked up at the sky warily. He had divided his men into teams to keep the wall of flame alive. Groups traveled back and forth to the nearby Iron Wood to gather fallen timber with which to feed the hungry barrier they had created. Others tended the fire, their faces glowing in its light while their bodies dripped with sweat due to the heat and the exertion the task required. Because of their efforts the flames continued to crackle between the cliffs, but the seheowks were not defeated. They had retreated, but they remained just outside the firelight, biding their time. Devrin's best and only course of action was a defensive posture, but the admission grated against his very nature. He would prefer no battle at all, but to wait for one that was certain to come was unbearable.

And then there were the storm clouds.

"Captain," Stephran said, coming up to stand behind him, "those clouds mean rain."

"I know."

Stephran swiveled between Devrin and the wall of fire a few times. He hesitated a moment more, and Devrin could tell he wanted to say something, but after a silent struggle the man sighed and retreated. Devrin watched him go, he appreciated Stephran's difficulty, but he was already aware of the peril posed by the coming storm. He had not spoken of it because he had no answer to it, yet.

Stephran continued on his way after leaving the captain. He came upon two patrolling officers, who stopped and acknowledged him.

"Rain coming," the first man said.

"Keep the fires hot," Stephran said. "And a sharp lookout for any activity out of the ordinary."

"Yes, sir," both men nodded and returned to their patrol.

Nearby, Stephran could hear snatches of quiet conversation from several warriors who were resting on their bedrolls. Most of the tents had been used up in the initial fire, but the men had adjusted without complaint, especially since their new captain was also without a tent.

"Think we can hold out?" one man asked.

"The creatures have become uncanny in their strategy and ferocity," another man answered. There was a pause. "I cannot be the only one who sees it?"

"We've all seen it," a third voice spoke up. "We're not just fighting senseless brutes any longer. This is an intelligent enemy intent on driving us back. Captain sees it, too. You can tell the way he's always got that thoughtful look, like he's calculating future strategies."

"If it rains, our best defense will be gone," the first man said, his tone glum. "The odds aren't good, lads."

"Captain will have a plan. He got us out of a tight spot before, he can do it again," the third man retorted. "Didn't I just say he's always thinking? He'll have it worked out before the rain comes."

Stephran moved away, satisfied that no mutiny was brewing this night.

"What do you know of this ancient enemy?" Oraeyn asked. Everyone was staring at the minstrel in surprise.

"'Tis a long tale," Kiernan Kane said. A pained expression crossed his face and made him look much older.

Kamarie looked up at him. "Will you tell it? If there is information in your tale that can help us defeat him..."

"Defeat him?" Kiernan interrupted, his voice full of weariness and a hint of despair. "I do not know if he can be vanquished. He can be driven away, yes, sent back beyond the edge of the world, certainly, but defeated? Who can say? He always returns. He uses different faces and bodies to do his bidding, willing accomplices that he sees as expendable, but no matter how often he is chained his power remains," the minstrel sounded dispirited. It sent a chill through Oraeyn to hear the man who was always so cheerful sound so downcast. Kiernan sighed. "Well, then, I shall tell you the story. But it is a mirthless tale, indeed."

There was a solemn silence, and when the minstrel began to speak he wove a spell around them with his words. His voice began in a low, whispering tone.

"Ages ago, before the war that stained the great sea, before the seheowks were created, before the wizards quarreled, before the land was split into island countries, even before there was a need for the first High King, the people of Tellurae Aquaous lived in peace and safety. The king of the dragons ruled all, but his rule was light and his judgments rarely needed. Tellurae Aquaous was young and fresh and sparkling with life. The world knew nothing but peace and all the races lived and worked side by side as friends. There was neither war nor bloodshed between them.

"But far beyond the Nameless Isles, beyond the edge of the world itself, something sinister began to gain strength. Haunting tales were told of the hazards that existed far away in those unknown lands, and thus nobody ventured beyond what was known. At that time, the lands were massed together and there were few ships and little travel upon the great oceans. Consequently, the enemy was allowed to gather power at his leisure.

"Perhaps it could have been stopped, had we heeded the

warning signs. Perhaps the dragons could have done something to change the outcome, but they did not. They cannot be blamed, they knew not for what to watch. This was an evil beyond any of them, and it wished great harm upon all.

"I shall not speak his name here, but for the purposes of this story I shall refer to him as the Ancient Enemy. Eons ago, he was chained in a prison beneath the eastern edge of the world. But his power is great, and it grows in spite of his imprisonment. He bides his time until he can reach out and touch a mortal being, then he offers the promise of power to one willing to work towards his evil ends. His first victim was the dragon king, Starnaugh."

"I've heard of Starnaugh," Brant interjected. "He was the last of the dragon kings to reign over all of Tellurae Aquaous before the Order of Wizards took power."

"Correct," Kiernan nodded. "The Ancient Enemy possesses a power unlike anything you have ever seen or dreamed of. He is full of his own strength and hungers always for war, death, and fear. Through Starnaugh's magic, he employed his puissance to create insidious creatures such as the seheowks and other creatures of shadow. They are not natural creatures to this world, and not even truly alive. Because of this he called them his werefolk."

Zara made a questioning sound in her throat, interrupting the minstrel's tale. "I thought the wizards created were-folk when they battled each other for power over the world."

"Many were led to believe that story," Kiernan replied. "Their true creator has worked hard to erase his existence from the memories of men. The were-folk were indeed used in that war. But even the greatest wizards possessed not the power to bring shadows to the merest semblance of life. It was the Ancient Enemy who performed that feat, and it was he who gave the wizards the knowledge required to compel the were-folk to do their bidding."

"What is this Ancient Enemy?" Arnaud asked. "A dragon? A wizard?"

"He is nothing ever seen in this world before or since. He is a being unlike any other, unique. More powerful than the dragons, more powerful than the entire Order of Wizards combined. Neither human nor myth-folk, he is the essence of all that is evil and villainous in this world. He feeds on greed, fear, hate. He breathes envy and pride. He draws his power from all that is caliginous. In addition to thriving upon it, he also creates and grows it by twisting and tormenting the hearts and minds of all creatures."

"But what is he?" Kamarie asked, she leaned forward, captivated by the minstrel's words.

Kiernan paused, and his face filled with an inexplicable sorrow. "He is a monster. He is vast, towering larger than anything you have ever seen, stronger than anything you've ever known..."

"Stronger than the dragons?" Yole asked, his voice rising with incredulity. "Is that possible?"

Kiernan Kane nodded, his face grave. "Very possible. There are few things in this world that a dragon will cower from, and this lost soul should be one of them."

Kamarie wrinkled her nose and exchanged a glance with her mother. She was dissatisfied with the minstrel's answer, and could tell Zara was equally discontent, but Kiernan was speaking quickly now, delving deeper into the story, capturing them all with his words.

"Starnaugh was ultimately defeated in his attempt to gain power in Tellurae Aquaous. A brave wizardess named Shannowhyn, with the help of a few friends, created a powerful object that destroyed Starnaugh and sent the Ancient Enemy reeling back to his prison.

"The repercussions of Starnaugh's reign were vast. Afraid of the power of the dragons, the people of Tellurae Aquaous turned to the wizards to lead them. The Ancient Enemy lay sleeping for many years, fed by the turmoil and hatred in the land above him. He worked his will on the Order of the Wizards next, not using any one individual, but corrupting the race as a whole. He whispered into their dreams. First he sent nightmares, visions that confirmed their deepest doubts and augmented their most secret suspicions. Those who listened to the nightmares grew haughty and cruel. And then the Ancient Enemy raised his voice again, but this time he spoke into their minds promises of power, prestige, and fame. The war—which Brant spoke of earlier—ravaged the land. The object of power that had defeated Starnaugh was now used once again in an attempt to stop the war. It succeeded, but it had a consequence no one could have foreseen. It shattered the land into fragments, scattering the were-folk and isolating the wizards to a single land: Llycaelon."

Brant looked surprised, and Zara's hushed intake of breath made it clear that this was new information to her as well.

"Yes," Kiernan nodded slowly at both of them. "That is the truth of why Brant's people live twice the span of a normal human. Drops of wizard's blood run throughout your entire race, Son of Arne."

A deep silence filled the room as each member of the group absorbed this unexpected information.

"It was then that the dragon wards came into existence," Kiernan continued after a pause.

"Gwyna and Keltarrka," Yole interjected, his voice excited. "I know this story! Gwyna was the daughter of a candlemaker. One day, she was out tending her family's bees when she met Keltarrka. His wing was hurt and he had fallen into the field and couldn't fly away. For some reason, Gwyna wasn't afraid. The story says she could see into his heart and saw that he meant her no harm. Either way, she tended his wing, despite the fact that his blood fell on her skin and burned her arms. She nursed the dragon back to health, and they formed a bond of friendship unlike any that ever existed before. When Keltarrka was healed, he offered Gwyna a ride on his back to thank her. It was then that they discovered the mystical link that tied their destinies together and allowed them to speak mind to mind. Gwyna became the first dragon ward, and others soon followed. None know why or how the link is formed, though a few of the older dragons think it had something to do with Gwyna getting burned by Keltarrka's blood, but if that's what happened nobody has ever been able to recreate it. There is no pattern, no heredity to it, all we know for certain is when it started and that the bond between dragon and ward is unbreakable."

Kiernan waited, an amused expression on his face until Yole finished. "The dragons like to add a bit of dramatic flair to the legend," he said, scratching his jaw just below his ear, "but the facts of the story are sound. Gaining superiority through the power of flight, young humans united with dragons and set out to establish peace once again. Surprised by the rise of the dragon wards, the Ancient Enemy remained quiet in his prison and nursed his hatred. Hundreds of years passed, but though he was forgotten, his purpose and power continued to grow.

"He filled the Nameless Isles with his followers and when he was once again certain of his own invincibility he strode forth. Using his power to deadly purpose, he found a new host in Acintya, who rode out upon a great, silver-winged werehawk across both land and sea. Close behind came all of his creatures, and together they conquered the named world. With fire and numbers they pulled the dragon wards from the sky. Thus began Acintya's long and terrible reign."

"How was he defeated?" Arnaud asked, caught up in the tale.

"Llewstor, a young boy orphaned by Acintya's conquest, was found by a wandering bard and rescued. Seeing something in the child that hinted at a greatness lurking deep within, the bard took Llewstor under his wing and raised him as his own, teaching him many things. The bard possessed great power and knowledge, and these he passed on to young Llewstor, along with all the lore he knew. As Acintya and the were-folk held dominion and fed the Ancient Enemy with their terrible reign, Llewstor also grew and learned the skills he would one day need.

"Though Llewstor was unaware, the bard knew there was one power in the world against which the Ancient Enemy could not stand. A gift, given to the world by Cruithaor Elchiyl himself, though all but a few had forgotten it existed. The bard remembered, and he hoped it would be enough. He led the boy to Emnolae. Deep underground this gift waited: the secret to defeating Acintya and the Ancient Enemy controlling him. The bard did not know if the boy could do what was required, but he hoped."

"Yorien's Hand," Brant breathed, almost in disbelief.

Oraeyn threw a brief look at Brant, puzzled. He did not know how Brant had guessed what was coming next in the story. But Brant's face was even more closed than ever. He stared with deep intensity at the minstrel. If Kiernan Kane's face was a puzzle, Brant was bent on solving it.

Kiernan nodded again, oblivious to the scrutiny that poured against him. "Llewstor made the long journey to Emnolae and found the gift there beneath the great mountain. Yorien's Hand, the fallen star. Wielding its might, he strode out to face Acintya. The battle was long and ruinous, the ancient enemy had used Acintya for many years, and much of his power resided within Acintya's frame. Their battle shook the earth to its core, but Llewstor prevailed and smote Acintya down. The warrior's death dealt the Ancient Enemy a mighty blow, severing his connection to the world outside his prison and leaving him weakened to the point of death. Llewstor then became the first High King to rule all of Tellurae Aquaous."

"What happened to the bard?" Kamarie asked.

Kiernan shrugged. "The story does not say. Perhaps he died in the battle."

"It seems strange that nothing more is said of him," Oraeyn commented.

The minstrel looked up from beneath a furrowed brow. "Do you wish me to continue?"

Oraeyn nodded. "Please."

"The High Kings come to power during such times of great need. The power buried in the depths of Emnolae can only be wielded by certain individuals at certain times. The throne of the High Kings does not pass from father to son as other crowns or titles might, and for many years now the throne on Emnolae has stood empty. The palace is in ruins and quite overgrown. But now… now that the need arises again, Yorien's Hand calls out to the next High King to come and free its power, to come and rebuild the palace and sit upon the empty throne once more. The Ancient Enemy has bided his time for many ages of men, and there has been no need for a High King since the reign of Artair. But now, he rises again to threaten the world. Only a wielder of the power of Yorien can hope to stand against this threat.

"Many have heard the story of Yorien's Hand, but few understand it. For though it calls out for the next High King to wield its power against the Ancient Enemy, it also calls out to the Enemy himself, drawing him towards itself. It was touched by Cruithaor Elchiyl, and above all who live on Tellurae Aquaous, the Ancient Enemy hates the Creator. There is nothing he desires more than to possess the power of Yorien's Hand, or, if he cannot possess it, to destroy it."

Kiernan Kane fell silent, letting the story fade away. The words echoed about the room long after he finished speaking.

"So… what does that mean?" Yole asked, his tone impatient.

Kiernan pursed his lips and stared meaningfully at his audience. "It means that the next High King must be found and he must journey to Emnolae, where he will find the only thing that can defeat this Enemy: Yorien's Hand."

"And what if a High King cannot be found?" Arnaud asked.

"Then Tellurae Aquaous will be conquered and enslaved forever."

"How do we find this High King?" Brant asked, one eyebrow raised.

"There are always clues," Kiernan Kane said, in a tone that was deceptively soft. "There are stories, songs, and prophecies that tell of what is to come, that aid us in finding the next High King when one is needed. In this case, I believe the clue lies in the verses of an old song." He took up his mandolin and struck a chord that sounded like breaking crystal, then he began to play, his fingers dancing across the strings. "The words go like this:

> *Black death rides on silver wings*
> *Thirsty for the blood of kings*
> *Only two can stand before him*
> *Only one can hope to fell him.*

> *The answer to the riddle lies*

In deepest, darkest, starless skies
The ancient foe quivers in fear
When the wielder of his bane draws near.

From far off crystal shores he strides
A golden blade hangs at his side.
The love of a sylph shall bind his heart
And gives him strength when they must part."

They were all still, as ones frozen in a trance until the words of the song faded completely away. At length, Oraeyn took in a long, quiet breath. His gaze locked with Kamarie's and she stared at him in obvious distress.

"The Fang Blade?" she whispered, the words filled with denial.

"It would appear so," Kiernan replied. There was a strange quality to his voice as if he were mulling over something that distressed him.

"You're talking about... about Oraeyn," Kamarie said sharply. "You're saying he's the next High King? That he must go to this land called Emnolae and fight this Enemy, an enemy so powerful he makes dragons tremble?"

The minstrel stood silent before her query, but he neither flinched nor backed down.

"And what if he loses?" Kamarie's tone grew harsh. "He's not guaranteed to win, is he?"

Kiernan shook his head. "The wielder of the blade might fail. The Enemy is crafty, he will know to watch the land of Emnolae, and there will be trials to face before reaching the star. Oraeyn will be tested; Yorien does not allow his gift to be taken lightly. Some may see the star, even touch it, but there is something more to a High King; he alone may master its power."

"A High King? Me?" Oraeyn asked. His voice sounded strange, and it echoed in his own ears. Nobody paid him any heed.

"Emnolae," Brant's voice came out in a hoarse whisper, "the ruined palace, and the star that lies beneath the mountains in a ring of..." Brant trailed off, sudden recognition dawning as he stared at Kiernan's face. He finished his sentence in a voice of steel, "In a ring of cool flames." He pressed his lips together in a tight line, and anger rippled in the air around him.

Oraeyn could not have said who frightened him more at that moment, Kiernan or Brant. The two men were locked in a silent stare and for an instant Oraeyn was not sure who would win. The intense blue eyes met the cold black ones with equal force; Oraeyn was amazed that there were no sparks where the two gazes met and clashed. Then Kiernan broke away from the contest and chuckled softly to himself. With a shrug of his bony shoulders he transformed from the confident, serious, other-worldly creature into nothing more than an awkward fool. But Oraeyn was no longer fooled. Although the minstrel backed down first, Oraeyn believed it was Kiernan who had won that silent contest, whatever it had been or signified. A tension remained in the air. Yole shifted from one foot to another as uncomfortable and confused as everyone else in the room. Just as Oraeyn felt he could not remain silent any longer, Brant spoke, his voice soft.

He directed his words towards Oraeyn. "I have been to Emnolae and returned safely. I have touched Yorien's Hand. I can guide you there."

Oraeyn struggled to take a breath. The ominous feeling that hovered around his shoulders closed in and his vision grew blurry. He swallowed hard, trying not to gasp for air, trying to remain calm.

"Are you sure it's me?" he asked, desperately wishing that someone would object, or point out how ludicrous this all was. He felt himself struggling to breathe under the new weight of this new responsibility. "Might there not be another who could carry this mantle?"

"There is no one else," Brant said, "you are descended from Llian, which might be pertinent, or it might not, but I cannot deny that you fulfill the words of the prophecy." Brant held up his hand and ticked off the points on his fingers as he spoke, "You carry the Fang Blade: *a golden blade hangs at his side.* You love a sylph: *the love of a sylph shall bind his heart*. As a mixture of human, merfolk, and wizard, Kamarie is as much a sylph as her mother. You may not know this, but Aom-igh is referred to in many lands as the crystal kingdom, partially because of its long isolation, and partially because of Calyssia's shield around Pearl Cove: *from far off crystal shores he strides*. You must be the one to whom the song refers. I can see our minstrel believes it is so, and I agree with him. Therefore, if our world is to be saved from this threat, you must travel to Emnolae with me, as Llewstor in the minstrel's tale, you are the only hope our world has."

Oraeyn's mouth went dry; he tried to swallow, without success. He opened his mouth to speak, but no words escaped. He was not sure he could even manage a whisper. He looked around the room at the faces of the people he loved. Yole was pulling at his lower lip and looking very much like he wanted to say something but was refraining. Zara's face was filled with worry and her arms were half-raised as if she wanted to embrace him and tell him it would be all right. Arnaud was looking after Zara, but his expression was downcast and apologetic. Oraeyn wondered if the former king of Aom-igh felt somehow responsible for the position Oraeyn now found himself in. Brant's face was more closed than ever, but there was no uncertainty in his expression, and his unspoken confidence in him spoke more than a thousand words and bolstered his spirit. Kiernan was staring intently at him, a look of expectation on his face.

He turned to Kamarie last, looking fondly upon the face he loved best in all the world. He wondered how she would take being left out of this adventure. He knew she would not like it, but he also knew with startling clarity that this was a journey he must make on his own. Her expression was a mix of worry and distress, sympathy and affection. He stared hard at her, trying to memorize her face, burning her image into his memory.

Silence hung in the air as Oraeyn fought to regain his composure. Everyone was watching him, waiting to hear what he would say. After a long moment, he cleared his throat. The sound rang out loudly in the room.

"I will go to Emnolae," he said at length, "if Brant will lead me there."

Like a downpour that has been hovering in heavy, threatening clouds all day which finally bursts forth, everyone spoke at once, their voices clamoring together to assure him that this was not necessary, that he did not need to do this. Zara stepped to his side and put a motherly arm around his shoulders. Arnaud pressed his lips together, but pride shone in his eyes. Kamarie and Yole shook their heads as they adjured him to reconsider.

Brant merely looked at him, and Oraeyn met his stare without flinching. His stomach fluttered, he felt that he stood on the edge of a cliff and was being asked to leap from it, but determination rose inside him and vied for dominance. He lifted his chin and felt the weight of the burden he had been carrying the past few weeks ease.

"I will go," he repeated, raising his voice and quelling the arguments, "if you will show me the way, Brant."

Brant nodded. "I will take you there."

Zara held him in a tight embrace for a moment more, but she could not argue with his decision. She left the room on Arnaud's arm, her shoulders hunched like a much older woman's.

Kamarie's face filled with misery and she opened her mouth to speak, but then she caught Oraeyn's look. He held her gaze for a long moment, and though he had made his decision, the look he gave her begged her not to argue. She closed her mouth slowly and nodded. She turned to leave, and Oraeyn sighed in quiet relief as she shepherded Yole towards the doorway.

Finally, only Oraeyn, Brant, and Kiernan remained in the room. Brant laid a strong hand on Oraeyn's shoulder and then turned to the story-teller.

"That was quite the tale, minstrel. I suppose you'll be staying behind, or perhaps disappearing... again?"

A mysterious expression played across the minstrel's face. "Oh, no, I think I shall be coming along on this adventure," he replied. "I believe I will be able to offer some help, to you, Sir Brant, in particular."

Brant grimaced and glowered. But Kiernan continued, turning his attention to Oraeyn. "Sire, please do be sure to pack plenty of food for the journey, for I shall sorely miss the palace kitchen while we are away, but such is the lot of heroes, and it is unbecoming to complain."

CHAPTER NINE

Yole flew straight from the palace to the Mountains of Dusk. He hoped to recruit two more dragons to carry Brant and Kiernan in their journey to Emnolae. Oraeyn had not asked Yole to come, but the boy-dragon knew time was precious and flying was the fastest method of travel. The young dragon was not yet wise in the ways of the Kin, but he had carried Brant to and from Llycaelon several times, and it was not a difficult task. Besides, he enjoyed helping his friends when they needed him. They had befriended him when he was nobody, adopted him in a way, and he would never forget that kindness. The other dragons were not so quick to offer flight to humans, but Yole was sure he could convince at least one or two of them of the importance of the mission. This Enemy was a threat to all of them.

As Yole approached his destination, other dragons wheeled above him and soared through the clouds. It was a beautiful day, and he could see the glint of scales on the mountainside where dragons rested in the open light of day, a luxury that many still reveled in, even after three years. As he landed, an older dragon exited the large cave in the mountain face above the enormous, flat shelf of rock that they called Gathering Peak. The other dragon climbed down to where Yole was standing, his sharp claws gripping the rock and his golden wings spreading slightly for balance as he descended the steep incline.

"Greetings, Thorayenak," Yole said, glad to see him responding so swiftly to the mental call he had sent out.

When Yole decided to take his rightful place among other dragons, Thorayenak had offered him a home within his own lair. He took the boy under his wing and mentored him, seeing it as his responsibility to instruct Yole in his new role as a dragon.

"Shentallyia is missing," Thorayenak said when he reached Yole, answering the younger dragon's unspoken question.

"What? Missing?" Yole asked in alarm. "What do you mean?"

Shentallyia was one of his closest friends among the dragons, and he had hoped to enlist her help. But if she had disappeared, Yole was not sure what to do. His first thought was to wonder whether Shentallyia's disappearance might be related to that of Dylanna and Leila. It was unsettling to discover that more people were vanishing.

"She left early this morning," the other dragon continued, "she felt the yearning. Said something about fire and rain and then just took off."

"The yearning?"

"For a ward." The response was given as if it explained everything.

Yole's alarm diminished and turned into curiosity. "I thought dragon wards didn't exist anymore?"

"They haven't, not for many years," Thorayenak said, his tone serious.

"I know the history of how the dragon wards began, but how does it work?" Yole asked. "And why would Shentallyia leave so suddenly?"

"I keep forgetting how new you are to the Kin," Thorayenak said in a kind voice. "When a ward is old enough, anywhere from fifteen to twenty years of age, the yearning begins. There have been rare cases where it began at younger or older ages, and typically these rarer cases have resulted in extraordinary matches. The moment it occurs, both dragon and ward begin to feel that a part of themselves is missing. When ward and dragon meet for the first time, they both know each other instantly, though a moment before they were complete strangers.

"Shentallyia has insisted that she has a ward since we emerged from Krayghentaliss. I don't think anyone believed her, it has been so long since dragons and their wards flew the open skies. There has been a great sadness in the hearts of many dragons since the last known dragon ward recently departed these shores, never to return again."

Yole knew the other dragon was speaking of Calyssia and he bowed his head in respect of the Keeper's memory. Then he spoke again, "So Shentallyia just left? Where did she go? I need to find her."

"We don't know," the other dragon's voice held a note of sympathy. "I'm sorry I can't be more specific. Why did you need to find her?"

Yole growled. Shentallyia would have been eager to help, and might have been able to persuade others. Now, he was at a bit of a loss. Though he was accepted by the other dragons, he knew they regarded him as barely older than a hatchling. Many felt he should not be allowed so much freedom, and most believed he spent far too much time with his human friends. He studied Thorayenak, pondering. He must start somewhere, and his mentor was one of the wisest dragons in Aom-igh. Thorayenak also tended to speak highly of humans, and had mentioned Kiernan with respect in the past, though why the older dragon would esteem the bumbling minstrel was a true mystery to Yole.

He decided it was worth taking a chance. Yole began to speak, raising his voice as he related all Kiernan Kane had said. As he spoke, a few of the dragons basking on the warm rocks lifted their heads to listen. Several others landed nearby and stood around Yole, their necks craning, their claws scratching at the mountainside. A few of the older dragons revealed glinting teeth as their mouths opened in silent snarls; they had heard parts of this story before.

As Yole finished, Thorayenak stared at him, the older dragon's eyes wide and unblinking. "I will come," the other dragon spoke in grave tones. "I do not normally involve myself in the affairs of humans, but to work alongside the Minstrel is an opportunity I dare not refuse."

Yole bowed his head. "Thank you, Thorayenak." He burned with curiosity about Thorayenak's choice of words, but it would be an unforgivable breach of etiquette to question the offer of help. A younger, more naive Yole would have blurted out questions, but he knew now that voicing those questions might cause the offer of aid to be rescinded.

A smaller dragon with green scales—Rhimmell, Yole recalled her name after a moment—moved forward, her body serpentining across the craggy mountain face.

"I will come too," she announced. "This threat is not to be ignored."

Yole nodded. "From what Kiernan Kane said there is no greater threat in all Tellurae Aquaous."

Thorayenak nodded gravely. "The Minstrel would know."

Yole wondered at that comment. Like Oraeyn, Brant, and Kamarie, Yole had been surprised by Kiernan's sudden appearance in the doorway and spellbound by his cryptic tale. Yole found himself wondering just who, or what, Kiernan Kane really was.

Yole had been the first of the group to meet Kiernan Kane, and because of their adventures together on the way to the Harshlands, he felt a kinship with the entertainer. But later he found out that he was like the man in other ways, too: Kiernan Kane was accepted among their group of friends like Yole, but he was also an outsider in some inexplicable way, different from the others. Yole supposed he had always sensed that though he had never truly pondered it before. He thought perhaps he had glimpsed a bit of that difference today though it had left him more confused than anything else. But Thorayenak did not act surprised at all. In fact, the older dragon appeared to take it for granted that Kiernan Kane would have the knowledge necessary to explain what was happening in the world. Yole pondered again: why did Thorayenak consider it such a privilege to get to work alongside Kiernan Kane?

But instead of asking, Yole merely bowed his great neck.

"Thank you both," he said to Thorayenak and Rhimmell as the other dragons dispersed. However, in spite of everything, he could not help but ask the most important question that burned in his mind before he returned to inform Oraeyn that he had a method for reaching Emnolae: "Thorayenak, you've spoken highly of the minstrel before. May I ask, how do you know Kiernan Kane?"

Thorayenak bared his teeth. "The dragons all know the Minstrel well. We have ever deemed him a friend. You will learn more as you grow into your heritage."

"What do you mean?" Yole asked, more confused than ever.

Thorayenak spread his wings. "I must make ready for our journey, and the Minstrel deserves to keep his secrets. He will tell you what you need to know, nothing more."

"But..." Yole began his protest.

Thorayenak shook his great head and with a mighty leap he took to the sky. "Tell King Oraeyn we will meet him near Fortress Hill," Thorayenak called down to him, and then he flew away.

Yole turned to Rhimmell, but she merely moved her tail back and forth in a dragon's version of a shrug. "I have no answers for you, youngling," she said, and then she beat her wings and was gone as well.

Yole stared after them for a few minutes, wondering. Rhimmell had not denied knowing the minstrel. There was a long journey ahead of them; perhaps he would gain some clues about Kiernan Kane along the way.

CHAPTER TEN

Brant bounded into the cottage, the door swinging open with a startling thud. "Food smells good," he commented as he strode into the kitchen. His strong arms encircled Dylanna in a hug. He picked her up and swung her around, causing her to gasp with surprise and laughter.

"It ought to smell good, after the time I spent preparing it," Dylanna replied through her merriment.

Together they sat down at their small table. Dylanna gave a satisfied sigh; everything was as it should be. She did not immediately begin her meal, but looked around, content to just observe her own life for a moment. The cottage was warm and homey, the man she loved was sitting across the table enjoying the food she had prepared, life was complete and as it should be. Except... there was that strange sensation again, the thought that something was out of place. Brant looked up and noticed the small crease of her brow, a tiny wrinkle just above her petite nose.

"Are you all right?"

Dylanna nodded. "I think so. I've just had this strange aura of confusion around me all day."

"What do you mean?" He put another bite of food in his mouth and leaned forward on the table, interested.

"Well," Dylanna began, then she hesitated, fumbling with how to articulate her thoughts. "I'm not sure. I almost feel as if I don't belong here, but of course, that's silly."

Brant reached out and placed his hand over hers. "You're working too hard, that's all. It's just your imagination, don't worry about it."

"You're probably right."

She took a bite and chewed, savoring the flavors of the vegetables. They were fresh, from her own garden. She had been so proud of her harvest this year. Which was strange since she didn't have a garden.

Dylanna stopped chewing, wondering where that thought had intruded from. She stared at her husband across the table, suddenly suspicious. His response did not feel right either. He should have been more concerned, or tried a little harder to figure out a reason for her uneasiness. The Brant she remembered would have put more stock in her anxiety whether it sounded silly or not.

Dylanna shook her head. The man at the table before her was Brant. And yet, he wasn't. He sat at the table almost too easily. No cares rested on his shoulders, no burden weighed him down. That was not right, Brant was always a coiled spring, ready to leap into action at a moment's notice.

"Where's your sword?" Dylanna asked.

Brant looked up from his plate, confusion written across his face. "What do you mean?"

"You never go anywhere without your sword," Dylanna said, the words bursting up from somewhere deep inside herself. "Why don't you have it now?"

Brant crossed his arms and leaned back against his chair, amused. "Dylanna, I've never owned a sword in my life, what are you talking about?"

"No, this is all wrong," she mumbled. She got up and stumbled back from the table. Her chair fell over when she pushed it away, but she did not pay it any heed. The room began to spin, and she felt dizzy.

Brant rose as well and moved forward as if to catch her. "What's all wrong? This is our home, everything is as it should be."

"No, it's not. It's wrong!"

Brant reached for her. "You're scaring me."

But Dylanna continued to shake her head, sobs rising in her throat. "Everything is as I wish it could be," she said, and tears now trailed down her cheeks. "But it's not real, it can't be real."

Darkness swirled up around her, and she cringed away from it. She was frightened of the place from which she had come; she did not want to go *back to it, but the dream frightened her more. It was a dream, she realized now. Her memories rushed over her in an overwhelming flood. She reeled back under their force. Familiar faces returned to her: Kamarie, Yole, Oraeyn, Leila, Zara, Arnaud, and Brant…. She looked up at the Brant who stood before her and felt tears wind their way down her cheeks.*

"I wish you were real," Dylanna said. "But you cannot be."

"You could stay," he whispered, a note of pleading in his voice and his eyes filled with a sorrow that mirrored her own.

"No," Dylanna's face crumpled in anguish as she turned away.

"Please, Dylanna, don't leave! Please stay!" his voice grew frantic. "Please stay! I love you!"

Dylanna began to run. Brant clutched at her arm but she tore away from him. She reached the door and plunged outside.

Dylanna awoke once more. Silent sobs wracked her paralyzed body. Frustrated tears rolled down her face and their salty flavor exploded in her mouth. The darkness laughed at her, she could almost hear its scratchy, cackling voice. She wanted to hunch her shoulders and wrap her arms around herself like a little child and hide. Nightmarish terror welled up in her heart and she could not push it down beneath the surface any longer. The horror of how she had almost allowed herself to be captured overwhelmed her and her heart shuddered.

She knew how narrowly she had escaped being caught in her own dream. It would have been so easy to stay there in that blissful semblance of life. The dream was her deepest desire, her every wish come true, and leaving it had cost her so much, but she knew that remaining in its clutches would have cost everything.

Shentallyia was not certain where she was headed. She knew little about her ward other than that he was far away and in peril. She knew which direction to fly, but that was where her intuition ended. She did not know how far she must travel. She had no idea of his name or what he looked like. She did not know how she would find him or even how old he was, she merely knew she would recognize him the instant she saw him. So she flew in the direction of her ward, following her yearning, filled with excitement, but also battling a rising anxiety.

Not for the first time, Shentallyia wondered if being underground had kept the dragons from being able to sense their wards. Certainly, she had never before suspected that she had one until after she emerged from the tunnels of Krayghentaliss.

What would it be like, she wondered for a moment, to meet him? Did he feel, as she did, the ache of being incomplete? Was he waiting for her, puzzling over what was taking her so long? Then a horrible thought occurred to her, what if he was afraid of her? Shentallyia banked and wheeled, flying in a helpless circle. She had already flown beyond the borders of Aom-igh, what if he belonged to one of those fearful countries that did not believe in dragons anymore? But the call was stronger than her disquietude. If he lived in such a country she would simply take human form until she discovered how he felt about dragons. Yole had lived as a human for most of his life: certainly it could not be very difficult.

Jemson's arrival in the camp of the Border Patrol caused a chaotic stir and a myriad of mixed emotions. Some were honored that their king would grace them with his presence on their battlefield, and heartened by his display of courage. Some, however, grumbled at his approach, believing they were being inspected, thinking he had come to search out their weaknesses and berate them wherever they might be lacking.

For his part, the young king was elated to be out on the field. He rode through the camp, surveying his men's work and congratulating them on it. Bit by bit, he dispelled the objections of those who did not want him there. By the end of the first day, the warriors had warmed to him considerably. Most had never met the young king, and had no idea what to expect, but Jemson was every inch the man Brant believed him to be. His three years on the throne under Brant's guidance had aged him and given him a confidence and a maturity not present even in men twice his age.

Jemson ended his tour of the camp at Devrin's headquarters. A pot hung over the fire, and Devrin sat on one of the logs that surrounded the small blaze, stirring the contents. Jemson cleared his throat as he approached and Devrin rose.

"Welcome, Sire," Devrin saluted, but his heart was not in it. He was not sure what Jemson's visit meant, and did not like that the king had abandoned protocol and not come to him before inspecting the camp.

"You have done well in your command here," Jemson said, taking a step forward.

"I do not look for your approval," Devrin replied, his voice terse. Then he bethought himself and cleared his throat. "Forgive me, we are all weary, and I am remiss in my duties. Would His Majesty like to sit? Are you hungry? The stew is ready."

Jemson stepped over to the log opposite Devrin and sat. He looked up at the sky and then back at Devrin.

"The story goes that the wall of flames over there was your idea."

Devrin shrugged, ladling stew into two bowls.

"Word is you started it by setting fire to your commanding officer's tent," Jemson continued. "Is that true?"

Devrin handed him a bowl and hesitated, wondering where the conversation was heading. "It is."

Jemson laughed. "I hoped it was true. Brilliant move on your part."

"I saw what needed to be done, and I acted," Devrin replied, his words clipped and angry in spite of his relief at Jemson's favorable reaction. "It was no more than anyone else might have done."

"But you were the only one who saw it, the only one who acted," Jemson returned.

Devrin opened his mouth to speak, then closed it again. He gave his head a small shake and put a bite of stew in his mouth, a scowl turning his lips down. Jemson watched him, curious. The man extended every courtesy, but something had him on edge. Jemson took a bite of his own stew and nearly gagged on the soggy, lumpen mess. With an effort, he managed to swallow the bite. He put his bowl down and wondered where the nearest stream was.

"Water?" Devrin raised a canteen without looking up from his bowl.

Jemson took the canteen and drank. The canteen stank like ashes and the water was warm, but it served to wash away the remnants of the stew. He took another swig and handed the canteen back. Devrin chuckled a little and continued to eat until his bowl was empty.

"It's better than nothing," he commented, taking a drink himself, and then using the rest of the water to rinse his bowl clean. "You'll get used to it, unless you're not staying long."

"I suppose I'll get used to it, then," Jemson replied, his tone even as he took another bite, this time, he managed to swallow without needing water to wash it down.

Devrin looked up, shock written across his face. Jemson saw, to his great surprise, that Devrin was younger than he had first assumed. The scowl aged him. The man ran a hand across his shaggy hair.

"What does that mean?" he demanded.

"I came to add my sword to your ranks," Jemson replied.

"Your Majesty cannot be serious," Devrin's tone was flat.

"The situation here has gotten out of control," Jemson returned. "It is high time the king of Llycaelon gave something to the men who have given so much for their country. I am here to fight the seheowks, Captain. I know the men believed I was here to inspect the ranks and give a critique, or perhaps they thought this was an appearance meant to boost their morale. They were mistaken. I am here to offer my sword, my arm, my bow, and even my life if need be to defend my country. It's time Llycaelon rallied behind a fighting king once again!"

Devrin felt his heart lift at Jemson's words. They were words he wanted to shout himself, but the earnest way the king said them left a bitter flavor in Devrin's mouth. He squashed the hope flickering to life in his chest and stood abruptly. He paced a few steps and stood with his back to the young king for a moment. It was unfair of him to be so angry at the kid, none of this was his fault, but Devrin couldn't help it.

"Devrin," Jemson's tone was serious. "Why did you ask to be transferred to the Border Patrol?"

Surprise made Devrin turn to look at the king.

"I thought I recognized your name on the report informing me of your appointment to command here," Jemson explained. "But I wasn't sure until I saw you."

Pent up emotions swirled in Devrin's thoughts. Part of him wanted to sit down and explain, unburden his soul to this insightful young man. Another part of him wanted to stalk off into the gathering night and leave the kid wondering forever. The duty-bound soldier within him would let him do neither, of course. He raised his chin.

"I felt I could be of more service to my country here, Majesty." The words felt stiff as they left his lips. Jemson gazed at him pensively across the embers of the cook fire. Devrin felt his shoulders tense, but Jemson did not press the matter.

Suddenly restless, Devrin took a step towards Jemson. "May I ask a question?"

"Of course," Jemson replied.

"Why did you come to me last?"

A muscle in Jemson's cheek twitched. "You requested a transfer the day before my coronation. That request was the only indication I had of how you felt about me. I am aware that the protocol in this situation would have been to come to you and have you at my side as I spoke with your men, but I must confess that I wanted a less biased report from them on your leadership, especially considering the unconventional way you came to hold that position."

Devrin felt a tendril of respect weave its way through his thoughts, followed by a sharp curiosity. "I see. I can understand that." Curiosity flared in his thoughts, and he couldn't prevent the question that sprang to his lips. "May I ask what you have discovered?"

Jemson sat back and took a deep breath. "Your men hold you in very high regard. To many of them, you are a hero."

Devrin was not sure what to say to that, and felt his throat close with emotion, preventing any words he might have come up with from passing into utterance.

Jemson seemed to understand this, and he rose. "Thank you for sharing your meal with me. I apologize if I caused you undue alarm by breaking with tradition, but I hope my findings are of use to you as you move forward. Your aid, Stephran, was kind enough to show me where I can place my bedroll. My sword is at your command."

The young man disappeared into the evening and Devrin was left with a battle of emotions warring within. He paced around his campfire attempting to sort out this strange encounter with his king.

"Kamarie will keep watch over things while I am gone," Oraeyn said, his voice quiet.

Brant's brow furrowed. "She will not appreciate being left behind, if that is your intent."

"I know, but she cannot come, it's not safe."

Kiernan Kane gazed at him, and Oraeyn wondered what was going on inside the minstrel's head. They had been making plans for the journey to Emnolae for several hours now, and Kiernan had yet to say a word. Oraeyn was used to the laughing, bumbling, singing minstrel, and this quiet, introspective side of him was quite unnerving.

As Brant described the journey to Emnolae, and what they could expect to find once they arrived, Oraeyn grew more curious about his mentor's first adventure there. Brant said nothing more about it, but Oraeyn was not surprised. Brant rarely gave out information about himself.

It was strange, Oraeyn decided, how alike the two men were. Could either of them truly be known? Kiernan wore a mask of joviality and chatter, but much of it was meaningless, a façade meant to distract, while Brant's mask was of silence, meant to discourage questions.

Just then the door opened and Yole entered the room.

Oraeyn looked up, puzzled by the dragon's sudden appearance. Consternation filled him at the unexpected interruption. He hoped Yole was not bringing more bad news.

"What is it, Yole?"

"We'll carry you to Emnolae," Yole said in an excited rush. "Thorayenak, Rhimmell, and I. We've discussed it. This Enemy is a force that threatens us all, not just the humans, and so you must get to where you are going as quickly as possible. You cannot get there any faster than by flying. In the old days, dragons carried humans all the time. I've taken Brant to Llycaelon a few times, it's not difficult."

"Yole, thank you so much," Oraeyn said, his voice filled with gratitude. "Brant said he arrived in Emnolae by ship on his first voyage there, but he was just recommending that I ask the dragons for their aid in traveling this time."

"We must use a certain amount of caution," Brant warned. "Three dragons carrying humans and flying straight towards Emnolae will not be something this Enemy will ignore. He has been defeated by High Kings wielding the power of Yorien's Gift before. He will be guarding that land with a watchful eye and it will not be easy to sneak past him. This is not a threat to be taken lightly, even by dragons."

Yole nodded gravely. "We understand."

Oraeyn knew Yole was a dragon, capable of taking care of himself, but he looked so young. Oraeyn had bonded with Yole when they had first met, he felt a tie of brotherhood to the boy from the beginning. Perhaps it was the Fang Blade, or perhaps it was because they were both orphans, or maybe it was because they had each discovered they were something more than they had ever guessed, Oraeyn did not know. The bond he felt with Yole could easily be explained by the simple fact that Yole looked up to him with such open admiration. Oraeyn was suddenly filled with gratitude and some emotion he could not define. He was intensely glad he had such friends around him in this time of desperate need, but at the same time he sincerely did not want to endanger any of them.

"Very well," Oraeyn said, the words felt heavy as they left his mouth. "I don't like asking anyone else to risk their lives on my behalf, but I understand the importance and urgency of this undertaking. Yole, if you and your friends are willing to carry us upon their backs, then the sooner we leave, the better."

"We are ready now," Yole's voice was eager.

"I recommend we set out at first light," Brant said.

Oraeyn nodded. "At first light."

At his words the door burst open again. Oraeyn spun in surprise, startled by the loud noise. When he saw the figure standing in the doorway his heart sank.

Kamarie stood there, her hands on her hips. An icy fist of dread clutched at Oraeyn's heart. He knew without asking why she was there. Everything in him screamed against it, he could not risk her life, he would not, but he also knew she would not back down. He stared at her, begging her not to speak, but she refused to meet his gaze.

"I'm coming too!" Kamarie's voice was quiet, but the words somehow filled the entire room.

In a flash, Oraeyn was caught in the midst of his dream again; he remembered watching Kamarie fall, recalled the awful knowledge that he could not save her or keep her from slipping away. The terrible helplessness he had felt as he came to that realization gripped him once again. His face twisted at the remembered pain of the nightmare. He could still see her face as she stared up at him, her expression a mixture of dismay and resignation, he could feel the horrible clenching in his stomach as her hand slipped from his grasp. Even though it had only been a dream, it was not one he ever wanted to experience in the waking world. Determination filled his heart. He did not know if he could be the High King Kiernan had spoken of, nor did he know if he was capable of the task required of him, but he did know he would do everything in his power to protect Kamarie.

"No," he said firmly. "I cannot allow it, Kamarie." It wounded him to say it, everything in him resisted the idea of leaving her. A chasm of grief opened in his heart as he spoke.

Kamarie lifted her chin stubbornly, never backing down an inch. It was as though she knew how much it cost him to say those words. "You can't tell me not to come, because I've already made up my mind. You need me. I won't let you go off alone, where you go, I go."

"You're right, I do need you. I need you to stay here and take care of Aom-igh while I am gone. I need you to do this for me. I need you to stay here where it's safe."

Kamarie tossed her head and Oraeyn knew he was in trouble; her blue eyes flashed with ire. "Justan can take care of things here. You told me you'd trust him with your life. Or my father. Don't give me any of this 'safe' nonsense, Oraeyn; with an enemy like the one Kiernan described on the loose, no place is safe anymore."

"The place we're going is far more perilous than here," Oraeyn argued.

"What about the prophecy?" Kamarie asked, turning to the others who all refused to meet her gaze. The tension in the room was uncomfortable.

"The prophecy?" Oraeyn asked.

"'The love of a sylph shall bind his heart,'" she quoted. "That's me, right? It means I have to come with you."

"'And gives him strength when they must part,'" Oraeyn shot back. "That means you stay behind."

"Brant?" Kamarie asked, turning to the warrior.

Brant ran a hand through his hair, his expression thoughtful. "If it is a prophecy—if there really is such a thing as a prophecy —it could mean you stay behind," Kamarie opened her mouth to object but Brant put up a hand, "or it could mean there will be a need to part later in the journey. I'm not an expert." He turned to Kiernan. "Well, Minstrel?"

Kiernan cocked his head, listening to a sound nobody else could hear. Absent-mindedly he mused, "Prophecies are tricky."

"Kamarie," Oraeyn said, his tone pleading, "please don't do this."

"You need me," she said, her mouth set in a stubborn line.

"No!" Oraeyn shouted, his desperate need to keep her safe making him speak much more loudly than he meant to. "I don't."

Anguish filled Kamarie's face and Oraeyn realized what he

had just said. The look of stunned pain in his beloved's eyes broke his heart.

"Kamarie," his voice was soft, "I didn't mean... that's not what I... I'm sorry."

After a moment Kamarie looked up; tears swam in her eyes but did not fall. Her expression was fierce. "I am coming with you, because you do need me, whether you think you do or not. I am honor-bound as the First Aelan to go with my king and defend him if I can and die for him if I must. It is part of my oath, and I take it very seriously. You cannot deny me the right to perform my duty."

Oraeyn sank into a chair in defeat. He could not argue with her on that point. She was within her rights to claim a place in the company on the merits of her rank in the Order of the Shield. Tears pricked, threatening to fall. He could still see her tumbling away from him, still hear her scream, the echoes of his nightmares overwhelmed him. He wrestled with his fear for a long moment, then straightened his shoulders, bolstered by a deep resolve. If the dreams were warnings, he would make sure he heeded them, if they were visions he would do everything in his power to keep them from coming to pass. In the deepest part of his heart he knew Kamarie was right, he did need her, and he was certain Brant would help him protect her. With Brant along, perhaps they would all be safer, no matter where they were.

Oraeyn sighed. "Very well. I will appoint Sir Justan to care for Aom-igh while we are gone. Kamarie will come with us. Yole, do you think there is another dragon who would be willing to come along?"

"I will carry both you and Kamarie."

"Are you sure?" Kamarie asked, concerned.

"I won't even notice either of you," he promised. "You forget how big I am as a dragon!"

They all chuckled at that, even Brant, and Oraeyn suddenly felt much better. He was surprised at how glad he was that Kamarie would be there, and he realized it would not have been the same, going on such a quest without her.

"At first light then," Oraeyn said. "I will go speak with Justan and give him the necessary instructions."

The group split up, each going their own way to prepare for the journey ahead. They would meet again at daybreak on the beach where the dragons would be waiting. Kamarie returned home to inform her parents that she was now part of this great effort that Kiernan had revealed in their hearing. Arnaud and Zara, already aware of their daughter's determination and tenacity, had made preparations for the journey on her behalf. Yole returned to the Mountains of Dusk to tell Thorayenak and Rhimmell when and where they were meeting. Brant retired to prepare his weaponry and ponder the many thoughts that had been stirred within him that day by the story of Yorien's Hand.

CHAPTER
ELEVEN

Devrin had been on edge all day. He had no idea of the source of his disquiet, but there was a definite uneasiness building within him. He was tense and jumpy; his nerves felt like the frayed edges of an old, well-used blanket.

The weather was not helping. The threatening storm clouds remained, but the rain was not yet falling. Devrin did not know how much longer his luck would hold. He had been racking his brain to find a solution to the looming problem of rain, but so far he had not come up with any particularly useful ideas. He was frustrated with his lack of ingenuity. And then there was his other problem: the king of Llycaelon.

Jemson had proven as good as his word. The young man slept on the ground amongst the men, carried firewood, took his turn tending the barrier of fire, patrolled through the night, and did everything else asked of him. The aethalons were heartened by his presence, and Devrin had to admit a grudging respect growing in his own heart towards the young king. Jemson accepted his share of the duties without complaint, never once acting as if he thought the work was beneath him.

Devrin's musings were cut short by a sudden commotion a few paces away. One of his men threw his sword to the ground with an angry grunt. His face was red as he shouted at two other warriors.

"Don't know why you all think this new captain of ours is going to figure out how to keep a fire burning during a Warm-Term deluge," the man bellowed belligerently. "It makes no sense, how everyone is falling all over themselves. He was raised to the position for one lucky move, not because he's a genius or a tactician. There's a long list of those who should've been considered first. Just because he commanded the Palace Guard doesn't mean he knows anything about leading men into combat. Don't know what..."

"That is enough," Stephran's voice rang out as he strode into the fray. His tone was tight and controlled, but tinged with anger as he put a restraining hand on the offending man's arm.

"I'm just saying what everyone else is thinking," the man was defiant.

"How dare you speak of your captain that way? Even at Aetoli, your rank does not grant you the privilege of disrespect. You, and you," Stephran's voice rose and two other men hurried over, "take this man and contain him until further notice. Captain Devrin will consider his punishment."

Silence fell as the man shuffled off between his guards. Stephran looked towards Devrin's campfire and saw his captain watching. The warrior pressed his lips into a thin line and strode over.

"Sir?" he said, when he reached his commanding officer. "I am sorry you witnessed that. It won't happen again."

"He's not wrong," Devrin's voice was low. "I don't have a plan. When that rain comes, our defenses crumble."

"That isn't an excuse for conduct unbecoming, in any event. You'll figure something out. Have you asked King Jemson if he has any ideas? A fresh perspective can often turn the tide of the most difficult situation."

"What could he possibly add that we haven't thought of?" Devrin growled, his patience snapping. "You really think a child can solve this? We don't need more suggestions, we need it to not rain."

Stephran's back straightened. "Sir, all due respect, but it's a fortunate thing for you Sir Brant was not here to observe such willful disrespect being demonstrated just now towards his nephew, and your king."

"I mean no disrespect to the lad. But he can't control the weather, and he couldn't even if he had endured his rite of passage, gone through the Corridor, or faced his questioning," Devrin's voice rose, and several warriors stopped what they were doing to stare at him. Not for the first time, Devrin regretted burning all the tents.

Stephran's voice was soft. "Begging your pardon, but none of that gives you the right to speak in such a way. He's been crowned king of Llycaelon, and you took an oath to serve him and this country, just like me, just like every other aethalon here. If you can't keep that vow, I can't follow you, sir, and that would be a shame, because I think you do have a chance of tipping the scales in our favor. But if you can't do that while being true to your word, then I have a duty to see you tried for treason, no matter what I think of your abilities as a captain. Just like it was my duty to have Aetoli Lance placed under arrest a few moments ago, even though we don't have a single warrior more skilled than him with any weapon you can think of. Begging your pardon, sir, but I'll leave you now. I hope next time we meet, your words will reflect the loyalty you owe King Jemson. You say you meant no disrespect, and our situation is dire, but we are aethalons. We are warriors. This is our duty and our life's blood: to overcome when all seems lost. And you need to understand the kind of impact a careless word or a thoughtless phrase can have. You betray your true opinion of the king by the way you refer to him."

Stephran turned and strode away, leaving Devrin alone once more. Shame flooded through him as he watched his most loyal supporter depart. Stephran was right, of course. He did think of the king as a child. There was nothing inherently wrong with that, but in a moment of frustration he had lost his self control and allowed that opinion to rise to the surface where others could see it. That could not be allowed. Devrin sat down on the log and put his head in his hands. It was becoming clear that he could not ignore the past, but he was unsure of how to proceed.

It was dusk when Devrin at last turned to his meal. As he stirred the contents of his pot with a long-handled wooden ladle, he heard a soft step behind him and felt the skin on the back of his neck prickle. His muscles tightened, and he gripped the spoon in his fist, prepared to defend himself. A wild thought passed through his mind that whoever stood behind him must be the source of the strange unease that had gripped him all day. The thought was ridiculous, of course, but Devrin whirled, ladle raised aloft.

At first light, Oraeyn made his way down to the waterfront. Brant and Kamarie were already there, waiting for him. Kiernan Kane was also present, his jaw open in a wide yawn as he stretched his neck from side to side. The man's hair stuck up wildly and his clothes were somewhat rumpled, but Oraeyn was relieved to see him there. Brant's face was void of emotion, and Oraeyn wondered what he was thinking. Brant was the only one who did not look tired or as if he had just awakened; Oraeyn envied the man's cool composure and not for the first time wished he could mimic Brant's exterior calm.

The minstrel, surprisingly, wore an unusual sword at his side. The hilt and scabbard looked old and battered and Oraeyn knit his brows together, trying to remember if he had ever seen Kiernan with a sword before. His mandolin was strapped to his back in its customary location. Kiernan never went anywhere without the instrument. Oraeyn felt comforted by its familiar presence. Even in this moment when they were about to walk straight into the inky heart of danger, in an attempt to overcome the greatest enemy ever to threaten the world, it was reassuring to know that some things never changed.

In a rush of gigantic wings and a hurricane of wind, three dragons descended. Although he had seen dragons many times before, Oraeyn was awed once again by their size and impressive appearance. Yole introduced his two companions as Thorayenak and Rhimmell.

Thorayenak was a beast of intimidating size with bright red

scales and copper-colored wings. His reptilian eyes were a deep copper with flecks of gold and Oraeyn remembered just in time not to stare too long into them. Rhimmell, on the other hand, was more petite, though still larger than Yole, who had not yet reached his adult size. Her scales were emerald in color and silver, translucent wings folded delicately along her back. Her eyes were a pale blue. She landed behind Thorayenak and ducked her head in silent greeting. Yole, in his dragon form had deep red, almost maroon scales, and golden wings. His eyes, however, still retained their human shape and size, albeit with very odd coloring. For whatever reason, perhaps because he had only learned he was a dragon three years ago, Yole did not have typical dragon's eyes. One could look into them and not become lost, no matter what form he took.

Thorayenak and Rhimmell nodded respectfully to Brant and Oraeyn, and then both dragons bowed low before Kiernan Kane. Startled, Oraeyn shared a confused glance with Kamarie. She shrugged, but looked intrigued.

"Minstrel," Thorayenak's voice was low, "it is my honor."

Kiernan's lips were quirked upwards. "As it is my own."

Rhimmell also inclined her head.

Oraeyn felt concerned. "We appreciate your offer, but are you both certain you are willing to endure this hazardous journey? We can go by ship if need be."

Rhimmell gave him a scathing look. "Do not be ridiculous," she snapped. "Young Yole was right to ask for our help, despite the indignity. Do not tarnish his request with inane suggestions. The Minstrel," there was reverence in her tone as she indicated Kiernan, "warns of an enemy that threatens all you know, and you would refuse a generosity that may be the difference between victory or defeat?"

Oraeyn stared. He was used to speaking with various dragons, but the ones he had interacted with all maintained a dignified regality, as well as a mien of esteem towards him and the position he held as king of Aom-igh. Rhimmell's sharp tone and sharper words took him aback.

"Forgive me," he stammered. "I did not mean offense."

"Then do not offend. Accept what has been offered with grace," Rhimmell replied. "Minstrel," there was that strange tone of admiration again, "if it please thee, I will carry thee on this quest."

Kiernan simpered vapidly. "Of course, of course, my good scaly one."

Oraeyn almost expected that to be the end of Kiernan Kane, but to his everlasting surprise, Rhimmell merely chuckled and lowered herself to allow the minstrel to clamber up her foreleg and settle into the spot between her shoulder blades.

"Is this all of us?" Thorayenak's deep voice questioned.

Brant, unruffled by the presence of the dragons, but rather disconcerted by their obvious deference to Kiernan, simply nodded. "It is."

"Very well. I shall carry you, Dark Firebrand, and Yole will take the King and his Sylph. It's a beautiful day for flying, despite the urgency of our mission," Thorayenak said. "Shall we be off?"

Without a word, the four travelers climbed up onto the dragon's backs, and Oraeyn felt a sudden excitement about the journey ahead as he settled himself between Yole's golden wings. Kamarie sat close behind him, her arms around his waist. He clasped a hand over hers, silently revisiting his vow to protect her, no matter what. Then the dragons lifted off the ground with several strokes of their powerful wings and all doubts and trepidation paled in comparison to the thrill of flying. Even the threat of facing a mighty, nameless foe, even the memory of his nightmares could not cast a pall over the excitement that mounted in Oraeyn's heart as they flew up to meet the morning.

Dylanna moaned. She had been trapped in this prison for an eternity. Every time she slept a dream rose up to ensnare her, but she was on her guard now and avoided the traps laid for her. She had seen her sweetest dreams come to life before her, but she had forsaken all of them. The pain of shattered dreams diminished with repetition.

So many dreams, and she had managed to deny herself all of them. She had seen herself high on a hill wearing a golden crown and wielding power that subdued the nations. She had been happily married to Brant. She had spent time as a mermaid, reunited with her mother and sister in the depths of the ocean. She had lived many lives and accomplished many things. She had been offered power, wealth, comfort, and love, but she had known the lies for what they were and had rejected them all. Better the uncertainty of reality than the guarantee of illusion.

The newest enemy Dylanna faced was boredom. The wizardess's muscles ached from hours of disuse. She burned up from the inside out. Her arms and legs screamed at her, begging for movement. She methodically tensed and released each muscle in her body, but the minuscule movement offered scant relief. Her mind was numb and lethargic. She had long since stopped caring about the passage of time.

There was no jailer; no one came to gloat over her capture. Dylanna had exhausted her ideas for escape, and besides the dreams nothing threatened her. She drifted, floating in her state of imprisonment. Thinking was a chore. The dreams left her weary and spent. She was being spread thin until there was nothing of herself left. Her emotions had been dulled by her endless hours—perhaps days, weeks, or even years—in this prison of nothingness.

Kamarie clung to Oraeyn, her arms around his waist, her face lifted up as the wind ruffled her long hair. She laughed, the joy of flying welling up within her and filling her completely. Everything else faded into mist as they soared high above the ground. She could not fathom how the dragons could have surrendered themselves to their underground prison for a single day, let alone centuries. After experiencing freedom such as this, how could they have willingly given it up?

Even as this occurred to her, Kamarie pondered. The dragons had fled the upper realm of Aom-igh and gone into hiding. But why had they chosen to do so? Surely they were more than capable of destroying a human enemy. Dragons were massive, powerful, and had the advantage of flight and magical strength. Few wizards remained in the world, even at the time of the dragons' retreat into Krayghentaliss. Why had they not fought for their right to live above ground?

She leaned forward. "Yole," she asked, shouting to be heard above the rushing wind and beating wings. "Why didn't the dragons fight to stay above-ground?"

"What do you mean?" Yole rumbled back.

"I mean why did they allow themselves to be herded underground to Krayghentaliss in the first place? They simply disappeared into the tunnels without a fight. Why?"

"I never thought to ask that," Yole replied.

Thorayenak drifted closer. "A few wished to do as you suggest and fight for our right to remain above ground, it is true," he said, entering the conversation. "But King Graldon preferred the way of peace. Most agreed with him. Humanity is frail compared to us, but the Minstrel holds your race in high regard. Our esteem for your people is an extension of our regard for him. To lay waste to your people would have caused him to be disappointed in us. And most of our people did not wish for that to happen."

"The minstrel?" Brant asked, from the dragon's back. "What minstrel?"

Thorayenak bared his fangs and snaked his neck to indicate towards Rhimmell, who was flying off to the left and just beyond hearing distance. The three riders and Yole stared at Kiernan Kane, atop the green dragon. He appeared to be constantly on the verge of tumbling from the dragon's back and falling through the air. Kamarie was not sure how anyone could be quite so awkward all the time. Riding a dragon was not as hard as the poor minstrel made it look. However, in spite of his apparent struggles, Kiernan seemed to be thoroughly enjoying himself.

"You cannot be serious," Brant said, his voice flat.

"Kiernan?" Kamarie asked. "That doesn't make any sense, Kiernan can't be old enough to have even been alive when the dragons descended into Krayghentaliss."

Thorayenak tilted slightly from side to side, but remained silent.

Oraeyn ran his hand across the back of his neck. Then he said, "For a dragon, you have a strange sense of humor."

"Believe what you wish," Thorayenak replied. "But I am sure you have noticed oddities about the Minstrel, things that cannot be explained. Someday, you may come to regard him as my people do." Thorayenak veered away, leaving Kamarie, Oraeyn, and Yole to reflect on what the older dragon had intimated about their beloved, bumbling Kiernan Kane.

The sensation that was stirred within Kamarie by their flight chased away all else. Her fears for Oraeyn and the implications of what he was being asked to do slid to the back of her mind. The minstrel's story and the chill its telling had sent creeping through her faded away into meaningless mist. The sky was a clear, bright blue, and they were flying up above the clouds. Kamarie looked down at the tops of the clouds and grinned. They looked like a white city, with peaks spiraling up to meet them. Some of the cloud-towers climbed so high that the dragons simply flew straight through them. Kamarie had been vaguely disappointed to discover that the great white fluffy things were merely a very thick fog. Her disappointment did not detract from her enjoyment of the experience, however.

"Just like the way we met, don't you think?" Kamarie whispered into Oraeyn's ear. "You and me, setting off on an adventure to who knows where?"

"I was just thinking that. This is almost our entire company, minus Dylanna, of course."

Kamarie sobered. "I wonder what happened to Aunt Dylanna and Aunt Leila," she said quietly.

"They know how to take care of themselves," Oraeyn said in reassuring tones. "Don't worry, we'll find them."

Kamarie sighed and then glanced over at Kiernan once more. She could not hear him, but she could see that he was laughing. She drew Oraeyn's attention to the bard.

"Why do you think he isn't more worried about Leila?" Kamarie asked. "Brant is distraught over Dylanna's disappearance, and Kiernan has a flare for the dramatic. It's surprising he hasn't mentioned her."

"I'm not sure what Kiernan Kane is, but I don't think that he is what any of us believed him to be. Did you see the way Brant's face changed when Kiernan was telling the story about Llewstor yesterday? And how the dragons esteem him? I'm still not sure what to think about what Thorayenak just told us. But if Kiernan's not worried about Leila, then it either means he believes she is in no danger or is capable of taking care of herself."

Kamarie nodded, appreciating Oraeyn's insight on the matter. She, too, had seen a subtle change in the minstrel and wondered at it. She had always liked the funny, awkward man, but now she realized he had a deeper, possibly darker side. It did not frighten her as she felt it should have, she believed with a surprising certainty that whatever Kiernan Kane was, he was not evil.

"Well, here we are again," Kamarie said lightly, changing the subject. "I wonder what this journey will bring us?"

"More than we expect probably."

Kamarie leaned her head against Oraeyn's shoulder, her heart full of something she could not express. She was still afraid for him, but she was glad they were together. Oraeyn felt the warmth of her cheek against his back and knew instinctively that he had been forgiven for his harsh words from the day before. He squeezed her hand wordlessly. He was suddenly fiercely glad she had insisted on coming along.

At first Devrin did not see her. Then the woman stepped into the glow cast by his cook fire and Devrin lowered the ladle he clutched in his hand, his consternation calmed and his curiosity peaked. He squinted, cursing the strange twilight which played tricks on his vision.

From where had she appeared? He could not picture her moving through the camp without raising some sort of alarm or curiosity, but there was no commotion to indicate that anyone else had seen her. She moved towards him another pace, her gait hesitant but graceful, her face open and innocent. He knew instinctively that she meant him no harm.

She was beautiful. Tall and slender with pale, almost translucent skin, with long, blond hair so light it was closer to silver than gold. She peered out at him from behind long lashes, her eyes a pale green; he could have sworn that as the light failed, they actually glowed. She was small-boned and fragile, her face that of a pixie or a fairy from the storybooks he had read as a child. She wore a dress made of a wispy, forest green material that flowed around her as she moved.

She seemed somehow familiar, her face similar to one he had seen in a dream that he could not quite remember. He stepped forward to take her hand and welcome her, wondering as he did so why she was there.

"Welcome, my lady," he said gallantly, and he would have continued, but then his hand met hers and he stopped short, his fingers tightening slightly about hers.

She was a dragon.

He did not know how the knowledge came to him, it was simply there. It sprang into his mind, unbidden. She certainly did not look like a dragon, he thought to himself. He tried to laugh away the ridiculous idea, but it refused to leave. It was a simple certainty that filled him, and he knew what she was as surely as he knew his own name.

The dragon did not appear to notice his sudden hesitation, nor his inner struggle. If she guessed that he knew her secret, she did not show it or seem concerned. Neither did she attempt to remove her hand from his grasp.

"I am called Shentallyia," her voice rang out like the gentle music of wind chimes. It burst through Devrin's ears and filled his head. He heard her name being repeated over and over again in his mind.

Shentallyia.

"Devrin. Me. I am, that is," Devrin blurted in a burst of eloquence. He stood there, tongue-tied and kicking himself, internally urging his mouth to speak, but unable to utter another syllable.

There was another moment of awkward silence. Shentallyia stared, her mint-green gaze bored through him, one delicate brow raised in a quizzical expression, a searching quality to her gaze. Devrin wondered what she was looking for. He hoped she found it, whatever it was. After a moment, he realized that she was waiting for him to speak. He also became aware of the fact that he was still clutching her hand in his own. He relaxed his fingers, releasing her from his grasp.

"Won't you join me?" he asked, the words coming in a rush. He gestured at the campfire and the logs placed around it. He wished, again, that he had not burned *all* the tents.

She ducked her head and seated herself primly on a log, her movements graceful. She surveyed his camp with a single, sweeping glance. Devrin shifted uncomfortably, hoping she liked what she saw. He did not know why it felt so important that she be impressed. She caught sight of the bubbling pot over the fire.

"You were about to eat," she sounded distraught, "I should have waited."

"No, no, don't worry," Devrin said quickly, wanting to put her at ease. "Please, it's all right, I don't mind. In fact, can I offer you some dinner? I would be honored to dine with you."

At his words, Shentallyia relaxed. "I would be most pleased to share a meal with you."

Devrin ladled the stew into two separate bowls and handed one to her, along with a chunk of hard bread. They busied themselves with the food for a while. Questions filled Devrin's mind, but they raced through his thoughts with such overwhelming force that he did not know what to say first.

"This is not the way that I imagined it would be," Shentallyia admitted, breaking the silence. "I did not realize you would feel like a stranger."

"Why are you here?" Devrin asked, his curiosity helping him find his tongue.

"To meet you," she said, her tone indicated that this should be obvious.

Caution flooded into Devrin's thoughts. The girl was a

dragon, he was sure of that. He no longer felt that incredible certainty he had experienced when he touched her hand, but he knew it, nonetheless. However, she must be hiding what she really was, or why else would she appear in human form? There was only one way to find out if she was hiding her identity.

"What are you?" he asked.

She seemed a bit taken aback. Her expression turned guarded, and she stared at him. Hurt and disappointment filled her face. Devrin felt the strength of her dismay overwhelm him and wished he had not asked.

"Don't you know?" her voice quavered.

Devrin was not entirely certain they were talking about the same thing anymore. The conversation was getting nowhere with both of them being distant and cautious. He decided it was past time for at least one of them to be honest.

"You're a dragon."

Her expression altered from disappointment to surprise. At length, Shentallyia nodded, her movements slow and deliberate. There was a bit of respect in her expression now, and Devrin felt he had regained a modicum of control over the conversation.

"What do you want?" Devrin demanded. "Why did you come here?"

Shentallyia swallowed hard. "I came because there was no other option. You called me. I came because you're my ward."

"Your what?"

Shentallyia took a deep breath. "I did not expect this to be so difficult. This is not the way they describe it—but then, none of the Kin alive have ever had a ward, perhaps they do not know." She caught Devrin's confused look and paused. "I will try to explain. Many years ago, when the world was still young, dragons and humans did not have such distrust between them. Some dragons were even linked to human children who were born with an innate empathy for dragons. These children were known as dragon wards."

"What could they do?"

"They could know a dragon by touching it," Shentallyia said, "no matter what form it took, among other things."

"What else?" he asked, his mouth and throat dry.

"They possessed an aptitude for our language: Old Kraïc, and they were always longing for the ability to fly. Dragon wards, Riders, Links, they were known by many names, but whatever they were called, they were always bonded to a dragon. A dragon ward's abilities come into full power as he approaches adulthood, and that is when his dragon comes to find him. The two are bonded for life."

"What happened to them?" Devrin asked, his interest rising. "If these children provided a link between humans and dragons, why were the dragons driven away?"

"Distrust and fear of my people sent us into hiding throughout the world. As we retreated from the world, fewer wards were born. The last haven for us was in Aom-igh, but even we have seen the last of the dragon wards: she departed from our land three years ago during the conflict between your country and ours. To my knowledge, you are the first ward to call out to a dragon in over two hundred years."

Devrin was overwhelmed. He could not contain all the information and he stood, bursting with energy. "So you believe I'm your ward. The first ward in more than two centuries. Why me? What brought you here? You come from Aom-igh?"

"The yearning led me to you," Shentallyia said simply. "I did not know anything about you. I did not know where you lived, what your name was, how old you were or what you looked like. All I knew was which direction to fly. So I came. Yes, I come from Aom-igh. My people have been underground for a long time, in the tunnels of a world we called Krayghentaliss. I believe being underground is what has kept us from sensing our wards. The fact that you are so much older than most wards at the time of their discovery would appear to uphold that theory."

"And what exactly do you expect me to do now?"

"I'm not sure. I did not expect it to be like this," Shentallyia admitted. "I did not believe I could be this uncomfortable around you. I thought perhaps you were waiting for me. Not necessarily that you would know who I was, but that you would have felt something at our first meeting."

Devrin was not sure what to think. But Shentallyia's story inspired him and he wanted it to be true. He remembered how seeing the dragon near the palace had not frightened him, how he had longed to ride it and battle the seheowks from its back, how he had known what Shentallyia was the moment he touched her. It all added up to... to something. The only problem was that Devrin was not sure what it did add up to. He felt like he was trying to connect mismatched puzzle pieces.

"Magic has not been present in Llycaelon for many years," he said at last. "If I am a dragon ward as you claim, then perhaps that is the reason our meeting was not as you hoped?"

"Perhaps," she hesitated for a moment, a thoughtful look crossing her fine features. "What you say is not true, though. Magic only lies dormant in Llycaelon, waiting for something to wake it from its slumber. I wonder..." she trailed off. "It doesn't matter. May I stay? I know the threat of seheowks, and I can help."

"Our situation here is precarious, although I'm sure you're aware of that, you seem to know everything else. Right now I wouldn't turn away any offer of help. Do you need anything?"

"Thank you, but I can fend for myself."

Devrin nodded, despite being completely confused. She rose to leave, thanking him for his time, and then she was gone.

CHAPTER
TWELVE

Kamarie had never seen such a sight. In a great, red ball of flame the Dragon's Eye sank into the sea. Its rays lingered long after it was gone, but eventually faded beneath the waves as well. The sky turned purple and stars began to blink into existence, a thousand sparkling gemstones dotting the heavens. Kamarie fancied she ought to be able to reach up and touch them.

"Wouldn't that be wonderful?" she asked Oraeyn. "This whole trip would be over if you could just fly up there and take down a star right now. Then we wouldn't have to go all the way to Emnolae, I mean, if Yorien's Hand really was a star, and not an enigmatic relic of power with unknown origins."

"Sure would be easier, if Yorien's Hand really was a star," he agreed. "But its origin appears to be wrapped in mystery. I'd never even heard of it until a few days ago."

The dragons glided down from the sky. Land had been spotted earlier, and they now came to rest on a deserted shoreline. It would have been easy to just camp out on the beach, but Brant insisted that they move away from the water and into a more wooded area to set up camp and spend the night.

"There is less chance of us being seen if we stay out of the open," he cautioned.

As they set up camp, the dragons took care of creating a

small fire. Oraeyn had not thought about how it would be beneficial to have the dragons along for reasons other than flying. He had never given much thought to traveling, and it occurred to him that this was the first time he had ever left Aomigh's borders.

He looked at Thorayenak, a curious expression on his face. "Do you know what Yorien's Hand really is?"

"I am afraid not," the old dragon replied. "There is, of course, the legend of Yorien that can be found in the lore of every land on Tellurae Aquaous, which gives a modicum of credence to the tale. My people have other theories, but that is all they are."

"What are the theories?" Kamarie asked, coming up and sitting next to Oraeyn.

"Some say it is a powerful object, given to the world as a gift by Cruithaor Elchiyl himself to protect us from the Ancient Enemy," Thorayenak said.

"Others believe it is truly a star, and that all stars possess the same power, though I think that is utter nonsense," Rhimmell added. "Yorien's Hand is unique, and no matter what else it is, I do not believe it is an actual star."

"A few of the other tales reference the beings called cearaphiym in conjunction with Yorien's Hand," Thorayenak said, "but those are much more obscure and were written by an extremely unreliable source."

"Have you ever seen it?" Yole asked the other dragons.

They both shook their heads.

"I have seen drawings and diagrams, of course," Thorayenak said, "but I have never been to Emnolae or seen the relic itself."

Oraeyn felt the little ball of worry that had worked itself into a knot in the pit of his stomach twist around a bit. He did not like being blind as to what lay ahead. Though he trusted Kiernan, he wondered if Yorien's Hand was even capable of defeating their enemies. What if it wasn't even a weapon at all? Brant had seen it, touched it, even, and yet he had been unable to use it. What if he, Oraeyn, also failed at this task? What if he succeeded, but they were defeated anyway?

"Thank you," he said to the dragons. "I'm going to go collect firewood."

As he left the camp, Brant fell into step beside him. Oraeyn felt himself relax in the presence of the warrior's strength.

"Where are we, exactly?" Oraeyn asked as they began searching for dry sticks and branches to use in the fire.

"A little island a few leagues east of the Barrier Islands. I don't think it has a name. It's fairly deserted, though there are a few people who like the isolation," Brant replied. "There are hundreds of tiny islands like this all across the sea, and we may need a few more of them during the course of our journey. Even dragons cannot fly from Aom-igh to Emnolae without rest."

They returned to the camp and Kiernan offered to prepare dinner. Oraeyn and Kamarie offered to scout around the perimeter of the camp together.

"It may be a small, mostly uninhabited island," Oraeyn said, "but best not to take chances."

"In any case, it is a good habit to form," Brant agreed. "But be on your guard, this is not a leisurely sojourn. We must stay alert at all times."

Oraeyn drew his sword and he and Kamarie ventured out into the forest, making sure to keep their fire in sight at all times. The night was filled with the sounds of creatures that come out after nightfall, but the noises were all familiar and comforting ones. The light of the Toreth filtered through the trees, lighting their path.

"Do you think we'll succeed?" Kamarie's voice was quiet.

Fears that Oraeyn had tried to leave behind threatened to overwhelm him and he gripped the hilt of the Fang Blade a bit tighter. "We have to at least try."

"Earlier I said that this was like the way we met, but it isn't, is it? Back then we thought we were traveling away from danger. This time, we can't pretend that we're doing anything but running straight into its heart."

Oraeyn reached out for Kamarie's hand. "I can't tell you it will be all right," he said, "but I can tell you that as long as we're together, I feel more confident of our success. I realize that doesn't make much sense, logically, but it's the way I feel. You were right, I do need you. And I'm glad you are here."

Kamarie's face softened, but she had the good grace not to gloat. The leftover tension from their fight the previous day dissolved into the cool night air.

When they returned from their scouting expedition, having found nothing worrisome, they discovered that Kiernan had prepared a small meal which they ate in hungry silence. Afterwards, they rolled out their blankets and retired for the night. Brant kept the first watch as the rest of the company attempted to fall asleep. Oraeyn soon found that he could not sleep. After a long hour of restless tossing about, he gave up and went to sit with Brant. The night was still. The two men sat together, content to keep watch in companionable quiet.

"Do you think that Dylanna and Leila are all right?" Oraeyn asked after a long while.

Brant looked worried, but his tone was even, "I hope so. If they were captured, perhaps we will hear word of where they are being held on our way to Emnolae, I for one plan on staying alert."

"I suppose that is all we can do, for now. Searching for them would be an impossible task."

"Any more impossible than the quest we are on at this very moment?"

"At least we know where Yorien's Hand is."

Brant made a strange sound in his throat. "We do at that."

"I'm worried about them, Brant."

The warrior took a deep breath and held it for a moment or two, and then he let it out slowly. "So am I, Oraeyn. So am I."

Both men sat brooding over a mystery that neither of them could hope to solve. They stared into the fire in quiet contemplation, each wrapped in his own worries, doubts, and concerns about the journey they were on and what it held for them all.

"Have you been here before?" Oraeyn questioned, uncomfortable with the silence and needing something to distract him from the thoughts whirling around inside his head.

"No, but we will probably visit many places I have been before this adventure is over. When I was younger I traveled through many of the lands this world holds. Not all of them, of course."

"How long ago was that? How old were you when you traveled across Tellurae Aquaous?"

"Several lifetimes ago. I was about your age when I set out, maybe a little younger. Of course, I had lived more years, but as you know, in Llycaelon we live longer lives and we age more slowly."

"Because of the wizard's blood. I remember Kiernan mentioning that."

"Yes," Brant said the word tightly as he shot a suspicious look towards the pallet where the minstrel was sleeping. "Though how Kiernan knows that, I should very much like to learn."

"Where did you travel?"

"Many places. The countryside of Kallayohm, the great city of Layrdon that is the heart of Yochathain, the treacherous forests of Emnolae, I even traveled to the Nameless Isles. You might say that I saw a little of everything."

"You saw the Nameless Isles?" Oraeyn asked, awed.

"What a place of mystery that is!" Brant spoke softly, his tone filled with sorrow at the memory. "A dear friend and teacher of mine died there, I was forced to leave him."

"I'm sorry," Oraeyn said quietly. A moment later he stirred. "What is Emnolae like?"

"I lost a friend there, too. She did not deserve her fate," Brant stared at the ground and spat out the words, which were filled with an emotion Oraeyn could not identify.

"Forgive me," Oraeyn said. He did not like seeing his friend in such pain. Though he desperately wanted to know more, needed to know what they were about to face, he stared at the ground and sighed. "I did not mean to dredge up painful memories. I will ask you no more questions."

Brant raised his head, his features softening in an unspoken apology. "No, it... it is all right. You need my memories, my knowledge of where we are going. Ask your questions, I will answer what I can."

Oraeyn looked at him askance, but Brant's face was once again calm. He hesitated to ask more, but he needed to know what Brant could tell him. At length, he asked, "Do you think the star, or whatever it is, is still there? You said before that you'd touched it; what's it like?"

"I spoke truly," Brant's voice was strained, like he was reluctant to let the words pass through his lips. "I once went on a quest in search of it, although you might say that I was sent to find it. What I discovered was not what I had expected..." he trailed off and Oraeyn kept silent, wondering if he would learn any more. Brant looked up and saw Oraeyn, his lips quirked upward but his face was haggard and weary. "No, not what I expected at all," he repeated.

"Will it still be there?"

"Yes, it will still be there."

"How can you be sure?"

"The Hand of Yorien is not at risk of being stolen," Brant chuckled a bit. "A thief would find himself dead before he even saw the star, and anyone else would be hard-pressed to get close enough to touch it. Those who make it that far are lucky, and once they reach their goal they will find that it is nothing like what they thought to find."

"Do you think I'm the person the song speaks of, Brant?" the question crept out, timid and hesitant, but Oraeyn could not let it go unasked.

"I have no idea, Oraeyn. All I know is this: my whole life has been governed by prophecies and the cryptic words of seers and mages, wizards and dragons. I have dealt with songs of the future and words of foretelling since before you were born. I have lived my entire life beneath their shrouds, they have dictated so many of my steps, and thus, I have learned one thing about them."

Brant leaned forward and lowered his voice slightly. Oraeyn instinctively leaned in as well.

Brant's jaw tightened. "Listen carefully, for this is the one insight that I have gained into the workings of prophetic words and those who speak them: they are never saying what you think they are saying. The meanings are never clear. When a prophecy seems straightforward, beware, for then it is most mired in mystery, obscured behind heavy curtains, and you can be certain that events will twist around beneath your feet and the ground you thought so firm will lurch out from under you. When the words of a prophecy are their most unambiguous, you will find they are filled with guile and misdirection and the very last thing you expected to happen will suddenly be what the prophecy meant all along. Best not to think too hard on the words of prophecy, they will only confuse you." Brant's voice sounded tight with anger, but then he winked and the corner of his lip twitched. "Of course, that particular insight is probably less than no help at all to you."

Oraeyn bit back a laugh, but his heart felt lighter. Brant was right, it was best not to dwell on what might happen, or on the ominous words of an unclear bit of poetry. Better to think about the path directly before him than worry about obstacles in the distance that might not even be there.

"I am afraid, Brant," he admitted, and saying the words helped to loosen the knot in his stomach.

"Fear can give you strength, if you do not let it control you."

"I'm not afraid for myself, though."

Brant glanced over at where Kamarie lay sleeping and he nodded in understanding. "I am afraid for the safety of others as well. We will watch after her," he kept his voice low, "I am sworn to protect you both. I promise I will do everything in my power to keep her safe."

"Thank you, my friend."

"You should try to sleep," Brant advised, "while you still can. We may not have many more opportunities to rest for an entire night after this. Already our Enemy may have noticed our movement. We do not comprehend the extent of his power, it may be he has already guessed that one of our company is a threat to him, or perhaps he knows nothing of us or our quest. In either case, we must continue to be cautious and remain alert."

Oraeyn nodded wordlessly and retired to his blanket. Brant's light touch on his shoulder halted him in his tracks. He turned and looked questioningly at the warrior. The firelight deepened the shadows that played across Brant's face making him look more intimidating and even more like steel. His eyes gleamed like the dying embers of coal, sending a chill through Oraeyn.

"Oraeyn," the warrior's voice was hushed, "keep a close watch on Kiernan Kane."

Oraeyn cocked his head quizzically. "What do you mean?"

"Be careful of him," Brant's voice was filled with a warning.

Oraeyn tilted his head to one side. "Kiernan is a mystery, but certainly he has proven himself to be our friend, and worthy of our trust."

Brant did not reply immediately. It appeared that the warrior struggled with a concern he could not, or would not, share. At length, Brant gave an almost imperceptible nod.

"Just stay alert."

"I think you worry about Kiernan too much," Oraeyn shrugged, standing up and stretching his legs a bit. "But I'll keep an eye on him if you want me to."

Oraeyn yawned and went to his bedroll where he fell into a deep and peaceful sleep.

From where he lay by the fire, Kiernan let out a loud snore and rolled deeper into his blankets. His eyes were closed, but had they been open the look in them might have been called amused. In the darkness he chortled softly to himself.

"So, our warrior does not trust the fool, eh? But then, he trusts no one easily, least of all himself." Then he sighed deeply and allowed himself to drift into sleep.

The Toreth was an hour past its zenith when Kiernan Kane woke to relieve Brant of his watch. As he approached, Brant moved slightly to allow the minstrel to sit next to him on the log, but he did not make any attempt to retire to his blanket. They sat in silence for a few moments, the warrior and the minstrel, alert for any sound or movement that was out of place.

Brant was barely tired. It felt good to be traveling again, good to be in a place where his skills could be put to their proper use. He felt more awake, more alert than he had in a long time. It had been too long since he had slept under the stars. At one time he had been content to live a simple life, to be a husband and a father. He had grown to love that life. But all of his reasons for remaining there had been stolen. Now he was where he was meant to be once more, and his heart was light, despite the threat they faced. He welcomed the risk; it reminded him that he was alive.

"You can sleep now," the minstrel said, his voice soft. "I will keep watch."

Brant had been so lost in his own thoughts that he had forgotten about Kiernan Kane's presence. There was a long silence. It stretched into the night, but it was not altogether uncomfortable. Brant squinted out into the night and when he spoke again he did not turn to look at the minstrel.

"A long time ago you wished to tell me a story about a second son who was destined to become king. I would hear that story now."

Firelight flickered across Kiernan's face in eerie patterns. "You do remember then, I thought perhaps you had forgotten that meeting."

"I did not forget the meeting, but I had forgotten the face of the minstrel. It was you who sent me on my first quest to find Yorien's Hand."

"You are mistaken if you believe that," Kiernan replied. "I did no sending."

"You knew I would go after the star, that's why you told the story. What I would like to know is what you thought to gain by sending me."

"I sought nothing."

"I do not believe that."

"Believe as you wish."

Brant still did not turn or look at the minstrel, but even so he was studying the other intently. At length he spoke again.

"What of the second son who was destined to become king?"

"I think you already know that story, Warrior."

"I would hear how your version of the story ends."

"Many people believe they would like to hear how their stories end, but when they are given what they wish, they cringe from it and spend the rest of their time and strength trying to deny or avoid what they have learned. Nobody ever really wants to hear the end of the story, they simply want to hear that everything will turn out all right."

"Will it?"

Kiernan sighed, and there was a world of meaning in that simple exhalation. "I can see much, Brant, but I do not see all. I have studied the stories and the ancient texts. Whether they are prophetic or not remains to be seen. Every story that I tell or pass along is true, and is intended to reveal that truth, but the result, the ending, is never clear. The stories shed light on what will come. They tell of the battle between what is hoped for and intended versus what is feared and altered. My stories are not for amusement, but if a story is not entertaining it is quickly forgotten, and that is never my purpose. I am not a wizard or a sage as you may wish to think. I am a minstrel. No more than that."

"You are more than a common minstrel," Brant accused softly. "You appear to be in your late twenties or maybe early thirties, yet you must be much older. I remember our meeting over thirty years ago and you look younger today than you did in Yochathain when first we met. I have heard many stories in my life, but none like the ones you tell. You speak of events from thousands of years ago, but they do not have the sound of stories passed down from father to son. Your songs make it sound like you were witness to these events, you tell the story as intimately as if you had been there. My whole life has been applied to training, studying, and working with little time for leisure or pleasure, and yet I could continue that effort for ten lifetimes and not have the command of so much knowledge and insight as you. The one conclusion that makes sense is that you have lived an unequalled span of life."

The minstrel shrugged, his bony shoulders rising in a fluid, nonchalant motion. "Some are bound by time, others are bound by something else, but in the end we are all bound. You are mistaken on several counts, but I shall only address two tonight. First, our encounter on Yochathain was not, as you suspect, our first meeting. And second, I truly do not know the end of this story. I may know more than you, but that does not have to mean that I am your enemy. And as for the caliber of my stories and songs, well, perhaps I am merely a better wordsmith than any other minstrel you have had the pleasure of hearing?"

Brant whirled on the minstrel in sudden anger. "You are just like all the rest of them, never speaking clearly, never saying what you mean! The prophecy that destroyed my life, the lives of my family, of everyone I held dear, what was its purpose? Will I ever be free of its curse?"

"It is a gift you have been given, not a curse. The knowledge of yourself and of what you can become is never a curse, and neither are its words binding unless you let them control you."

"I could not control the way others interpreted their meanings though," Brant muttered bitterly.

Kiernan shook his head and there was deep sadness etched in every line of his face. "No, but then that is the nature of things. You cannot control the reactions of others, only your own."

Brant sighed, his anger fading, replaced by a deep weariness. "So what have you sent us on then, with your words of the past and your hints of the future? Do you take us to our deaths? Oraeyn believes so. He has not said as much but I can see it written plainly in his movements and expressions when he believes no one is watching, perhaps he has had a vision of his own. Are you leading us to glory and triumph or to ruin?"

"Brant, I seldom lead... and never to glory or triumph. My hope... my purpose, is only ever to safeguard Tellurae Aquaous and its people. I do not know if this journey leads us to our deaths or to victory. I do know for certain that this quest is our best course of action and, in fact, our only hope."

"I don't understand what game you are playing, Minstrel, but I warn you to consider with care who you are up against if you mean to do harm. My life has been dictated by prophecies and the consequences are very real and very painful. I despise people like you who play with the lives of others and then leave them to deal with the ruin and clean up the mess you create with your words."

"The words are not mine. I merely carry a message."

"Not this time," Brant returned fiercely. "Not this time."

The minstrel met Brant's gaze steadily and without flinching. His expression reflected care, not fear, at Brant's harsh words. He blinked and turned away.

"Your strength will be needed," Kiernan replied quietly, "but not against me, my friend. You judge me by things you have seen in the past. You believe I am playing games and you would like to accuse me of attempting to rearrange lives, of using your friends as pawns—but really you give me far too much credit. The pieces may be moving, but not by my hand. Our paths are indeed different, but our purposes are joined towards the same end. You are correct in believing me a fool, but I am not only a fool."

"You must think me a simpleton then, if you expect me to believe that."

Kiernan waved a hand in an expansive gesture. "As I said, believe what you will."

"Whatever else you are, you are not what you seem," Brant said firmly. "You would have sent us off on this adventure alone if you could have."

Kiernan's shoulders shook with silent laughter. "I never protested coming along. I only let you believe I would, because I knew it was the only way you would let me join this quest. Be honest with yourself, would you have agreed to let me be your guide had I eagerly volunteered?"

Brant scowled into the fire. But after a moment, he had to admit the truth of the minstrel's words. "I would not," he muttered.

"You are worried about the wizardesses, and much of your anger towards me springs from that. Do not forget that one of them is the woman I love, too."

Brant peered at the minstrel's face, his gaze burning with the intensity of his stare. "I know who you are."

Kiernan Kane cocked his head, unconcerned. "Do you? You

really ought to sleep," Kiernan said, "morning is closer than you think."

THIRTEEN

A tiny, golden-haired child stood in the midst of the rubble and sobbed. Frightened tears streamed from his brown eyes and ran down his cheeks as he gazed about in shock, unable to move. He barely understood what had happened. All he knew was that he was scared, and he had been left alone. The creatures had come in the night; no one had been prepared for the horror that had been unleashed.

They had left nothing standing, sweeping through like a blanket of death, breaking things and hurting people with as little effort as thought. The destruction had been mindless and thorough; and above it all swooshed the glittering wings of the werehawk and his dreadful rider. It was just a town on the outskirts of Kallayohm. There was nothing special about Chensar. It was merely one of the many towns unfortunate enough to be in close proximity to the capital city. Except for this one child there were no survivors.

The child wiped a grimy hand across his face, leaving a smear of dirt and tears. Surrounded by the destruction of what had once been his home, the boy had no idea of what he should do next. A rush of wind ruffled the small boy's hair as a large, winged creature swept across the sky. The child cowered in fright, thinking the evil creatures had returned. He had seen the werehawk, and it had filled him with unescapable dread. Its chill, unfeeling glance had grazed the boy and their cut had probably saved his life. His mother had shoved him towards the outside cellar, trying to get her baby to safety, but the boy had stopped, frozen as he watched the horror unfolding around him. It was then he had noticed the giant creature circling above him. He shrank away from its gaze, panic sending him stumbling backward; he had tripped and fallen down the cellar stairs and tumbled into a corner, hitting his head and losing consciousness. The were-folk had not seen him fall and did not believe anyone had made it to the laughable safety of the cellar. When the child had awoken, night was over and he was alone.

The little boy hunched down behind a piece of rubble, doing his best to hide beneath it; he gazed upwards, cowering. The large form passed over again, blotting out the cold light of the Toreth, closer this time. Then there was the soft thump of something large landing nearby. More tears escaped from behind the boy's eyelids and streaked his dirty face.

"Hello, what have we here?" the voice was friendly.

"Go 'way, go 'way," the little boy whispered pleadingly, his voice tiny and trembling.

"Come on out little one, I won't hurt you."

The child took a shaky breath. He was tired, he was scared, and he was alone, but the voice was kind. After a moment, he risked a peek out from beneath his piece of rubble. He gave an ear-piercing shriek at what he saw, and scrambled backwards away from the creature before him. A piece of rubble twisted between his legs, causing him to fall again. He sobbed, a wild, despairing sound, still scrabbling with his arms and legs to get away.

"Shhhh, shhh, little one, I am not one of the creatures that did this," the dragon nodded his head at the destruction. "I am a friend."

The child's voice rose in a wail, his tiny hands held up in front of his face in a feeble effort to protect himself. The dragon leaned down and touched his hand with his hard, scaly nose, an unbelievably tender gesture for such a massive creature. It blew a warm, tender breath on the boy's face and then pulled its head back, giving the child space.

The little boy's sobs slowed; he peered up warily, wondering why he had not already been eaten. The dragon looked at him, making no threatening movement. Finding himself unharmed, the boy sat up and wiped a hand under his nose. Then he regarded the dragon quizzically. The creature's eyes gleamed silver like the werehawk's, but the face was warm and wise, and its gaze did not slice through him with that same icy malice. Although this creature was every bit as terrifying as the others, the child calmed as he began to realize that this beast meant him no harm.

"I am not one of them," the dragon assured him again, keeping his voice to a quiet rumble. "I'm from Llycaelon, I was just out stretching my wings a bit when I saw what had happened here."

The child's face turned serious. "Lie... Lie... Liecane?"

The dragon sighed. "Do you understand what I am saying to you?"

The child looked confused. "You talk," he said abruptly.

The dragon nodded his great head. "Yes, I talk. What is your name, little one?"

"Shane," the child replied. "What your name?"

"My name is Khoranaderek."

The boy cocked his head to one side. "Drek."

"I suppose if that is the best you can do, you may call me 'Drek.' I come from Llycaelon."

"Drek," the child said proudly. "Liecane."

"How old are you?" the dragon asked curiously.

The little boy scowled and raised a hand. After a moment of struggling to get it right, he raised two chubby fingers. Then he made a chopping motion with one hand on the other.

"Two and a half?" the dragon asked.

Shane nodded and made the motion again, a proud grin lighting his face. The dragon found the smile contagious. Shane cowered back from the sudden appearance of so many teeth and for a moment it appeared that he might flee. With an effort,

Khoranaderek closed his scaled lips and pulled back once more, so as to appear less threatening.

"Well, Shane, would you like a ride? We can go back to Llycaelon and get you food and a warm, dry bed. And the king must be warned, whatever did this to your home may be on his way towards mine even now."

There was a pause, then Shane seemed to decide that this creature was a friend, regardless of his intimidating size and number of teeth. After a moment, he reached up his tiny arms to be held. He looked pleadingly at the dragon.

"Drek, Liecane, hungwy."

The dragon looked at the child with compassion. Then he plucked the child off the ground and swung him up onto his back, placing him securely between the large wings so he would not fall. With a flap of those great wings they lifted off the ground and into the sky. The boy squealed with delight and terror as he found himself lifted very high off the ground.

"Hold on!" Khoranaderek said, worried that the child was too small to understand. "Don't fall!"

Shane leaned forward and squeezed his arms against either side of the dragon's long neck. Then the dragon turned towards Llycaelon and began to make his way home.

Dylanna, her thoughts were listless and required a great amount of energy to form, *I must remember. I must remember my name. My name is Dylanna… why is that important? Dylanna… Dylanna… that is who I am… why do I care? What is so important that I must not forget? Why… Dylanna…*

But it took so much effort to remember, and all she wanted was rest.

Dylanna… her mind clung to the name, but she did not know how much longer she would be able to remember.

The night on the small island was uneventful, and when dawn arrived the company ate a quick breakfast and set out again. The rest brought renewal with it, and they all felt much better for having gotten food and sleep. They had been flying an hour when Kiernan cried out with a shout that was a mixture of triumph and distress. The others turned to look at the minstrel in concern, Oraeyn half expected to see that he had tumbled from Rhimmell's back, but the man was still seated on his mount.

"Down, we must go down!" he shouted to his companions. "We must land now!"

His voice was frantic, and he waved his arms as if he could make them all descend from the sky by sheer willpower. Oraeyn shot a questioning look at Brant to see what his mentor thought of Kiernan's antics. Brant caught his glance and shrugged.

"Follow Kiernan," Oraeyn said, making the decision. "But be cautious," he added quietly to Yole.

The dragon began to spiral downwards. They broke through the clouds and Oraeyn saw a very small landmass below them. It was hardly even large enough to be called an island, it looked more like a large rock that the waves had not quite managed to cover.

"Kiernan," Brant shouted, "there's nothing down there!"

"Trust me," the minstrel shouted back.

"It's just a big rock," Brant yelled. "There's not even enough room for the seven of us to stand on it once we land. What could possibly be so important?"

"Leila and Dylanna are down there," Kiernan's voice floated to their ears above the whistling wind around them and the lapping of the waves below.

Oraeyn heard Kamarie catch her breath in surprise and hope. He looked down at the small landmass again, wondering if he had missed something. The small protrusion of rock had not changed, it was still tiny and bare and empty. He shook his head in disbelief, wondering what the minstrel had sensed. It did not seem possible that Dylanna or Leila could be hidden anywhere on the face of that ledge, but he decided it was worth a try.

"It can't hurt to look," Oraeyn called out, wishing he did not have to shout to be heard.

"Our time grows short," Kiernan cried. "If we do not find

them now, it will be too late."

Brant nodded in ready agreement. "Everyone stay alert," he added.

Jemson sat atop his horse, sword drawn and ready. The rain had begun to fall several hours before daybreak and it now drizzled continuously. Heavy clouds obscured the sky, forbidding any daylight to penetrate. A strong wind whipped its way in from the sea; Jemson shivered within his leather armor and stared out at the fire which sputtered and hissed.

The warriors entrusted with the fire worked in desperation to keep the wall of flame intact, but they were losing the battle to the rain and would soon need to take up their weapons. The fire was dwindling, dying. The sentries had given the alert that the time was at hand and the battle would soon be renewed. Jemson was impressed by how the men reacted to the bad news, taking it in stride. There was no uproar, no frenzied or aimless scampering about as by those with no idea of what to do with themselves. The camp remained orderly and quiet.

A sign of good leadership, Jemson thought, heedless of the water that dripped down his back and rolled along his spine. *These men know their assignments and what is expected of them.* He applauded Devrin, and the captains before him, for the evidence of good training and discipline.

Jemson felt nothing but admiration for the young captain, but he could sense that the emotion was not reciprocated. There was a tightness to Devrin's jaw, a clipped tone to his words whenever Jemson sought him out that betrayed his true feelings. Jemson was not sure what he had done to elicit this sort of response from the captain. At first he had assumed it was due to his own youth and inexperience—he had encountered plenty of that kind of attitude since taking the crown—but as the days wore on, Jemson came to understand that Devrin's behavior towards him stemmed from elsewhere. Whatever it was, it didn't interfere with the man's duties. The captain acted with courtesy and respect, listening to Jemson's opinions and even incorporating a few of his ideas into the daily routine.

Jemson surveyed the camp. The rain plastered his hair to his head and every inch of him was thoroughly soaked. His ears caught the hiss of the fire as the rain pelted it. He tasted the thick, acrid smoke as the wind blew it back over the camp. Now was not the time to question Devrin's motivations. There would be time for that later if any of them survived the coming battle.

Despite the terrible army waiting with mounting impatience on the other side of the dying flames, Jemson felt excitement stir within him. Though he was young, he had trained to become a warrior for his entire life, and like his men, there was a part of him that despised the safety of the fire wall which offered protection and asked nothing of him in return. He was trained to do battle, and it was to battle that his entire being now yearned. There was no doubt of his purpose or course of action. He had come to the borders to fight the creatures that now threatened the safety of his kingdom. He faced the wall of fire, every muscle tensed and ready. He tightened his lips in determination, his expression cold and hard. He did not know it, but in that moment, he was the mirror image of his uncle.

Devrin rode up beside him. Jemson noticed that a young woman rode with him. She sat on a white mare and rode a few paces behind Devrin on his great roan stallion. Her face was impassive, and she was unarmed, yet she exuded confidence and calm. Jemson rubbed his chin, confused. Devrin noticed and nodded at the girl.

"Her name is Shentallyia," he said briefly. "She may be able to aid us in fighting the seheowks today."

Jemson studied the woman, peering through the rain. She was slight of build and Jemson could not imagine her posing a threat to anyone, but there was something about her that supported Devrin's assertion. Her hands were steady on the reins of her mount, and Jemson felt he understood her. She would not shrink from the seheowks, they would learn to cower before her.

"How much longer do we have?" he asked, still staring at the woman who rode behind Devrin.

"Minutes, at the very most," Devrin's voice was quiet. "Are

the men ready?"

Jemson nodded.

"Stay near me when they break through," Devrin continued, "the first rush will sustain the greatest losses."

With an effort, Jemson tore his gaze away from the woman's face. It was more difficult than he would have imagined. He clenched his teeth angrily and gave Devrin a hard stare.

"I don't need your protection."

"Perhaps not, but you are my king and I am sworn to protect you. It is my Oath. All aethalons take it, and it is the one thing we hold most dear. Its words are binding in a way that few understand," Devrin said the words with careful enunciation, staring intently at the fires. He did not notice the fury building in Jemson as he spoke.

Jemson bristled. "I have taken your Oath," he declared heatedly. "And I am apprenticed these past three years to Brant of the House of Arne. Perhaps you have heard of him. A few of the elders have argued that a younger king or a younger apprentice has never been seen in Llycaelon, but none have argued that there has ever been a greater warrior than Brant. He declared me ready. Because of his teaching, it is likely that I know more about the Oath of our people and what it means than even you. I may be king of Llycaelon, but I doubt that I am *your* king. I do not know why this is, but I do know that now is not the time to belabor the point. Look to yourself and your men, I am no concern of yours."

Devrin turned to the young king, his mouth open slightly and surprise written across his features. "I meant no disrespect to your age, Majesty. I only meant that while you are here in my command, you are under my protection. Were you old and gray, ten full ranks above me, and completely capable of besting me in every contest imaginable, I would still be bound to protect you, my liege. As to the rest of your accusation, you are right, now is not the time for it. But rest assured, it is my own problem, and no doing of yours."

Jemson's jaw tightened, but he nodded tersely. "Very well, forgive me for misunderstanding."

A horn sounded, and Devrin stiffened. "The dry wood is gone. The seheowks will soon attack."

His voice was steady. Jemson peered at the captain cautiously, trying to discern what the man was thinking. Devrin's face was full of determination and purpose, all held carefully beneath a mask of imperturbable calm.

We are not so different, the thought flitted through his mind, *perhaps...* Then he drew his focus away from the captain. He could not afford to try puzzling the man out now; there would be plenty of time for that once the seheowks were defeated. *If such a thing can be accomplished,* Jemson thought ruefully.

He hazarded another glance at the mysterious young woman. She sat like a statue, her pretty face devoid of all expression. She caught his gaze and looked away swiftly. Before she did, however, Jemson recognized something in her eyes that startled him. There was no time to pursue this new knowledge, though, because a moment later lightning streaked across the sky and the rain began to pour down in earnest. The great fire struggled, sibilating as if in anger and frustration. Smoke billowed into the sky and mingled with the clouds as the flames flickered to ash. Jemson tightened his grip on the hilt of his sword. Smoke and fog intertwined, creating a new wall as impenetrable as the barrier of flame had been. The aethalons hesitated, peering through the murky air, waiting to see what their enemy would do. Jemson felt like a tightly coiled spring just waiting to be released. His heart pounded in trepidation and excitement as he waited, poised and ready to strike.

With a wild, screeching cry the first line of seheowks rushed into the gap. They pounded through the smoke, ash, and rain, furious and impatient after long days of waiting caged between the fire and the sea. As the sinewy creatures reached the dying embers, the fire flared to life again with a brightness and intensity that caused Jemson to catch his breath. He heard his own surprise echoed across the camp as the rest of the aethalons witnessed the strange scene unfolding before them. The flames, which had dwindled almost to nothing, leaped up around the seheowks with a vengeance, licking at their limbs and engulfing them in hunger. Jemson stared in fascinated horror as the line of enemies burst into flame and died with bone-chilling shrieks of terror and agony. The rest of the creatures shrank back, unwilling to hazard the death that had consumed the first wave of their company.

Jemson turned to Devrin, searching for an answer, but the look on the captain's face told him that he was just as startled by this turn of events as everyone else. Jemson swallowed hard as the last cries of the seheowks dwindled away, muted by the heavy rain. After a long silence he found his voice again.

"Well, no wonder they fear it so."

Devrin nodded, his expression dazed. He opened his mouth to speak, but words did not come.

"Does fire always do that to them?" Jemson asked in a dry whisper.

"I have never seen anything like that before," Devrin replied.

Shentallyia tossed her hair back, a tiny smile upon her lips. Jemson caught her movement out of the corner of his vision and turned to her.

Dragon!

"You're a..." he stopped, interrupted by a shout that swept through the ranks of the aethalons. Perceiving the reluctance on the part of the seheowks to join the battle, men and horses charged down through the gap, trampling through the ashes and bearing down on the enemy with all the force they could muster.

Devrin unsheathed his own sword. Holding the blade high in the air he let out a cry of his own. Then he pointed his great blade forwards and spurred his horse into the gap. The aethalons stampeded to the attack. The hooves of their horses churned the ash and sent it flying into the misty air where it hung like a gray sheet.

Forgetting Devrin's charge to stay close, Jemson raced into the midst of the enemy. The many years of exacting training under his father's demanding eye and the more recent years under his uncle's watchful one bore fruit as he brandished his sword, the king's sword. His blade flashed again and again, and with every stroke one of the terrible creatures met its end.

Nothing could withstand his fury or deadly precision.

Sensing the threat that he posed, the seheowks turned their attention to the young king. Ignoring the army of aethalons before them, they surged their energies towards Jemson, placing him at the center of the quickly shifting battlefield. Time and again the seheowks attempted to pull him down, but nothing would slow or stop his battle rage. Like a berserker of old, the ringing of Jemson's sword would not be silenced and the cries of the evil creatures echoed out into the night as they fell before his every stroke.

From a distance, Devrin could see the seheowks beginning to rally and surround the king. Cursing the tide of the battle that had separated them, he struggled to return to Jemson's side. The king fought like no living man, but the captain knew no one could stand alone against so many for very long. In that instant, Devrin's mind was made up. His brother's dishonorable death had not been Jemson's fault, and to hold it against him was wrong. Jemson had proven himself. In spite of his youth, he had worked alongside the Border Patrol without complaint. And now, here in this battle, he had proven that he was no coward.

He is *my king.* The thought struck Devrin like the flat of his master's blade across the back of his head.

At the same moment that this thought swept through his being, Devrin saw the king's horse stumble. Jemson fell from view as the seheowks pulled him down. Fear clenched in his gut. For a heart-stopping moment, he lost sight of the boy, but then the great horse regained its feet and the aethalons raised a cheer when they saw King Jemson still firmly seated in his saddle and wielding his blade.

"To Arne! To Arne! For Llycaelon!" the king shouted the battle cry of his forefathers to rally the aethalons, now truly his aethalons, as his sword found its mark again and again. His eyes were ablaze and his face was like lightning. He was, in fact, a warrior king of old. Those who saw him took heart and redoubled their efforts to push the loathed enemy back into the sea. The seheowks fell away once more. The aethalons rallied to their king, taking up his battle cry for themselves. They surged towards him, attacking with a new vigor and defiance. Devrin fought desperately to reach Jemson and fight by his side. There was no hesitation now; he was caught up with his brother warriors in the battle cry of their king. He was almost there, at his king's side, when Jemson was pulled down again. This time, he did not reappear.

FOURTEEN

The land was dying. Zara held up a handful of brown grass and looked at Arnaud in confusion.

"I can't stop it," she said. "I don't have the power." Her voice was filled with frustration and despair in equal parts. She buried her face in her hands. "I feel so helpless. I don't even know why this is happening! I wish Dylanna and Leila were here. I wish I knew where they were! I'm so worried, so scared, I-I..." her words trailed off as Arnaud pulled her close in a strong embrace. She pressed her faced into his shoulder and leaned on his strength.

"It's okay," Arnaud whispered into her hair. "You'll figure it out."

"I don't know," Zara moaned in defeat. "I've tried everything."

"Do you know why it's happening?" Arnaud asked.

"Not really," Zara mumbled, still clinging to her husband.

Arnaud stepped back, but kept hold of her hands, giving them a gentle, reassuring squeeze.

Overnight, the land had changed from a vibrant, lively green to a sickly brown. It was as if Change-Term had gotten confused and come early. But there were none of the brilliant reds and golds and purples of that season. This change was all limp grays and browns. Tree limbs dangled lifelessly, weakened and weary. Flowers wilted. Even the wild animals had disappeared, as though retreating into early hibernation.

Zara tried on her own to put life back into the land, using every last trick she knew, but whatever was draining the land of life was too powerful for Zara to counter. It was frustrating for her to admit defeat. She had the most raw power and talent of the four daughters of Scelwhyn. Leila had once commented that Zara possessed the potential to be even more powerful than Calyssia, perhaps even stronger than Scelwhyn himself, but Zara had given up her life as a wizardess when she met Arnaud, and thus never realized her full potential.

"If only I had paid more attention to Calyssia when I was younger," she said now. "If only I knew more."

"Perhaps it is the work of the Ancient Enemy," Arnaud said. "Have you read the messages Oraeyn received from Yochathain and Kallayohm?"

"I have. None of them mention a blight on the land," Zara pulled her hands out of Arnaud's grasp and rubbed her fingers along the bridge of her nose. "It must be the Ancient Enemy, though, nothing else makes sense."

"Then Aom-igh must be different in some way from the other countries," Arnaud replied. "If the Enemy is using a different tactic on our land, he must be worried about his ability to conquer us."

"But what do we have that makes us different or a threat?" Zara asked. "We don't have the numbers that Kallayohm has. We don't possess an army like Llycaelon's."

Arnaud squinted thoughtfully. "We have dragons and gryphons and pegasus. We have wizardesses. We have magic."

Zara stared at him for a moment, then she chuckled ruefully. "I must be very tired not to have figured that out." She pressed the palm of her hand against her temple and sighed heavily. "Of course. A magical attack against us is logical. How could I not have seen it?"

"When is the last time you slept?" Arnaud's voice was soft but stern.

"I don't remember. I can't sleep. I need my sisters, I worry about what awful fate has befallen them. I can't do this on my own... I've lost one sister already, I cannot bear the thought of being the last one, all by myself... if only..."

Arnaud walked around behind Zara and rubbed her shoulders gently for a moment. "Would you give up the life you chose in order to have the ability to counter this threat today?"

At the tone of his voice, Zara turned and took Arnaud's hands in her own. She stared up at him. His expression was sad and tired and she reached up to touch his face with gentle fingers.

"Even for the power to heal the land and drive this Enemy out of Tellurae Aquaous once and for all, I would not have chosen differently. You and Kamarie are my world, and I would not trade either of you. Not for anything," she said the words firmly.

Arnaud did smile then, a gentle smile. He did not speak as he brushed the stray wisps of golden hair from her face. Zara gazed at him for a long moment.

"I would not have chosen differently," she spoke the words with quiet resolve. "But that doesn't make what I have to do now any easier."

"What is that?"

"I have to speak with Rena. I fear she must play the dragon pipes once more."

"No!" Devrin shouted his fury into the murky, ash-filled air. "No!" He was not aware of what he was yelling, the words tore their way out of his throat with no conscious effort on his part.

He forced his way through the swarm of seheowks, his blade glinting with their blood. With their prey in hand, the seheowks fought with renewed frenzy, but other aethalons reached the king and beat them back. Devrin reached the spot where Jemson lay and defended the king's body with every ounce of strength and skill he possessed. Together with his fellow warriors, they formed a shield around the king and retreated slowly, allowing him to be carried from the battlefield to the relative safety of the camp. Behind them, the fighting continued.

Devrin stayed by Jemson's side as the king was placed beneath a makeshift shelter, a length of canvas held up by tall posts. A few other wounded men already lay on pallets inside the shelter, tended by a few Kestrels who worked in the camp but were kept out of the fighting. Rain pelted the canvas roof with a pitter-pattering crackle. Devrin knelt by the pallet upon which Jemson was laid and watched uneasily as he was tended by one of the physicians who traveled with the Border Patrol.

"Is he dead?" Stephran's voice was heavy and dejected as he came up to stand beside Devrin.

"No," Devrin replied. He felt slightly awed by the word. It was so simple, and yet so filled with hope. "No," he said it again, savoring the beauty of it. A heavy word. A freeing word. "Though he should be, by all accounts. He's unconscious and badly hurt, but he's alive."

"The king had them retreating," Stephran said, his tone filled with wonder.

Devrin nodded, a strange mix of emotions coursing through him. He could not untangle them all, and there was little time to do so. Envy, admiration, and confusion mingled in his mind along with a sensation of urgency. The enemy had drawn back during the king's sally, but already Devrin could hear the sounds of battle rejoined. He had to get down there, lead his men, but he also had a duty to his king.

"It was like he was King Artair stepped out of the storybooks," Stephran continued speaking, his words waxing eloquent. It was odd, hearing flowery language coming from the man who usually spoke in such plain, simple language. "Riding the wind on his great steed that was no real horse at all, but something great and majestic…"

"Well, he was riding a real horse all right," Devrin snapped, a bit irritably, cutting off Stephran's monologue, "and it's dead now."

Stephran noted the frustration in Devrin's voice and his brow furrowed in confusion. "The king held his own quite well in his first battle. The men rallied to him and are now holding their own; we were nearly defeated before Jemson took the field. I would have thought you'd be a bit more pleased at the turn of events."

Devrin curled his lip. "The king is injured. He disobeyed my orders and dove into the enemy lines without a care for his own safety. That wasn't heroic, it was foolish. I could not protect him. He should be dead now, not just unconscious, and the battle still goes on." He pointed down to the field where the seheowks had regrouped and gathered for their next attack.

The physician looked up at Devrin. "He'll be fine," the man assured him. "He took a blow to the head, but he is otherwise unharmed. When he wakes up, he may have a nasty headache. But overall, he's lucky."

Devrin nodded solemnly and rose to venture back out into the rain. The mixture of emotions within him solidified into a single flame of determination. He had been prepared to hate this boy, prepared to despise him for his rank, his title, and for all the mistakes made by his family. What had happened to Kelan was unforgivable, and Devrin had been ready to hold Jemson personally responsible.

What he had been unprepared for, however, was for Jemson to win his admiration or his respect. He had not been ready to watch his men stirred to action by a young man—who was little more than a child—riding into battle with reckless courage. And yet, that was exactly what Jemson had done. The men had found the standard around which they could rally: a king who fought beside them, who slept on the hard ground without complaining, who weathered the elements and did his share of the work shoulder to shoulder with them. It hit Devrin with the force of a battering ram: Jemson would lead these men to victory, not Devrin.

The island was only a bit larger than it appeared from the sky. As the dragons landed, they discovered it was little more than a large rock sticking up out of the water. It was approximately twice the size of the throne room in Oraeyn's palace; there was plenty of room for the dragons to land, but no hiding places. As the riders dismounted, Kiernan informed them that they were standing on the top of an underwater mountain; Oraeyn wondered how the minstrel could possibly know such a thing. But since he had no better explanation, he accepted Kiernan's words as truth.

The rock's surface was gray, smooth, and domed. The sides of the tiny island sloped gradually down to the sea in all directions. An occasional wave would sweep over its face, making their footing slippery and treacherous. The dragons dug their claws into the rock and everyone else hung onto a dragon to keep from falling. Everyone, except Kiernan Kane. The minstrel paced about the small island, nodding to himself and muttering unintelligibly under his breath. There was no awkwardness about him now. He did not encounter any trouble with his footing or the slippery ground. Oraeyn noticed this and filed it away as information that might be important later. Brant was growing impatient.

"There's nothing *here*, Minstrel," he growled. "Our time is short and such a delay could do irreparable damage to our chances of completing this quest. There is nothing here."

Brant's disappointment at the emptiness of the island was acute, making him snappish. A wild hope had gripped him when Kiernan announced that the wizardesses were below them, and the reality of this barren, desolate rock in the middle of the ocean was now more than he could bear.

"Nothing you can see," Kiernan Kane replied, his tone mild.

"Exactly," Brant retorted, "because there is nothing to see."

"Perhaps."

Brant ground his teeth in frustration as the minstrel continued to mutter and pace; the rest of the company looked on, wondering if Kiernan Kane had lost his senses.

At length the minstrel looked up. "Oraeyn, bring your sword."

"What? Why?"

"I need you to use your sword to cut open this hidden

doorway," the minstrel pointed down at the rock upon which he was standing.

Oraeyn was completely mystified and wondered if the minstrel had finally taken complete leave of his senses. Sighing in exasperation, Kiernan paced out a door-sized rectangle in the middle of the island. Then he turned to Oraeyn.

Slowly, and enunciating his words precisely as if speaking to a child, or a very thick adult, Kiernan said, "Use the point of your sword to etch a doorway for me. Quickly, boy, we haven't much time. The shape I just paced out, that is where the doorway is, I cannot open it without your sword. Only the Fang Blade can unlock this prison."

Still confused, Oraeyn obediently drew the sword from its sheath. The great, golden blade gleamed in the light of the Dragon's Eye that blazed overhead. Though the moment was tense, Oraeyn was captivated yet again in a moment of awe as he held up his sword. He still could not quite believe the blade was truly his to hold, and often fancied that the sword was simply his to care for until its true owner reclaimed it. Oraeyn often wished that the true owner would come soon so he could be rid of its burden.

The entire world paused as Oraeyn held the blade. The other members of the company stared at it. The great dragon-tooth blade glinted with an inner fire. The silver, dragon-scale hilt fit perfectly in his hand. Oraeyn gazed at the sword with trepidation, he was always a bit loath to actually use it. The last time he had wielded the blade had been in the battle with the Dark Warriors. He remembered how the sword made him feel: as if nothing in the world could touch him. But when the battle was over, he had been overwhelmed by the sobering realization that he had perhaps enjoyed using the sword too much. Now, Oraeyn picked his way over to Kiernan. He nearly lost his footing twice, but he made it to the minstrel's side without falling and touched the blade to the surface of the rock.

There was a great screeching sound, like that of rusty metal bars scraping together, and the ground threw off sparks where the Fang Blade touched it. Behind him, Rhimmell hissed. Taking a deep breath and tightening his jaw, Oraeyn gripped the hilt of the sword with hands that were steadier than he felt they ought to be. With quiet resolve he began to slice into the rock with the sword, creating a deep gash in the face of the island.

A cold wind poured from the cut. Oraeyn felt his heart begin to race and his palms grew clammy with apprehension as he continued cutting out the rectangle that Kiernan had paced out. He kept his gaze down, focusing on the task. He looked at the blade and the rock he had yet to reach, ignoring what was happening to the rock he had already disturbed with his sword. Just before he completed the task, Kiernan put a hand on Oraeyn's shoulder.

"Wait," the minstrel said. "I need to pry open the door, but you must keep the Fang Blade firmly inside the rock or I will not be able to do what I need to do."

Without questioning, Oraeyn pressed the blade deeper into the cut and Kiernan reached down to the ground. He grasped the edge of the door Oraeyn had drawn and pulled. The muscles on the minstrel's arms and neck bulged with the strain. He panted with the effort he was expending until at last they heard a hideous groan and the door cracked open at their feet. Beyond the door yawned a deep, rectangular hole that appeared to lead straight down into the heart of this strange, underwater mountain in the middle of the ocean.

They all stared at the gaping doorway. Kamarie wrapped her arms about herself and shivered, huddling closer to Yole's warm, scaly side. Kiernan looked at Brant.

"Help me open this the rest of the way," he gasped.

Without hesitation or questions the warrior sprang to assist the minstrel, pressing his shoulder against the underside of the door. Together they heaved the slab all the way open until it lay flat on the ground next to the opening.

Thorayenak stretched out his neck and peered into the doorway. "What is it? I have never seen anything like it before."

Rhimmell reared away from it. "There is a stench of malice here. No kindness was lost in the creation of this place."

"I have never seen anything like it either," Brant added. He turned to Kiernan. "I owe you an apology."

They all looked at Kiernan Kane. The minstrel gazed into the hole, then he looked up and met their curious stares with a gaze that was neither blank nor empty.

"It is a portal," Kiernan's voice was barely more than a whisper. He paused. "How do I explain it so you can understand? It is like a hole in the fabric that makes up Tellurae Aquaous, but no, I doubt that will make sense to you. Brant, do you understand how the Corridor in Llycaelon works?"

Brant rubbed his chin. "I know a little of what it does, but I have never entered the Corridor myself, and I do not know how it works. I didn't think anyone knows much about the Corridor, it is a tradition nobody questions or attempts to decipher. There are many things like that in my country."

Kiernan nodded. "That is true. Very well, I will try to explain. Perhaps using a concept you are familiar with will help a bit.

"Think of the Corridor like a tunnel. Its entrance is a crack in reality itself. A person steps through that breach and finds himself outside the limits of this world, and yet still within the confines of the Corridor. At the end of the tunnel is another crack, this one leading back inside the limits of Tellurae Aquaous once more. What all that means is unimportant. What is important is that the Corridor has two ends: an entrance and an exit. It was created to serve a distinct and beneficial purpose— though it comes with its own hazards, one can still get lost within the tunnel.

"This portal, on the other hand, is one-sided. Think of it like a closet, but the handle is only on the outside, and there is no exit."

"A prison." There was a slight tremor in Kamarie's voice. "If you place an object or person inside a portal like this it cannot get out unless someone opens the door from the outside?"

Kiernan nodded. "Exactly. But it is not a finite closet, with walls. Anything left inside for too long will slowly slip farther and farther outside the limits of our world until it is irretrievable."

"And you believe Dylanna and Leila are inside this... prison?"

Brant asked, the look on his face said that he believed it too, though he did not want to.

Kiernan stared at Brant with a penetrating gaze. "Truly, I do not know. I sensed the presence of this portal, and I can think of no other reason for one of these to be hidden out here in the middle of the ocean. Nor any other logical reason for Zara and the dragons to have failed in being able to locate our two wizardesses than if they were inside one of these. But even if it is not Dylanna and Leila, somebody is being kept prisoner here, and whoever is keeping them prisoner is cruel and ruthless, of that I can assure you."

Oraeyn stepped back from the portal. The memory of his nightmares clung to him and for an instant he thought he could see Kamarie falling into the portal, her face disappearing from view. His sword hung loosely from his hand, dangling carelessly. Kiernan noticed the pallor of Oraeyn's face and the limpness of his hand and acted quickly. He leapt to the king's side and closed his own fingers over the hand that gripped the Fang Blade. He tightened his own hand over Oraeyn's.

"You must hold the doorway open for me," he commanded.

Oraeyn froze, his hand tightening reflexively around the hilt of his sword; he stared at Kiernan Kane in disbelief. "How?"

"Keep the blade inside the opening until I return. The sword will hold the doorway open. If the portal closes behind me, I will not be able to get back out, do you understand? You must hold it open for me. You can, you *must* do this."

Oraeyn nodded wordlessly and tightened his grip on the sword even more. Kiernan Kane's face brightened and then he took a jaunty step forward. Brant grabbed the minstrel by the shoulder before he could take another step.

"What are you doing?" he asked harshly, a mixture of concern and accusation in his voice.

"I am not leaving you," Kiernan whispered, looking at Brant with a steady gaze. "I am going to enter the portal to see if I can find whoever is being held captive here and bring them out."

The concern on Brant's face grew deeper. "Should I come with you?"

There was a hint of amusement about Kiernan's mouth. "Stay here with them," he nodded at the others. "They will need your strength if I do not return."

Brant stared at the minstrel and the tension on his face and concern in his eyes spoke volumes, then he released his hold on Kiernan's shoulder and stepped back. The minstrel glanced at Oraeyn, who met the minstrel's gaze and lifted his chin in calm resolve. Kiernan's face turned grim, and he stepped into the darkness and disappeared. Suddenly, Oraeyn caught his breath in a gasp and fell to his knees, holding the hilt of the Fang Blade in both hands.

Kamarie reached out to him in concern. "What's wrong?"

"It's trying to close," Oraeyn said, his voice coming through his teeth in a gasp. He said no more, unable to expend the strength for another word.

Brant knelt next to him and pressed both hands against the slab of rock, holding it open. He knew in his heart that no amount of effort on his part could secure the opening if Oraeyn failed, but he still felt he must do something.

Oraeyn's muscles strained as he struggled to keep his sword in the doorway. Kamarie threw a worried glance at Brant and saw her own helplessness reflected in his face. She felt her stomach clench. All they could do was wait.

Devrin plunged into the battle. He fought like a man who no longer cared whether he lived or died. He waded into the enemy on foot with reckless abandon. He had no notion of where he was and gave little thought to his situation. He had no idea what had happened; something inside of him had snapped. He spun and slashed with his blade, carving a path through the seheowks with no thought other than to fight.

Shentallyia watched her ward in concern. With the fall of the king, the Border Patrol had lost their driving force. The contagious fire ignited by the king's intrepid charge faded to embers with his injury. The seheowks were no longer retreating, and the aethalons were incurring heavy losses.

Everything within Shentallyia screamed at her to take action, to dash to her ward's defense, but something else held her back. She could not explain why she hesitated. Devrin got farther and farther away from her, whirling and slashing, cutting a senseless path through the seheowks. It was unbelievable that he was still standing. In spite of his recklessness, his enemies fell back before his battle rage. But Shentallyia could also see that he was tiring, weakening. As he pressed his way through the enemy horde, it was clear that he was not unscathed. He bore many wounds, and the loss of blood was draining his strength. Shentallyia could feel his pain, and it was blinding. She could not understand how he could keep moving; she could not see why he did not succumb.

As she watched, Shentallyia encountered a horrible truth: she was afraid. She felt ashamed. She had been so quick to judge Devrin, so quick to be disappointed in their meeting, swift to believe that he had not seen her as she truly was. But now she realized that she had not seen Devrin as he truly was. She had ignored the courage and the heart and the strength residing within him.

Nothing about her first meeting with Devrin had gone the way that she had planned, and her disappointment eclipsed everything else. In her own mind, she had judged him unworthy to be her ward because he had not welcomed her with open arms. She had shown up and expected him to change his mind about everything he had been taught to believe his entire life. She had heard disbelief in his words, and the wound they had inflicted had kept her from seeing the longing that was also there. She had missed the clues that showed how much he yearned for her story to be true, or how much he truly wanted to be her ward.

She was angry at his reaction, and more than a little anxious that Devrin would shrink from her and shun her if she appeared in her true form.

As she stood at the edge of the battlefield, mulling over these thoughts that troubled her mind, Jemson appeared at her side. He had a white cloth wound around his forehead and he looked unsteady, but he wore his leather armor and his sword was buckled at his side. Shentallyia scrutinized him in concern, taking in the pallor of his face.

"Are you well?" she asked. "Should you be up and walking around so soon after an injury like that? Many have given you up for dead."

Jemson nodded carefully. "I'm all right. What happened?"

The dragoness looked mystified. "You rode into the fray and demanded the attention of these creatures. The battle centered on you as you fought like none I have ever seen. The seheowks fell by the dozens at your feet. And then you shouted the battle cry of your fathers and the Border Patrol rallied to you. The seheowks saw how you inspired your men and became desperate to pull you down. Though you fought them furiously, they overwhelmed you. Your men rescued you and brought you to safety."

"I did all that? I don't remember much of it."

"You fought like a warrior king of old."

Jemson grinned ruefully and shook his head. "Unfortunately I'm simply me, not some unconquerable hero stepped out of a legend... obviously," he touched the bandage on his head and grimaced. "Where's Devrin?"

Shentallyia gestured towards the place where she had last seen Devrin, but he was no longer there. Frantically, she scanned the battlefield until she spotted him. Her breath caught in a gasp. Devrin was cornered on a ledge that jutted out into the gap. His back was against the stone of the cliff wall. There was no retreat. The seheowks surrounded him, just as they had surrounded Jemson. Shentallyia felt frozen as she watched the scene unfold before her. She wanted to change shape and fly to her ward's rescue, but she could not make herself move from where she stood.

Jemson followed her gaze, his eyes catching sight of the captain's peril. In a moment he assessed the situation and understood that the probability of Devrin's survival was slim. He took a hasty step towards the battle without hesitation.

"What are you doing?" Shentallyia shouted at him. "You are in no condition to walk, let alone fight. Don't you see the danger?"

Jemson threw a smile over his shoulder. "The only danger I see, is his."

"He hates you."

Jemson nodded, a quizzical look on his face. "I know. I haven't figured out why... but it doesn't matter. I don't hate him."

His words jerked Shentallyia out of her numbness. She looked at him in amazement, stunned by his courage, his quiet acceptance of the peril he faced, and his determination to run to battle when one of his men was in need. His bravery shamed her. She grabbed his arm, halting his progress.

"No, Jemson, young king of Llycaelon, it is my turn. You recognized me from the moment you saw me, but you never asked for help. You are a different kind of king. You seek to bring help rather than demand it. Well, Sire, my help is yours to command."

Jemson looked at her in grim defiance, his lips pressed together in a determined line. Then he nodded. There was a sudden blinding light in the air around her and Jemson blinked. His eyes were only closed for a fraction of a second, but when he opened them again, Shentallyia was gone.

A gust of wind on his face made Jemson look up at the sky. An enormous, scaled dragon soared across the battlefield, its body glinting like emeralds as lightning flashed between the clouds.

Jemson looked back to where Devrin was fighting and he saw that the battle had become a desperate struggle against overwhelming odds. Devrin had come out of the frenzy that had gripped him and become aware of the dire straits into which he had plunged. Even from where Jemson was standing he could see that Devrin's entire manner had changed. The captain of the Border Patrol was now fighting for his life, struggling to get away from the enemy creatures that swarmed about him and attempted to pull him from the ledge down into their midst. No longer caught up in his battle rage, Devrin's movements bespoke exhaustion and desperation. Jemson gazed skyward once more , searching for Shentallyia, and breathing a sigh of relief as the dragon reappeared.

Shentallyia hurled herself down from behind the clouds, bathing the enemy in waves of flame as she neared the ground. The seheowks checked their advance at the onslaught of this new threat. A few of them cowered at the sight of their greatest and most dreaded enemy bearing down upon them. The aethalons stared up at the great beast with expressions of mingled dismay and hope on their weary faces. Jemson wondered briefly if any of them had ever seen a dragon before, or if any of them but he even knew the name of the creature.

The dragon swooped towards Devrin in a streak of green and silver. The aethalons watched in horror, fearful for their captain's safety, but too stunned to make a move towards him. She clawed her way through the seheowks, crushing them beneath her mighty talons until she had cleared them away from Devrin. She turned, shielding him with her body. Fire poured from her mouth, making the seheowks reel back in terror. The orange flame consumed any who were not fast enough. The dragon fire was not affected by the rain, and the flames Shentallyia breathed did not die but swept through the ranks of the enemy, devouring any that stood too close to those who were already burning. Jemson found himself jabbing his fist into the air as he recognized the crackling flames from earlier in the battle and realized that the sudden burst of fire had been Shentallyia's doing.

Next, the dragon reached out a huge, silver-clawed foreleg and scooped up the nearest seheowk. She tossed the creature in the air and caught it between her sharp golden teeth. The seheowk disappeared down the long, green neck, and the rest of the creatures retreated swiftly, stumbling over each other in their terror.

Then the dragon rose up into the air again with powerful strokes of her silver wings. The aethalons strained to see what had become of their captain, but Devrin was gone. Somebody among the Border Patrol let out a wail that was a mixture of grief, anger, and despair. Someone else caught up the wail and it soared into the sky, only to be cut off by sudden shouts and gasps of disbelief. Devrin was seated astride the dragon, perched securely between the great wings.

"What is it?" one of the men near Jemson cried out in terror. "Yet another kind of monster? It will take the captain back to its lair and then return to finish off the rest of us!"

"No," Jemson replied, his strong, calm voice ringing out over the dismayed wails of the men of the Border Patrol. "It is a dragon, a friend from Aom-igh. See how the seheowks fear her?"

And as the aethalons watched, they saw that what the king said was true: the seheowks were scrambling back to the ocean, dropping their weapons in their haste to get away. The dragon swooped down again; pouring flame into the midst of the enemy. Devrin's broadsword flashed, this time from the back of the dragon. Together, the two of them thoroughly routed the seheowk horde. The aethalons, heartened beyond compare by what they witnessed gave a mighty cry and returned to battle. Slowly, but with steady certainty, the seheowks were driven from Llycaelon back into the sea.

CHAPTER FIFTEEN

The small company stared down into the yawning maw that gaped up at them from the ground. Oraeyn gritted his teeth. Sweat beaded on his forehead. His muscles strained as he gripped the sword, holding the door open.

Kamarie pushed against Yole's great, scaled forearm in nervous desperation, wishing she could help. Brant stood on the edge of the portal his neck craning, searching for any sign of Kiernan's return. Even the dragons were tense as they waited. Rhimmell's tail swished back and forth, beating an anxious rhythm through the air and intermittently slapping into the water. Time moved with interminable stiffness, seconds turned into years that dragged by with agonizing sluggishness.

"I see him!" Brant's exclamation broke through the tension.

They peered into the portal. The form of the minstrel appeared. He was small, as if still a long distance off, but there was a light around him that pushed the gloom away. He moved slowly, struggling against the portal that gripped him, denying his escape with all its strength. As he drew closer, Oraeyn felt a great pressure on his arms. The doorway was trying to close. He fell to his knees, and the sword slipped a few more inches into the mouth of the portal.

"I... can't... hold it anymore," he gasped.

Brant looked at him sharply. "You have to."

"Brant, I... it's too heavy, the portal is pulling the sword away from me! I can't hold it!"

"Be strong, Oraeyn," Brant commanded, "you have to hold the doorway open or our friends will be stuck inside forever."

Oraeyn stared at Brant, his face anguished, his breath coming in great gulping gasps. Brant met his gaze quietly, his expression filled with confidence and calm assurance. Oraeyn gritted his teeth and lowered his head in determination. As the minstrel came closer, the sword was yanked into the portal all the way to the hilt. Oraeyn cried out in pain. Kamarie took a step forward, forgetting her own terror in her concern for her beloved. Yole wrapped a great claw around her, stopping her in her tracks.

"He must do this alone," Yole said. "I do not know much about magic yet, but I do know that you must not interfere with it until it is finished."

"But I can help him."

"No," Yole replied, "you can't."

"Please, Yole."

Yole shook his head solemnly and Kamarie buried her face in her arms to hide her frightened tears. Oraeyn cried out again and Kamarie dropped to the ground in an agony of helplessness.

"The Youngling is correct," Rhimmell added her voice to the discussion. "Oraeyn must hold the door open alone. You would only hinder his efforts."

At last... at last... Kiernan Kane stepped out of the portal. He was holding Leila up, helping her walk. Her arm was draped around his neck; she barely had the strength to put one foot in front of the other. The minstrel's face was worn and haggard. As he emerged through the doorway Oraeyn gasped with relief and the strain lifted from his features. The blade of his sword remained inside the portal, but he no longer struggled as if against an unseen foe.

"Where is Dylanna?" Brant demanded.

Kiernan laid Leila down with exceedingly gentle movements and then stood. His shoulders slumped and his expression was sorrowful.

"Portals are abstruse," he said. "Like the Corridor they have their own set of rules. I assumed this one would be similar... and I have paid the price for my arrogance. You see, the Corridor can only accept one entrant at a time and escape is offered with every decision; however, this portal will take many entrants and escape is never an option. When I stepped inside, I could sense Leila immediately. I assumed Dylanna would be with her. But once I found Leila, the sense that guided me vanished. I had no idea which direction to look. Leila was on the verge of death, and I had no star to direct my course. I was blind to any path but the one I had already taken, for I went willingly into the portal, while the wizardesses did not.

"I believe a certain kind of awareness or sensibility can alter the portal's intent. Though the portal did not want me to find Leila, it could not prevent me. But once I had found her, it could prevent me from all else except escape."

Leila groaned and shuddered violently. Her face was ashen and drawn. Kiernan knelt next to her. He dipped a small handkerchief into the ocean and began wiping her forehead gently with the damp cloth.

"Are you going back inside?" Brant asked after a moment.

Kiernan looked up, defeat and anguish on his face, his chest heaved as he attempted to catch his breath. "Brant... I wouldn't even know where to begin. I could walk right past Dylanna and not even know she was there. I cannot sense her presence inside the portal."

"But I know she is here," Brant pleaded. "I can feel it..."

Kiernan gazed up at the warrior, his blue eyes full of many things he did not say, but his gaze told Brant all he needed to know. He knew what he must do, and it was the only thing he cared to do. Before anyone could stop him, Brant dove into the yawning maw.

Justan paced along the top of the wall surrounding the palace, his gaze turned to the east, out across the sea in the direction King Oraeyn had flown with his companions. He sighed and surveyed the surrounding land. Though it had only been a few days since Oraeyn had left him in charge of Aom-igh, the once-vibrant greens of the forests and rolling hills of grass had sickened, turning yellow and brown. The strange disease spread with eerie speed, and Justan worried that it was a forerunner to the armies of were-folk King Oraeyn had warned him might be coming.

He felt someone approach and then a gentle hand was placed on his shoulder. He put his own hand over Rena's, comforted by his wife's presence. He sighed slightly, remembering how they had met.

It was the night of the great feast to celebrate the new alliance with Llycaelon. Rena was standing against the wall, not really taking part in the celebration. Justan saw her and felt his heart skip a beat. He did not know she was the one who had played the Dragon Pipes and renewed the hearts of the knights, he only knew she was lovely and he wished to learn her name.

He crossed the room and asked her to dance. It was then that he saw the little girl who stood next to her.

"I'm sorry, I cannot leave my daughter. She needs me. Thank you for asking though," Rena said gently.

Justan nodded and then knelt down to speak to the child. "Hello, what is your name?"

"Kaitryn," the little girl replied shyly.

"Well, Kaitryn," he said with a smile. "I think your mother is almost the most beautiful lady here, but she has refused to dance with me."

Rena frowned, her expression flustered and quizzical, not sure whether he had just complimented or insulted her. Kaitryn stared at him, her eyes wide; they pierced through him, her gaze too wise and too sad for her youth. It was as if she had already seen enough of the world and decided she did not like it. Pain for the sorrow she had endured pierced his heart.

"What do you think of that?" he asked.

Kaitryn looked at him contemplatively for a moment. "I don't know."

Justan's expression was full of mischief. "Well, since your mother will not dance with me, I must summon the courage to ask the most beautiful young lady here to dance with me. Kaitryn, would you honor me with this dance?"

Kaitryn's face lit up, and she giggled, understanding the joke. Rena chuckled but then her expression turned concerned and haunted, but Justan grinned at her winningly.

"Don't worry, I'll take care of her," he said.

"Please?" Kaitryn begged her mother.

Rena paused, then relented. He would find out later that Kaitryn had neither smiled nor laughed in weeks, and that hearing her giggle at Justan's small joke was what had warmed Rena's heart towards him.

Justan took Kaitryn's tiny hands in his own and led her out onto the dance floor. She stood on his feet and they danced around the room. He picked her up and spun her around and she giggled, her youthful voice full of the joy of the moment that only a child can truly experience. When the song was over, he brought her back to her mother and Kaitryn grabbed Rena's hand excitedly.

"Did you see me?" she asked animatedly. "I was out there dancing, just like a real lady! Did you see?"

Tears glimmered in her eyes, but did not fall. Rena pulled her daughter into a tender embrace. "Yes, darling, I saw you." She looked up at Justan, gratitude on her face. "She hasn't laughed in so long. How can I thank you?"

"May I see you again?" Justan asked, a little nervously.

Rena hesitated, then she looked down at her daughter who was still chattering away about her dance. The woman's face filled with tenderness. She looked up at Justan, who was waiting apprehensively for her answer.

"Yes."

"Have you spoken with Zara and Arnaud?" Rena asked, seeing the worry he was trying to hide, her voice pulling him out of his memories.

"A bit, they have been busy trying to determine a solution to the problem of the land dying. It has only been a few days since this creeping disease began. Surely it is too soon for them to have an answer."

"Excuse me," one of the servants appeared in a doorway. "Sir Arnaud and Lady Zara are here to see you."

"Or... maybe it's not too soon," Justan chuckled, his tone wry.

Arnaud and Zara were waiting in the Great Hall. Justan was

once again amazed by the fact that both of them looked so much younger now than they had just three years ago, especially Arnaud. Putting aside the crown had taken years from his face, restoring to him a youth he had been forced to forego when he became king.

"What have you discovered?" Justan asked as he and Rena entered the Great Hall.

"We must call on the aid of the myth-folk," Zara replied, her tone serious and weary. "I have tried everything I know, but I cannot touch the sickness that eats away at our land. It began just after Oraeyn left, but I do not know if that was coincidence or cause."

"It will also be beneficial to reach out to our contacts and allies," Arnaud added. "It would go a long way to understanding the problem if we knew whether this has occurred in other lands that have come under attack, or if this phenomenon is isolated to us."

"I have already sent messages out, and am waiting to hear replies," Justan confirmed.

"Whatever else is going on, this is not a natural occurrence," Zara said. "I have not the strength to counter it myself."

"Very well, we should contact King Rhendak immediately," Justan agreed.

"Yes, that is a good place to start." Zara turned to Rena, and her voice grew gentle, "We may need you to play the pipes again."

Rena let out a small sigh. "Very well."

Justan looked at her in concern. "You swore you would never play them again."

Rena nodded. "I know," she whispered.

Justan turned to Zara. "She can't control them," he argued. "You cannot ask her to do this!"

Rena's face was pale, but she laid a reassuring hand on her husband's arm. "I know what I said before. But our land is dying. We cannot see our enemy, but we are being attacked as surely as if an invading army stood on our shores. If it is in my power to help, I will do it. Even if it means letting the instrument control me again. Yes, I am afraid of the pipes, I am terrified of them! But they were given to me. Perhaps it was sheer blind chance that they came to me, or perhaps fate twisted so the pipes would be placed in my hands, but either way, they came to me. It is a responsibility I must bear..." Rena trailed off, remembering that day.

"Kitry! Kitry!" she screamed over and over again. The commotion atop Fortress Hill overwhelmed her. A steady beat like the pounding of a war drum pulsed in her temples. Nothing was more important than finding her small daughter. She darted through the crowd, searching frantically. "Kaitryn!" the word burst from her throat in a scream.

A hand on her shoulder halted her frenzied hunt. Cold metal pressed into the palm of her hand.

"Play!" a voice commanded her.

"My daughter! I cannot find her!" Rena replied, but the crowd of people surged around her and whoever had handed her the small object disappeared from view.

She stared down at the item in her hand. It was a set of shepherd's pipes, small, unassuming. Captivated by the music she knew was contained within, Rena lifted them to her lips. Thoughts of her daughter faded as the first note was released from its captivity within the instrument and floated out into the air.

It hung there, and all of creation paused, frozen in awe at the perfection of that single, pure note.

Then more music poured from the instrument. It started with an old, familiar melody, a song Rena had known since she was a child. But when it ended, another began, this a song that Rena had never heard. It sprang from the pipes, tearing its way out into the air and bursting across Aom-igh. A strange shudder coursed through Rena's body and she felt wild and free and strong all at once, and yet also strangely powerless. In that moment she realized that she was the true instrument, not the Dragon Pipes.

She played on and on until in exhaustion she fell to her knees, barely able to draw another breath. The precious pipes slipped from her nerveless hand, releasing her. As the song ended, the melody cut off abruptly, and Rena collapsed. All that was left within her was a shadow of her former distress concerning the disappearance of her daughter.

"Kitry," she whispered just before losing consciousness.

Rena remembered with a shudder that sensation of being drained of self. She had poured more than breath into the pipes. It terrified her, and she had no wish to experience that again. She winced, but knew there was no way she could withhold her aid if it was needed.

"I will play the pipes again," Rena managed to keep the tremble out of her voice as she spoke, "if they are the only way."

"Hopefully we will not need them," Zara replied, understanding more than she could express.

Rena nodded, hoping her face did not betray the relief she felt. The music still called to her. She could hear it, an ever-present whisper of temptation to get lost once more in that exhilaration of complete power. But she resisted it, ran from it. She believed that if she ever gave into its song, she would be used up completely, becoming little more than a memory of a melody the powerful instrument had once sung.

Inky blackness surrounded Brant, closing in on all of his senses, attempting to drive him mad. His first reaction was to lash out at it, to struggle against it and wrestle it away from him, but he doubted this enemy could be defeated by brute strength. Instead, he forced himself to remain calm. He was blind, deaf, and dumb, and more helpless than he had ever been, but he continued walking, placing one determined foot in front of the other, down into the unknown chasm. Then the images began to come.

One by one they approached, assaulting him with emotion and lies. They dangled in front of him tantalizingly, just out of his reach. Memories rose up to haunt him in the forms of familiar and beloved faces. A few called out to him, beckoning him to follow them, enticing in their promises. Others were frightened or lost or alone and they cried out to him to help them. He turned a deaf ear to their pleas, but still he saw them. He steeled his heart, forcing himself to plunge through the specters, stopping for no one. He tried uttering his oath, but found that his voice had been stolen. He gritted his teeth, telling himself the people were not real. He clung to what Kiernan had implied, summoning an image of Dylanna, filling his mind with the sound of her voice, the fragrance of her hair, the way she pursed her lips when she was angry or annoyed, how she tapped her foot when she was impatient. For a moment, he felt it, the tenuous glimmering of a path before him, and an unshakable knowledge that Dylanna was at the end of it.

The other images faded, becoming more subtle, more surprising. No longer did he hear cries for help or see playful faces beckoning him to follow. Instead, he found himself transported to an eerily familiar place. He stopped, gazing about in shock. A green field lay spread out below him and before him sat a small, but quaint, little cottage. He recognized the shutters he had painted with such painstaking care as a surprise for Imojean. He heard the burbling of the little creek that ran through one of his pastures where his son Schea and his daughter Kali had once played with the happiness that only children can summon. His nose caught the scent of bread baking and lamb stew cooking over the fire. He reached out and touched the little door that he had carved himself. He could feel its smooth wood beneath his hand. He was home.

For the first time that anyone could remember, the seheowks were gone. The men of the Border Patrol looked around in wary triumph and disbelief. A few muttered about the dragon and wondered where their captain had gone, but Jemson walked among them and reassured them that Devrin would return. They looked to him with trust as they turned to the sad task before them of honoring their fallen brothers.

Jemson worked alongside his men as they buried their dead and tended to the wounded. He wondered what had become of Devrin, but did not worry for his safety. He had learned about dragons and their wards from his uncle, and it occurred to him that Devrin might be a ward. Whatever the case, he believed the man would return. Though Jemson was still unsure why the young captain's attitude was so chilly towards him, he understood that Devrin had too much invested in his identity as an aethalon to desert his post. Whatever issues Devrin needed to work out, Jemson could afford him the time he needed. He had earned the love and esteem of his men. Regard from the warriors now surrounding him far outweighed the regard of a single captain. And though Jemson hoped he had earned Devrin's respect as well, he now understood that he did not need it.

Devrin threw his head back, reveling in the feel of the wind on his face. His battle wounds were forgotten and his worries faded as he felt himself lifted up into the sky. Night had fallen above the clouds, and the twinkling stars were brilliant against an obsidian sky.

There was no fear now, no uncertainty about the things Shentallyia had told him about dragons and wards. The confusion was gone, shattered perfectly. They belonged together, dragon and ward. An emptiness within himself that Devrin had not even known existed was filled to overflowing. He realized how lonely he had been, but the loneliness was gone, replaced by the bond tying them together. They could share thoughts without speaking aloud. There were no walls between them, no guards or doubts, simply an understanding of each other, a friendship that had flared to life. It was unexplainable. It was magic.

My dragon, Devrin thought, elated, *and I am her ward.*

He felt a brush of answering fondness from Shentallyia.

Where are we going? he asked.

It doesn't matter, she answered, *I just felt your longing to fly.*

His heart soared. Life had been nothing more than fragments and dust before, without the dragon. Sudden fireworks burst before him and all around them, lighting up the sky. Lightning arched across the heavens and stars fell around them.

What is it? he asked.

Like it? The dragon's voice in his head sounded playful and Devrin could feel Shentallyia's delight at his awe.

It's beautiful.

It's your magic.

My magic? But I don't possess any, Devrin was confused. *Nobody in Llycaelon does. It has been gone from our land for many years, most people have forgotten it even exists.*

Magic never left Llycaelon. And even if it had, you are a dragon ward. Shentallyia's thoughts were filled with mirth. *Magic would re-enter your country through you.*

As if that explains everything, Devrin thought wryly.

Doesn't it?

Devrin was silent for a moment. He did not understand everything, but suddenly it did not matter anymore. He had been born a dragon ward, and while it was hard to accept such a simple explanation, he found that he had to. Maybe that meant magic was part of his heritage as well, he reflected absently.

You are beginning to understand, Shentallyia said, sensing a small part of his thoughts. *You did not become my dragon ward, you were born into that calling. It is your heritage, passed down through the generations without ever taking root, and somehow it has been handed to you to use. Devrin...*

Yes?

Use your gifts wisely.

I will, he said solemnly, his shoulders drooping beneath the weight of responsibility that came along with his newfound identity, *I will.*

A startling thought struck him. This was what it had always been like for the royal family. A crown, a responsibility, handed down through generations. The throne was a heritage, and the man who took his place upon it was no more or less worthy of the chair he sat upon than Devrin was the dragon he now rode. A person couldn't choose his heritage, he could only attempt to be worthy of it. Shame at the way he had acted around King Jemson flooded Devrin's thoughts, and true repentance began to grow. If Shentallyia could hear or feel what he was thinking, she wisely refrained from comment.

The moment Brant stepped into the portal Oraeyn's head

and arms were yanked in after him. The unexpectedness of the warrior's move had left Oraeyn unprepared for the sudden weight of the doorway attempting to close again. His head and shoulders were pulled inside and he nearly lost his grip on the Fang Blade. He began to slip even further into the portal. He let go of the sword with one hand and flailed wildly for something to anchor him to the tiny island, but there was no purchase, nothing for his searching fingers to grip.

Then he felt a strong hand grasp him by the shoulder, and another wrapped around the hilt of the Fang Blade alongside his own. Steadily, he was pulled back until he was firmly on solid ground once more. Only when he was safely kneeling at the portal's edge, with both hands once more wrapped tightly around the Fang Blade's hilt, did Kiernan let him go. Oraeyn gasped for air and felt that he had forgotten what it was like to breathe freely.

"Thank you," he whispered, the horror of what had nearly happened overwhelming him.

Kiernan Kane nodded slightly and looked down into the portal. Oraeyn's hands began to shake, and he clenched them around the sword, trying to hide his unsteadiness.

"Will Brant be all right?"

The minstrel shook his head. "I don't know. If you can hold the portal open, if he can fight his way through all the traps within, he might be able to find his way out again."

"You said it would be more dangerous for him. Why?"

"I have encountered chambers like this before. Brant has not, and therefore he has no idea what to expect or how to counter it. I did, that is how I could enter the doorway safely and be fairly certain that I would return. I was not sure, mind you; there is always the risk of being trapped, but I at least knew what awaited me."

"Is there any chance he will return?" Oraeyn asked.

"I do not know," Kiernan replied, "he is strong, and his strength comes from both his heart and his mind. Perhaps he is strong enough to do what is needed. Perhaps he is even stronger than I."

"Can't you go in after him?" Kamarie demanded, stepping forward and clutching Oraeyn's arm with both of hers.

She glared at Kiernan accusingly as if to say that all of this was the minstrel's fault. Yole attempted to urge Kamarie to come back away from the portal, but she was holding onto Oraeyn's arm protectively and her eyes flashed blue fire daring anyone to try to pull her away. Kiernan gazed at her for a moment and the princess's defiant glower slipped slightly.

"I cannot go in after Brant," Kiernan Kane said. "Unless you want him, Oraeyn, Dylanna, and me all trapped on the other side with no way to get out."

"No, of course I don't want that. But you went in and came back out why can't you go in and find him? You brought Leila out why not Brant and Dylanna too?"

The minstrel put a gentle hand on Kamarie's shoulders. "There are many reasons why I cannot go after Brant. I would lack the same awareness for Brant that I did for Dylanna. Two may enter the portal together, but they will not walk the same path. Brant and I would not even know or recall that we had entered together. I already know I cannot find Dylanna, and I am certain I would not be able to find Brant. Also, do you see how Oraeyn strains to keep the door open?"

"Yes."

"Were I to re-enter, he would be pulled in as well. Brant's sudden rush inside nearly caused Oraeyn to fall in as well. The portal became unstable when I entered it, and I damaged it even worse by leaving and bringing Leila with me. Right now it is incredibly fragile. Even without me re-entering, I do not know if Brant can make it out before it collapses completely.

"But I will offer this: I may not know for certain whether Brant can succeed. For any other man there would be no doubt, and I would have shut the portal immediately upon my escape. My doubt has less to do with Brant, and more to do with how long Dylanna has been trapped inside, if indeed she is inside. I was certain Leila was there, but have no sensation of Dylanna at all. In this matter I choose to trust Brant. He has earned that trust, wouldn't you say? If I have a fear for Brant it is not because of any weakness in him, but rather because of the strength in him which could fuel the trap into which he has plunged. For just as a sword has no power of its own other than the skill which belongs to the person wielding it, so the portal has no more power than what it can gain from the person who enters. In this case, Brant's strength will be the only thing that can help him return to us, but it is also the thing that gives the portal the greatest chance of preventing his escape."

Kamarie's face grew even more worried. "What can we do?"

"All we can do is wait," the minstrel said, his voice gentle.

The waves lapping against the tiny island were the only sound to be heard for a long moment.

"You can trust the Minstrel," Thorayenak rumbled.

Oraeyn looked at him, then nodded. "So we wait."

CHAPTER
SIXTEEN

Brant stared at the door of his home in disbelief. For one moment he allowed the memories to flood over him. They were familiar and achingly welcome; he could slip into them as easily as breathing, these visions of the only time in his life when he had been content to be still.

He could see his wife, beautiful Imojean, standing in the kitchen, hair wrapped around her head in a braid. Long skirts swished around her feet as she moved with gentle grace about the kitchen, turning housework into an art. He ached to hold her in his arms as she welcomed him home once more. The light of his life: she made him content to remain in one place, taking away his need to wander. He could hear her sweet voice, scolding him for trying to steal a bite of whatever she was cooking and then he could see her pretty face turning soft as he leaned over to kiss her on the cheek.

Golden-haired Kali sat on the window seat, brilliant daylight surrounding her and making her appear as if she belonged in the fairy world. And there was Schea, his first-born, clomping around the house with an ear-to-ear grin, bright eyes twinkling with mischief and an intense love of life. His skin was browned and his hands were continually stained and dirty from all the time he spent outside.

A sudden pang throbbed in Brant's heart, an ache he had thought buried deep beyond his consciousness. But here, in this strange world where anything was possible, the pain rose to the surface. Tears he had believed long since passed welled up within him and he found he could not breathe around the lump that had lodged itself in his throat. He reached out a hand, touching the doorknob, longing to open the door and step into the picture he knew was on the other side. Beloved faces awaited him there. He yearned to reach out and touch them, he ached to turn his memory into a reality. He longed to kneel on those wooden floorboards and embrace his children, hold them close to his chest, and protect them forever. He could hear their laughter, smell their sweet breath, and feel their little hands patting his cheeks in search of any whiskers he might have missed while shaving.

For one moment of joy-filled agony, he let himself consider opening the door and slipping back into the life he had lost, and losing himself inside those happy memories forever. With a monumental effort Brant forced himself to lower his hand. With an exertion that left him weakened he turned his back on the door.

He roared into the hollow emptiness that greeted him, his voice tearing its way out of his throat and shattering the silence that tried to hold him captive in a thundering cry that felt like it might never end. He screamed his anger and pain until his throat grew raw and hoarse, and then he slumped to his knees in a kind of exhaustion that can only be brought on by despair.

"It's not real," he rasped through a broken sob. "It would never be real. I would gladly remain here, lost in this dream, but it would be a lie. My wife and children are dead, and you will not trap me here with their faces. You will not defile their memories in this way. They have been laid to rest, alongside so many others I have loved and lost, and you cannot keep me here with deceptions about them being alive again. I would rather remember them as they were and move on than disrespect all they meant to me by taking part in a charade that does not let them rest."

No sooner had he spoken, his sobbing voice echoing into the nothingness that surrounded him, than the little cottage disappeared. Though he knew it was not real, Brant was not prepared for the grief that swept over him at its leaving. He swallowed, forcing the tears back down into their place deep in his heart. He raised his hand in a gesture of farewell and continued on towards his goal.

Moments passed, or hours, or weeks—Brant had no concept of time in this place—when the air around him began to glow. He hesitated, on guard against whatever new threat might rise up to distract him from his quest. But nothing happened. The light merely grew brighter, making the darkness flee from him, hiding itself in corners and deep holes. And then he saw her.

Dylanna's face floated before him and he dove towards her, forgetting all caution. She flitted from his grasp and he followed her image. The light about him grew brighter the farther he walked, but he could not get any closer to Dylanna. Her face taunted him, always before him but never in reach. Brant's efforts became frantic as he raced after her, never noticing how he was being guided and shepherded deeper and deeper into the depths of the prison.

Panting and gasping for air, Brant was forced to halt and rest. Dylanna disappeared from sight and the thought occurred to him that she might have been yet another trick.

"Truth," he gasped, weakly, knowing it was useless, knowing there would be no help from his oath in this place.

To his surprise, the word escaped from his lips and reverberated around him powerfully, bouncing into the depths of the cavernous portal. He stood still, waiting. Then, there she was. Dylanna. This time Brant knew it was no trick. The wizardess was suspended in midair before him, bound in a net that prevented her from moving or having any awareness of her surroundings. Brant could see the net clearly, and he understood how to unravel it. Dylanna's face was pale. She looked weary to the point of death. The resignation in her expression frightened him; he could tell she was near the end of her struggle.

Brant stepped forward and touched the net. Carefully, ever

so carefully, he began to untie the threads that bound it together. He worked slowly. It was deliberate, difficult work, but he knew one slip could cost him everything, so he did not hurry. After what seemed like hours of painstaking work, the net fell away and Dylanna was free. Brant slipped his arms around her and eased her to the ground gently. He knelt beside her, his arms wrapped around her.

"Dylanna," he whispered. "Dylanna, wake up."

The wizardess stirred and blinked up at him. She squinted through the brilliant light, peering at Brant's face. Then she recoiled, shaking and moaning. She raised her arms defensively, pushing at him with feeble gestures and shaking her head in denial.

Brant looked down at her in confusion. "Dylanna," he whispered again, "it's me. Come on, wake up, I'm going to take you out of here."

Dylanna moaned but did not respond. Grimly, Brant gathered the wizardess up in his arms. Setting his face in determination, Brant turned back the way that he had come and began to make his way out of the portal.

He journeyed a long time. Dylanna slipped in and out of sleep as he carried her. The light he had encountered at the end of his search did not leave, it shone around him and guided him. Though he was watchful, Brant encountered no more tricks or illusions. With Dylanna in his arms, the portal no longer held any power over him.

At long last, he stepped through the doorway and into the true light of day once more. The position of the Dragon's Eye told him that less than an hour had passed outside of the portal, though it had felt like an eternity within the terrible confines of the prison. His companions rushed towards him, concern and relief written on their faces. He could hear Kiernan Kane telling Oraeyn that he could let the doorway close now. Kamarie said something about Dylanna, and Oraeyn, although he looked exhausted, was asking about whether or not Brant was all right. He was vaguely aware of all of them, but he felt that he was watching them from a great distance.

"Is he all right?"

"Take Dylanna, he's about to fall over."

"Careful."

"Brant? Brant are you all right?"

"What happened in there?"

"Help him lie down, he needs to rest."

"What happened in there? Will he recover?"

The worried voices mixed together, a barrage of repetitive questions and concern. Brant wanted to nod or speak or find a way to tell them that he would be fine. He wanted to tell them to look after Dylanna, but he could not make his voice work. He staggered forward, still holding the unconscious wizardess in his arms. He felt her being taken from him and for a moment he struggled against it, but then he numbly realized that whoever was relieving him of his burden was a friend, and he should let them help. He let her go and felt at peace. He stumbled a step more and then felt himself falling. Strong arms encircled him, helping him lie down. He wanted to thank whoever it was, but he did not have the energy.

I'll thank them after I sleep for a little while… but I'll rest now, just for a little while, he thought. Then he fell out of consciousness.

When they returned to the camp, Devrin and Shentallyia found everything quiet and in order. Sentries were posted, but there was no movement around the various cook fires and the horses were picketed and grazing quietly. The battlefield was silent and bare.

Devrin looked around, his brow furrowed. "Where is everyone? More importantly, how long have we been gone?" While in flight, Devrin had lost all sense of time and did not realize that a full day had passed since the battle ended. His stomach rumbled, and he became aware of a dryness in his throat reminding him that it had been a while since his last meal. He retrieved a canteen and drank the water inside it thirstily.

Shentallyia shrugged. "We have been gone for a single turning of the day, though it may feel as if it has been only moments to you. I have heard that is often the way of the first flight and mindshare between a dragon and its ward. The revelations and exhilaration cannot be contained, and thus, not measured in mortal time. It is a one-time experience that cannot be captured again... it cannot be captured at all, it merely runs its course." Shentallyia tilted her head to one side. "Do you hear that?"

Devrin listened for a moment but heard only silence. He opened his mouth to say as much when he heard the noise Shentallyia's ears had already picked up. It was coming from a valley between the camp and the Iron Wood.

"Come on," he said.

He strode away towards the forest. When he reached the top of the rise overlooking the valley he stopped short. The men of the Border Patrol were assembled below by rank. As soon as he appeared, someone pointed and let out a cheer that resounded its way around the valley and was echoed back by the rest of the aethalons. Shentallyia stepped up to Devrin's side, and another cheer shook the valley floor as the aethalons recognized her. Embarrassed, Shentallyia took on her human form once more.

"What is going on?" Devrin wondered out loud.

Before Shentallyia could make any sort of answer, a younger aethalon appeared at his side.

"Captain," the young man said, saluting smartly, "follow me, if you please."

Devrin hesitated for a brief moment before both he and Shentallyia followed their guide. As Devrin passed, each aethalon saluted him. Whispers of "dragon" and "hero" susurrated through the air as they walked. Devrin felt a lump of emotion welling in his throat as he passed through the ranks of these brave and noble men. He had been their captain for so short a time and already he felt a strong camaraderie with so many of them.

He reached the end of the rows of aethalons and found himself standing before Jemson. Devrin blinked and had to look twice before he recognized the young king. Jemson was standing up on a mounting step, dressed in formal armor. He wore a scarlet cape with the crest of Arne embroidered upon it. A golden crown adorned his head. His face was stern, the wisdom written upon it belying his youth. Two aethalons holding flags flanked the king on either side. One depicted the crest of Llycaelon, and the other depicted the crest of the Border Patrol. In his hand Jemson held his great sword, the sword which had passed to all the kings of Llycaelon. Some had used it wisely, some ruthlessly, some with pride, and some with humility, but all had held it. It was the legacy of the kingship as surely as the crown itself. Jemson held it with familiarity and ease.

Devrin looked up at the young king and felt an overwhelming flood of shame wash over him. Then Jemson raised an arm, his hand balling into a fist. Devrin shifted slightly, ready to either block a blow, or receive it as he now knew he deserved. He looked at the king askance. Then Jemson saluted, fist over heart and bowed deeply at the waist. Devrin's felt his stomach lurch in surprise and he could hear the gasps of the aethalons behind him. That particular salute was reserved for the king of Llycaelon only, and the king himself saluted no one.

"Devrin of House Merle?" King Jemson's voice filled the valley as he straightened, but he did not appear to be speaking any louder than normal.

"Yes, Sire," Devrin managed to choke out the appropriate answer.

"You are a true leader of the Border Patrol. You have demonstrated great courage, creative and flexible strategy in the course of battle, and loyalty to your oath in spite of your misgivings about your king."

The aethalons burst into a deafening roar of applause and cheering. But Devrin winced. He knew he deserved that last statement, but it hurt in a way he had not expected. He hung his head. Jemson raised a hand and the Border Patrol fell silent once more.

"Our borders are safe, largely due to this man. Devrin of House Merle, I charge you with command of the King's Helm."

Devrin blinked. "What?"

Jemson continued: "The King's Helm was once reserved for

the most elite aethalon warriors in our country, and in my view, in all of Tellurae Aquaous. It wore a stain of dishonor upon its name in the last days of my father's rule, but those days of sorrow are behind us." He looked at Devrin and said softly, "I hope?"

Devrin nodded, overwhelmed.

Jemson raised his voice once more. "And so, I trust you to restore the Helm to its former stature. If any man can do this, it is you.

"With this honor and corresponding responsibility, I am giving you another task as well."

"What is that?" Devrin asked warily, unsure how many more surprises he could take this day.

Jemson beckoned for Shentallyia to step up to the platform. The girl-dragon glided forward to stand next to Devrin. A hush fell over the aethalons as they noticed her. They stared in awe, remembering who and what she was. Shentallyia shifted in obvious discomfort, and Devrin could feel her shy embarrassment at being the focus of so much attention.

"Shentallyia, Dragon of Aom-igh," Jemson began, "we are in your debt. Is it your intention to remain with your ward?"

Shentallyia nodded firmly. "I could not leave him, the dragon ward bond is for life."

"I thought as much. Your presence is very welcome in Llycaelon."

The aethalons raised another cheer, and Shentallyia blushed furiously. She looked down and mumbled incoherently.

"It is my wish, and that of my uncle, that Llycaelon remember its heritage once more," Jemson said. "We have remembered much, but we have also forgotten what ought not have been lost. We have banished the myth-folk, and by doing so we brought the seheowks down on our own heads. I welcome the myth-folk back to Llycaelon. Not as they are now, disguised as humans, no, but as they are in Aom-igh, out in the open, living side-by-side with us."

Shentallyia looked at Jemson in disbelief. "Is it possible to change hundreds of years of distrust in a single day?"

Jemson shook his head in solemn gravity. "Certainly not. I make no such presumption. However, it only takes one step to begin a journey, and I would like to initiate that step with you today. Shentallyia of both Aom-igh and Llycaelon, you are the first. It is my hope that many more will follow and that we can be of service to your people as you have been to mine. I have seen dragons return to Aom-igh, I believe, with time, it can happen here as well."

The aethalons cheered again and Jemson raised a hand. "Shentallyia of Aom-igh, Devrin of House Merle, will you rebuild the King's Helm? Will you work to restore trust and friendship between our peoples?"

Devrin felt dizzy and his face flushed with shame. "Sire... I..."

Jemson raised his chin slightly and Devrin found a well of courage within himself he had only hoped he possessed.

"A few days ago, Sire, you said that you believed you were not *my* king. You were right." A hush fell across the ranks of aethalons at his words. Face flaming, heart racing, Devrin pressed on, "You see, my brother followed King Seamas to Aom-igh. He fought in the invasion at your father's command. He died dishonorably and stained our family's name. I blamed you and your father for Kelan's fate. Worse than that, I disrespected you because of your youth and inexperience." Devrin took a deep gulp of air and rushed on, "But then I met you. And I saw that you were a king willing to fight and die with his men. A king not only full of courage, but also full of daring and pride and strength. Here today, I see more. You bear authority and power, but also humility and gratitude. Your Majesty, you have broken down every belief I had about royalty. You are not what I expected you to be, and at first I hated you for it. I resented you for your lineage and the authority I did not think you had earned, but I did not understand the corresponding responsibility and agony that walks alongside that heritage. Now I do. I am truly sorry for my behavior. You have extended a patience and a mercy towards me that I do not deserve, but that I will try to be worthy of." Devrin paused and glanced out at his men. Then he knelt before King Jemson.

"If you still wish for my service," he said in a loud voice, "I will serve no other. I can follow no other. I will do my best to merit the honor you have placed upon me, not from duty, not from virtue, not from need. I pledge my sword to you in humble gratitude to the king I always longed for, but was too blind to see at first. If you will forgive me, I will be your loyal servant... forever."

Jemson reached down and lifted Devrin to his feet. The warmth of forgiveness washed over Devrin as his king stared down at him. There was no reproach in that gaze, only acceptance. Then Jemson turned to his countrymen and said, "Then let the celebration begin." He pulled Devrin and Shentallyia before him and stepped back, leaving them in front of the entire Border Patrol. The aethalons there saluted and then unleashed thunderous applause.

Devrin gazed about at the sight in astonishment and pleasure. He turned to Shentallyia and offered his arm. She took it and together they joined the rest of the Border Patrol at their feast. It was by far the most satisfying meal Devrin had ever eaten. A few of the warriors had instruments, which they began to play once the meal had ended. There was jesting and merriment long into the night as the warriors celebrated their victory as hard as they had fought for it.

But deep below the celebration, a sinister presence watched. He had touched all the other lands, and Llycaelon was soon to come. He had not forgotten Llycaelon as so many had. He did not care that the seheowks had been defeated, they were the least of his creatures. He did not even care that the myth-folk were being welcomed back, although it did make his goal harder to achieve. His lips stretched into a stiff, sickly smile, Llycaelon would serve his purpose in the end. Let them celebrate their little victory now, he thought, it would merely serve to make their fear that much greater in the future. He licked his lips, he could almost taste the sweetness of their fear, but he could wait, he would feed soon enough. Llycaelon and Aom-igh had stood together for a time. Now they would fall together.

With the merest thought the great werehawk lifted off the ground, carrying its rider up into the clouds on sharp, argent wings.

Dylanna opened her eyes experimentally. The light did not hurt as much as it had before. She had gotten somewhat used to its brilliance again, and after the darkness of her prison, she welcomed the light, no matter how painful. She felt that perhaps at one time she had lived always in the light, and that her time in that hateful cage had only been a few moments in comparison, but it was hard to believe. The caliginous prison was still so prominent in her memory.

Dylanna took a deep breath and sat up to survey her surroundings. She was in an unfamiliar place, but she was comfortable and warm. She curled her fingers up and then stretched them out again, delighted to have movement back.

She was in a large room that was richly decorated, and resting on a bed covered with fluffy blankets, which had been pulled up to her chin. She snuggled her face down into them, inhaling their warmth and noting the faint scent of lavender that clung to them. The room was full of bright colors: crimson and gold was the theme, though muted blues accented here and there. Memories began to return to her, memories of the time before her imprisonment, but they were fragmented and broken.

At length she noticed Brant sitting in a chair next to her bed and more of her memories came back in a rush, her mind putting the broken images of her life back together. He was slumped over with his head resting on the edge of her bed. His hair was tousled and his clothes rumpled. She stared at him for a long moment, not quite sure if she should believe that he was really there. But the light streaming in through her window was too real not to be believed.

"Brant?" she whispered.

At her quiet voice his head jerked up, and he stared at her, relief and concern chasing each other across his face. "You're awake," he breathed, hope and disbelief mixed together in his whisper.

"You rescued me," Dylanna whispered.

She had the strangest idea that if she tried to speak above a whisper everything around her would disappear again. The visions from the portal rose up in her mind. She shook her head, trying to clear it. This was real, she was certain of it, but a tiny whisper of doubt hissed in a corner of her thoughts.

Brant, having seen just a fraction of what the portal was capable of, understood her struggle. He leaned forward and kissed her. Dylanna felt a jolt of surprise and she stared at Brant as he moved away again. He looked a little startled himself, and his face, usually so impassive, flushed red.

"I'm sorry," he said hoarsely, somewhat brokenly. "I just… I'm not sure why I did that… I…" he searched for the words, but they would not come.

"You are no dream," Dylanna said in a wondering tone. A teasing note entered her voice. "In my dreams, you did not stammer or apologize for kissing me."

"I… erm… no," Brant shook his head. "This is not another one of the portal's tricks. I am real, and so is all this."

Dylanna reached out to touch his hand, to assure herself that this was, in fact, no dream. As she did so, Oraeyn and Kamarie entered the room. Dylanna pulled her fingers back, embarrassed. She smiled warmly at her niece and the man who would soon be her nephew as they bounded to the side of her bed, relieved to see her awake. Kamarie sat down on the edge of the bed and wrapped her arms around Dylanna.

"We despaired of ever seeing you again," she said. "Kiernan was able to rescue Leila, but then he couldn't find you. Brant jumped into the portal…"

Dylanna looked confused and interrupted Kamarie's broken retelling of events, "Kiernan Kane? Portal? What are you talking about?"

"I'm sorry, I'm going too fast. All will be explained later tonight. Get some more rest now."

Dylanna crossed her arms and glowered. "Excuse…"

"Come on Brant," Kamarie urged. "Kiernan said if she woke it would mean the worst is over. Come away, let her rest."

"But…" Dylanna tried to argue, but felt her initial burst of strength and energy fading.

Brant nodded. His hand found Dylanna's, and he squeezed it wordlessly. Behind the relief apparent on his face, there was a haunted worry. Dylanna noticed that all three of them looked disheveled and haggard. She wanted to ask so many questions, but found she only had strength for one.

"Where are we?"

"I'm sorry, we should have told you that," Oraeyn answered. "We're in Llycaelon, in King Jemson's palace."

Dylanna allowed herself to sink into the pillows, wondering. How had they gotten here? How had they found her? Where had she been? Was Leila all right? Why were they in Llycaelon of all places?

"Come on Brant," Kamarie said again. "You could use some rest yourself, we all could. We will see you at dinner tonight," she said to Dylanna.

Dylanna nodded and the three friends left her room. When they were gone, Dylanna wiggled her toes and chuckled to herself. A sensation of freedom flooded through her and she breathed a deep sigh, letting it wash over her, lulling her to sleep. But this sleep was different from before, and it did not frighten her. This was a deep and peaceful rest; the ghosts and dreams that haunted her in the prison did not exist here.

She did not know how long she slept, but when she awoke again, Dylanna felt much stronger. The sleep had renewed her and restored her clarity of thought. She wondered how Leila was and whether or not she was nearby.

After a moment, she sat up and saw that she had slept straight through the afternoon. The horizon was awash with brilliant splashes of orange and purple. A pang gnawed in her stomach, and Dylanna hoped dinner would be soon. At the thought of dinner, her mind skipped to the idea of sitting next to Brant and she felt a little dizzy. She put a hand to her head and firmly told herself to stop acting silly.

Dylanna stood up, finding her legs to be stronger than she would have expected. She walked across the room and opened the large wardrobe that stood there. When she looked inside, she found that several choices of magnificent garments had been provided for her. After a moment of indecision, she chose a pale blue dress worked with gold embroidery and laid it out on the bed.

A maid entered, humming. "Oh!" she said, upon finding Dylanna up and about. "Would milady like me to prepare a bath?"

Dylanna smiled. "I can think of nothing more delightful."

Luxuriating in the hot, cleansing water restored her spirit. However, her stomach protested that she had not eaten in far too many days, so she did not linger in the water as long as she would have liked. She emerged and slipped into the gown she had chosen. The dress was a little too long, but it fit well other than that. The sleeves were little more than strips of fabric over her shoulders though sheer fabric hung down from them and wrapped in tiny bracelets around her wrists. It was not a style she had ever seen in Aom-igh, and at first it made her feel uncomfortable, but the evening air was hot and thick, and having her arms bare was pleasant. She resolved not to let the strange style of Llycaelon bother her and turned to the mirror where she began working on her hair.

It was a woeful mess of knots, and at first she despaired of ever working them out, but she eventually had it tamed. She pinned it up on top of her head, allowing a few tendrils to escape and frame her face. Then she gazed at herself in the mirror with a critical eye. Her cheeks were sunken and her face was too pale, but on the whole she felt that she had come through her ordeal better than she had any right to.

Kamarie entered the room. She was wearing a dress similar to Dylanna's in style, but it was a light shade of lavender with no embroidery, just a little fancy stitching at the neckline, and it fit the princess perfectly. Her hair was down, flowing around her shoulders in a cascade of silk, looking both casual and elegant at the same time. Dylanna was amazed to notice how grown up her niece appeared. It was hard for her to remember that Kamarie was no longer the wild little girl with rips in her dresses from climbing trees and mud on her knees from playing out in the fields with the squires.

"You look lovely," Dylanna said.

"Thank you. And you look quite well yourself. There isn't anybody that you're trying to impress is there, Aunt Dylanna?" Kamarie's eyes twinkled with a teasing light, and a smile danced about her mouth.

Dylanna tried to hide the blush that rose up in her cheeks, Kamarie was just as impish as ever, she reflected. But then, that was what made her Kamarie.

"If you had been trapped for days on end with no hope of escape, you'd feel like dressing up a little when you got out too," she said loftily, but there was no sharpness in her tone.

Kamarie just nodded knowingly. "Well, I came in to tell you that dinner is ready."

Dylanna looked in the mirror one last time. "And I am ready for dinner."

Together, the two women made their way to the small dining room. Brant, Oraeyn, and the dragons were already there when they arrived. The dragons had taken human form for convenience's sake—so they could fit at the table—and also so as not to burden their hosts overmuch with filling dragon-sized stomachs. A few seconds later, Leila appeared with Kiernan Kane. Compared to Dylanna, Leila still looked quite shaken. Her cheeks were hollow and sunken and a haunted look resided deep in her violet eyes. She clung to Kiernan's arm and took slow, faltering steps. She brightened a bit when she saw the others, however.

Hugs and greetings were exchanged as the group entered the dining room. Yole greeted everyone with his usual enthusiasm. Thorayenak and Rhimmell hung back at first, but Dylanna put them at ease by offering them hugs as well and thanking them for their part in her rescue. Leila relaxed noticeably, but she still hovered near Kiernan. Kamarie thought this strange since Leila had never quite seemed to care for the minstrel anywhere near as much as the minstrel claimed to care for Leila. She looked over at Dylanna and saw that her aunt had noticed Leila's strange behavior as well. They shared a worried look, but there was no time for more than that because dinner was being served and its arrival made all other thoughts fly away. The room filled with the delicious aroma of warm food, and all conversation halted.

A tall, regal woman entered the room. Her hair was white as sea foam and her face was heavily lined, but her back was straight and she was dressed in an elegant gown of deep maroon. Brant crossed to greet her, and the two embraced, then he led her into the room on his arm.

"Please let me introduce my mother, Queen Fiora," Brant said, his voice filled with more warmth than any of them could ever remember hearing before.

The old queen gazed around at the party, her expression soft. "It does my heart good to meet these friends my son has spoken of so often and with such fondness. You are the family that took him in when his own had turned its back on him, and for that I thank you. I am sorry my grandson could not be here this evening, but he had urgent business at Caethyr Gap with the Border Patrol. In his stead, please, allow me to welcome you to our home. I hope your stay is comfortable. If you need anything, just ask one of the palace staff."

Brant led her to the head of the table and helped her sit. Then he turned to the others.

"I am happy to have you here, in the home of my youth. I know we all have questions, but I'm sure everyone is hungry, so let's eat."

The others voiced their agreement and together they sat down. Servants glided around the table, filling their plates with food. Several of the dishes were unfamiliar, but all of it was delicious. Dylanna and Leila devoured their food with a hunger borne of days without a meal. The rest of the company ate heartily as well although not with quite as much zeal.

When dinner was complete and everyone's hunger had been satisfied, Brant suggested they move to the adjoining room to relate their stories, answer questions, and determine their next course of action. Queen Fiora bade them good night and retired to her chambers. Brant kissed her on the cheek before she left and she pulled him close for another hug.

"Your wizardess is lovely," she whispered.

Brant looked startled and the old queen's lips twitched with a hint of amusement.

"Jemson has told me all about her," she said. "I want you to know, Son, that I approve."

Brant cleared his throat. "I see. Thank you," his eyes crinkled at the corners. "Good night, Mother. I love you."

"I love you, too, my son. Good night. Don't forget to say goodbye before you leave."

"Never."

The company retired to a charming, comfortable study that was furnished to encourage relaxation and conversation. Oraeyn sank down into a couch with a grateful sigh, though he felt a pang of homesickness for the Cottage Room back in Ardura Palace. For a long, awkward moment, nobody knew quite what to say. The silence grew decidedly uncomfortable, so Kamarie spoke up.

"Well, let's start at the beginning then," she said, "when we discovered that Dylanna and Leila were in trouble."

She related to the two wizardesses everything that had occurred in the past two weeks. She spoke at length, and nobody interrupted, content to let her tell the story.

"Brant staggered out of the portal carrying Dylanna, and then collapsed," Kamarie said as she concluded. "With Dylanna, Leila, and Brant all unconscious, we knew we had to go somewhere we could rest. Oraeyn suggested Llycaelon, so here we are."

"So," Brant said, when Kamarie was done speaking, "what of your side of the story?" He looked first at Dylanna and then Leila. "How did you end up in that portal out in the middle of the ocean?"

CHAPTER
SEVENTEEN

Myth-folk gathered atop Fortress Hill in a carefully organized pattern of circular power. Those with the greatest strength were furthest from the center, while those with lesser, but perhaps finer, strength were near the core where they could control their attempts with a deftness and a delicacy the strongest could never hope to equal.

King Rhendak, in dragon form, hung in the air overseeing the entire effort. Justan watched with mounting curiosity, wondering what the endeavor would look like, wondering if he would even be able to see was happening. Zara and Rena stood together on either side of the stone from which it was said Artair had retrieved the legendary sword once upon a time. Rena held the dragon pipes in shaky hands, a look of quiet resolve on her pretty face.

Rhendak had agreed at once with Zara's assessment of the situation and he insisted they should do everything in their power to counter the disease that crept across their land and drive it back. He had summoned the most powerful creatures under his rule to Fortress Hill where the greatest magic in Aom-igh still slept. Now, with everyone assembled, Justan realized that he was useless to this great gathering. He possessed no special abilities and had little to contribute to this particular fight. The time might come when his sword was needed, but here, all he could do was watch. He felt both excited and helpless as he stood at the outskirts of the circle.

"Take care of Kitry," Rena said to him, just before she went to join Zara at the center of the assembly, "in case..." her throat closed on the words. "Just in case."

Justan's throat was dry. He wanted to ask what could happen and what she was afraid of, but he could not. He simply nodded, his heart full of fear for her; she kissed him and turned away. He watched her walk among those gathered, her head high, her step never faltering. Nothing of her outward appearance betrayed any of her hesitation.

Now the dragon king looked at her. "Rena, Song Bearer, will you begin?"

Rena's outward expression was calm, though her heart hammered out a steady beat of nervousness within her chest as she lifted the pipes to her lips and began to play.

The music welled up into the air. The song spun around the circle of myth-folk and then spiraled up into the sky. At first, everything about this experience was different from the previous time; this song was more controlled, more directed.

Rena could feel the power of the myth-folk as they directed the song where they wanted it to go. She could feel their hands as they sent the magic into the ground in an attempt to heal the land, and as they formed the shield they would place over all of Aom-igh when they were done. Like skillful weavers they caught the notes as they left the pipes and wove them into an intricate and predetermined design. For an instant, Rena allowed herself to relax and believe that all would be well.

But then the music welled inside her and she knew the pipes were taking control of her once more. She struggled to contain the melody, but it could not be restrained. Despite her best efforts it burst forth, all of its wildness and power overwhelming her and racing through her and into the song. She could hear gasps as the dragons and gryphons surrounding her were overwhelmed by raw power that surpassed all other experiences. She could see the troubled look on Zara's face, but it seemed a trivial matter. Rena was being carried away on the wings of that sweet refrain, and she was already out of the reach of those who surrounded her. Now she was being used; she had the strange sensation again that she was the true instrument, not the pipes. But this time she did not reject the power that rushed through her; instead she welcomed it, embracing it with her entire being.

Rena had known before she began that she might lose control. She knew that if the rings of myth-folk failed there was no way for her to protect herself from burning up like a candle inside a dragon's flame. She had told Rhendak not to let his people stop weaving the shield if such a thing happened. Rena would not give any less than Wessel had given. Her heart ached at the thought of leaving Kaitryn and Justan, but they had each other, and they were strong. They would face the world together, and they would hold each other up and comfort one another in the midst of whatever storms might come.

From outside the circle Justan watched in horrified fascination. He did not know what was happening, but it frightened him. Rena shone like dragon fire. She overflowed with life and its brilliance flooded out of her. She was ethereal; light spilled from her body and she lifted off the ground, caught up in the breath of the song. She held the pipes to her lips and the beautiful, bewitching music poured out of her like lifeblood.

A cool breeze rustled through the assembly. It was sweet and fresh and bore the tang of morning rain and fresh flowers. The scent of fruit wafted through the air. The grass covering Fortress Hill rippled and turned a vibrant green, a green that spread down the hill and across the land in every direction, pushing back the terrible rot and wilt.

Rena felt herself floating up into the sky. She watched as the land was healed and felt content. Then she felt a new burst of power as the shield was raised in a massive dome high above them. It glistened with her life force, and she knew it would keep the enemies at bay for a time. Not forever, but she hoped it would last at least until King Oraeyn could find Yorien's Hand. Most importantly, it would keep her Kitry safe.

Rena continued to play long after she should have stopped,

testing the shield, searching for weaknesses. When she found none, she felt relieved. Then she saw Justan, he was standing on the very edge of the assembly. She reached down and brushed his face gently. Then she ended her song.

Justan felt a tiny breeze brush against his cheek, and he raised a hand to his face, hoping to hold the sensation in place. He stared up at the empty sky. Somehow he knew she was saying goodbye. He reached out to stop her, to beg her to stay, and then the song ended. The pipes clattered to the ground as they fell from Rena's lifeless hand. Zara caught her before she collapsed and laid her gently on the now-green carpet that covered the top of Fortress Hill.

"How did you end up in that portal out in the middle of the ocean?"

For a few moments there was no response to Brant's question. Oraeyn began to think that perhaps the wizardesses would refuse to answer the question all together.

Surprisingly, Dylanna spoke first. She told her story in broad strokes, without emotion, recounting the days she had spent inside the portal and how she had struggled against losing herself. As she concluded her story, she drew her brows together in confusion.

"I do not remember how I got into the portal, though," she said.

"It was my idea that caused our imprisonment," Leila said, her voice soft. "I was reading some of my father's writings and came across several references to an obscure piece of lore that could allow two people to talk across great distances as if they were standing right next to one another. Of course, such a feat would require a lot of power and effort, especially on the first attempt. I meant no harm," she whispered. "Magical beings of considerable strength can do this already, but I thought it would be beneficial if, for example, Brant were here in Aom-igh and needed to speak with his nephew in Llycaelon. I simply thought it would be a useful ability, especially with the new alliance. It could save a great deal of time and effort, and we could free up the dragons from their generous offer of transportation."

"I don't mind," Yole interrupted.

"No," Leila shook her head, "but you might not always have the time to fly across the ocean. Your people have their own duties and affairs to worry about. In any case, I believed the matter was worth looking into. I contacted Dylanna and asked for her assistance. From the journals, I had a fairly good idea about how it could be accomplished. Dylanna was more hesitant than I, not wanting to stir up anything too grand, but she came anyway. I wanted to test my understanding in the Harshlands, a place full of wild magic similar to my own. I understand it and can make use of it, which is why I make my home there. I thought it would aid me in my attempt to rediscover this lost art."

Leila's shoulders slumped for a moment. Then she looked up at each of her friends in turn. Her expression pleaded with them to understand and not judge her for what she had done.

"Leila," Dylanna spoke up. "What happened was not your fault. It had nothing to do with the Harshlands. The experiment should have worked. There was something more powerful than us in play, something you could not have planned for or even expected to find."

Leila managed a watery smile of gratitude. "Dylanna arrived and we set up the experiment. I had my father's journals ready, though I had memorized every word. Since I was most familiar with what we would be doing, Dylanna agreed to provide the power and let me handle the delicate details. We had just begun when," Leila paused and took a shaky breath, "I felt something go wrong. It was like someone else was grabbing hold of my power and twisting it out of my control. I tried to pull it back, but I wasn't strong enough." Leila faltered and Kiernan put an arm around her shoulders.

The others waited, giving the wizardess time to compose herself.

Leila took several slow, deep breaths. "Everything grew very cold. I could feel myself growing numb. I tried to shut down the experiment, but I no longer had control of it. I tried to cut myself off from Dylanna, but I found myself powerless. The numbness spread until I lost consciousness. When I awoke..." Leila's voice broke, but she visibly pulled herself together and continued, "When I awoke, I was in the prison where Kiernan found me. But... it was different for me than it was for Dylanna." She paused, her face twisted in anguish.

Kiernan laid a gentle hand on the wizardess's shoulder, "It's all right," he whispered, "just tell them."

Leila squeezed her eyes shut and when she opened them again tears clung to her long lashes. "I've seen the Enemy," she said, her voice a hoarse whisper.

Kamarie and Oraeyn exchanged startled glances. Brant shifted slightly, his hand reaching for his sword in an involuntary motion. The three dragons leaned forward in interest.

"Did you discover his name?" Kiernan asked, his voice low and quiet.

"Ghrendourak," Leila shuddered and her face turned pale. She turned and buried her head in Kiernan's shoulder, her shoulders shaking with deep sobs. She remained that way for a few moments, and then she turned back to the others, her face streaked with tears, her nose and cheeks red. "His name is Ghrendourak," she whispered, "and he does indeed possess the power of the Ancient Enemy. He is reaching into our world once more, just as Kiernan warned you about."

"What does he look like?" Oraeyn asked, unable to contain his curiosity.

"Like anything he wants," Leila snapped. "The power controlling him is ancient and devastating. I do not know who or what Ghrendourak was before the Enemy touched him, but he is that creature or man no longer. He is not bound to any one flesh or shape. The way he prefers to appear is as a giant of a man, taller than Brant, with a long cloak wrapped around him and a crown upon his head. His face is hidden by a great hood. But there is an intensity in that shadowy chasm where his face ought to be. His gaze may be hidden, but yet it seared into my heart, seeking out all my weaknesses and revealing them one by one. I cowered before him. I do not know why he kept me alive. He rides a great werehawk, a bird like none other. It is fierce and cruel, with razor sharp claws and silver wings."

Kamarie and Oraeyn shared a meaningful glance.

"He came into the portal, as you call it, and taunted me," Leila said. "He told me I had been in his prison for years and that all those I had once known and loved were long since dead. He told me he had taken over all of Tellurae Aquaous and enslaved all the free people. He showed me visions of the world he would create.

"He told me I had been long forgotten, that nobody even remained alive to come rescue me, nobody even remembered that I existed. He wanted me to join him. Often he came, offering me a place at his side. It grew harder to disbelieve what he was saying. He showed me countless visions of the world he claimed he had already created, and they haunted me when he left. I could not join him, but I no longer doubted him. I was resigned to an eternity of hopelessness and despair; a torment of life with no hope of death.

"When Kiernan arrived and tried to rescue me I fought him, thinking it was a new trap. I thought he was just another lie… I fought him…" Leila broke off her story.

Kiernan Kane wrapped his arms around her, and Leila leaned into his embrace. Great, shuddering sobs wracked her slight frame. The sorrow and compassion of her companions was reflected in their own tears. To see their beloved Leila, who so loved life and filled it with her delight and laughter, broken so cruelly was unbearable for them to watch, let alone endure.

"He fed on my fear," Leila said, her voice full of bitterness, "I helped make him stronger."

Suddenly Kamarie could bear it no longer. She crossed the room and wrapped her arms around Leila, adding her embrace to Kiernan's.

"Leila, you are not to blame. Ghrendourak selected you because you represent all that is best in this world; you are life itself and you bring life wherever you go. Why else do you think that you alone can thrive in the Harshlands when no one else would even try? You inspire life, and Ghrendourak, or the power controlling him, desires only death."

Kiernan continued to hold Leila as Kamarie stepped back.

"We will stop him, this Ghrendourak," Oraeyn said.

Everyone turned to look at him. He had drawn the Fang Blade and was standing there, like a hero of old.

"Tomorrow we travel to Emnolae. We must continue our quest to retrieve Yorien's Hand and use it to put an end to this threat. We will use any means necessary to defeat this Enemy. Even if it means we die trying, we must not give up. Here on this sword I swear I will not halt in my quest until Ghrendourak is no more."

"You will not go alone," Kamarie said quickly, speaking for all of them.

"Indeed, you cannot go without me," Kiernan whispered softly, but not quietly enough.

Brant turned to him, a quizzical look on his face. "Minstrel?"

"Indeed, he cannot go by himself. This task may belong to Oraeyn, but not to him alone," Kiernan replied smoothly. "Watching and waiting is over. At long last, the time for action has arrived."

Oraeyn turned to the wizardesses. "Dylanna and Leila, neither of you is in any condition to travel with us to Emnolae, and I hate to make this request of you, but we have no one else to call upon."

"What do you need?" Dylanna asked.

"One of you must find King Jemson and explain to him the events that are transpiring throughout the lands, and one of you must return to Aom-igh and report what you learned within the portal so as to help Justan prepare the defense of our beloved home. We await battle against an enemy unseen, with the exception of Leila. Hopefully, her vision can help find a weakness in his attack. Will you do this for us?"

Dylanna nodded firmly. "We can do that."

Oraeyn squared his shoulders. "It's settled then. We shall say our goodbyes tomorrow morning. We leave at first light. There is not a moment to lose."

With that, the small company retired to their beds. The three dragons went out into the yards and took their true forms, preferring to sleep in the open air.

Despite the events of the past day, Yole was not tired. His thoughts churned like the oars on a great ship and he could not get comfortable. At length he stood up and prowled around a bit. Thorayenak sat up and shook out his wings.

"Is everything well, youngling?"

"No," Yole replied. "Who would do such a thing to Dylanna and Leila? They are two of the kindest, best people I know. I find it hard to believe that anyone could be so cruel to someone so good. Hearing their story angers me. There are things in the world I never dreamed of, and they are disturbing." Heat flared in his chest as he spoke, and Yole raked his claws into the soft dirt of the ground.

"Truly," Rhimmell's voice burst from her as she sat up. "But there is great beauty in the world, as well, young one. Do not let yourself be overwhelmed by the evil you see. You must cling to the light you know exists, even when it appears to be blotted out by the darkness. The love of Cruithaor Elchiyl, the kindness of the wizardesses, the loyalty of your friends, the wisdom of the Minstrel, these are the reasons we continue."

Yole scratched at the ground with his claw in frustration. "I wish I understood more. I wish I knew why you both speak of Kiernan with such awe."

"Your eyes are open, are they not?" Rhimmell's voice held a slight hint of reprimand. "Did you not see the way he located the portal none else could see or sense? Did you not watch him enter that prison and return with the Wilding wizardess in his arms? Were you truly blind to the assistance he gave the young king when his strength was almost spent, allowing the Wanderer enough time to rescue his beloved? Youngling, you have spent three years amongst your own kind, have you not yet learned to trust your own insight? It is not our way to teach by telling every answer. You must divine the truth of such weighty matters for yourself. If Kiernan seems but a fool to you, is it because you truly believe him to be one, or because your human friends dismiss him as such? Does the esteem of dragons yet bear no weight in your human-trained mind?"

Yole felt a thrill of shock at Rhimmell's words. It had never occurred to him that his opinions might be influenced by his human upbringing. He stared at the green dragon, pondering her words.

"I," he paused. "You are right."

"Watch, observe, test," Rhimmell replied. "Learn. And come to your own conclusions. Do not be swayed overmuch by the voices of others. Especially humans."

"If you care so little for them, why did you come on this quest?" Yole asked.

Rhimmell blinked one long, slow blink. "It is not that I care not for them. It is that I know them to be shortsighted. There is a difference." She gave him a hard look.

"They have a different kind of wisdom," Thorayenak admonished gently. "But it is still wisdom."

"So you say." Rhimmell bowed her head. "But to your question, Youngling. Why do you think I came on this quest?"

"Because it's important?"

"That is true."

"Because of the minstrel?"

"That is also true."

"I still do not understand," Yole huffed.

"That can be remedied with time," Rhimmell's eyes danced with amusement, but there was no unkindness in her tone. "You have much to learn, young one. But you have good instincts. They will serve you well if you can learn to trust them." Rhimmell turned and prowled away, searching for a good place to sleep.

Yole stared after her and shook his head. She had given him much to ponder.

The night was too short, and morning came swiftly. As the sky began to turn a pale pink, the company of friends stood outside the palace, ready to set out once more. They were traveling light, their goal being both stealth and speed. Kiernan warned them that Ghrendourak would now be on alert. The rescue from the portal had saved Leila and Dylanna, but it had also most assuredly forewarned Ghrendourak that his prison had been breached and his certainty of victory was now threatened. This might motivate him to act swiftly as he turned from his conquests of other regions towards Aom-igh and Llycaelon; thus the urgency of gaining Yorien's Hand was heightened. Kiernan believed that the imprisonment of the wizardesses was not a random act, but a calculated strategy on Ghrendourak's part to remove anyone who might threaten his power. Having failed in this plan, Ghrendourak's malice would only be inflamed. Rescuing Leila and Dylanna multiplied the hazards they raced towards. As they assembled, Dylanna and Leila came out to see them off.

"I still feel I ought to come with you," Dylanna said, sounding a little uneasy.

"No," Oraeyn returned. "You and Leila must warn Aom-igh, and Jemson should be made aware of the tenuous situation as well."

Dylanna nodded, a hint of tears in her voice. "You take care of my niece, do you hear me?" she spoke with teasing sternness, but there was true concern there as well.

Oraeyn embraced her. "You have my word." He turned and climbed up onto Yole's back, and Dylanna found herself facing Brant.

He took her hand in his own, pressing her fingers together gently in his grip and looked down at her wordlessly. He opened his mouth as if to speak, but then appeared to change his mind.

"Take care of them," Dylanna's voice came out in a whisper and she grimaced, hearing herself repeat the same thing she had just said to Oraeyn.

"Always," Brant replied.

Another moment passed, neither of them speaking, until Thorayenak growled and Brant released her hand so he could climb up on the dragon's back.

As the dragons lifted off, Dylanna watched them as they flew away, growing smaller and smaller. "Come back to me," she whispered softly, "when all this is over. Come back to me."

She gazed after them until they disappeared from view, and

then she sighed. Shaking herself slightly, Dylanna clapped her hands together once and took a deep breath. Much of her strength had returned and she was ready to tackle new tasks.

"Well, we need to make contact with King Rhendak and hopefully he can communicate with Zara and Justan. Then we need to get some horses and find King Jemson to warn him of the coming threat," Dylanna said.

Leila nodded timidly, then she looked up. "Dylanna..." she hesitated.

"What is it?" Dylanna caught the strange note in her sister's voice and turned her full attention to her sister.

"My magic is gone," Leila whispered.

Dylanna's reply was quick and fierce. "No, it's not. The portal just made it seem that way. I was afraid to reach out for it at first too, but it's there, just as it has always been. You simply need to muster up the courage to reach for it again. Try it, you'll see, it's still there."

Leila's lips quivered. "No," she whispered. "I have reached for it. It's gone. All of it."

"That's not possible."

"I didn't believe it at first either, but it's true."

"How?"

"When Ghrendourak imprisoned us, I told you it felt like my magic was being drawn out of me and I couldn't stop it."

"Yes?"

"Well, I couldn't. And in the end whatever Ghrendourak did to imprison us left me unable to even touch it anymore."

"It's gone completely?"

"Yes, I am merely a shell of who I was before," Leila said bitterly. "Ghrendourak didn't kill me, but he may as well have."

"Don't say that."

"Why not? It's true," Leila's voice was both cynical and resigned. "I should have died in that prison. Better that than to live like this, this... this is a hollow life compared to what I once was. It's like both of my arms have been cut off, or a part of who I am has been ripped away from me."

"Perhaps there is a cure," Dylanna forced cheerful hope into her tone. "Have you spoken to Kiernan?"

Leila shook her head. "No, I couldn't." Her brow furrowed. "What do you think he could do?"

Dylanna patted her arm reassuringly, feeling more helpless than she had ever been in her entire life. "That minstrel is far more than he seems, is all. Well, don't worry. Perhaps it will just take time to heal."

"Maybe," Leila did not sound at all hopeful. "In any case, you will have to contact King Rhendak on your own, I will not be able to help."

"Don't worry about that. I have the strength to take care of this."

"I know."

For a moment Dylanna stood very still, concentrating on something Leila could not see. The former wizardess felt tears welling up, but she refused to let them appear. She had always been strong enough to cope with anything; she could deal with this, too. Dylanna's brow furrowed in confusion and she shook her head.

"I can't reach him, something is blocking me," her tone was frustrated.

"Maybe you still need rest?"

"No, it's not that. I'm strong enough, but it feels like I'm coming up against a wall. It's puzzling."

"Well, perhaps you shouldn't try again for a little while. Let's find Jemson, maybe you are tired and just don't know it. In any case, it won't be any harder to send the message from the borders than it is from here."

Dylanna agreed that her sister's logic made sense, so they set off to find the horse-master. The stables were pristine under the care of a man named Rhian, who had been instructed by Brant to assist the two wizardesses who would be needing horses that morning. Rhian was eager to help, and he led Leila and Dylanna through the rows of stabled horses, pointing out which were the fastest, strongest, and gentlest.

"Brant said you were to have whatever help you needed. You may take any horse in the stable except for Hawkspin there," he pointed out a great chestnut horse, taller than any Leila had ever seen, standing well over seventeen hands.

"If we're to have any horse we want, why can't we take Hawkspin?" Leila asked.

Rhian chuckled. "Because you wouldn't want him, plain and simple. Ain't nobody can ride him, he's that wild, and mean spirited, too. The king's been trying to gentle him, to no avail. King Jemson is as good a rider as we have in Llycaelon, for all his youth, but I think he's met his match in Hawkspin. That horse will never submit to a rider, that is certain."

Leila stared at the great horse. Sensing her gaze, he tossed his elegant head proudly and his long copper mane rippled behind him. He was one of those horses that was never truly still. His muscles rippled with his every movement and he shifted restlessly. Leila had never seen so magnificent a creature. Without quite knowing what she was doing, she walked up to Hawkspin's stall. She opened the door and stepped inside.

"Lady, no!" Rhian shouted, rushing to stop her, but it was too late.

Hawkspin reared up in surprise at Leila's unexpected move. His great hooves kicked out wildly. Dylanna gasped and raised her hands as if she could ward off the blow for Leila, sure that the huge horse would trample her sister. Then Leila's voice rose up, quiet and gentle, and Hawkspin's hooves clattered harmlessly to the ground once more. The horse's ears twitched forward, listening to the wizardess's voice. Leila reached up and placed a gentle hand on the great horse's neck. Hawkspin's muscles quivered at her touch, but he did not shy away. He stood still as Leila continued to talk, her voice soothing and calm.

"Easy there, quiet now, Hawkspin," Leila murmured. "What bothers you so? Why are you so afraid?"

The horse nickered and made a chuffing noise. He put his soft nose down near Leila's ear and blew air out through his nose. The wizardess giggled a little.

"That tickles," she said, and there was joy in her voice again.

The horse lipped at her shoulder and snorted. Leila stroked his nose and nodded seriously. After a moment she spoke again.

"I need your help," she said. "Will you carry me to find King Jemson? An enemy is coming and he must be warned."

The horse gave a questioning whinny and Leila nodded. "Yes, I know how to ride bareback."

Hawkspin bobbed his head and Leila patted his neck once more. Then she stepped out of Hawkspin's stall and looked at Dylanna and the dumbfounded horse-master. Leila's chin was raised, she had regained some of her old fire and she looked mightily pleased with herself.

"Apparently I haven't lost my touch with animals," she said in a triumphant tone. "Dylanna, find yourself a horse. Hawkspin will be my mount; he has agreed to help us find King Jemson. He says that the king is a good man who takes great care with men and animals alike. Hawkspin is simply afraid of losing his freedom and becoming tame. He has no problem with the king or any man, he just wishes not to be contained."

"You... you spoke to the... the horse?" Rhian's voice was filled with disbelief.

"Yes," Leila said casually, brushing a strand of stray hair back from her face.

"And you're going to ride him?"

"Is that a problem?"

"Lady, if you can *ride* that horse, he's yours!"

Leila snorted sternly. "Hawkspin isn't a creature to be possessed," she lectured. "A beast this noble may be an ally, but never owned." Then she giggled, her face flushed and her heart giddy. "We'll see what King Jemson has to say about you giving away one of his greatest treasures, anyway."

"He'd say the same thing as me. He's all but given up on old Hawkspin here."

Leila's face quirked. "Well, I suppose we'll see. Dylanna, have you picked your horse?"

Dylanna nodded that she had. She told Rhian her choice. The horse master looked approving as he tacked up the small, palomino mare.

"You know your horses, my lady," he said. "This little girl is named Spun Gold, though we all call her Goldie. She looks small, and she's as gentle as they come, but I've never seen a horse built better for stamina. She won't let you down."

"Thank you, Rhian."

Then Leila opened up the door to Hawkspin's stall. The horse stepped out, all power and muscle. He moved lightly though, with a fluid grace in spite of the nervous energy he had been displaying just moments before. He stood in full view, his neck arched and his head high. Then he buckled his front knees, allowing the wizardess to mount. Leila swung up expertly and settled herself on the horse's back, sitting sidesaddle.

"Milady," the groom said, a look of concern in his hazel eyes, "I don't need to tell you that's not the most secure way to ride."

"Do you really fear for my safety Rhian?" Leila asked.

He stared at her with a considering look, then he turned his gaze to the giant horse, standing there as quiet and gentle as a steady old mount who has been ridden for years. Rhian chuckled then, a little self-consciously, and shook his head.

"No, milady, I don't suppose I do."

With that the two wizardesses rode out into the fading daylight. Rhian shook his head, he had never seen the like of that, and he doubted he ever would again. With a cheerful whistle, he returned to his duties, and as he worked he would often look up and stare out towards the border and shake his head in disbelief.

Several hours after the wizardesses left the stables, a strange dragon landed on the lawn in front of the palace. Once, this would have caused a stir among the servants, but now dragons descending upon the courtyard were almost commonplace. Word was sent throughout the palace until it reached the ears of Queen Fiora. The elderly queen descended regally from her apartments to greet this newcomer. Her body was frail, but she held herself with a hint of her old grace as she stepped outside.

"Greetings, dragon," she called out.

"Greetings," the dragon rumbled back. "I have come to lend

my aid to the king of Llycaelon, where can I find him?"

"He rides to battle at the Caethyr Gap," the old woman called out in a firm voice. "I am confident he would not turn you away."

The dragon nodded in reply. "I also bring a young charge." He lowered himself to the ground and a small boy clambered down from his back and took a few shaky steps forward. "This is Shane, sole survivor of a small village on the island of Chensar. Will you care for him?"

The queen stared down at the child and a strange light filled her face. She descended the remainder of the steps and knelt in the dust, arms outstretched towards the little boy.

The child gazed up at her solemnly for a moment, one finger in his mouth. Then, appearing to find in this woman a spark of much-needed motherly sympathy and tenderness, he toddled into her embrace. Fiora wrapped her arms around him and held him close. A silent tear wound its way down her face, and their was healing in that sparkling trail.

"Shane," she whispered. She rose, still holding the child tenderly, and looked up at the dragon. "I will care for him as if he were my own son."

"Very well," the dragon replied. "My thanks. If you will excuse me, I must away."

The dragon leapt into the air and soared away. The old queen turned, holding the child to her breast and humming snatches of an old nursery rhyme, and went inside. The lines receded from her face and everyone who saw her whispered that she was much changed. She took the little boy and held him on her lap, rocking him to sleep while the servants prepared a room for him.

EIGHTEEN

Zara descended from Fortress Hill, Rena's limp body in her arms. The wizardess looked weary, and Justan rushed forward to take his wife from her. Rena was surprisingly light, almost weightless.

"Is... is she...?"

"She is not dead," Rhendak answered the unspoken question, appearing at his side.

The king of the dragons strode majestically down the hill with Justan and Zara in his full form. The dragon offered his fore claw to Zara, and she accepted, leaning on it gratefully. Rhendak looked at Justan, his gaze serious.

"The Song Bearer is not dead," Rhendak continued, "but neither is she alive. She poured too much of herself into the song. Her life force emptied into the melody and she herself is what now gives the shield above us its strength. That was not supposed to happen, we had planned to control the magic, to prevent this very phenomenon. But Rena allowed herself to flow into the song and held nothing back."

"Will she come back when the shield is no longer needed?" Justan asked.

Rhendak pondered. "I do not know if she will survive. If the shield is broken, there is no saying whether she will return to this shell. Though her heart still beats, the object you hold is but her body. Her spirit is elsewhere. So few have done this before, I do not know what her chances for survival are."

"But she might yet wake again?" Justan asked, desperate for any hope the dragon might give him.

"I do not know."

"I understand," Jemson felt crestfallen.

The rest of the myth-folk had crowded down around behind them. Rhendak turned and spread his wings, blocking their view, though his people still strained curiously, trying to see what had happened to Rena, the one they called the Song Bearer. Rhendak rose up on his hind legs and they fell silent as death.

"The Song Bearer yet lives," he said, his voice booming out. "But her life hangs by a perilous thread. She has stolen us a little time. She has given everything for the chance of our safety. We must do everything we can to make sure her sacrifice was not made for naught."

The myth-folk raised a cheer, their voices mingling together into a song that floated up into the sky. Power surged upward as their voices touched the shield, strengthening it even further. Zara looked at Justan sadly.

"They sing for her," she murmured. "And they now attempt to anchor her here, so that when the shield comes down she will return to body."

Justan nodded to the powerful creatures before him in a grateful acknowledgement of what they were trying to do. His heart was full of gratitude he did not know how to express and he struggled for a moment, trying to find the words. Rhendak noticed the look on his face and he inclined his head regally.

"They know how much she means to you," he said, "she means a great deal to us as well. She was the one meant to play the Song that has been locked in silence since before the reign of King Llian."

"I just want to thank them," Justan said.

"They know. They can feel your appreciation, it echoes their own. They honor one who gave up everything for our safety."

Justan nodded, his heart too full for words. He looked down

at Rena, lying lifeless in his arms. She could not be gone. Her face was calm and peaceful and full of color. She appeared to be merely sleeping. His heart was heavy with the knowledge that his wife was much farther away than she appeared. Her body was lighter than breathing, but Justan's shoulders were bowed under the weight of the loneliness she had left behind. To hide the sudden tears that rolled down his face, Justan turned and strode away towards the castle, bearing his burden alone.

The small company had been flying all day without seeing any kind of landmass at all. Oraeyn was beginning to wonder if any land even existed south of Llycaelon. Every time he looked down, all that could be seen was water. Llycaelon was far behind them, and ahead of them all he could see was endless ocean. He had never dreamed the world could be so big, and he had barely seen any of it yet. They were all weary of flying, but there was nowhere to land or rest. Daylight faded and stars blinked into existence like tiny pinpricks in a vast ebony cloth overhead. Suddenly Brant waved to the others from the back of his dragon and pointed.

"There," the warrior said confidently, "Emnolae."

Oraeyn and Kamarie peered in the direction Brant was pointing. At first they thought there was nothing to be seen. Then they saw what Brant was indicating. On the horizon, a dusky purple landscape rose up out of the cerulean ocean. Against the sky, the landmass looked like a low cloud formation, but Oraeyn's heart leapt up into his throat at the sight of it anyway.

There it is, he thought to himself excitedly, *our goal: Emnolae. The home of the High Kings.*

"We should not approach too obviously," Kiernan Kane suggested. "Ghrendourak will be watching for us."

"True." Before Brant could consider how this might be accomplished, Thorayenak surprised them all.

"If we wait a bit until true nightfall we can approach the island by sea. Dragons can swim as well as they fly. If you lie down flat on our backs or on top of our wings, we can approach the island without being seen. We will appear as little more than driftwood to anyone who might be watching."

Brant pursed his lips. "Let's do it. I can guide you to a secluded beach I know of where there will be fewer prying eyes, and we can perhaps acquire some help, as well. Keep a sharp watch out for hydras and sea monsters."

"There will be no hydras in these waters," Kiernan replied.

"How could you possibly know that?" Brant asked.

Oraeyn thought it odd that Kiernan would contradict Brant's concern. If anyone would know the perils of this area it would be Brant, who had traveled here before, and yet, surely Kiernan would not make such an assertion out of thin air.

Kiernan was unconcerned by Brant's question. "I know these waters," he said, as if that explained everything.

After their experience with the portal, no further challenge was offered, and once night had fallen the dragons dipped down to the ocean. They sank beneath the surface of the waves until only their wings remained above the water. Thorayenak's head came up out of the water and he twisted his neck around to look at Brant.

"We will need to come up for breath occasionally," he informed them, "but we can do so without lifting our heads entirely out of the water. Do not worry, you are perfectly safe."

Oraeyn turned to look for Kiernan Kane and was astonished at how difficult it was to spot him. He and Kamarie followed his example, lying down on Yole's wings, content to rest until they reached the shores of Emnolae.

Oraeyn wondered what it would be like, to set foot on the same sand the High Kings had walked upon, to see the castle in which Artair himself had lived. His thoughts drifted to the star. What would it look like? It was hard for him to build up any amount of excitement about touching Yorien's Hand; the one real emotion he could summon was trepidation. Brant had seen the star, even touched it, but had said very little about the experience. Oraeyn knew it would be difficult, even painful. Brant had not spoken of it, but his expression of distaste and sorrow and barely controlled anger whenever the star or Emnolae was mentioned spoke volumes. Something had happened there, many years ago, and the memory was not pleasant for the warrior; that much Oraeyn could discern.

He wondered again if he was truly the one about whom the prophecy spoke. Would he be able to bear the weight of the words the minstrel had spoken? Already that morning on which the minstrel had revealed to them the truth about their situation seemed so far away. Oraeyn wondered how much of himself he would retain throughout this journey, and if he would be able to do all that was expected of him. So much rested on his shoulders, so much depended on him.

I am just one person, he thought in despair, *what can I do? Tellurae Aquaous is so immense why am I the one chosen to stand up and save it? Surely there is one better equipped than I.*

But there was no one, and Oraeyn was not about to flinch from the duty he had been assigned. He was determined to see this quest through to the end, no matter the outcome. He did not even care for himself anymore, his thoughts were all for Kamarie. In his heart, Oraeyn vowed to keep her safe at all costs.

"Prophecies are never saying what you think they are saying," Brant's words echoed again in Oraeyn's memories. Something pricked at the back of his mind as he remembered what the warrior had said. Suddenly things did not add up as neatly as Oraeyn thought they had. He was not sure what was wrong, but he was overcome with a sense of urgency, and he felt they had misunderstood something important.

This sensation was not altogether new; something had seemed out of place about their interpretation of Kiernan Kane's words since they had left Aom-igh and it had been bothering him all along. Oraeyn focused his thoughts as much as he could, straining to decipher what mystery the words were hiding, but it flitted from his grasp. It was like trying to capture a cloud.

"Kamarie," he whispered across Yole's back. "Do you think we've interpreted the prophecy correctly?"

She turned her face to him though he could barely discern

her hazy outline.

"Which part?" she whispered back.

"I'm not sure. I just have this uneasy sensation that we're missing something. Something important."

Water lapped up over Yole's wing and Oraeyn shivered at the sudden cold.

"I don't know," came the response. "Have you talked to Brant or Kiernan?"

"I tried to talk to Brant about it, but he just said that prophecies are not to be trusted. Which I guess is part of my problem. This all seems too easy."

"Perhaps that's true," Kamarie replied. "But regardless of whether we missed something in the prophecy, Ghrendourak is real, and Kiernan said the only way to defeat him is with Yorien's Hand, and Brant has seen it here on Emnolae. We can't exactly change course now."

"You're right. And it's not that I think we're headed in the wrong direction. I think maybe it's just... I'm not sure the prophecy is really talking about *me*," Oraeyn confessed.

A soft laugh emanated from the other wing. "And that's why I love you."

"I'm serious," Oraeyn whispered, a hint of vehemence in his tone. "I'm not a hero. I just keep falling into these roles; responsibilities pile on top of me, honor and duties I never sought."

"Oraeyn, I'm sure every High King in history felt the same way. Heroes don't realize they're heroes when they're in the midst of things. Don't worry, everything will turn out fine, I'm sure of it."

Oraeyn was not so sure, but he knew that he wasn't going to solve all the riddles that plagued him this night. He sighed and lowered his head onto his hands just as more salty water sloshed over Yole's wing and bathed his face. He spluttered and coughed and heard muted giggles coming from Kamarie. He sighed, it was going to be a long, cold, wet night.

It was the most uncomfortable night Oraeyn had ever experienced. Water lapped over Yole's wing intermittently, and before long, Oraeyn was completely soaked. Long before morning, a wind picked up, causing Oraeyn to shiver uncontrollably. The cold and the wet and the fear of rolling off the edge of the dragon's wing and sinking into the ocean's depths made sleep impossible. When morning dawned once more the travelers were only a mile from their destination, and Oraeyn had never been more glad to see the Dragon's Eye. The only blessing to be found was that a lack of sleep meant no nightmares.

As the new day dawned, Emnolae rose up, filling Oraeyn's vision. The beach glistened white in the morning light, reminding him of Pearl Cove. A wild and tangled jungle-forest rose up in the distance, its emerald depths both inviting and forbidding. Beyond the forest the peaks of mountains stretched up into the sky: dormant volcanoes, Oraeyn remembered from Brant's brief story about his first trip to this island. One peak, in particular, dwarfed the others, towering above them. That volcano, in the center of the island, was the very heart of Emnolae. It was there they must go.

Thorayenak's head came up, just enough so he could ask Brant which point they should aim for on the island. Brant indicated a small cove and the dragon's head disappeared beneath the waves again.

Dylanna and Leila camped for the night on the trail and woke early to continue riding towards the Caethyr Gap. They rode well into the afternoon before they reached their destination. The aethalons' camp was not far from where they emerged from the Iron Wood, and Dylanna sighed to herself, relieved that they would not have to search.

Scouts rode out to stop them. There were three of them, all dressed in the familiar armor of the aethalons. It was still strange to think that these men were now friends and allies when not so very long ago they had been enemies. There was no time to ponder the odd twists of fate, however, for the scouts had reached them and brought Leila and Dylanna's progress to an abrupt halt.

The scouts were all tall and their faces were hard and stern; they were men who had seen battle and killed to survive, men who saw death as a necessary evil, a side effect of their orders. They approached warily, but there was a lightness about their expressions as well, like people who had lived under stormy skies that had recently cleared. They asked for Dylanna and Leila to identify themselves, their voices guarded.

"My name is Dylanna, and this is my sister Leila," Dylanna informed the scouts. "We come from Aom-igh. We bear a message for King Jemson. Can you take us to him? Our message is urgent."

"We will need something more convincing than your word on who you are if we are to let you see our king," one of the warriors said bluntly.

Dylanna sized the man up. He was obviously the head scout and had the look of a man who took his job seriously. The expression on his face said he would not budge one inch on the matter. Dylanna respected his dedication to duty, but wished it did not complicate her errand.

"What proof can I give that you will believe?" she asked. "I am from Aom-igh, so I know none of your passwords, and any names I might give you I could have picked up from overhearing idle gossip."

The scout's face took on a look of respect and thoughtfulness. "Well now, I don't know about that, but you'll have to come up with proof that you mean no harm before I can let you come any closer to the camp or King Jemson."

At that moment Leila urged her horse forward. The scouts had been focusing their attention on Dylanna and had barely noticed the second wizardess. They noticed her now though. Leila saw the astonished looks of recognition on the faces of the men as they saw what horse she rode.

"Sir," she said boldly to the scout leader, "Hawkspin is all the proof you should require to know that we are friends. I can see from your expression that you know him. Your king's horse-master, Rhian himself, gave me leave to ride this horse on our urgent errand to bring the king a message of utmost importance."

"That horse is one I would know anywhere, he is the king's pride and joy. But it's not possible that you should be riding him," the scout sputtered.

"Why not?"

"No man can ride Hawkspin. He's as wild and vicious as they come."

"Is there any way you can be sure this horse is indeed the Hawkspin of which you speak?" Leila pressed.

"Of course there is. Hawkspin is legendary. If it's him, there'll be a scar beneath his left front leg. The story goes he got it when he tried to jump the fence of his paddock as a colt."

One of the other scouts looked skeptical. "How could you possibly know that?" he scoffed.

"You haven't heard the story?" the first man's voice was surprised. "The fence was eight feet tall! Hawkspin nearly made it, too."

His comrades shook their heads.

"Huh," the first scout shrugged. "I thought everyone knew that tale. It was all anybody was talking about for months."

"Take a look then," Leila challenged.

"Lady, you could easily have stolen this beast," the scout argued. "How is knowing the identity of the horse you ride going to convince me that you are friends?"

"If this is the horse you believe it is, then you can know we are who we say we are," Leila said, authority filling her voice. "Who but friends could have taken this particular horse? Would enemies have chosen to steal the wildest horse in the royal stables in order to come and kill the king?"

"You have a point there, Lady."

The man swung down from his own horse and advanced upon Hawkspin with wary apprehension. The great chestnut stallion pranced in place nervously at the soldier's approach, but Leila soothed him and he quieted. The scout checked beneath the horse's left foreleg and then nodded at his companions.

"It's him all right, but how you are riding him is a mystery to me. And without a bit or a saddle either!"

Leila raised her chin triumphantly, but said nothing. The scout looked up at her again, trust and respect evident in his expression. He patted Hawkspin idly for a moment.

Dylanna cleared her throat in satisfaction and impatience. "If you are thoroughly convinced that we mean your king no harm, would you please escort us to speak with His Majesty? Our message is urgent and time is not our friend."

The scout bobbed his head in a swift apology. "Follow me."

Leaving two of the scouts behind to continue their rounds, the rest of them rode into the camp. The aethalons stared at the wizardesses as they rode past. A few of them recognized the legendary colt and they pointed him out to each other with mutters of astonishment.

From his campsite King Jemson heard the commotion. He looked up to see what was causing the disturbance and caught sight of the odd procession approaching. After Shentallyia, he had thought nothing would ever surprise him again. He had been wrong.

"Sire, friends from Aom-igh, bearing a message. They say it is urgent," the scout announced as they came closer.

"Dylanna! Leila!" Jemson called out, catching sight of his two visitors. "This is a welcome surprise! What brings you here? And riding my most unruly mount, I see. What should I expect from a pair of wizardesses? You look tired; come, sit, let me find you something to eat or drink. Pieter will take your horses. Leila, whatever you did to Hawkspin, make sure he doesn't take Pieter's arm off once you dismount, will you? It is good to see you. What's so urgent that you came all the way out here?"

Jemson paused, pulling his shoulders back. A look of maturity passed across his face and he took a deep breath. Dylanna was amazed at how much older he looked. Jemson had grown quite a bit since the war in Aom-igh that had claimed his father's life and given him the throne. Brant believed in the young man, and at this moment Dylanna could see why.

"Pieter," Jemson said, getting his curiosity under control, "please make sure these horses are cared for."

The two wizardesses dismounted and Pieter took hold of

Spun Gold's reins. He looked questioningly at Leila and the woman whispered in soothing tones to Hawkspin. Then she turned and addressed the scout.

"He will follow you, as long as you make no attempt to put a halter or a rope on him."

Hawkspin tossed his head and snorted and Leila chuckled. "Do not worry," she said reassuringly.

After Pieter and the horses had left, Jemson held out a hand to both of the wizardesses. "Won't you come sit down or accept a bite to eat, perhaps something to drink? You must be thirsty at least. If I don't miss my mark, you've been traveling since dawn."

"And part of last night too," Dylanna affirmed. "I, for one, could do with a cup of water, or perhaps tea."

Leila nodded in agreement and Jemson gestured for them to find seats on the logs surrounding his fire. Then he poured them each a cup of tea.

"It's not as hospitable as the palace, but this has become a sort of home, and it's all I have to offer right now," he commented.

"How goes the fight?" Dylanna asked, taking a sip from her tin cup.

"It's over for now," Jemson replied. "The seheowks have been destroyed, or at least, this batch of them is gone."

"Destroyed?" Leila almost choked on her tea in disbelief. "How?"

"Apparently one of my Aetoli captains is also a dragon ward," Jemson replied. "It was only with the help of his dragon that we were able to beat the vile creatures back."

"Dragon ward?" Dylanna asked. She and Leila shared a startled glance, then both wizardesses leaned forward in sudden interest.

Jemson stared at them. "You didn't know? You didn't send her?"

Dylanna crossed her arms. "There is much to explain, and very little time. First, we must give you Brant's message, then you will tell us more about this dragon ward."

CHAPTER

NINETEEN

The small company stretched their legs, relieved to be standing on solid ground once more. Everyone was waterlogged, and the warmth of the Dragon's Eye felt good as it beat down on them, helping them dry out.

Kamarie twisted her hair in her hands, wringing out the excess water. "Ugh, I hate the way sea water corrupts everything it touches. I'll never get the taste out of my mouth. I think I'd rather face Ghrendourak than travel like that again."

Kiernan pulled his mandolin off his back and began examining it and tuning the strings to make sure it had not gotten wet or suffered during the journey. "That is because you have not met Ghrendourak yet."

Kamarie nodded, her expression sobering a bit. "True. That was a thoughtless thing for me to say. I do hope I never meet him although avoiding him altogether does not seem very likely at this point."

Oraeyn chuckled, admiring her straightforward sense of humor and amazed all over again at her unflinching courage. He could tell she was scared—they were up against an enemy they knew little about, with enough power to take over all the known world and set dragons shuddering in trepidation—and yet she would never back down. Oraeyn almost pitied Ghrendourak if

Kamarie ever got a hold of him. His jaw clenched; he would make sure that evil being never got close to the woman he loved. He had made a promise to keep her safe, and keep her safe he would, even if it meant his own death.

The dragons stretched as well, their sinuous necks and tails straightening and then curling as the water dripped from their massive bodies. When they had finished, the three magnificent creatures transformed so as to be less conspicuous. Oraeyn decided that he would never cease to be amazed at a dragon's ability to shape shift. After giving them a few moments to rest, Brant told them there should be a cabin not far ahead.

"I once received help from the family that used to live there. I doubt they would begrudge us the use of their shelter," Brant informed them.

"Lead on," Oraeyn replied.

They followed Brant as he made his way across the beach, towards a deep and ominous line of trees. It was slow going in the soft sand, as they followed the tree line and skirted sand dunes.

"What are we looking for, Brant?" Kamarie asked after they had hiked some distance.

"A cabin," Brant replied tersely. "I seem to have misjudged our landing. It is farther up the beach than I remembered."

"What is in this cabin?" Oraeyn inquired.

"A family helped me last time I was here. We may need their help once more. Come on, it's just a bit of a walk around that way," Brant pointed and continued trudging.

They were all quite dry and weary by the time they came within sight of what they sought: a quaint little cabin tucked into the forest edge. A patch of green grass surrounded the home, and wildflowers grew up around the stone path leading up to the wooden door.

The company's spirits lifted to see the cabin still standing. Oraeyn had been secretly thinking that it had been a long time since Brant had visited this land, the cabin could have been destroyed while he was gone. None of them knew it, but Brant was worried about the same thing, and he was relieved to see the cabin still intact and exactly where it had been almost forty years ago.

The weary and bedraggled group made their way cautiously up the path to the front door. Kamarie felt soothed by the sight of the wildflowers bordering the little path. They were pretty and reminded her of home.

Brant strode up to the door and knocked. Nothing happened. Oraeyn blew out a breath he had been holding and opened his mouth to speak. Then the door swung open and whatever words Oraeyn had been about to utter died on his lips. At first they could not see who was standing in the doorway because the light inside the house was so dim. Then the person moved out of the doorway and stood in the full light of day.

It was a woman in her late forties. She had auburn hair that was streaked with grey, but her face was smooth, bearing no wrinkles and possessing a child-like quality. She had a pleasant mouth, and she stood with her head held high. Her chill gaze swept over them, raising goose bumps on Kamarie's arms. The woman's eyes seemed strange, wrong in some way. Kamarie looked closer and started in consternation. Her eyes were not just pale, they were the milky-gray color of blindness.

"Excuse me, ma'am," Brant began. "I was wondering if you could tell me what became of the people who used to live here? They were kind to a young boy once who passed through here."

The woman's face turned secretive and amused. "Welcome back, Rhoyan. I have been expecting you."

Brant tilted his head to one side, raising an eyebrow in surprise. Then he peered more closely at the woman. "Ina?"

"The same," she replied. "How are you?"

"You were just a child when last I saw you!" Brant stepped forward and took her hand, pressing it warmly between his own, his expression full of joy.

"Are you so surprised? It has been many years since you left here. We don't all have the privilege of aging as slowly as you."

"Look at you now, all grown up! And your mother...?" Brant's question trailed off at the sorrow that passed across the woman's face. "I'm sorry," he whispered.

Ina patted his hand. "There is much to tell. And you're one to speak of age, you weren't much older than a child yourself when last you visited our shores. Won't you come in? Colas will be back soon."

"Colas is still here as well?"

"As I said, there is much to tell, much to catch up on before you continue on your quest. Come in, I just started dinner, there is enough for all, and Colas will want to see you. You can take a moment for old friends."

They followed Ina into the cottage. The house was much bigger on the inside than it looked from without, and Oraeyn marveled at how comfortably all of them fit. There were chairs enough for everyone, and even the dragons looked at ease in their lanky human forms. Ina bustled about the kitchen; she was remarkably adept at finding things quickly in spite of her blindness. Oraeyn found himself watching her closely, trying to figure out her secret.

Although he was eager to keep moving, Oraeyn kept his restlessness to himself. Brant appeared to be content to stay where he was, and Oraeyn had no reason to doubt the warrior's judgment. This place felt safe, and whatever Ina was preparing in the kitchen smelled wonderful. Oraeyn's stomach was very much aware of the long days of travel and the small, cold rations it had been resigned to, and it complained loudly. Oraeyn's face flushed, but no one else noticed.

Then Ina brought out the food, a veritable feast of bread and cheese, cut-up fruits, and a hearty stew filled with vegetables and thick pieces of meat. The travelers attacked it hungrily, and for a while all were silent. When he had eaten enough to slow down a bit, Oraeyn mentioned his astonishment at the amount of food the woman had brought them. Ina winked at him and Oraeyn had the uncomfortable notion that she could see him quite well.

"We have visitors here on the outskirts of the Wylder Wood more often than you might think," she said, her voice placid. "My mother taught me to always be prepared to offer hospitality to anyone who might need it."

"A good standard to live by," the minstrel said approvingly between bites.

Ina turned in the minstrel's direction and nodded. As she did so, the front door swung open.

The travelers looked up from their meal to see who this newcomer was. Ina's face lit up. There was a patient and welcoming look on her face and Oraeyn understood that whoever had just arrived was no threat. He looked over at the door, wondering what manner of person this was.

A man entered the room, closing the door behind him. He appeared to be approximately ten years older than Ina though there was no gray in his light brown hair or the beard that covered part of an old scar running down the length of the right side of his face. He carried a small sack over one shoulder and he walked with a bit of a limp. But there was strength and wisdom in the lines of his face, and he moved with spirit. He took in the sight of the company seated around the room and his lips turned up in a welcoming grin.

"This is a change," he said in a cheery tone. "Ina dinner smells good, who are our guests?"

Brant stood. "Colas," he said taking the man's hand in both of his own, a warmth in his expression that Oraeyn was unaccustomed to seeing.

Colas took Brant's hand with a puzzled tilt to his head. "Do I know you, sir?" he asked.

"We met once before," Brant said. "My name now is Brant, though you knew me by my childhood name. Do you not recognize me?"

Colas peered hard at Brant's face and recognition dawned. "Rhoyan?" he asked incredulously.

"I have returned."

"But... but you've barely aged ten years, though it was no less than forty since you were here before!" Colas looked wondering. "Truly, the same amount of time must have passed for us both, yet now I appear to be your senior, though you must certainly be at least as old as I."

"Older," Brant responded.

"Ina, the man looks no different than he did when he last visited."

Ina nodded, her gaze was distant and unseeing, but her voice was strong. "Perhaps he does not look any different, however, we are all of us changed since last we met in this very room. We have all grown much since then. You have grown too, Rhoyan. I can tell that you have endured trials of your own although the years might have been kinder to you than they have to us."

Brant chuckled. "It's in the blood."

Ina's answering smile was fierce. "Yes, I know."

Oraeyn cleared his throat and half rose from his seat, unable to abide not knowing what was going on any longer. "Brant, I don't mean to be rude, but who are these people?" he asked, keeping his voice even. "What are we doing here?"

"Yes," Ina said demurely. "Introduce us to your friends, please."

"Forgive me," Brant said. "I was so caught up in the joy of finding you still here... of course I need to explain. Ina, Colas, these are King Oraeyn and Princess Kamarie of Aom-igh, the minstrel Kiernan Kane, and Thorayenak, Rhimmell, and Yole, dragons of Aom-igh. They are my friends." He bowed his head slightly and then turned to the rest of the company. "I told you that I journeyed here once before. There is not time to explain the entire story, but I met Ina, Colas, and their mother when I first came here. Ina's mother was a guardian of sorts and she helped me find Yorien's Hand."

Oraeyn sat back down, mollified, though not completely satisfied. Colas and Ina joined the small company by sitting down and relaxing with them. Ina and Colas were warm, hospitable people, and the small company soon felt very much at ease. Colas regaled them with tales of his adventures at sea. He had apprenticed under a man named Captain Delmar a few years after Brant's first visit to Emnolae, and the two men were mutual acquaintances of the gruff sea captain. Though the others did not know Captain Delmar, the stories Brant and Colas shared were ones they could all enjoy. Then Brant told brief snatches of how things had turned out for him, and they all listened intently,

Oraeyn most of all. The warrior did not talk about himself often, and Oraeyn was always eager to find out more about the mysteries that wrapped themselves around Brant in a heavy, impenetrable cloak.

"Ah," Colas said after Brant finished telling about the battle between Aom-igh and Llycaelon. "It is good to see you again, Rhoy…" he caught himself. "I mean, Brant. But what is it that brings you back to Emnolae? Surely you did not come all this way with six companions, three of whom are dragons, to catch up with a remnant of your past."

Brant's face turned serious. "Have you heard of Ghrendourak?"

Colas's friendly look turned strained. "That is an ill name to speak so freely, even in daylight. Word of that evil creature has reached us even here."

"You are right, the name is a fell one, but my speaking it cannot summon him. Though he would have wished to stop us from arriving here, he will be wary of Emnolae. The greatest threat to his power rests here."

Ina stirred and rubbed her arms. "You have come for Yorien's Gift once more, have you?"

"We intend to destroy him before he gets any stronger," Kiernan affirmed.

"So that's what you've come for, eh?" Colas nodded. "Come to see if you can't master the star a second time around."

Brant shook his head. "Not I," he gestured to Oraeyn. "If the prophecies are to be believed. Oraeyn, show them your sword."

Oraeyn hesitated, but Brant nodded his encouragement and Oraeyn stood reluctantly. He drew his sword and held it up for Colas to see. The golden blade flickered in the light cast by the fire in the hearth, and Colas caught his breath sharply. It was Ina who moved first though.

She walked over to Oraeyn, her steps careful but certain, staring blankly. She stopped in front of the young king and touched the blade. Then she laid a light hand upon Oraeyn's arm. Oraeyn shuddered, a sudden chill sweeping through him. The woman turned her blank gaze around the room and she stopped when she came to Kiernan Kane. Meaningful wordlessness passed between them, and Oraeyn ached to know what was communicated in that strange, sightless gaze.

"Guide them well, fool," Ina said in a hushed voice, "but do not be misled yourself, the prophecy is not as clear as you believe it to be."

"Something is wrong, Sire," Devrin exclaimed as he dashed up to Jemson. He was panting and his voice was hoarse. When he saw the two wizardesses he drew himself to a halt. He made an apologetic bow. "Forgive me," he gasped. "I did not know you had visitors."

"You must be Devrin, the dragon ward," Leila said. "Please, join us."

Devrin made a strange face and looked to the king for clarification. Jemson nodded.

"Yes, this involves all of us. You should hear what they have to say. And I would like to know what it was you were about to say as well."

"It's Shentallyia, Sire, she says she can feel an ominous presence approaching, an evil that threatens all the lands. She tried to reach King Rhendak in Aom-igh with her thoughts, but could not find him. I don't really understand it, but she said I should come talk to you."

Jemson turned to the two wizardesses. "I get the idea that this has to do with what you came to tell me about?"

Dylanna nodded. "As I said, there is much to tell, Your Majesty."

Jemson's face tightened and he raised his hand to his chin, then swiftly dropped it back down, letting his fingers play with the pommel of his sword instead. "I see."

"Who are these people?" Devrin asked suddenly.

"Forgive me," Jemson said. "Devrin, this is Dylanna and Leila, they are wizardesses from Aom-igh and dear friends of my uncle."

"Ah," Devrin replied, "pleased to meet you."

"You said that your dragon cannot contact anyone in Aom-igh?" Dylanna asked.

"That is correct. She is very concerned, and I am worried for her."

Dylanna crossed her arms. "This is the very reason we were sent to you. An ancient Enemy has risen from beyond the Nameless Isles and the safety of all Tellurae Aquaous is threatened. We received reports of his armies marching uncontested through Yochathain, Efoin-Ebedd, and Kallayohm."

Jemson's expression grew worried. "Tell me," he said.

Dylanna explained about how she and Leila had gotten trapped in the portal. Then she informed Jemson about how his uncle and the rest of the company had come to find them and told of their continuing quest to Emnolae in the search for Yorien's Hand.

"Then no one is safe," Jemson said. "And the seheowks are not really gone."

"The seheowks are the least of your worries, Majesty," Leila replied. "I have seen this enemy, he calls himself Ghrendourak. I have seen his plans for our world. The seheowks are the smallest and most insignificant of the were-folk that comprise his army. There are monsters that make dragons look small, creatures so warped and twisted that what they once were is impossible to even guess. His power is fell and terrible indeed, based on lies and hate and cruelty. He feeds on our vices and wields them as his weapons."

Jemson rose. "We must ready the men and warn our people. We do not seek war, but neither do we run from it." He turned and met Dylanna's steady gaze. "The two of you must speak with Shentallyia and see if you can discover what is happening in Aom-igh. Surely this enemy cannot have moved so quickly as to overwhelm our sister country in so short a time."

"I hope not, Sire." Dylanna replied gravely.

"Captain Devrin," Jemson said, "take the wizardesses to meet with Shentallyia. Perhaps their combined strength can reach the dragon king. We must unite our efforts to fight this threat."

He turned to the wizardesses. "Do what you can, and thank you for the warning, without which we would have no hope at all."

CHAPTER TWENTY

Though Oraeyn had been eager to set off towards the mountain right away, Ina and Colas had urged them to spend the night in their cabin first. In light of the lack of rest any of them had gotten the previous night, it had not taken much convincing. The next morning the travelers gathered once more in Ina's kitchen to eat. An air of peace permeated the cabin, surrounding them and easing their cares while bolstering their courage and determination.

Ina had food waiting on the table. As the travelers ate, they snuck glances at Brant, wondering how long he was planning on remaining. For the first time since departing Aom-igh they felt safe; however, they were also anxious to see the end of their journey.

Brant, however, did not appear to be in any kind of hurry to resume their quest. He sat at the table and ate slowly, savoring each bite. Oraeyn noticed him shooting furtive glances about the room. A while later, Brant got up and paced about, tilting his head and examining first the books on a desk and next the large shells that adorned a small shelf. When everyone else was finished eating, Ina busied herself washing the dishes and Kamarie helped.

The conversation of the previous evening between Brant

and Colas had paused because the travelers were exhausted, but Brant seemed eager to return to it now that they were rested and fed. The small company stayed silent for the most part.

Kiernan brooded in a chair that he had pushed back into a remote corner of the room. Oraeyn sat and listened, wondering when they were going to get back to their quest. The dragons eventually got up and stalked outside, edgy and restless. Ina and Kamarie finished the dishes and returned to the main part of the room. Ina sat, straight-backed and prim, next to her brother, but Kamarie remained standing.

"So what are you doing back here on Emnolae?" Brant asked Colas.

Colas shifted in his chair. "I stayed with the good captain for a long while. He was always like a father to me, and when he offered to take me aboard as part of his crew I jumped at the chance, though it nearly broke my heart to leave my mother and Ina behind. We sailed all over the named world and I saw more wonders than I ever could have dreamed. But Captain Delmar could not stay away from Emnolae forever, and after several years, we returned here.

"He came with every intention of marrying my mother and retiring from his life at sea. He had saved up quite a good sum of money, and he felt he had enough to offer her—enough to live comfortably anyway. But we were almost too late as it was. Mother was very ill when we returned, and Ina herself had a horrible fever. Mother had obviously been caring for Ina when she caught the fever herself and collapsed on the floor. Ina was so weak all she could manage was to drag herself out of bed and curl up on the floor next to our mother. How long they had been like that when we found them is anyone's guess. Ina doesn't remember, already the sickness had taken her sight and day and night blurred together for her in feverish dreams.

"We did everything we could, but Mother never recovered. The fever eventually broke, but it had done its damage. She was blind then too, and she could hardly breathe without pain. Ina had pulled through, and though she was weak we believed she would continue to improve. Mother drew her close and passed her legacy on, and then she begged Captain Delmar to take care of us. He agreed to do whatever she wished, all the while promising that she would get better soon, all the while knowing it was a lie. She was dying. He kept his promise though. We buried her out next to Father and Delmar stayed with us and raised us. He never went back to sea. He died four years ago, and it has just been Ina and me since then."

"How do you do it? All by yourselves way out here?" Kamarie asked.

"We get by," Colas said. "Neither one of us likes the bustle and busy mood of even small settlements. I've been in cities and don't care for them. Delmar took us into town once, but Ina received such a negative reaction that we never went back. The younger ones pointed and whispered that she was an evil that should have been destroyed rather than let live. The older ones hurried by like prolonged contact might contaminate them. The bolder ones threw rocks and hurled insults.

"She was just a child, and neither Delmar nor I could bear to see her tears. So, we grew our own food, made our own clothes, and if we ever needed anything, Delmar would go into town to get it for us."

Kamarie made a sympathetic noise and moved forward to take Ina's hand in her own. Ina leaned against Kamarie and murmured a comforting word in her ear. Then she straightened.

"I was stronger than my brother or Delmar believed," Ina said in a clear and steady voice. "Yes, I cried, but not for myself. They will never see as clearly as I do. I merely lost my eyesight; those who jeered at me had lost all their sight. Their insults stung, true, but more than that I pitied them their loss."

Kamarie stared at the woman. "How can you say such a thing? They were so awful to you."

"They hurt themselves more than they ever could have hurt me," Ina replied. "You have a gentle heart. Your young man is very lucky to have such a woman for his betrothed."

Kamarie blushed and peeked across the room at Oraeyn. She half hoped that he had not heard the comment because she did not want him to feel self-conscious or awkward. He did not look embarrassed by the woman's words.

"Yes, I know," he replied simply.

"And whatever happened to Dru?" Brant was asking. "Did he stay with Captain Delmar after they left Llycaelon?"

Colas laughed. "A real pirate, that one. Better seaman than most I've seen, but a thief through and through. He sailed with us for a time. I think he felt obligated to look after me, he knew it was what you would have wanted, but his only real loyalty was to you, Rhoyan... Brant, sorry. After a time he acquired a ship of his own..."

"You mean he stole it," Brant guffawed.

"Of course," Colas replied, his shoulders lifting in a hint of a shrug. "Then he gathered his own crew and left with Captain Delmar's somewhat dubious blessing. The last I heard the man was terrorizing the western seas. Anyway, I believe he's a wealthy old pirate now. He's not quite as noble as he'd like people to think, certainly he keeps a portion of that which he steals for himself and his crew, so he's probably living like a king on the high seas. He's more of a name to frighten children with than anything else these days. I haven't heard tell of any real attacks in several years. They probably pulled into an obscure port and retired once they were all rich enough."

"Captain Dru, the pirate. It sounds about right," Brant mused in a fond tone.

"Brant," Ina spoke up. "What are you here for? I know why you have come to Emnolae, but why did you come here, to this house? Surely you came here for more than a place to sleep and a meal. You had no idea we were still alive, let alone still residing here; what did you hope to gain by returning? Your quest is of great importance, time presses at you, and yet you linger, much to the perturbation of your friends, I might add. Why?"

"You truly have your mother's sight," Brant sighed. "Your mother had a key. She was a gatekeeper, in her own way. She not only kept the memories of Emnolae alive, but protected its greatest treasure as well. A long time ago, she trusted me with that treasure enough to aid a young boy in a foolish quest for the ignoble goal of glory and an exciting adventure. What she saw in that boy I'll never know or understand. But I had hoped she might trust me with the key once again, this time not for glory or honor, and not for myself at all, but rather to save Tellurae Aquaous from that which threatens to destroy us all. But since she is no longer among the living, I suppose we will just have to find another way into the mountain."

Ina shook her head, a sad, quiet look on her fine features. "No, you shall have what you seek. My mother passed her legacy to me, along with her memories and the treasures of Tellurae Aquaous she was bound to protect. Emnolae is the center, it always has been. Here High Kings have risen and fallen. If Yorien indeed existed and is more than merely a legend, then this is where he decided to place his gift, the one weapon he could grant against the evil that has threatened from the edges of the world throughout time. This is where the heart of our world beats, and I guard it. The key is mine to protect and to give."

"You have the key to the tunnel under the mountain? Your mother once trusted me with it, will you trust me once again?"

"You are a very different person than the impetuous boy who wandered into this house by accident so many years ago. Rhoyan came seeking glory and adventure, but Brant seeks healing and truth. I said then that Rhoyan would bring the healer, and he has, he has brought the new High King to Emnolae. Long ago my mother trusted Rhoyan with the past, now I shall trust Brant with the future," she reached into the pocket of her apron and then held out her hand, a simple, rusty key lay in her outstretched palm and she offered it to Brant. "Take it, Brant. May you find freedom for us all."

Brant clasped the woman's hand in his own for a moment. Then he bent down and kissed her forehead.

"Thank you," Brant said, his voice harsh with emotion.

"Safe travels to you, Wanderer," Ina whispered. "I know you will not stay a moment longer. You have what you sought, now go. The Enemy already creeps towards those you hold dear. Enter the Wylder Wood, and be not dismayed, for it counts you as a friend."

Brant nodded and looked at his companions. "Let's go."

Ina and Colas accompanied them outside, bidding them farewell and all speed on their journey. As they turned to leave, Ina reached out and grabbed a hold of Brant's shoulder, halting him mid-stride. She pulled him close and put her mouth by his ear, whispering so that none of the others could hear, Brant listened closely and after a moment she released him.

"Go with speed," Ina said loudly. Then she turned and walked confidently back into her house.

Brant rejoined the rest of the company and led them into the vast, tangled forest, following the same trail he had walked some forty years before. The path would take them to the ruined palace of the High Kings, and there was an excitement building in the small company. They had reached the last leg of their journey.

"What did Ina say to you before we left?" Oraeyn asked, falling into step beside Brant once they got a ways into the forest.

"What she told me was for my ears alone." At Oraeyn's crushed look, Brant laid a hand on the young man's shoulder. "Do not worry about it. She was simply reminding me to be on my guard and not to trust what seemed clear. She wanted to make sure I only trust in the truth I can be sure of—that is all."

Oraeyn accepted this though he could not help but continue wondering. He slowed and fell behind the warrior once more, walking beside Kamarie. They did not speak. As they ventured deeper into the forest the air grew thick and warm. A deep silence enveloped them the farther they went. Oraeyn took Kamarie's hand, glad of her presence in this gloomy place.

To Brant, however, the forest did not feel as oppressive as he remembered. Perhaps it could sense the urgency of their quest, or maybe it remembered him and how he had spoken with it so many years ago. Forty years would not have felt so long to the forest, Brant reflected. He could hear the whisper of restless wood nymphs; they knew something was amiss, but they left the travelers alone.

As they made their way along the trail and deeper into the forest the light diminished until it disappeared altogether. Kamarie clung to Oraeyn's hand as they stumbled along the path, squinting in the dim, murky light. It became hard to discern their way in the gloom. They were both having a difficult time keeping their footing, the sounds around them made it clear that the others were not doing so well either.

"Is this normal?" Oraeyn asked loudly.

"I don't remember it being quite like this," Brant's reply sounded like it was coming from a great distance away. "But then, that was a long time ago."

"It's impossible to tell where we're going," Kamarie called out.

"Make sure you stay on the path!" Brant's voice warned them.

"I can't even *see* the path," Oraeyn grumbled.

"We could have strayed from it a long time ago and never noticed," Kamarie said, her voice trembling.

Oraeyn raised his voice again, "Can't we light a torch or a lantern? Surely we brought one."

"We did," this time it was Kiernan's voice that answered. "I tried lighting one of the lanterns; it's no use, lad, the light won't pierce this murkiness. There's magic at work here, if not Ghrendourak's, then something very much like it. Be on your guard."

"I've lived underground," Rhimmell growled, "but this is intolerable!"

Thorayenak made a noise of agreement. Something about the dragons giving vent to their frustration made Oraeyn feel a bit better about his unease. He pulled Kamarie close, determined not to lose her. Doggedly he pushed on, placing one foot in front of the other with stolid resolution.

"Come on," he said. "Let's just keep moving. The path must end at some point."

"It's like being back inside that portal," Brant commented absently. "But without..." he trailed off, whatever he had been about to say was lost in Kamarie's sudden scream.

Oraeyn heard Kamarie scream even as he felt her nails dig into his arm. The sound that ripped its way out of her throat was one of pure terror and it pulled him to an abrupt halt. Oraeyn whirled about, drawing the Fang Blade to defend against the unknown attacker.

It took him a moment to ascertain what was happening, but as his eyes adjusted Oraeyn saw that Kamarie was struggling with an overgrown tree branch that had tangled itself in her long hair. He exhaled deeply in relief and helped her get herself untangled. He pulled her away from the branch and into a one-armed hug. She saw her attacker and her face flushed in embarrassment as she realized what it was that had frightened her so.

Desperate to put her at ease, Oraeyn glowered sternly at the tree branch. "You shouldn't do such things," he reprimanded. "I thought you knew better than that."

Kamarie chuckled. At her small laugh, Oraeyn pointed his sword at the branch and pretended to challenge it to a duel.

"On guard," he said grandly. The branch remained still and after a moment, Oraeyn straightened. "Aha! Chicken, are you? It's easy enough to grab a lady's hair but you won't stand up to a man with a real weapon? I see how it is! Well, I'll let you off with no more than a warning this time, but don't let it happen again!"

Kamarie laughed out loud and Oraeyn turned to her, his expression bright with affection. The others had rushed to converge upon their location at Kamarie's scream, but had stopped short and were watching in amazement as Oraeyn challenged the tree. Now it was Oraeyn's turn to feel foolish. He looked down at the ground, embarrassed to have been caught in such silliness. He started to put his sword away when Rhimmell stopped him with a word.

"Don't!"

Oraeyn paused. "What?"

"Don't sheathe your sword!" she commanded.

Oraeyn's expression grew mystified. "But why…?" Then he realized why everyone was staring at him in such amazement, and why he could see their expressions of wonder. He raised the Fang Blade higher, the wan light that emanated from it cast a glow over the entire company. The golden blade flickered with a glowing translucence like that of a million fireflies trapped within.

Brant stepped towards the young king. "You must lead us now," he said. "The sword will light our way."

"But you're the one who knows this wood and where we're going."

"You hold the golden blade from the prophecy, you must lead us. Do not worry about leading us astray, just make sure you stay on the path and we will be fine. This path only leads to one place."

Oraeyn nodded, but he was not at all encouraged by the turn of events. With a sigh, he stepped to the head of the company and hesitantly raised the Fang Blade. Its light flickered brighter, and he pointed it forward into whatever awaited them.

The light of the Fang Blade improved all of their spirits. Oraeyn welcomed the light, but his heart was heavy. As if she sensed his thoughts, Kamarie moved up to walk beside him and she slipped her hand into his.

"I don't want this," he murmured.

"I know. But it is what you have been given. We trust you to lead us truly."

"No, I don't mind leading the company," Oraeyn paused. "It's just I feel I should go on alone, and it scares me."

"You're not alone."

"I know," he stopped to gather his thoughts. "But soon, I may be."

"What do you mean?"

"I'm afraid for you," he admitted. "Back in Aom-igh, I had nightmares every night for months. I dreamed about this adventure. This place. I dreamed that you died here. Every night, this quest ended in your death, in Brant's death, in everyone's deaths. If I let you continue much farther..."

"You didn't tell me," Kamarie's voice was low. "I didn't know that was what your nightmares were about. Why didn't you tell me?"

"I didn't want to give them any attention. I thought they were just ordinary nightmares; I saw no reason to worry you about them. And besides, they were so horrible; I couldn't bear to speak of them. Besides, usually I couldn't even remember what they were about, except for the foreboding sense they left behind. But now... now that we are here they press down around me at every turn."

"They were just dreams," Kamarie reminded him. "They cannot touch you in the waking world."

"I know. But they felt so real. They just... they felt so real. They frightened me. They still do."

Deep in the forest, between the massive trees, a monstrous form glided in silence, malice dripping from its jaws and hatred stirring in its heart. The creature that stalked them was patient, waiting for its quarry to make a mistake. There was no thought behind its instincts. Its master had promised that there would be food soon, and so it had waited, spinning its gloom over the forest like a spider spins its web. It only knew the hunger, but still it waited. The glowing torch was deadly, the creature knew. But a mistake would be made, a mistake was always made, and so it waited patiently, hunting its prey, eager to feed upon the meal it had been promised.

CHAPTER
TWENTY-ONE

Justan sat like stone next to Rena's body. He had carried her back to the palace and laid her on a couch in one of the private chambers and he had not moved from her side since. Zara brought him food, but he hadn't touched it. The servants tried to remind him that he still had a duty to the people and to King Oraeyn, but he sent them away without listening. He had lost the will to live, and he was as unreachable as the woman over whom he kept vigil. Rena remained unconscious, her face light and peaceful. But Justan's grief consumed him and he could not find the strength to do anything more than watch over her.

"This cannot continue," Zara told Arnaud after returning from the palace several days later. "Oraeyn gave him a charge to take care of the kingdom, and Justan is the most capable person I can think of to carry out such a responsibility, but Rena's sacrifice is sapping his will to survive. Even Kitry has been neglected."

Arnaud rubbed his chin. "Have you spoken to Rhendak about this?"

"Rhendak has his own concerns. One of his own has gone missing and the shield is preventing him from contacting or locating her. Apparently the shield doesn't just keep everything out of Aom-igh, but it keeps us in as well. But I'm worried that

Justan is acting like we are invincible behind this shield. I know for certain that the shield cannot hold forever; Rena bought us time, and he is squandering it."

"What about the unicorns?" Arnaud asked. "Have you spoken to them?"

"What can they do?" Zara asked miserably.

"They are healers," Arnaud said.

"So?" Zara asked, her shoulders slumped with exhaustion.

"Well," Arnaud spread his hands in a meaningful gesture, "Rena helped heal the land. Perhaps the unicorns can be persuaded to establish a bond with her to bring her back. She's still here, she isn't dead. As I understand it, as long as the shield remains intact, she is still alive, which means there is still a connection between her body and her spirit, however tenuous."

"Perhaps the unicorns can strengthen that link," Zara finished his thought. "It could work, in theory."

"And if you can offer that theory as a ray of hope it might give Justan the boost he needs to snap out of this depression he's fallen into. The people will be warned, the troops will be placed, and Rena has a better chance of waking up when it's all over."

"Why didn't I think of that?"

"You would have thought of it sooner or later. Sometimes you just need a fresh perspective to come up with a new solution to an old problem."

"That sounds like my father talking," Zara accused.

"A wise man, your father. Go visit Kessella."

The unicorn's refuge was deep within the Aura Wood. The most wary and skittish of the myth-folk, unicorns preferred isolation. When they departed Krayghentaliss, the unicorns continued to keep to themselves hidden in the woodland regions. The forests were immense, mysterious, and tangled, and these beautiful, delicate creatures found safety in this untraveled wilderness. Their chief talent was that of healing, and while they did not seek patients, neither could they refuse to utilize their healing art if a need was presented.

Zara had befriended Kessella in a strange chance meeting, and the unicorn had taken a liking to the wizardess. Kessella found it intriguing that Zara had given up her life as a wizardess because she had fallen in love with a human. Their unlikely friendship had grown over the past two years and Kessella had begun to teach Zara about healing. The rest of the unicorns came to accept Zara's presence in their midst, mostly because they trusted Kessella's judgment. Though there was no hierarchy among the unicorns, Kessella's age and wisdom was highly respected.

Zara now made her way along the path into the *Ionell*. The trail was such that it would disappear behind her without a trace, leaving it impossible for anyone to track her. The unicorns had left nothing to chance when it came to concealing their home. Though she had visited many times, it always took Zara's breath away when she first stepped into their secret domain.

The *Ionell* was beyond description. Although the trail led straight to the deepest part of the wood, Zara emerged from the path into giant, rolling pastures of emerald grass that swayed peacefully in the wind. Unicorns frolicked and danced across the plains in front of them. Tall patches of grass hid foals, and shady copses of trees provided shelter in bad weather. A turquoise-blue stream ran through the plains and a great rock cliff rose up on the eastern edge of the realm. A veil of water cascaded down over the rocks, glittering like a bead curtain of diamonds.

Though not the strongest of the myth-folk, the unicorns were unique in their abilities. The dragons could permeate the land with their power, as they had done in the Harshlands, but the formation of the land itself remained unchanged. Wizards could create and sustain an incredible illusion as Calyssia had done in Pearl Cove. The unicorns did neither. Their magic was spun in such a way that they could create and alter the very fabric of the ground.

"It never gets old," Zara breathed. She often found it difficult to speak above a whisper in this place; any real sound might shatter the fragile picture into a thousand precious, tiny shards that could never be reassembled.

Zara stood still, waiting. She was allowed to find this place, but it would be rude to go further than the doorway without an escort. She did not wait long. Kessella had felt her presence and now the unicorn appeared, racing fluidly across the rolling hills to greet her.

Kessella was as black as an aethalon's armor, but her mane, tail, and horn were as white as the sands of Pearl Cove. Her coloring was unusual, even for a unicorn, but it cost her no respect, she was too strong and too wise for anyone to disrespect her for such a superficial distinction.

"Zara!" Kessella thundered up to the wizardess, her white mane flying behind her. "What brings you here today? More lessons?"

"No, Kessella, I have come to ask for your aid."

"What sort of aid do you require?"

"I'm sure you've heard of Rena," Zara began.

"The Song Bearer? Of course." Kessella raised her horn to the sky. "She's responsible for that."

"Yes. But I fear it came at too dear a cost," Zara said. Then she related to Kessella all that Rena had done to create the shield.

Kessella listened until Zara was through and then she bobbed her head. "You were right to come here. My people cannot ignore this cry for help. I shall return to the palace with you, but I must call council first and alert my people. Will you stay and tell them what you have told me?"

"Of course."

Kessella did not hesitate. "The council will want to hear your story. If a battle approaches many may need healing, which will require others of my race. Up on my back, dear friend. Time is precious."

Zara slipped onto the great back of the unicorn and Kessella took off towards the grove of trees where the council would be held. The unicorn lifted her great neck and trumpeted into the air, a long, loud, clear call that echoed throughout the *Ionell*. Every unicorn within its borders would find themselves compelled to answer.

"We must act now," Dylanna's voice was all business.

"Ghrendourak has wasted no time conquering our world, he must be stopped."

Shentallyia agreed. "There is no time to lose. Aom-igh could already have fallen, I should not have left."

Leila huffed in exasperation. "What could you have done? What could any one of us have done? At least you are safe and capable of helping from the outside if our country is under attack."

They were gathered together and had been discussing plans and options for two days, far too long already, at least in Dylanna's opinion.

Jemson sensed Dylanna's impatience and asked, "How do we defend against an enemy unseen? How do we attack when we have no idea where the battlefield is located? Leila, you tell us that this Ghrendourak leads an army of creatures that make the seheowks seem like puppies. You know yourself the close call we recently had with these same 'puppies.' This close call took all of our training, resources, and many of our best men, and even then the difference between victory and defeat was provided by Shentallyia—who is now departing with you for Aom-igh. Certainly you can see the desperate plight we face, and we will indeed face it, but we cannot race into battle with an enemy that cannot be found."

Dylanna sighed. "Of course, I see that as plainly as you."

A young Kestrel approached. "Sire, a dragon is waiting to speak with you in the Iron Wood." His voice trembled with excitement.

Jemson looked up from his plans, surprise flitting across his face. "Thank you, Nethua. I will be there directly."

The Kestrel nodded sharply, standing a bit taller as he left. Leila watched him, noticing that he stood a little straighter and walked with a more confident stride. That boy would never forget the moment when his king called him by name. She considered Jemson with new respect.

Jemson rose and gestured to his companions. "Please come with me. This sounds important."

They followed Jemson through the camp and, curiosity

peaked. It was a little distance to the tree line. When they reached the forest edge, the dragon moved out of the trees and into view, striding gracefully on his four strong legs, wings folded along his back. His neck arched up to his enormous, horned head. He was covered in scales of obsidian and his eyes were like two argenteous stones. He was the largest dragon either of the wizardesses had ever seen, and even Shentallyia reacted with awe, bowing her head in deference to this majestic creature who bore age and wisdom in every line of his body.

"Welcome," Jemson greeted the dragon. Dylanna was impressed that the young king's voice bore no hint of tremor.

"Are you King Jemson?" the dragon asked, his voice a thunderous growl.

Jemson nodded. "I am."

"I received your message. My name is Khoranaderek, and I am here to do my part in this battle."

"You are more than welcome," Jemson beamed. "I had hoped for a verbal response, but I never dreamed you would come here, much less prepared for battle. You, my new friend, are unbelievably welcome."

The dragon bared his teeth; they glinted like sharp rows of spears. "I was already on my way here when news of your message reached me," he said with a deep chuckle. "I came to bring you warning of an enemy that marches towards Llycaelon, but I believe the news has already reached you," he nodded to Dylanna. "Wizardess, you are known to me."

Dylanna bowed back, stunned.

"There are others," Khoranaderek continued. "And they bring with them survivors from many nations already left desolate by this foe. We know of the power that rises behind this Ghrendourak; he will not be ignored. I hoped to persuade you to welcome my people as allies, and shelter these survivors. They follow and will be arriving here soon."

"Others? You have brought others?" Jemson asked, and now his voice did tremble. Unashamed tears clouded his vision. Jemson turned to the others, each of whom was also suddenly misty-eyed. Their faces provided all the assurance Khoranaderek needed to make his long flight worthwhile. "Any refugees who have survived the destruction wrought by our common enemy are most welcome here," Jemson spoke around the lump in his throat.

"Excellent. I had hoped you might say that." Khoranaderek stretched his long neck up into the air, muscles rippling beneath his scaled armor. "Ah, but it is good to take this form again," he said, his teeth snapping as he worked his jaw. "You show wisdom, young king, in your decision to bring us back out into the open."

"Not everyone will think so," Jemson's voice was regretful.

"That is true," Khoranaderek replied. "But your open support of our people will make most of those think twice before they complain out loud. Yes, you show wisdom, especially in the friends you keep," he nodded towards the three women. "Yes," the dragon continued in a thoughtful tone, "I think I might like you, Jemson, king of Llycaelon."

"Justan," Zara's tone was no-nonsense as she entered the room where Rena lay, the room felt old and stale and Zara reeled back at the stench. It had only been a single day, but the darkened chamber reeked of sickness, death, and despair.

Justan looked up, his expression dull and vacant. He did not even acknowledge Zara's presence as he continued his vigil. Kessella knit her brows together. She had taken human form in order to navigate the stairs better and she remained in that form now. She appeared as an elderly woman—full of wisdom and experience—though her back was straight as an oak tree. Her hair was pure white, but there was a youth about her as well: her dark face was smooth and her hands were steady.

"I see what you mean," Kessella said, her tone grave.

She strode over to Justan. He did not look up at her approach. She spoke his name once, but he did not react. Then she reached out her hand and touched his chin, drawing his gaze gently away from Rena. At first he resisted, but then he gave up and looked at Kessella with impatience and a touch of anger.

"I'm sorry, do I know you?" he asked.

Kessella shook her head. "No, but I can help you anyway."

"I don't need help," Justan said. "It's my wife."

"I know. I'm a healer. Zara has told me about the situation and I have come to see what I can do."

For the first time in days Justan's face filled with life. "Is there hope?" His voice lost a bit of its toneless quality and his cheeks flushed with color.

"There is always hope. But you must choose to see it."

"I don't understand."

Kessella sighed. "I will try to help her. But you must do something for me if there is to be any chance of your wife returning to this side of wakefulness."

"I'll do anything," Justan said.

Kessella's tone was icy. "Do I have your word on that?"

"You do," he replied firmly.

"Good. The first thing you must do is open that window and let the outside air into this room, it's stifling in here. Even healthy patients would languish in such a place."

Justan obediently hurried to the window and flung it open. A cool breeze entered and Kessella took a deep breath. Zara felt a bit of the oppressiveness of the room fade and she relaxed slightly.

"That's much better," Kessella murmured. "Now, you must go down to the kitchen and get a bite to eat, and you must not return to this room until I send for you."

Justan's face darkened. "What? But..."

Kessella raised a stern hand. "You gave your word. If I cannot trust that, I will turn around and leave this place without ever looking back and you can attempt to bring your wife back on your own."

Justan clamped his mouth shut on the arguments he wished to make. With a glower at Kessella he turned and left the room. He muttered under his breath as he left, but he obeyed. Zara shut the door behind him.

"That was well done," she said.

Kessella nodded brusquely. "Yes, the healing process for that one has begun. You must go to him now. Speak to him, ask him questions. But make sure you don't tell him what to do," Kessella cautioned. "Just ask him questions—about the coming war, his duties, it doesn't matter, really. Even questions you don't know the answers to might help. His own curiosity will do the rest, and he will attend to his duties once more. I will stay here with the Song Bearer."

"Do you think you can help her?" Zara asked.

"I am unsure. Whether or not I can help her remains to be seen. She is very distant. It is hard to explain. It is like she is sleeping, or in a deep dream. I might be able to establish a link to her, maybe even communicate; I do not know. She isn't gone, you know, she's not even unconscious, she's just focusing all of her effort in one spot and has no energy to perform any other autonomous acts."

Zara nodded. "I know. I have formed such a shield before, it drained me as well, but not like this. Rena was right to avoid using the dragon pipes. I never should have asked it of her."

"You cannot blame yourself for doing what needed to be done. Who knows how many lives your actions may save. Rena sacrificed herself willingly, it was not your doing," Kessella said. "I will see what I can do for her. You must go to Justan. He will find himself somewhat at a loss, and you need to help him find balance."

"I will. Perhaps he will work so hard looking for answers that he might actually find them."

"That is what I hope for," Kessella said, her voice softening. "Go now, I will tend the Song Bearer."

From where she stood in her small kitchen, Ina turned her face towards the window. Golden rays of light bathed her skin. She stopped in the midst of her dishwashing and stretched her hands up to it. She was beautiful, innocent, standing there in the glow; younger too, resembling a child despite her forty odd years. She twirled around, arms flung wide, her face tilted upwards, an expression of beaming delight on her lips as she felt the warmth caressing her skin.

Colas sat across the room, whittling a piece of wood into what would soon become one of many carvings that he would take into town to sell, or perhaps use to trade with the occasional passing ship. It did not matter where he sold it; most people considered his work the best they had ever seen, and merchants paid him well for the trinkets.

He took his time as he carved, his body relaxed as the creativity in his fingers guided the knife across the little piece of wood. There was no hurry in his motions, no intensity in his concentration. The carving gradually took shape in his expert hands.

"It's a lovely day," Ina said, beaming with wonder and excitement, as if she had only just discovered that she was alive.

Colas paused in his work to look up at his sister. Every time he looked at her she surprised him again. He always expected to see an adult when he looked at her, but he doubted he would ever see anything but a little girl of five. And yet she was a woman, with their mother's gentle tone and her own wisdom and grace. It was a startling combination. She bore their mother's burden with such poise. The memories never dragged Ina down; she never struggled under their weight. Colas wished he had such a talent.

"Do you think Rhoyan and his friends have any chance of completing their quest and bringing all of this to an end?" Colas realized as he posed the question that he had no hope for it, himself. Suddenly he felt very old.

"Of course they have a chance," she replied, her tone indicating it should be the most obvious thing in the world. "There is always hope."

Colas sighed and turned his attention back to his carving, but his pose was no longer relaxed, and the knife felt clumsy in his hands. He grunted in frustration.

Ina walked to him and patted his head. "They have the minstrel with them. They will find their way."

Colas looked up at the window. "I hope so. I don't know much about what is going on, not as much as you do, I don't have the sight like you. But I know that we are all at risk. And I know that those seven travelers are our best and only hope for survival."

"Our best hope, yes. But not our only hope, never that."

"If you say so," Colas shrugged again. "But I don't see anyone else volunteering to save the world."

"If they fail, another else will rise up to carry their burden," Ina said.

"How can you be so sure?" Colas asked.

"I'm not." Ina's words were ominous, but her tone was carefree. "But I have faith in Cruithaor Elchiyl. He has a plan, and he will not let the world fall to this darkness."

Colas shrugged and shook his head with a sigh and returned to his whittling. When Ina spoke like this it was best to stick with the things he understood best, those he could touch and shape himself. Ina saw what could not be seen, and while Colas respected her gift, it also frightened him. The piece of wood began to take a shape under his skilled fingers, but Colas did not pay much attention. Carving was his gift—he had discovered it while passing long hours on Captain Delmar's ship. Oftentimes he had watched in fascination the wood-carving of a fellow sailor. One evening, the man had handed Colas a block of wood and a small knife, telling him to give it a try. The sailor only meant to be kind to a lonely boy, but something marvelous happened to Colas when he began to whittle away at the little wood block. It had practically formed itself in his hands, taking on a life of its own and turning into something beautiful. Ina called it magic, though others referred to it as skill or talent. Colas did not care which it was; the carvings made him happy, it was how he relaxed and found peace. Living on an isolated island was not always easy. It got lonesome in their little cabin. Storms and wild animals often threatened their tiny garden. And then there were the rumors about Ina that sometimes troubled them in the form of unwelcome visitors. Their trials were different than those of many, but that made them no less real.

"What are you making today?" Ina asked.

Colas shrugged. "I don't know yet."

It was his usual response. Colas rarely ever began a carving with a clear idea of what he wanted to make. The wood knew what it wanted to be, he often said, he just helped it along. Ina moved about the little house, cleaning and straightening. She went outside and picked a bouquet of the wildflowers that she had planted along the path, bringing them inside to decorate the table.

"Do they look pretty?" she asked.

Colas looked up. "Beautiful," he affirmed.

"Are you finished yet?"

"Almost."

Ina was always excited for him to finish a project. One of her favorite things was to take the carvings and try to guess what they were before he told her. When Colas finished this one he held up the piece of wood and stared, amazed and a little unnerved by the image he had made. Ina tilted her head, missing the sound of the knife scraping away at the wood.

"Are you finished?"

"Yes, it…" he swallowed hard, not quite sure what to say.

Ina held out her hand and Colas placed the figure in her outstretched palm. She traced the lines of the carving with her fingers, exploring it with a curious expression on her face. At length she shrugged and handed the carving back to Colas.

"I can't tell. What is it?"

"A mandolin," Colas murmured, "like the one the minstrel carried. My fingers must have remembered it. But there are tiny carvings all over it, a sword, a dragon, and a star."

Ina nodded, a look of wisdom clung to her face. Colas looked at her warily for a moment, but she did not speak.

"Ina, what does it mean?"

"And in the end, the fool will guide them all," Ina intoned.

She may have been responding to Colas' question, or she might have been reciting a line from an old story, Colas could not tell and her words did not answer any of his questions. But the look on her face was faraway, and she spoke in dulcet tones, her mind filled with memories that were not her own.

Justan was pacing the castle walls like a caged gryphon when Zara found him. She walked across his path and stood looking over the stone wall at the sea. Her face was calm; she appeared to take no notice of Justan at all. After a few minutes he came over to stand by the wizardess. He placed his arms on the top of the wall and leaned on them with a sigh.

"What should I be doing?" he asked as he joined her in staring out over the ocean.

"It always helps me find calm," Zara said, "coming out here and watching the waves roll in. I can't remember how many times I've stood here, feeling like the world was either about to crash down upon my shoulders or bestow upon me all my dreams. I was never quite sure which would be worse."

Justan turned, his expression anguished. "Zara, please, tell me what to do. Don't play wizardess games with me. I am without direction and I cannot abide it any longer."

Zara pursed her lips, her gaze pensive. "You need to look to the defense of Aom-igh," she said the words tentatively. "Our enemy will not be stopped by the shield for long. And we ought not be taken by surprise. It will not help Rena if she wakes to find our country in ashes. It would be a waste of her sacrifice."

Justan flushed and looked down in sudden shame. "You are right. I forgot my responsibilities in my despair. There is no excuse for that; the world is bigger than me, and I was left in a position of authority. King Oraeyn trusted me to serve the people, and I forgot about them in my grief."

"But you have remembered them now," Zara reminded him softly. "And it is not wrong for you to grieve over your loss."

"I will not forget again," Justan's voice was determined, although sorrow still clung to his words.

Zara looked at the knight with compassion, his heart was breaking, yet at last he was standing strong in the face of it. "Yes, King Oraeyn knew what he was doing when he left you in charge."

"Zara?"

"Yes?"

"Do you believe Kessella can help Rena?"

"She has determined to try," Zara replied, "and that is all we can ask for now. She will not give up if that is your question."

Justan's mouth twisted, but he did not speak. He turned and left Zara standing at the castle wall by herself. She watched after him for a moment, noting how the strength had returned to his stride. He had been reminded of his duty and his mission was now clear. Justan had returned to himself. Zara hoped that Rena could be persuaded to return as well. She stood there for a moment by herself, staring out at the sea. A moment later, Arnaud joined her. He came up behind her and slipped his arms around her waist, resting his chin on the top of her head.

"I remember standing here with the weight of the crown pressing down upon me so hard that I thought I might as well just sink to the ground and give up, and there are days it is still a wonder to me that I did not," his voice was soft and full of many things he did not say, but Zara understood.

She leaned back against her husband. "You never did," she watched the birds wheeling above the sea, contentment on her face.

"How is he?" Arnaud nodded in the direction Justan had gone.

"He mourns still, but he is returned to his duties," Zara's voice faltered. "We are asking so much of him."

Arnaud fell silent, knowing that Zara meant more than just Justan. Their thoughts were ever with Oraeyn and their daughter, far beyond their reach. Arnaud kissed her hair.

"They will be fine."

Zara turned a little and craned her neck to look up into her husband's face, seeking comfort in his strength. "I am so scared," she admitted. "I honestly do not know if I believe there is any hope for us in this coming war, and yet I am the one who keeps reassuring everyone else that there is." Tears blurred her vision, threatening to spill down her face. "I don't know if I can do this any longer. I don't know if I can pretend to be this strong."

Arnaud squeezed his arms around her a bit more tightly.

"You are the strongest, bravest, most caring person I know. If anyone can lift the spirits of the entire country, it is you. But you do not have to do it alone. And you do not have to always be the one extending hope to others. I am here. I believe there is hope, I believe that Oraeyn will succeed. We stood against the invasion from Llycaelon and triumphed. We welcomed the myth-folk back into our realm when the very prospect of such creatures terrified most of our countrymen, and yet we have prospered and lived peacefully side-by-side with dragons and gryphons for three years. We will overcome this newest challenge as well. And we will do it as we ever have: together."

Zara buried her face in Arnaud's chest and he wrapped her in a strong embrace. "What would I do without you?" she whispered.

"Come home," Arnaud said. "You've done enough for today, as have I."

Zara turned and allowed herself to be led away from the wall.

TWENTY-TWO

The creature that stalked the company through the Wylder Wood struck just after Toreth-set during Kamarie's watch. As she stood, straining her senses in the inky gloom, she felt a light movement of air on her cheek. Without questioning her instincts, Kamarie flung herself to the ground and rolled to one side. Her quick movement saved her life. A shadow passed overhead, but what it was she could not guess.

Brant was awake and crouched next to her, blade drawn, before Kamarie could even raise her voice to sound the warning. He looked down at her. She could barely make out the shape of his face.

"Did you see it?" he hissed.

"I can't see anything," Kamarie whispered through clenched teeth, trying to prevent her voice from shaking, "but I definitely felt a menacing presence a moment ago. I felt the air move as it passed overhead."

She rose to her knee. Her sword drawn and nerves taut she peered into the surrounding trees. She strained her senses to their limits, attempting to determine from which direction the creature would attack next. She whistled a warning that woke the others. Oraeyn was next to her in an instant.

"What is it?" he asked.

"Something's out there," Kamarie responded. "I didn't see it, but I could feel it."

Oraeyn drew the Fang Blade and held it up and ready. The sword gave off its dim glow, once more lighting the surrounding area.

The company formed a protective circle, backs to each other as they faced outwards, waiting for the creature to attack again.

Swiftly, silently, a huge creature lunged out of the woods at Yole. Quicker than thought, Yole changed into his true form. The creature swerved in midair, avoiding the dragon but crashing into Kiernan Kane. Yole's great jaws snapped together on one of the creature's legs. It screamed in pain, a hideous sound that echoed through the forest.

Kamarie caught a glimpse of a sinuous body, skeletal wings, and a spiked tail, and then darkness like an extra, unnecessary blanket spewed out from the creature as it wrenched its way free. They could hear it tearing its way through the trees into the darkness it had created.

"What *was* that?" Kamarie asked, her voice shaky and filled with disgust.

"I believe it is a whyvren," Brant said. "I have heard of them, although I've never met anyone who has actually encountered one. I do not believe we have seen the last of it."

Rhimmell nodded. "Dragon lore tells much of these creatures. It will stay with the hunt until death. Ours or his: that is the way of the whyvren."

Kamarie shuddered.

"Well, there's no sleeping now. We might as well push on for a few more hours," Brant said. "Best if we are all alert the next time the creature strikes."

The others agreed with that sentiment, and they quickly struck camp and began following the trail once more. Oraeyn kept the Fang Blade out until at long last dawn pierced through the canopy overhead. But even then there was a gray haze that covered everything it touched.

Travel was slow, their movements stiff and tired. Doggedly, they trudged on, allowing Brant to lead the way.

The whyvren attacked again near the middle of the day. The creature pulled Rhimmell down from behind, its claws and teeth sinking deep into her unprotected back. Its tail lashed, striking her several times with its stinger. The dragoness was at the back of the company, and she fell with a cry of surprise and pain. She did not have time to shape shift, the attack was so sudden, so silent, so brutal. Thorayenak heard Rhimmell's cry. He was upon the creature in an instant, hacking at its legs with his sword. In the immediacy of Rhimmell's need, he did not have time to shape shift either, confident in his abilities no matter what form he took.

Oraeyn raced into the fight, striking at the whyvren with his sword. The blade flashed in the gloom and the whyvren hissed in pain, recoiling from the Fang Blade.

Kamarie took a running step but found her progress halted by an iron hand on her shoulder.

"Stay back," Brant's voice shouted in her ear as he passed, pushing her away from the whyvren even as he raced toward the battle.

The others joined the fight as well, but even with Thorayenak's battle rage they were no match for the mighty creature.

The whyvren was much larger than they remembered from the night before. It was the size of a full-grown dragon and it fought with deadly ferocity.

It wrapped its front claw around Oraeyn, pinning him down and striking with its stinger. Oraeyn managed to block the blow with the Fang Blade. Brant leaped to his aid, sword flashing as he swung it with all his strength. The whyvren shrieked in pain as the sword cleaved through its tail, but the creature did not release Oraeyn. It snarled and pressed its claw down, crushing Oraeyn beneath its weight. Oraeyn gasped and scrabbled at the enormous talons, but he could not free himself, and the pressure on his chest was making it difficult to breathe.

"Kiernan!" Brant called out. "To me!"

Together, the two men attacked from opposite sides of the monster. What was left of the whyvren's tail lashed at Brant, but the warrior ducked and rolled beneath the creature's belly, driving his sword deep into its abdomen, then wrenching it free and scrambling out of reach. The whyvren screamed, more from anger than injury, and released Oraeyn to focus its malice on this new attacker. Oraeyn rolled away and pushed himself to his feet. He retrieved the Fang Blade and retreated a few paces to catch his breath.

Thoraeynak, now in dragon form, flew at the enemy in a furious assault. Fire streamed from his mouth, but the whyvren did not even flinch. It rose up and batted the dragon from the sky, knocking him into the trees where he lay stunned. Then it focused its gaze once more upon Brant.

"The Fang Blade is our best chance against this creature!" Kiernan's voice rose above the battle.

The whyvren made a swipe at Brant, but the warrior leaped out of the way. Then Yole charged at the creature from the other side with a mighty roar. As the whyvren lunged toward's Brant, the warrior dove between its legs. Using the monster's lunge, Yole crashed into the whyvren from behind, bowling it over with the force of a mighty oak falling to the woodcutter's axe.

Kiernan drove his sword into the fallen creature's neck and Brant's sword joined it. The whyvren flailed and gasped, gurgling its defiant cry.

"Oraeyn, now!" they both cried.

Oraeyn was at their side in an instant and he plunged the Fang Blade into the heart of the whyvren. As quickly as it had begun, the struggle was ended.

Kamarie shuddered as they saw the creature clearly for the first time. Even dead, the beast radiated a malevolent hatred that Kamarie found unnerving. Its twisted features made a mockery of the partial life it had contained.

"Is it one of Ghrendourak's?" Kamarie asked.

Kiernan Kane nodded. "Without a doubt."

"Rhimmell!" Kamarie cried, remembering the dragoness.

The company rushed to Rhimmell's side. Thorayenak was already there, crouching close to her head. Rhimmell, in full dragon form now, lay motionless where she had fallen in pools of dragon blood that had scorched the ground with their heat. Thorayenak lowered his great muzzle to her face.

"Will… will she be ok?" Kamarie was afraid to ask.

Thorayenak shook his head and golden tears poured down the scales of his face, hissing and steaming as they dripped to the ground. "The whyvren's bite is poison," he whispered brokenly. "Rhimmell is dead." He arched his neck and roared into the sky, his voice filled with grief and fury. Then he bowed his great, horned head. "Rest easy, dear friend."

Kamarie voice was strangled as she reached out a gentle hand. She felt the enormity of the dragon's grief wash over her. "I'm sorry," she whispered. "She will be sorely missed."

"That she will," Thorayenak breathed sorrowfully. "That she will."

Aom-igh was visible in the distance and Dylanna was relieved to see that all appeared to be quiet. There were no great forces amassing on the borders, and the land appeared greener and brighter and more alive than it had before her imprisonment. They flew towards it, the landmass growing clearer with every beat of the dragon's great wings. Shentallyia sighed, echoing the relief that Dylanna was experiencing.

"All looks well," the dragoness commented.

"Yes. I only hope that everything within the borders is as peaceful as it appears. We need to speak with Zara, Justan, and Rhendak as soon as we can. Let's get to the palace as quickly as possible."

Shentallyia made a noise of agreement and flew directly towards the castle which was growing larger by the second. Soon they could make out the city and its buildings. Dylanna felt anticipation rising up within her as they came nearer the border. About a hundred feet from the shore, Shentallyia veered sharply and wheeled away. She turned back and faced Aom-igh but did not attempt to approach again.

"What's wrong?" Dylanna asked, fighting a rising trepidation.

"I can't go any farther," Shentallyia replied, her voice

frustrated.

"Why not?"

"I'm not sure. I'm trying to figure that out."

Dylanna waited, confident of the dragon's ability to determine what was wrong. After a moment Shentallyia shook her head. Dylanna could feel the dragoness reaching out again, and she thought that perhaps her first attempt had not satisfied her. At length, Shentallyia let out an exasperated breath.

"Well?"

"I know what it is," Shentallyia said. "I just don't understand how it came to be here. There's a shield about the border, it stretches up like a dome over the entire land. I've never seen anything like it before."

"Well, I suppose that's our answer as to why we cannot communicate with King Rhendak," Dylanna mused. "Is there no way to get through it?"

"Not without attacking it, though I do not think that the barrier was put up to keep *us* out. We need not worry about warning those inside, it is obvious that they are already preparing to face Ghrendourak."

Dylanna put her hands on her hips. "I still need to communicate with my sister, but I doubt the barrier will be any easier to pierce here than it was from Llycaelon."

"No, it is even more forbidding now that we are closer. What should we do?"

"Well, we could return to Llycaelon and help King Jemson."

"You believe that is the wrong choice?" Shentallyia asked.

"We have information that could tip the course of the coming battle in our favor. I cannot abide the thought of leaving without completing our mission," Dylanna replied. "I worry for our people, I wish I had some way to warn them."

"The caves!"

"What?"

"If I dive into the ocean, how long can you hold your breath?"

"My mother was one of the merfolk. I can breathe under water as easily as above, but what does that have to do with anything?"

"There are underground entrances into Aom-igh through the caves near the palace shoreline," Shentallyia explained. "They used to serve as an entrance into Krayghentaliss. The shield may not cover those entrances."

"It's worth a try. If it works then we will have to warn Justan about them. If we can get in that way, then the enemy can as well."

Shentallyia nodded her head in agreement. "Hang on!" she cried as she plunged down into the deep, blue waters of the ocean.

"Zara!" Dylanna entered the palace with all of her usual no-nonsense air about her.

"Dylanna!" Zara's face showed mix relief and wonderment. "What happened to you? Where have you been? Where is Leila? How did you..." she paused and took in Dylanna's bedraggled appearance. "Why are you soaking wet?"

"Slow down, Sister," Dylanna said, her voice calm and patient. "There will be plenty of time for stories later, and I promise that I will explain everything, but right now we must speak of more important things. Tell me what has transpired here."

Zara's face sobered. "Much as happened. But first, explain how you circumvented the barrier." Her face paled. "Did anyone see how you got in? Were you followed?"

Dylanna put up a reassuring hand. "The Enemy has not yet reached our shores. We did not lead them inside the barrier, but that is something we need to discuss. The shield only touches the water around Aom-igh, and it does not go all the way down to the ocean floor. We were able to come in through the caves."

"We?" Zara noticed Shentallyia. "Who is this?"

"This is Shentallyia," Dylanna explained, "she left before the barrier went up, because she heard the call of her *ward*."

Zara leaned forward as she caught the full meaning of her sister's words. She shot a sharp, questioning glance at Dylanna who nodded. When Zara looked back at Shentallyia it was with new respect.

"A dragon ward walks the land once more," Zara murmured, her tone filled with awe. "You must be anxious to get back."

Shentallyia bowed her head. "I am first and foremost loyal to Aom-igh and to King Oraeyn."

Zara gave a vexed little shake of her head. "No, you're not, and you shouldn't be. You are first and foremost loyal to your ward. Your bond is unique to this world and transcends most others."

Shentallyia breathed a sigh and stood taller. "If that is the case, my lady, I must admit I am eager to get back to Devrin."

"Go then," Zara replied. "Your greatest service to Aom-igh will be in concert with your ward. The great histories of Tellurae Aquaous shone brightest when dragons and their wards patrolled the skies. May our shared histories be so once more."

When Shentallyia had gone, Dylanna turned back to her sister, her expression sober. "Now, tell me the situation here."

The savage werehawk circled high overhead, its shadow sweeping across the ground far below. Ghrendourak stood on a cliff overlooking his legions of were-folk. Tens of thousands of them filled the valleys of Quenmoire. Had Ghrendourak's face been visible beneath his hood, he might have been smiling. His troops stamped and bellowed until he raised a great, armored hand and all fell silent.

"Today we begin our final conquest," his voice thundered down into the valley, filling the silence, "many have fallen to our dominion, but there are two kingdoms that yet resist our mastery with feeble attempts to stand before us in defiance. Their efforts are pitiable, and yet their brazenness must be punished. They will be brought to know the error of their ways."

The swarming horde shrieked their agreement. Ominous clouds filled the blue sky, echoing the werehawk's bone-chilling scream.

"They will not fall easily," Ghrendourak said, when his

armies once again fell silent. "They stand strong, and they stand united in purpose. But they also stand alone, separated by an ocean. We attack both tonight. We will catch them off guard, and we will crush them into submission. We will feed on their nightmares! We will feast on their pain. Come my armies! Come my children! Come my whyvrens, I have need of your talents. You must spin a web tonight, the like of which has never before been seen by mortal men! Come, follow me and together we shall rule all. The darkness we create will be such that the great light above shall never again shine in this land!"

The armies roared at this, and the werehawk shrieked in triumph. Ghrendourak made a quiet signal, and the creature swept down and allowed its master to step onto its back. They soared up into the sky and the were-folk on the ground began their march.

"It begins," Kiernan's voice was heavy, his face turned to the north-west.

Oraeyn laid his stone upon Rhimmell's cairn and peered up at the minstrel, wiping sweat from his brow. "What begins?"

"The great war," Kiernan Kane answered. "Our enemies have begun their assault."

"How can you tell?" Oraeyn asked.

"I cannot explain in any way you would understand. But I know it to my very bones, our enemy begins his attack this day."

The world paused around them. Oraeyn heard a rushing sound in his ears like that of a great waterfall. The moment he had been dreading was upon them. *Now!* His thoughts exploded inside his head. *Leave now, before you get them all killed!* He pushed the thought aside. Brant still held Ina's key, without it and Brant's directions he would never find Yorien's Hand on his own.

"How will it end, Kiernan?" Kamarie asked, breaking the silence.

Night drew close and the travelers were exhausted: physically by their battle with the whyvren, and emotionally by the loss of their companion. It was strange, Oraeyn thought, that they were not more eager to leave the ominous forest path. But then, it was the whyvren who had tried to kill them, not the forest itself. Besides, Brant believed that they need not fear the woods, and he had traveled here before.

"How will it end?" Kiernan's face was filled with sorrow. "With death and blood and tears, the way that wars always end, king's daughter."

"Do you think it is wrong to fight, then?" Brant asked.

Kiernan shook his head. "I did not say that. Sometimes those deaths and tears are needed to wash us clean, but that does not make it any more pleasant."

Oraeyn felt himself nodding. He stared back at the path they had travelled and wondered how he had gotten to this spot. He remembered the day King Arnaud had charged him with protecting Princess Kamarie on her journey to Peak's Shadow. It had been just another day. How differently things might have turned out if another had taken his place back then. Oraeyn wrapped his arms around himself. The air was not cool, but he shivered anyway.

"Brant, do you think we will encounter any more of those whyvrens?" Kamarie asked.

Brant nodded solemnly. "I would assume so, but let us hope we have not alerted them to our presence. Come, let us continue a little ways. We can rest soon, though I think none of us will sleep well this night, weary as we may be."

They left their sorrowful work at the cairn with a few murmured words of farewell. Thorayenak and Yole lingered a few moments after the others had gone. The air of Emnolae was cool and filled with mist and gray clouds. As the small company continued wearily down the path Rhimmell's face floated in Yole's memories, haunting him as he trudged through the never-ending forest. She had not spoken much, but when she did her words had been sharp and keen. She had a way of getting at the heart of things and making him re-evaluate his stance and choices.

He hadn't known her very well though he felt a kinship with her because of their shared journey. His mind reeled in shock regarding recent events. Rhimmell had been a dragon. How could she be gone? How could any creature kill a dragon so effortlessly? Since discovering his true heritage, Yole had begun to believe himself invulnerable. Surely, as the largest and most powerful of the myth-folk, dragons were invincible?

He had spent so much of his life alone and afraid, a lost little boy. The revelation of his birthright changed everything, at first. But lately he had been feeling a little lost again. He did not fit in either world. His human friends had their duties and responsibilities, and the dragons were occupied with restoring their place in Aom-igh. In dragon terms, Yole was still a youngling which might have been fine, except that there were very few other younglings for him to befriend other than the hatchlings that had been born since the dragons moved above-realm, but they were just babies.

Thorayenak had taken Yole under his wing and filled a gaping void in the young dragon's heart. And it was because of Yole that Thorayenak's friend was now dead. If he hadn't asked them to come on this quest, Rhimmell might still be alive.

He wanted to speak to Thorayenak, apologize, but he did not know what to say. Thorayenak's obvious grief pierced Yole through the heart. He trailed along, listless and sorrowful, wishing there was something he could say to make it better, knowing that he never could.

"I barely knew her," Yole whispered brokenly, falling into step with the older dragon. "But she came on this mission because I asked her to. She offered me counsel when I needed it. It's my fault she's dead."

"It is not your fault," Thorayenak replied. "She comprehended the risks as well as we. She had her own reasons for joining the quest. You cannot blame yourself."

"Thorayenak?"

"Yes, Youngling?"

"I have seen death and cruelty before. And I have faced foes who wished to kill me and my friends. But this is the first time I've ever been truly afraid."

"There is no shame in that," Thorayenak said, his voice kind.

"I would be worried if you were not afraid."

Yole nodded, and they turned to follow the others. The older dragon turned his head to the side.

"Have I ever told you about my daughter?" he asked, a strange quality in his tone.

"No," Yole replied, startled.

"My mate and I had one hatchling," Thorayenak continued walking and Yole jogged a bit to keep up with the other dragon's much longer strides. They were both in human form for ease of travel, though they were alert for any danger that might require the use of their true forms. "It is unusual for dragons to produce only a single offspring, but we had Elenika fifty years before our kind descended into Krayghentaliss. We did not as yet know how being underground would affect our population growth, and thus did not understand how precious every hatchling was." Thorayenak heaved a deep sigh. "When King Graldon decided that we should retreat into hiding, my Elenika and a handful of other younglings determined to stay above-realm in human forms. They were barely old enough to make the decision, but it was agreed that we should let them follow their own course. They had to promise to remain in human form and never tell anyone of their true natures. We assured them that the doors of Krayghentaliss would always be open to them if they wished to come home, but made it clear that if they ever did change their minds and return, there could be no going back.

"So, we left her behind, our Elenika. The light of our lives, the love of our hearts, she stayed behind and became one of the Lost. My mate and I never saw her again, the only hatchling we would ever know."

Yole felt a burst of sympathy for this dragon who had mentored him the past three years. "I am sorry," he said.

Thorayenak turned to him. "Do you know why I am telling you this now?"

Yole shook his head.

"You remind me of my Elenika," Thorayenak rumbled softly. "In many ways, you resemble her."

Yole wasn't sure how to respond to this revelation.

"I do not know if anyone has told you this, Yole. But you are very odd. For instance, your eyes do not hold the same power over other creatures that most dragons possess. In many ways, they almost seem... human," Thorayenak paused. "I do not tell you this as a slight or to make you feel uncomfortable. I do it to explain to you why you were so completely unaware of your heritage all those years. I believe you are half-human. You must understand, such a thing is unheard of, which means that if my theory is correct, you are completely unique. Beyond that, though I have no proof, I choose to believe you might be the son of my dear Elenika."

Yole stopped walking, his mouth agape at this unexpected information. A wellspring of emotions burst to life in his chest like a volcanic eruption. He was too overwhelmed to form words. He had been alone and confused for his entire life. The concept of friendship had been foreign to him until he had met Kamarie and Oraeyn, and though he felt included in their warm circle of friends, the possibility of family had never crossed his mind. Family was an idea other people got to experience and enjoy, but never Yole.

Fiery heat pressed behind his nose and Yole shook his head, terrified at this unexpected sensation. Thorayenak put a hand on his shoulder. It was a strange gesture for a dragon, but Yole found it comforting.

"I know it is a great deal to comprehend all at once," Thorayenak said. "I should have told you a long time ago. But I did not want you to feel obligated in any way. You did not know me, and I did not wish to force a relationship. You have been independent for so long, I believed that learning of a possible family connection might make you feel stifled."

"Family is all I've ever wanted!" Yole burst out. "I never dreamed it was even possible."

Thorayenak nodded. "Forgive me. I knew you had grown up amongst humans, and I guessed at your heritage long ago, but I did not understand how much of a difference that would make in the way you see the world. I wanted to tell you, but I hesitated because I was only thinking like a dragon."

Yole looked up, tears filling his vision. "Did you only offer to mentor me because you felt an obligation to do so? I have learned much from you, but there is so much about the Kin I still do not fathom. What is family to a dragon? You have not taught me this."

"Family is precious," Thorayenak assured him. "We guard it fiercely. To answer your question: in many ways, yes. I did put myself forth as your guide because of the resemblance you bore to my Elenika. But it was not that I felt an obligation or a sense of duty towards you, but rather a ferocious hope that the resemblance was more than just strange coincidence. Then, as I grew to know you, I began to wish you were part of my brood for your own sake, and not just because I was clinging to memories of my lost daughter. I tell you all of this now, because I understand I erred in not informing you before, and because I have become convinced that my first intuition about your relationship to me is, in fact, correct. But whether or not you are my true blood, young Yole, you have become as dear to me as a son."

Yole's head spun, and his heart overflowed with more emotions than he could name. His throat felt tight, and a pressure in his chest threatened to overwhelm him. "And I regard you as the father I never knew," he spoke past the lump in his throat.

Thorayenak squeezed Yole's shoulder, and the two dragons hastened their steps to keep up with the rest of their companions. There were no more words between them for the moment: none were needed.

The horn of the tower guard sounded as evening fell over Aom-igh. Arnaud and the wizardesses joined Justan on the wall and together they peered out into the unnatural darkness that had come too early for nightfall. Together, Zara and Dylanna wove a light that barely penetrated the gloom, but its feeble beam did help them see what was happening below. The myth-folk were gathering outside the castle walls, and the knights of the realm were forming ranks, with the grizzled knight, Garen, at their head. Members of Kamarie's Order of the Shield were taking their places about the castle wall itself, their duty purely defensive but no less important than those who would be in the front lines. And out beyond the border a mass of fell creatures approached. Their pace was unhurried, but they advanced steadily, creeping towards Aom-igh. The enemy had no ships, but the water proved no difficulty to them at all. No numbers could be estimated yet, but what could be seen promised overwhelming odds.

"Will the barrier hold?" Dylanna asked.

"It will hold for a while," Zara replied, her voice tight. "My concern is: what will happen when it falls?"

"Do they attack only us tonight?" Dylanna wondered out loud. "Or have they divided their forces, attacking Llycaelon as well? There was no army advancing on their shores when I left."

"It would be too great a burden upon our shoulders to believe this is only half of Ghrendourak's army," Arnaud said. "But either way, the time is past for looking to Llycaelon for help. If we had been able to communicate with King Jemson sooner, perhaps the aethalons could have come to our aid, but as it stands, the distance now is too great. There will be no hammer coming to crush the enemy against our anvil."

Justan straightened. "This battle is ours to be fought and won. If standing together with Llycaelon was indeed the wiser course of action, it is not a course available to us. Our men must be made aware that this is our stand, our challenge to win or lose. Arnaud, will you come with me to speak to the knights? They will be heartened to see their former king in the absence of their current one. Your added presence may well give them the courage they need to purchase the time King Oraeyn requires to succeed in his quest."

Arnaud nodded. "I will be proud to walk and fight at your side, Sir Justan. Our sole hope for victory lies with Oraeyn's quest. Our part is to defend Aom-igh. We must hold this line until he succeeds."

"And if he doesn't?" Justan did not want to ask the question, but it sprang unbidden to his lips.

"Then weep for the world we knew," Arnaud said. "For this will be its final chapter."

Justan had no response for such bleak words. Together, they strode down to the courtyard where the knights of the realm had assembled. It was a time for grand speeches full of honor and glory. It was a time for cheers and a rallying, clarion call to arms. But Justan could not stomach the idea of speaking lies to these brave men. Instead he went to tell his men that they could not expect any help, that they must stand alone, and that if they lost, dawn may never return for free men. All he had were cold, joyless words for men facing a hopeless situation, but all Justan could do was tell them the truth and hope the courage that had won them their shields did not shatter in its icy blast.

King Jemson had done all he could to prepare Llycaelon for the attack, and although confident in his own abilities and the courage of his countrymen, he still wished fervently that it was his uncle leading them instead. But Brant had a different duty. The hope of Llycaelon might rest with Jemson, but the hope of all Tellurae Aquaous rested on Oraeyn's shoulders and that meant Oraeyn had more need of Llycaelon's greatest warrior than Jemson. He realized the weight Oraeyn carried must be immense, but a part of him was still envious of Oraeyn's position.

"Sire," Devrin's voice broke into Jemson's concentration.

Jemson turned. "Yes?"

"Shentallyia has returned, I thought you might want to hear of what she discovered in our brother country."

Jemson liked the term. Whispers of it had started shortly after what the Border Patrol was calling the "first flight of the dragon ward," when Shentallyia and Devrin had secured the defeat of their seheowk enemies. Aom-igh truly was their brother country now. The link began with Brant, but now that one of Llycaelon's soldiers was ward to one of Aom-igh's dragons, there was no doubt as to the ties that bound the two lands together.

"You thought correctly," Jemson replied. "Where is she?"

As Devrin led the way, Jemson thought back. Was it only days ago they had essentially been enemies? It seemed years. In an incredibly short time, Devrin had become one of his most trusted soldiers, Captain of the King's Helm, the King's Champion, as it were. The Helm did not yet exist, of course, since Jemson had only just reinstated them a few days ago. But Jemson was glad Devrin was now an ally, nonetheless.

When they reached Shentallyia, the dragon quickly explained the barrier that had been forged around Aom-igh. "They know it cannot endure a prolonged assault. Their primary hope is that it may buy time for Oraeyn."

"Buying time for Oraeyn seems to be the only option remaining for Tellurae Aquaous," Jemson said after hearing all that Shentallyia had to report. "Aom-igh has a shield, and Llycaelon has a dragon and her ward, not to mention the dragons Khoranaderek says are on their way here to assist us in the defense of our nation. Who can say which will be most effective? At any rate, it is our only hope."

"So it would seem, Sire," Shentallyia said. "But there may be one other hope as well. I do not believe the Song Bearer sleeps. The barrier itself may become a weapon before this war is ended."

"The Song Bearer?" Devrin asked.

Shentallyia explained, "One woman created the barrier by playing music on a set of shepherd's pipes that the dragons crafted centuries ago. A High King of Tellurae Aquaous once came to the dragons and asked for aid in a time of great peril. The pipes were fashioned and presented to the king with the warning that he must not play the pipes himself, but was charged with finding the one to whom they belonged. That person alone would awaken their power."

"What happened?" Jemson was intrigued.

"In his search, the High King stumbled across a young woman, nameless and homeless. He took pity on her, caring for her as a daughter. He asked her name and she told him that she had none, or none that she could remember. This was a mystery to the king, who lived in a world that still comprehended the power of names. So he asked her what he should call her and she replied, 'You may call me Song.'

"The High King wept for joy, because he knew he had found the one who would help him in his quest. He brought the woman to his household where she was cared for and restored to health. Then he asked her to play the dragon pipes. She played them and the enemy that threatened their world fell before the power that was unleashed in the music."

There was a pause. "But what happened to the woman?" Devrin asked.

"I do not know," Shentallyia replied. "There is no more mention of her in the histories, though some believe there was a flaw in the design of the relic, and that though Song won the battle, she did not survive to see its outcome."

"And you say that Rena now lies at the edge of death," Jemson said. "Let us hope the legend about Song does not imply that this gift cannot be used without the sacrifice of an innocent life."

TWENTY-THREE

Ghrendourak's forces arrived off the North-Eastern coast of Aom-igh in the night. They swam and flew up to the barrier and stopped, a massive horde of horrible creatures. Above them all flew Ghrendourak atop his mount, his power forcing the monsters below to batter themselves against the barrier. After several long hours of testing the shield and finding no weaknesses, Ghrendourak swooped through the ranks and called for his creatures to rest from their assault. Then he rose up into the air on the back of his great werehawk and raised his arms.

Blinding light poured from his hands, crackling against the shield and sending a wave of sparks skittering across its surface in all directions. A roar of sound followed, and those inside the barrier clapped their hands to their ears. The roar was followed by a tidal wave of flame and then a rain of hailstones. The wind outside the shield whipped up, throwing waves of water crashing into the barrier. But the shield held strong. A battering ram of solid darkness came next, pounding against the shield again and again, but still the shield did not waver.

Ghrendourak uttered a sharp cry and a score of fell warriors rose up on winged mounts of their own, joining him in the air. Spears of lightning hurtled from them towards the barrier, hitting it with resounding thuds like the footsteps of doom. Yet, the barrier held. Invisible to their sight, yet as solid as steel, the protective dome stood strong.

Rena could sense the enemy horde, could feel their attempts to penetrate the shield she and the dragon pipes had wrought. She strengthened her thoughts, holding strong against their assault. She would protect her people, her country, her family, though it cost her all she had.

"He watches," Leila shivered, wrapping her arms around herself, appearing small and vulnerable. "He watches, and he sees." Her words tinged the air with a chill that belied the warmth of the evening.

"Who?" Jemson asked, not turning his head from the reports he was reading. As soon as Leila and Dylanna had informed him of the coming battle, Jemson had sent messengers to every post in Llycaelon, commanding them to meet at the Caethyr Gap where they would make their stand. It was a fairly defensible location, and Leila was convinced that her presence would lead Ghrendourak and his army to attack wherever she was.

"Ghrendourak," Leila replied.

"He's watching? Now?" Jemson looked up, startled. "Us?"

"No, the battle. He rides on his winged steed and sees the battle through the eyes of his creatures. He attacks both us and Aom-igh tonight, there will be no help for us, no help anywhere."

"How can you possibly know that?" Jemson turned to her. "I thought you said you lost your magic."

"I don't know. I just get glimpses of him, of what he is doing, what he sees." Leila rubbed her hands up and down her own arms briskly. "Maybe it was something to do with the portal. I was the one he spoke to directly though I don't know why."

"Who is stronger, you or Dylanna?" Jemson could not keep his question silent, he was too curious.

Leila sniffed and then cleared her throat, her face flushing. "Dylanna always said I was strongest, after Calyssia. Zara might have been stronger, but she abandoned her studies for Arnaud and a normal life."

Jemson snorted. "Normal. What's that?"

Leila tried to maintain a straight face, but it was to no avail. The young king's amusement was contagious, and they found themselves sharing a moment of levity. Everything they cared about would come under attack tonight. They knew what the reports said: the army they faced was larger than their own. Ghrendourak and the Ancient Enemy who controlled him were more powerful than they. But still they laughed, their voices raised in defiance of despair.

When they had spent their laughter, they stood together in silence. The night was still, but Jemson knew the attack would come soon. He knew that there was no hope of defeating this enemy, and surrender was unthinkable. The choice was to fight as free men and die, or live enslaved to Ghrendourak forever. He found his mind drifting.

If I come through this alive… if anyone comes through this alive, I will take my true-name from this experience, this battle. If I can lead my men through this, if together we can walk through the darkness that threatens our world and out into the light on the other side—there must be light on the other side—we will come through stronger and more complete than we were before. No one will be left unchanged after this night. The songs of our courage will last forever, the ballads of how we won through the hopeless situation will be comprised of numerous and lengthy verses hailing our deeds.

"They are coming," Leila's voice reverberated in his ears after the long silence.

Jemson glanced around quickly, but his senses registered nothing new.

"Not the enemy," Leila assured him, "friends."

"What friends?"

"More of the myth-folk… come, we must meet them."

Leila turned and walked up the path to the high ground above the camp and towards the forest. Jemson followed Leila, uncertain as to what he ought to expect.

There were not many dragons in the clearing, but he felt his mouth drop open in astonishment. He closed it quickly, feeling foolish, and embarrassed by his youthful reaction. Gazing around at the myriad of enormous, powerful beasts, Jemson rubbed a hand across his chin, then berated himself for it, dropping his hand to his side and forcing it to stay still. As his eyes searched the glade, he caught sight of gryphons and pegasus mixed in with the dragons. They were fierce and proud, necks arched and faces noble. He edged closer to Leila. His first inclination was to turn around and run as fast as he could away from these strange creatures who would surely eat him as soon as acknowledge his kingship.

"Do not be afraid," Leila's voice whispered in his ear, "they are here to help, if you will have it."

"Monarch Jemson," the largest of the dragons stepped forward and addressed the young king with polite formality, "my name is Alynyack. Khoranaderek told us of thy plight."

Jemson's thoughts unexpectedly turned to an image of his father and uncle. He saw them together, as clearly as if they were watching over his shoulder, waiting to see what he would do. He understood that this moment was a test of his ability, a test of his worthiness. As quickly as it had come, the urge to run vanished; Jemson's shoulders straightened, and he took a step towards the dragon. He summoned up every lesson that Brant had taught him of Llycaelon dragons and put what he had learned to good use. *Remember not to stare directly into the creature's eyes*, he thought as he bowed his head in a polite gesture that allowed the dragon permission to continue speaking.

The dragon's teeth bared in an awful expression that Jemson knew was supposed to be friendly. "Thine uncle hath taught thee well in our ways, youngling."

Jemson bristled a bit at the term, "youngling," but he bit his tongue, realizing that to the dragon, *anyone* under the age of three centuries was probably considered "young."

"How dost thou know mine uncle?"

"Many of those with me hail from other lands, but I was born in Llycaelon, and ever has it been my home, though I walked its surface in a different form to hide my identity. Thine uncle is well known to me though I have never met him in person."

"You said Khoranaderek told thee of our situation?" Jemson searched the faces before him until he picked out Khoranaderek's familiar scales. The dragon bobbed its head at him.

"Verily," Alynyack replied. "We have come to offer thee our aid in the coming battle."

"With gratefulness I accept thy offer," Jemson replied, working hard to make the strange wording and accent sound natural and correct.

The dragon's face lightened with pleasure at Jemson's effort and subsequent success. "This will, methinks, be an agreeable alliance."

"If we live to the end of the day, aye," Jemson agreed.

"Deploy our forces as thou wilt, my liege. We are thine to command."

"The fire of the dragons will surpass any weapon we can provide," Jemson said.

This acknowledgement pleased the elder dragon, and he inclined his head. "Thou grantest honor to my people. Our fire is indeed effective against the fell creatures we must face."

Jemson drew a crude map of the battlefield on the ground, pointing out where his battalions of aethalons were positioned. "Thou and thy people can provide cover from the air when the battle joins. A strong front may cause our enemies to hesitate."

An older gryphon strode forward, bowing his head slightly, his mottled feathers rustling. "My name is Kanuckchet, and I speak for my people. I believe thou wilt agree that my people would be best put to use in squads that can strike and retreat with great swiftness. In truth, speed and agility are our greatest strengths. If some of us wait inside the tree line here, and others hide on the cliffs, I believe we can surprise the enemy with devastating effect."

"Very well," Jemson agreed. "I trust thou knowest where to place thy warriors. I will leave their command to thee."

A mighty sorrel pegasus stepped forward then. Snorting and tossing his head, the pegasus introduced himself. "I am Hynfwyn, and my people would be honored to carry thy men into battle."

Jemson felt his jaw go slack yet again. He tried to cover his surprise by rubbing his chin and then bowing his head. "That is a generous offer, noble Hynfwyn," he replied. "I know what it costs thee to make it, and I assure thee I will not forget it."

Hynfwyn gave a short, high-pitched whinny. "We are not so proud as the stories make us sound, Majesty," he assured Jemson, speaking in a less archaic vein. "We have carried men into battle many times and consider it a most virtuous duty. Do not believe everything you read."

Jemson fought back a grin and managed to pull off a solemn bow from the waist. "My thanks and that of my people are yours forever." He straightened and gazed at the three mighty creatures who spoke for their powerful races and had come to pledge their aid to him. "I am young, even by my own people's standards, and I have little experience in the matters of war. I fear I must rely heavily upon your vast wisdom to lead me in this coming battle. Will you guide me in the events to come?"

Alynyack rose up to his full height. "We would count it an honor, Majesty."

A mighty gust of wind swept across them, and Shentallyia alighted on the ground near them. Devrin swung down from her back and raced over.

"The attack is begun, Sire," the words tumbled from his mouth. "The enemy has been sighted coming across the ocean. They will be here soon, we must prepare ourselves."

Alynyack lowered his head in curiosity, his nostrils flaring as he took in Devrin's scent. Then the great dragon reared back in surprise.

"A dragon ward?" his voice thundered. He swiveled his head to peer at Jemson. "Thou hast a dragon ward in thy midst?"

"How did you know?" Devrin craned his neck, peering up at the dragon. "Can you smell it?"

Alynyack's glowing orbs narrowed to slits. "Sense, more than smell, though not every dragon is able to do so." He swung his head from side to side. "This could mean..." he paused. "But time enough for that after. If we are not victorious this day, it will no longer matter in any case."

"Uplifting," Devrin commented out of the side of his mouth to Jemson, who felt his lips twitch with amusement.

"Sound the alert," Jemson commanded. "The hour is nigh." He felt grand and commanding as the words welled within him, but once they had reached the open air he wondered if perhaps he sounded a bit silly using such archaic, grandiose speech.

Nobody else took issue with his choice of words. Devrin dashed back to Shentallyia and clambered onto her back. Together, they leapt into the sky.

Hynfwyn strode forward. "I will carry thee, Majesty."

Jemson felt his heart beat a bit faster, but he hid his apprehension and swung onto the back of the great pegasus as gracefully as he was able. He settled himself in front of the enormous, folded wings and clung to Hynfwyn's mane as the pegasus surged forward, racing down the hill to the battlefield where the ranks of aethalons were gathered and waiting.

They did not wait long. At Toreth's-height, the first wave of were-folk stormed through the Caethyr Gap. The aethalons fell back as one, allowing the dragons to flood the gap with their fires. Enemy creatures pulled back, screaming and burning, dissipating like mist in a stern breeze.

A wind swept over Jemson and he looked up to see Shentallyia and Devrin passing by overhead. He raised his sword to them, and Shentallyia roared in answer.

On the great dragon's back, Devrin felt his emotions kindle into intrepid temerity. Flying over the enemy with Shentallyia he felt invincible. It was incredible to think how quickly his life had changed. Was it only weeks ago he had been defending this self-same gap against the seheowks? It felt strange to think how the turn of events had brought him to this position. He focused on his dragon and felt her cunning and fury surging through the link they shared. Were her emotions bleeding over into his own, tinting them? It was an astounding thing, to be linked to a creature so vast and powerful. She would change him in ways he was unprepared for, it was certain. That thought gnawed at him with a tinge of apprehension, but Devrin knew there was little he could do to stop it. Perhaps he would change her as well.

The dragon arched her neck, and he felt the blaze of her fire wash through him as she breathed death upon a score of seheowks. And then he was swept up into the battle, the all-consuming ferocity of it, as he defended her back from creatures above while Shentallyia slashed and tore and rained fiery demise upon the enemy below.

The aethalons on the ground plunged into battle to defend their country from the malevolent foe that threatened their land. Not a man faltered or cringed. They met the enemy with faces of steel and impassive, courageous hearts.

At the back of the field, astride Hynfwyn, Jemson's heart filled with pride. He paused, witnessing the bravery of his aethalons. Next to him, riding Hawkspin, Leila surveyed the field below with cool composure.

"All our hopes rest now with Oraeyn," she said.

Jemson nodded his agreement. Their only hope of seeing the end of this war lay in Oraeyn's success. Gazing out at the sea of were-folk his heart rang with excitement. He should have been afraid, he knew he ought to be quaking at the size of the enemy's army, but the cry of battle and duty called him and his heart responded with a leap. With a roar that was echoed by his aethalons, a roar that made the ground shake with its furious defiance, Jemson cast his fears to the wind and charged into battle, followed by his loyal men. There would be a dawn.

"It's not a game anymore, is it?" Kamarie asked Oraeyn quietly, coming up beside him and taking his hand, more to comfort herself than anything else.

"What do you mean?"

She gestured at Yole, who was obviously still in distress over Rhimmell's death. "I always just sort of assumed that the people I knew and cared about would be safe... you know, like in the storybooks where the heroes always win and never get hurt?" She raised her free hand in a helpless gesture. "It isn't that way in real life."

"I know what you mean. You read about adventures and how people risked their lives, but they always come out fine in the end. In real adventures it doesn't all end up that way."

"Oraeyn?"

"Yes?"

"I'm scared."

"So am I, Kamarie."

"I wouldn't choose differently, though," Kamarie said after a short pause. "I'd rather be here with you than anywhere else."

Oraeyn squeezed her hand. "I'm glad you're here, though I also wish you were safely at the other end of the world."

They walked in silence after that, comforted by the understanding they shared.

The forest was quiet, but it no longer loomed over them with hostile or threatening intent. Oraeyn found that even in the silence and peace his guard was still up; not against the forest, but against the creatures that might lurk within it. He kept the Fang Blade unsheathed as they walked, and its light was soft and comforting to the entire company. The dragons wore their true forms, determined not to be taken by surprise again.

"How long are we on this path, Brant?" Oraeyn asked about mid-morning. The days felt endless beneath the canopy of branches and leaves. The darkness of the day was indiscernible from the darkness of night. The Dragon's Eye was but a distant memory, for the only light they knew was the soft glow of the Fang Blade.

Brant appeared thoughtful. "The end of the forest should be coming soon. I don't remember exactly—it was a long time ago —but my memory leads me to believe that we shouldn't have to be on this path much longer."

Kamarie sighed with relief. "Good." She spoke quietly, but Oraeyn heard her.

The sky above them turned inky, and the air grew thick and caliginous. Kamarie screamed, for the air above them was filled with a swarm of whyvrens. The fell beasts dropped from the sky and landed on the path before them.

Yole stared at the swarm of monsters, there were perhaps a

score of them. Not as many as he had at first thought, but still
more than they could hope to defeat. Despair and determination
twined together to form a cold knot in the pit of his stomach.
They would not survive this assault, but Rhimmell, sweet, quiet,
uncomplaining Rhimmell would be avenged at any and every
cost.

Of that, he would make certain. And he would protect what
remained of his family to his last breath.

Shoulder to shoulder, Yole and Thorayenak charged into the
enemy. The dragons roared and fire streamed from their open
jaws. A whyvren lashed its deadly tail at Yole's face, but he caught
it in his claw and gave a mighty heave, throwing the monster into
several of the other whyvrens, knocking them from their feet.
They staggered to rise, hissing and snarling, but Yole propelled
himself into their midst, his talons flashing, his fiery breath
blazing. He became a swirling typhoon, dealing death to the fell
creatures.

Thorayenak was right beside him, roaring. "Run!" his voice
bellowed to the humans. "This is not a fight you can win. Run!
Go, NOW!" his voice thundered through the wood.

Oraeyn raised the Fang Blade, not wanting to leave
Thorayenak or Yole, but Brant and Kiernan knew it was madness
to stride into that frenzy of teeth and claws and stinging tails.
They would merely get in the way of the enraged dragons. They
might be able to join forces to defeat one whyvren, but they
stood no chance against an army of them. The two men shared a
glance through the dim light, and for the first time, they were in
complete agreement, understanding one another perfectly.

"We won't leave you!" Oraeyn shouted.

"GO!" Thorayenak shouted. "There is no time! Brant, you
must go! Minstrel, take them while there is yet a chance."

Oraeyn felt strong hands grasp his shoulders and suddenly
he was being dragged along in a wave of strength. The world
spun out of his control and all he could do was allow himself to
be carried away with it. For a split second he considered resisting
and fighting this helplessness, but something in his heart warned
him that he and all he cared about would be destroyed if he gave

into such a desire. After a moment's hesitation he ceased struggling and allowed the sweeping strength surrounding him to bear him away. A moment later, and without quite knowing how or why, he was running. He ran with every fiber of his being. He pushed himself to the very limits of his strength and beyond, dashing faster and faster. If he stopped, he would die. He pumped his legs, his breath coming faster and faster; sweat dampened his forehead, but he could not stop. Salty warmth dripped down his face, blurring his vision and wetting his lips, but he could not spare the energy to wipe it away. His vision blurred but still he could not stop. The sense of urgency pressed inwards making it harder and harder to breathe, pushing him to continue even as his muscles burned and screamed for him to stop. Air dragged through his lungs in painful surges and he gasped, hating each life-giving breath as it passed through his lips.

Then, the forest ended. With an explosive gasp, as if he were a caterpillar bursting from its cocoon, Oraeyn slowed and staggered drunkenly in the blinding twilight. The urge to run vanished like a mirage in the desert. Oraeyn's legs buckled beneath his weight and he sank to his knees.

"Wh... what just happened?" a trembling voice near him asked.

Oraeyn found the strength to turn his head. Kamarie was a few paces away, sitting on the ground with a bewildered expression on her face.

"I—I don't know," he gasped, tearing ragged words up out of his chest and spitting them through his lips with great effort.

"That was my doing," Kiernan Kane said, and as the minstrel spoke Oraeyn found that his head felt less fuzzy and disoriented.

Oraeyn looked up, startled by the tone in the minstrel's voice. The tall man was not out of breath. Oraeyn's eyes darted around at what was left of their small company. Kamarie was to his right, still gasping for air. Brant was on his left, breathing heavily, but still on his feet and glaring sternly at Kiernan Kane. Kiernan himself stood directly in front of Oraeyn, completely unconcerned by the curiosity of his companions as they waited for his next words.

"You left them!" Oraeyn shouted. "Thorayenak and Yole, you left them to die! And you dragged us along with you! You made us leave them! How could you?"

"Oraeyn," Kiernan's voice was mournful. "I left no one to die. I brought you, to live. It is our only hope."

Oraeyn's face hardened and his hands clenched into fists. "You left them," he growled.

"They knew the risk," Kiernan Kane said, his voice low and intense. "They knew it the day they agreed to come. I warned you," the minstrel lifted his hands in a questioning gesture. "Did you not listen? How could you not understand? All might have been lost had we stayed."

"They are our friends!" Kamarie put her face in her hands, her shoulders shaking.

"And they did what they could to help you, their friends. They believed in what we are trying to do... you must do the same!" Kiernan knelt beside Kamarie, placing an arm around her shoulders. "The Enemy moves, his forces spread to your homelands, your loved ones are fighting and dying to keep his attention focused away from here, to give you the time you need to succeed in your quest. You must not waste their efforts."

"We left our friends in trouble," Oraeyn gritted. He felt he was being unreasonable, but the heaviness in his heart was more than he could bear.

"You would risk all for the lives of a few? What we are doing is of utmost importance. The Enemy will stop at nothing to gain all. You think Ghrendourak is bad? If the Enemy manages to rend a hole in his prison and escape, the power he has lent to Ghrendourak will seem but an imperceptible breath compared to the exhalation of evil that will be unleashed upon our world. He would reign supreme and none, *none,* would be able to stand against him. All would be enslaved to his great lust for power. Only now, now when he is still weak, now when he does not expect our attack, now when he is still caged and has use of but a fraction of his power through the shell that is Ghrendourak, only now will the next High King be able to stand against him. You would risk this chance, the sole chance we have, for the sake of two? Yorien's Hand alone holds the key to defeating him and the Enemy would like nothing better than to destroy the one for whom it is destined, for he knows our mission would then fail. You would risk the entire world's enslavement for your own selfish wishes?"

Oraeyn hung his head, his shoulders bowed under the burden of Kiernan's words. He gazed at his companions and there was an apology in his face, but there was also the fire of new understanding and strength that had not been present before.

"You should go back, all of you. I have put you at risk; I should go on from here by myself. I am sorry for not understanding before."

"You can't make us leave. You can't make *me* leave!" Kamarie rose from the ground and stepped forward with a strong, determined stride.

"I will if I have to," Oraeyn said, and there was the strength of iron in the words, "it's too dangerous for you. Kiernan is right, I would have risked all... I *have* risked all, everything, because I was scared, I am afraid to let go of my friends, to go on by myself, but it's the only way you will be safe. It's the only way I can assuage the despair I've been carrying. This island is familiar to me, I've seen it in my nightmares and I know we are drawing close to our goal. And if my dreams are to be believed, then I cannot risk any of you going further, because it could mean your lives. And that is something I cannot bear. Please, let me continue alone."

"No," the metal in Brant's voice was solid steel. "You cannot go on alone, there is too much before you for which you are unprepared. You do not know what you are going to face, I do. You do not know where to look for Yorien's Hand, I have been here before. I can lead you and I can help you.

"We each have our part yet to play, the only reason you have gotten this far is because of your friends, you would never have made it to Emnolae this fast without the dragons, you would never have found the key to the entrance without my guidance, you would have been killed by the whyvrens if it weren't for Kiernan Kane. At the very least, I must come with you. And if I come, then so must the minstrel and Kamarie, for I will not leave them unprotected.

"If you come under attack, you will need us to fight for you so you can continue the quest. Your goal is the pinnacle, the sole reason for undertaking this journey, for facing these perils. Kiernan is right, our lives are forfeit if we do not succeed here. Defeating Ghrendourak is worth our lives, we all made that decision the moment we agreed to come with you back in Aomigh. You cannot ask us to leave you now, not when you need us the most."

It was, perhaps, the longest speech any of them had ever heard Brant make, and Oraeyn was not sure how to respond. Brant was right though Oraeyn hated to admit it. He stared helplessly into the faces of his three remaining friends. There was the same quiet determination in each of them. Kiernan's face had gone impassive and unreadable, Brant's expression was hard and determined. Kamarie gazed at him with love, but there was a stubbornness in her expression that wrenched his heart. He thought about his dreams and he shuddered as he realized what they had foretold. He knew that at the very end, he would be forced to choose between her and the fate of all Tellurae Aquaous, and he did not know if he could make that choice. His heart lurched as he looked beseechingly at Kamarie.

"Please," it was half gasp, half sob, and he knew before he spoke that it would do no good.

Kamarie stepped forward and wrapped him in an embrace. "Oraeyn, I cannot leave you. My place is here, at your side. When will you realize that?"

"We waste time," Brant unsheathed his sword and took a step, looking back over his shoulder, his head tilted to the side questioningly.

"Very well," Oraeyn's shoulders slumped. "Lead on, Brant."

There was no need for more words; all had been said. As one, the four of them turned to continue their journey. Together they had set out, and together they would remain.

All through the long, weary night, the shield held, repelling attack after attack. However, as the Toreth, obscured by the web of darkness, sank below the horizon, the barrier also came crashing down with a deafening rumble, causing the ground to shake and tremble beneath the knights of Aom-igh. Rena had held the enemy at bay with the shield for as long as she could, but Ghrendourak's power was far too strong for her to hold his forces back forever.

Justan sat with his wife until the end. He had made his peace with the inevitable, and as news reached him that the shield was failing, he leaned down to kiss his wife's pale lips.

"Goodbye," he whispered brokenly. Then he rose, fighting past the lump in his throat and the despair in his heart, and strode from the room to face the battle that awaited him.

As he appeared amongst his men, they whispered that something was different about their leader. His face looked older, and a strength and peace surrounded him. He spoke to the men, building their hope and courage, reminding them of their many preparations. As Ghrendourak's army surged up onto the shore there was no cowering, no blanching from what they faced, only the knowledge that what they had been waiting for had happened and it was time to fulfill their duty as knights of the realm.

A hideous cry arose from the army of were-folk as they swarmed to the attack with a vicious malice and overwhelming force. Justan, Garen, and Arnaud had prepared well for an assault from the sea. Barricades, defenses, and numerous traps had been laid in place, and the men were well-trained to move as directed. Justan signaled the order and the sand beneath the first wave of were-folk collapsed, tumbling many of the creatures into the deep pits the knights had prepared. The were-folk did not hesitate in their charge and showed no concern for their fallen. With another signal, sharp spikes erupted from the sand, impaling more dark creatures and removing them from the battle. However, the size of the army continued to grow.

Monsters crawled out of the roiling sea like an unstoppable wave.

Justan climbed up the stairs that led to the top of the ramparts and gave yet another signal as more men raced up to stand on the walls with him.

Dragons roared across the sky from behind Fortress Hill and swooped towards the enemy army. A torrent of fire poured from their mouths, sending many of the creatures in the front lines scattering and fleeing in unorganized panic. Those behind cringed away from the deadly flames, but Ghrendourak's commanders urged them on, giving them no time to hesitate or ponder their own impending fate.

Winged beasts rose up from the ranks of the were-folk and soared into the sky to challenge the dragons, putting a stop to their ability to rain fiery death down upon the enemy unchecked. The dragons were massive and powerful, but they were too few compared to Ghrendourak's army. They crashed into this new threat, and the sky was filled with the sounds of snarls and roars and eerie screams that would haunt the dreams of the men below for the rest of their lives.

Justan gave another order and the gryphons and pegasus joined the dragons, lashing out with talons and hooves. The myth-folk fought furiously, and the archers on the ground did what they could to help, though it soon became apparent that no defense, regardless of how valiant the warrior or accurate the archer, could withstand the forces delivered by Ghrendourak.

Another trap on the beach was sprung and scores of arrows flew from disguised locations, felling another line of the dark creatures, but still they continued to advance.

Justan turned to the old knight standing at his side. "Garen, we can't hold them. There are too many. What should we do?"

Garen unsheathed his sword, his face hard and strong beneath his white hair. "We don't need to hold them, we just need to fight them. King Oraeyn needs more time, our job is to make certain he gets it."

"What if we do all we can and it's not enough?" Justan stared at the battle below as it crept towards the wall.

"Then we lose."

The older knight hefted his sword, adjusting his grip on the hilt. "But I'd rather lose battling that army than surrendering to it. And that's true of every man fighting here today."

A line of whyvrens emerged to stand together. Darkness spewed out of their tails like streams of blood, blotting out the faint light of dawn that peeked tremulously over the horizon and plunging the armies into deepest night once more.

"What is this?" Justan whispered, unable to see the approaching enemy. He peered through the gloom, hearing the twanging of bow strings, and the tramp of many feet on the ground. How could they fight blindly? How could they hope to maintain a defense in such conditions?

Something struck him from behind and Justan whirled, his blade swinging.

"Easy, lad," Garen's voice stayed Justan's hand. "I did not mean to startle you. I wasn't sure you were still there. King Rhendak said this might happen. Whyvrens, he called them. They've got an ability to create darkness in daylight, and they're poisonous, so don't let one sting you or bite you."

"What do we do?"

"Watch."

As Justan watched, a tiny light appeared. Then another, and another. As the light spread, he began to see rows of torches spread out across the ground. Their glow was weak, but effective. It pierced the inky web, allowing the men to see the battlefield and their enemies. As he peered down at the ground, he saw the adumbral figure of a dragon, then he saw a stream of light and several more of the torches coughed into existence.

"Whose idea was that?" Justan asked, impressed.

"A dragon named Tellemyack," Garen replied. "I guess he's Rhendak's son. It was after the battle plans were all drawn up, he came to me about the idea and I told the commanders to help him put up the torches while we waited to see how long the barrier would hold. I guess dragon fire is a bit more resistant to whatever it is the whyvrens do."

"It's ingenious."

A sound made them both glance down. The enemy had reached the moat below the walls. The men looked at each other, and then there was a sound of a thousand swords ringing in the murky air as the men atop the wall drew their weapons as one.

CHAPTER
TWENTY-FOUR

A deep weariness clung to Oraeyn's soul as he approached the broken gates leading into the overgrown courtyard of the palace. Due to extreme amounts of rust, it was impossible to even speculate as to what the once intricate design adorning the gates had depicted. Patches and flecks of gold plating lingered, but most of it had flaked off through the many years of neglect. Brant led the way through the gates, which creaked so loudly Oraeyn was sure the sound carried all the way back in Aom-igh. Inside the gates was a vast and sprawling castle that might have once been glorious, but now was merely ruins. His heart sank at the sight.

Centuries of disuse had left their mark. Whole sections of the walls had been broken down by the elements and forest creatures; only one of the three towers was still standing. Huge windows stared out at the company: empty holes with no glass in them. Only bits remained of the roof, which had caved in long ago. Wind and rain had worn away the once mighty marble steps, leaving them chipped and broken. Weeds sprouted up between the cracks. The courtyard was overgrown and twisted in a veritable jungle of green, like a small extension of the forest from which they had recently emerged. Oraeyn stared in disbelief and not a little dismay at the sight of it.

If I truly am the High King, the dismal thought flicked through his mind, *will I be expected to live here? This may be the Palace of the High Kings, but it is not my home.*

He had not given much thought to what might happen after they retrieved Yorien's Hand, but now his mind spun beyond the current quest as he tried to imagine what his life would become if they defeated Ghrendourak. He grimaced at the toppled walls and wondered if this was the true nightmare.

He had been forced to accept so much: creatures that should not have existed outside of children's stories, a presence in the forest as though the trees were alive, a blind woman who could see much deeper than he. Oraeyn had left behind friends to face death or worse on his behalf, and now, at the end of their great quest, he was confronted with a ruined castle, an overgrown courtyard, and the fear that he still had to make a terrible choice. The choice from his nightmares.

He tried to swallow, but his throat had stopped working. Oraeyn gave a silent gasp as his chest tightened. He was a man by everyone's standards; he had held the position of king of Aom-igh for three years, he was a full knight of the realm, and mere months away from getting married.

And I'm supposed to leave all that—my friends, my home, everything familiar—to accept a broken-down throne that hasn't existed in centuries, a second crown that I desire even less than the first one, and rule over subjects whose countries I've never even heard of, much less visited? Kiernan Kane must have been mistaken. I am not the person for this job. The castle is in ruins, it would take the work of the rest of my lifetime just to get it into good enough shape to live in it.

Kamarie looked around in awe. "It must have been beautiful, once," she gave a sorrowful sigh. "It looks so lonely now."

At the sound of her voice, Oraeyn found himself staring. She was so lovely it made his heart ache. Her long ebony hair glistened in the dying light of day, and her blue eyes glistened with sympathy for the dilapidated castle grounds. At that moment, he knew what his choice would be when it came. He could not abandon her like he had the others, like he had in his nightmares; if he could save her, he would, and neither Kiernan Kane nor Brant himself would be able to change that.

If the minstrel had any thoughts about the state of the palace, he kept them to himself. Oraeyn realized that Kiernan had not bumped into anything, fallen over, tripped, or stumbled once lately; in fact, the minstrel had proven extremely capable and even deadly with a sword in his hand. Kiernan had certainly been anything but a fool in the past few days.

Brant's voice interrupted Oraeyn's thoughts. "It wasn't this bad when I was here the first time... though that was a good many years ago. The place has deteriorated since I was here last." There was a sadness in his voice. "Come."

The others looked at him questioningly, but Brant had sunk deep into fell memories that he would not share. All they could do was follow him as he fought his way through the undergrowth towards the great marble steps that led up to the doors.

Doubtfully, the rest of them trailed along behind the warrior. With long strides, Brant ascended the steps to the once-mighty oak doors. There were paint peelings and chips on the steps. It was obvious that the doors had once been adorned with lavish artwork, but whatever decoration once existed had long since been lost.

Aom-igh was in flames and their defenses were melting before the enemy assault. Each courageous man or woman who fell was a barb in Justan's heart. They could not withstand this battering much longer. Justan could see the city walls being overrun. Savage were-folk landed inside the palace courtyards spewing devastation wherever they touched the ground. His heart fell with the realization that they were indeed powerless against Ghrendourak.

Crackling sounds filled the air as the ground shook and a chasm formed outside the city wall. The earth split beneath the were-folk and snaked all the way back to the water. Both the enemy forces and the sea poured into the opening. Then, just as suddenly as it had appeared, the chasm closed, burying its victims. At the same moment, a gale-force wind of sleet, ice, and bitter cold swirled through the air, bringing the battle on both land and in the air to a screeching halt as everyone, warrior and were-folk alike, shivered in the face of the storm. Thunder rumbled in the distance and the wind whipped over the land with no mercy. The sand on the beach, driven by hurricane-force winds, blinded the were-folk and sent them screaming towards the water in search of protection. Justan watched in fascination as their enemies ceased fighting and bowed to their simple need to protect themselves from the relentless elements. A sudden warmth enclosed Justan like a brief embrace. The sensation lasted for a fraction of a moment, and then it was gone with the wind, but Justan recognized the touch.

"Rena!" he shouted, his voice trembling. "Rena! It's Rena! Zara, it's Rena!"

Zara stepped into the storm at his call. "What? Justan, what are you talking about? What about Rena?"

"It's her," he said firmly. "The barrier fell, but she is still there, still wielding the power of the pipes. She's using the elements themselves to fight for us. The earthquake, the wind, the storm, it's all her doing. She must have known the barrier could not hold, and so she channeled the power into a different kind of weapon. She's still here, she still fights for us."

Zara's face took on a thoughtful expression. The enemy below was hampered by the wind and driving sand, but they pressed forward in spite of the storm. The desperate plight of Aom-igh was not yet over.

"You may be right, Justan, but Rena's power must reach its limit before long."

Justan sobered. "Yes." He knew that victory was beyond Aom-igh's capabilities, but hope had been resurrected in his heart. Rena was alive! He turned to face his enemies with new strength. Oraeyn would have the time he needed.

Brant reached out his hand to push the door open. As his fingers touched the wood he was enveloped by the same sensation he had noticed the first time he had ventured to this place. It was an impression that the palace had once been beautiful and cared for, and that it would care for its inhabitants if it were just given the chance. Brant was aware of the emotions of his companions; there was pity and disgust and horror in their minds. They had not expected such disrepair, such a bedraggled castle with all of its walls tumbling down. Brant found himself fighting down a sudden, unreasonable urge to defend the Great Hall, to tell them what the place had been like once. *But I don't know how the place once was*, Brant reminded himself; *they would be confused and would not understand.* The urge passed and Brant shook his head and lifted his hand from the door.

"Follow me, but carefully; we do not know if the Enemy has been here or if traps have been set."

The rest of them nodded and Brant pushed open the great doors. They proceeded with caution, allowing Brant's memory to guide them through the palace. After a few minutes Brant stopped.

"Each of you, take a torch," he said, pointing to a wall that had a row of sconces attached to it. "We will need the light where we are going."

"Where *are* we going, Brant?" Kamarie asked, a little hesitantly.

"We are going to enter a secret tunnel that leads from this palace to the heart of the mountain that you saw from the air. It will be a long walk and we will sleep in the tunnel at least once before we reach the chamber where Yorien's Hand is kept. The tunnel is not lit, and the torches may burn out, which is why we need several of them."

Kamarie's face took on a pained expression. "That doesn't sound very appealing. Are there spiders in the tunnel?"

Brant chuckled. "My memory is good, but that I do not remember."

Kamarie wrinkled her nose in distaste, then stepped forward and lifted a torch from the wall. "Very well, let's get it over with then."

The rest grabbed torches as well.

"This way," Brant said, pointing to a set of stairs leading down towards the cellars. "The entrance to the tunnel is at the bottom of these steps."

The companions followed Brant down the stairs and stopped at the door. It was small and simple, as unremarkable as the old key Brant held. The sole noteworthy thing about the door was the fact that the carving upon it had escaped the same wear and aging the rest of the castle had suffered. Brant hesitated as he looked at the door.

"'Keep this safe and use it well; it will get you through the door you seek,'" Brant whispered.

Anguished memories chased one another through his thoughts. He stared at Kamarie, but did not see her. Faces of people he had left behind long ago, faces of people he had loved, and faces of people who had died haunted him as he stared at the door.

"Calla. Imojean. Kali. Schea," his lips formed their names, though no sound came out. Iron bands wrapped around his heart and he gasped for breath, a drowning man with no hope of salvation.

"Brant? Come back," Kamarie's pleading whisper broke through his memories.

At her soft touch on his arm Brant shuddered. "Calla." He shook his head. "I mean, Kamarie. Forgive me, I didn't know the memories would be so hard to face." He looked up and met Kiernan's gaze, and for once, there was only sympathy in the minstrel's eyes. Wordless understanding passed between the two men, and Brant felt himself strangely comforted.

He took a deep breath and pushed the key into the lock. Rusty and old as it was, the key turned without complaint and the door swung open. After the loud creaking of the front gate and the big oak doors, the silence was eerie. A blast of warm, humid air washed over them.

"Well," Oraeyn spoke at last, "we might as well get started if we're going to do this."

Brant lit the first torch and then stepped into the damp, musty murk. The rest of the companions accompanied him. No one thought to close the door behind them so that they could not be followed.

The floor of the tunnel was packed earth, but the walls were made of jagged stone. Kamarie gasped and Brant halted, turning in concern.

"It's nothing," Kamarie's voice sounded embarrassed. "I just brushed against the wall... it was slimy," she explained.

Brant heard Oraeyn choke back a laugh.

"We're under the mountain now. I believe there is an underground stream running near this tunnel, there's a bit of a waterfall when we get to the end of it, if I remember correctly."

Kamarie edged closer to him and Oraeyn. "I can't believe you came down here alone the first time, Brant."

"I wasn't alone," Brant replied quietly.

"But I thought you..."

"Two friends accompanied me to this island. Only one of them survived to leave it at the end of our quest."

"I'm sorry." Kamarie's voice was soft. "Is that what you meant when you spoke of memories earlier?"

Brant nodded shortly.

"That name you called out at the doorway... Calla? Was she the one who...?" Kamarie found that she could not finish the question.

"The one who didn't make it," Brant's voice was filled with regret. "I couldn't save her from the seheowks, even though I had touched the great Hand of Yorien. She died anyway, horribly, and all I could do was mourn her loss."

"It... it wasn't your fault."

"I brought her here, and she died, if I hadn't, she would have lived." The words were tight and clipped, indicating that the conversation was over. Oraeyn tightened his arm around Kamarie's shoulders, but did not speak.

The small company traveled on in a stiff, uncomfortable silence for the rest of the day, though there was no real way to tell if the day had come to an end by the time that they stopped to rest. Burying the end of one of the torches in the hard ground, they managed to create the semblance of a campfire. As they rummaged through their packs for what was left of their food supply, Kiernan Kane sat down and began strumming a few chords on his mandolin.

Munching on a chunk of bread, Kamarie sat down close to the minstrel to listen. After a moment Oraeyn and Brant joined her. The minstrel's fingers danced across the strings of the mandolin. Then Kiernan began to sing:

> *The minstrel draws you*
> *The minstrel calls you*
> *The minstrel beckons*
> *Come listen, come hear.*
>
> *When the days turn dark*
> *And the firelight dim,*
> *When cold are your hearts*
> *Come listen to him.*
>
> *The minstrel sings*
> *And strums his strings*
> *Let your heart take wings*
> *Come listen, come hear.*
>
> *When the road seems long*
> *When your strength is gone*
> *You've forgotten his song*
> *Come listen, draw near.*
>
> *Let the minstrel remind you*
> *With his song let him find you*
> *From the darkness unbind you*
> *Come listen, come hear.*
>
> *With his song he draws you*
> *As he strums, he calls you*
> *As he hums, he beckons*
> *Come listen, come near.*

As the last notes of his song faded, so did a portion of their weariness. It was like Kiernan Kane had found a way to bring the Dragon's Eye into the tunnel with them. Not that the passageway was any brighter, but *something* had changed, though none of them could have explained exactly what.

From where he was sitting, Oraeyn picked up an unlit torch and tapped Kamarie's shoulder.

"On guard!"

She danced backwards, then picked up her own unused torch and parried. They batted the torches back and forth for a bit until Kamarie got through Oraeyn's defense with a fancy flick of her torch and sent his flying through the air.

"I surrender," Oraeyn called out, holding up his hands. "Take your prize, my lady."

Kamarie grinned triumphantly and leaned forward for a quick kiss, but lost her balance and nearly fell on her face. Oraeyn caught her and they dissolved into laughter and giggles.

Kiernan continued to strum his mandolin. Brant leaned back, listening to the music and the laughter of his friends, and his thoughts turned to Dylanna. How he wished she could be there with them. His memories of this place were not happy ones, but thoughts of Dylanna gave him the strength to face them and move past them.

Oraeyn came over to sit next to Brant.

"How much farther do we have until we reach Yorien's Hand?" he asked.

Brant squinted. "I'm not sure. It's hard to keep track of time down here. I think it's about a day's journey to reach the door, and we haven't gone very far yet, but we expended a fair bit of energy already today. I think it would be best if we tried to get some rest before continuing on."

Despite Kiernan's song, none of them slept surpassingly well. The ground was hard, the sound of dripping water echoed in the stillness, and concern for Yole, Thorayenak, and all the ones they had left behind plagued each of the travelers. Nobody complained when Brant said it was time to move on. They ate an unsatisfying meal of nuts and dried fruit, and then they rolled up their packs and began the tedious march once more. After long hours of travel and a few brief stops for food, the travelers were touched by a breath of fresh air.

"Nearly there now," Brant announced.

His words, and the sudden breeze, urged them forward. A moment later, the tunnel ended abruptly and spanned out into a much larger cave with a clean, sandy floor. The sound of dripping was clearer now, and they saw the stream of water Brant had mentioned earlier dribbling down from the ceiling in a steady trickle. At the far end of the cave was the outline of a door in the rock wall. It was from this outline that the unexpected breeze appeared to be emanating.

"There it is," Oraeyn breathed.

Brant strode to the center of the cavern. "Just as I remembered it."

Kamarie was the first to reach the door. She looked at it quizzically. "How does it open? There is no latch."

Brant did not react as if he had heard her, he lifted his torch and stared up at the ceiling. Glittering gemstones were embedded into the roof of the cave and the firelight of the torches made them shine as convincingly as real stars. To those who had not seen starlight in what felt like centuries, this wonder was awe-inspiring indeed. After a moment, the others noticed that the pebbles were not scattered randomly or by chance. The stones had been placed with care across the ceiling of the cave in the exact shapes and locations of the constellations in the night sky.

"Yorien!" Oraeyn exclaimed, pointing towards the ceiling. "And Ethalon, and The Gryphon... they're all here!"

"Is it just artwork, Brant? Or is this the key to getting through that door?" Kamarie asked.

"Chareel is the key to Yorien's heart," Brant murmured. He reached a hand up to the ceiling and touched a stone that was a part of the Chareel constellation. It turned and the door of the cave swung open with a quiet click.

A strident screech filled the air. The noise was excruciatingly loud, but the terror it introduced into their hearts was worse than the torture to their ears. The awful sound hung in the air for a moment and then it was gone as quickly as if it had been whisked away by the wind. Kiernan and Brant shared a concerned look.

Kiernan Kane was the first to speak. "The Enemy has not forgotten the power of Yorien's Gift. He has been alerted to our presence."

"Then we must move with even greater speed," Brant replied.

TWENTY-FIVE

Rhendak led a charge against Ghrendourak's army. As Rena battered the enemy with rain and howling wind, Rhendak dove at them with fire and tooth and claw. His bright green body swept down over the were-folk again and again, flames pouring from his mouth. In the midst of the rain, the light of the dragon-fire sparkled and shimmered along his silver wings. He was a truly marvelous sight, a creature of ferocity, he winged across the sky like a storm of fire.

The dragon king soared and plunged. He dove into the seething enemy army and struck with outstretched claws, his powerful tail sweeping through the ranks and wreaking havoc. Then he lunged into the sky, a seheowk clenched in his teeth as he hurtled higher and higher. When he reached the barrier, he paused. Then he opened his jaws and released the filthy creature; it plummeted back to the ground with an unearthly wail.

Though many of the creatures below cringed and cowered before the dragon's attack, a dozen whyvrens rose on skeletal wings to meet the dragon king in the sky. Rhendak did not know it at the time, but two of his own, many miles distant, were engaged in their own death struggle against these same creatures.

The dragon king let out a roar of challenge and met the whyvrens as they ascended. Thick, inky clouds poured from the monsters' tails, surrounding Rhendak and momentarily blinding him. In his moment of weakness, the creatures attacked. Together they dove at the enormous dragon, their stingers whipping towards him. Dragon fire erupted from the unnatural cloud and Rhendak streaked upwards, out of reach of the venomous stings.

The whyvrens snarled in fury and pursued the dragon. To those on the ground it appeared that Rhendak could never be caught. He was speed itself, and the whyvrens, swift as they were, seemed clumsy in comparison. The sight of the great dragon heartened those fighting below, renewing their courage.

Rhendak exulted in his strength. Warmth filled his body, and he turned to face his pursuers, greeting them with even more fire. The whyvrens were not as afraid of fire as their seheowk brethren, but they were not immune to its power. Two of the whyvrens screamed as they were engulfed in flames. They hurtled from the sky like falling stars.

The other whyvrens paused, circling the dragon king at a safe distance. Rhendak flamed and darted towards first one, then another of the creatures, but they danced away and then closed back in, staying just out of reach, their fell wings beating a hideous rhythm in the air. They hissed and spat, spewing darkness at him. They flew at him and then away again in infuriating feints that clouded the dragon's vision with a red haze of rage.

Two whyvrens attacked at once from opposite sides of the dragon king. Rhendak darted his head forward and snapped his teeth down on the neck of the creature in front of him, killing it instantly. Then he twisted, catching the one behind full in its twisted face with a burst of flame, but not before the venomous stinger had embedded itself in his shoulder between two scales. Rhendak roared in pain. He felt the poison burning through his veins, weakening him. He beat his wings harder, but the effort soon became more than he could manage. Dipping and faltering, he fell to the ground. The remaining whyvrens followed.

Rhendak landed with a heavy thud in the middle of the enemy army. The creatures near him let out a victorious howl as they caught the scent of the whyvren's poison working its way through their foe. Rhendak raised his voice in a trumpeting, clarion call of defiance.

Deprived of flight, the dragon king became a cyclone of death. Whirling and whipping his tail through the ranks of the enemy, he amassed their carcasses around him in a barricade. Other dragons flew overhead, jaws snapping and claws ripping at the enemy between bursts of fire in a tremendous effort to protect their king, but the whyvrens were too numerous and they overwhelmed the great dragon. They swarmed over him, clawing and biting and stinging him without mercy or restraint. Even as other dragons tore them away from their king, more werefolk piled into the fray.

At long last, the great dragon, King Rhendak roared his last, desperate challenge. He surged up from underneath the mass of enemies in a vicious and desperate struggle for survival, but a snarling wulfban clamped its jaws to Rhendak's great neck, its fangs tearing through the great dragon's throat. With a gasp, Rhendak spurted one more magnificent burst of flame that reduced the were-creatures around him to ash, and then he fell, shaking the ground as he collapsed.

The dragons sent up a mighty roar as they saw their king fall amidst his enemies. From the wall, the knights of the realm watched in quiet shock.

The battle did not cease for the fall of the dragon king. The enemy gained confidence with this victory and redoubled their efforts. Though the myth-folk fought with great courage, their spirits collapsed with their king. Then Justan's battle cry rang out over the field.

"Rhendak!" he cried, his voice rising to the sky. "Rhendak! For Rhendak, for Aom-igh!"

Justan's blade whirled and slashed, and his enemies fell before him and the plunging hooves of his war horse. The knights of the realm roused themselves at the sight of their leader fighting with such daring. They followed him into the fray, taking up his cry. The myth-folk rallied to the call as well and delayed once more the defeat that was sure to come.

The battle raged through the day, and Justan fought with his comrades, leading them, encouraging them, until his sword arm ached with fatigue and his throat was raw and hoarse from shouting. A sudden rain of arrows poured from the sky, causing the enemy to fall and recoil.

"Take a breather!" a voice shouted over the din of the battle.

Justan looked up to see a wave of fresh men plunging into the fray on either side of him. The reserve forces had moved to the front of the line to give the men who had been fighting the longest a short respite. Gratefully, Justan saluted and turned his horse, urging the beast to retreat to the back of the lines.

When he had reached a place of relative safety, Justan paused to take a long swig of water from his nearly empty canteen and survey the battle. The vile creatures were everywhere, and the death of his countrymen followed in their wake. Knights, women of the Order of the Shield, and now farmers, tradesmen, families, and even children lay dead among the ruins. It sickened Justan to understand that this scene that brought heartache and sorrow to his own soul brought delight to their enemy.

That is why we fight, he thought to himself. *Win or lose, the only choice is to fight.*

He brought his hand down and noticed distantly that it glistened with his own blood. He was vaguely aware of numerous wounds covering his body and a hazy pain that gained in intensity with every movement. Warm blood trickled across his skin in more than one spot, but there was no time to have his wounds tended.

The storm, sustained by Rena through the barrier's power, had subsided long ago. The last they had seen of the shield was an eruption of flame from the ground that claimed many of the were-folk's numbers. Then nothing. Rena's power vanished. Justan had no way of knowing whether or not his wife was fading away from him or if she was simply resting, and he fought as if he did not care. He could not remember seeing anyone he recognized in what seemed like hours; although he could not have said for sure how long ago it had been since every minute of the battle raged for what felt like an eternity. He sighed and readied himself to charge into combat once again.

"Justan," a soft voice halted him.

He turned in his saddle, half raising his sword instinctively. It was Dylanna. Justan relaxed at the sight of a familiar face. Breathing a deep sigh he let his sword fall to his side.

"Dylanna, you startled me," he commented needlessly.

Dylanna's gaze swept over him in concern. She took in the weariness about his face and the wounds he had sustained. "How are you holding up?"

"Does it matter?" Justan asked. "I must continue the fight. While I still have strength, I must remain."

"You need to *keep* your strength," Dylanna cautioned. "You must not use yourself up, you will be needed..."

Justan raised a hand. "I have the strength, Dylanna. Please understand me: my men are dying, our castle is overrun, and the day is almost done. I must continue to lead the fight or the men will lose hope. If they do not see me, they will assume I have fallen and that will break their hearts, taking away what hopes they do have. Dylanna, look around. We are defeated, we cannot avoid defeat. Our numbers are too small, we are too weak to stand before so vast an enemy. There will be no victory march for us, no triumph at the end of this day. We fight now merely to give the king more time. If he succeeds, then our deaths will have meaning, our deaths will be worth the cost of this day. A free world for our children?" Justan scowled. "My death is worth that."

An unearthly scream rent the air above them, and both Justan and Dylanna froze, staring at the sky. The silver-winged werehawk flew in a giant circle. Its rider, the one they had identified as Ghrendourak, was emitting bellows of pain and anger that shattered their way across the battlefield. For a moment, all fighting ceased. Then, the werehawk wheeled and winged its way out across the ocean, away from the battlefield. It flew swiftly, disappearing in an eye-blink.

Justan turned to Dylanna, his eyes wide and questioning. She paled.

"My guess? King Oraeyn reached his destination."

"I only hope we've given him enough of a head start," Justan replied quietly.

Before either of them could say more, the battle reached them and Justan pushed Dylanna back, away from the fight, raising his sword to the attack. He spared a quick glance for the wizardess and saw that she was preparing to enter the conflict as well.

"No!" he shouted. "You have skills no one else does. Go back inside the castle! Help Zara. We need your magic more than we need your sword."

Then the enemy was upon him and he did not have time to see if she heeded his orders.

Dawn did not come to Llycaelon. Instead, ominous clouds covered the sky and enemies surged over and through the land. The sheer number of were-folk pouring onto the battlefield through the gap in the cliffs was overwhelming. The aethalons fought fiercely, but even their warrior skills seemed pathetic against the great enemy facing them.

Early in the fighting, Devrin led his troops in and smashed them against Stephran's anvil. The ploy had worked brilliantly, and any other enemy would have fallen to it, but the fact remained that there were not enough aethalons to make a difference.

Leila had never felt so helpless as she did standing on the hill watching everyone else fight. She had been left to guard the refugees, the women and children, and those too injured to continue fighting. Everyone else had gone to battle. She tried to watch Jemson, and for a while she had been able to spot Devrin and Shentallyia, but now they all blurred together in a sea of battle.

"We just have to hold their attention long enough for my uncle to succeed in his quest," Jemson had said to her mere days before.

"And if they don't succeed?" she had asked quietly.

"Then there is no hope for any of us anyway," Jemson had

replied. "I prefer to die fighting. Perhaps we can hold them back; perhaps there are not as many as we anticipate."

But there were so many more than they had feared. Leila stared down at the battle and desperation filled her. It was only a matter of time before they were all dead. Defeat was inevitable, it hemmed them in on all sides.

"Steady, Wizardess," a clicking voice said.

Leila turned and faced the old gryphon that had come up behind her. "Hello again, Kanuckchet. And I am no wizardess."

The gryphon's beak parted. "You wish to be something else now? What wish you to be?"

Leila shook her head at the misunderstanding. "No, I do not wish to be something else, but I am forced to find something new anyway."

The gryphon's feathers rustled, and he jerked his head in a sort of twisting motion. "Foolish wizardess. You do not *lose* magic like you can lose your memory or misplace a beloved object. It cannot be torn away from you like a limb, nor can it be stolen from you like a possession. Wizardess is what you are: as much a part of you as your name; it cannot be lost, merely forgotten. Even the Ancient Enemy cannot make you lose what you are; he can merely make you forget. Speak your true-name and possess its meaning, and you will find yourself again."

"I have tried, I cannot." Leila's hands lifted of their own accord, a poor attempt to convey the depths of the misery that consumed her. "I must find a new function."

"You are who you are and you must find a way to remember. We have great need of you this day, Wizardess."

"Stop calling me that! I am no longer a wizardess!"

"No," the old gryphon said. "It is you who must stop. Stop binding yourself to the lie that has blinded you."

Leila stared at the great myth-creature and began to shake her head in denial, but she paused. There was a knowing look deep in the gryphon's bright gaze that caught her attention, a memory that tugged at her mind. She stared into his wise old face and he returned her stare with unflinching faith.

"Who are you?" she asked wonderingly.

The gryphon threw his head back and clacked out a long name in gryphonese. "My name is Kanuckchet, which means 'guide.' My parents named me well, for I have learned to find what is lost and return it to where it belongs. Now, I have told you my name; what is yours?"

Leila felt foolish and her cheeks flushed. "We don't really hold with true names where I come from…" she began but Kanuckchet cut her off with a sharp click.

"It matters not. Tell me who you are."

"I am Leila."

"*Who are you?*"

"I am Leila," the wizardess said it louder.

"What are you?"

"I am a sylph: part mermaid, part wizardess. My father was a great wizard named Scelwhyn and my mother was a creature of the sea, a mermaid. I am a bridge across worlds, a combination of two races. I am full of their strengths, but I must always remember that I bear their weaknesses, too."

As she spoke, the gryphon stared at her with a frightening intensity. She felt the world begin to spin around her. Her own voice thundered in her ears and she reached out with her mind, attempting to grab hold of something solid. As she did so, she heard her name being repeated over and over again, and then like a door swinging open everything came flooding back. In horror she remembered how she had locked her magic away when she had been floating in that awful portal. She had hidden it where the Enemy could not reach it, but then he had made her believe that he had stolen it instead. After days of endless imprisonment, she had believed his lies. Kiernan Kane had come to rescue her, but not before she had accepted the lie as her own truth.

Now the real truth sprang up before her. She was not defenseless. Nothing about her was broken or defeated. She was whole and strong and capable. She felt power surge within her, bursting forth and begging to be used. As truth washed over her, Leila fell to her knees, salty tears of relief and healing streaming down her face.

"My name is Leila," she repeated. "My name is Leila," her

voice grew stronger as she said it again. "My name is Leila. And I... am a WIZARDESS!"

CHAPTER
TWENTY-SIX

Despite Brant's admonition to move quickly, Kamarie found it impossible to hurry. Slowly, reverently, without making a sound, she followed the others through the doorway and into the great cavern beyond. She gazed around in the sudden light, experiencing an overwhelming sense that she was small and inconsequential. No longer did they stand in an earthen passage, but in a palatial hall designed by the obvious hand of a master architect. The floors were a gleaming obsidian and the walls were of polished silver. Massive pillars led the eye upwards to an expansive ceiling of pure, brilliant gold so bright it was painful to look at it. As they emerged into the spectacular hall, the secret door slammed shut behind them with a crash that resounded and echoed throughout the chamber.

"Well, that cuts down on our options," Oraeyn commented wryly.

Kamarie chuckled nervously, then fell silent. She stepped up to his side and slipped her hand into his. Together they stood still, taking in their new surroundings and gazing about in awe.

"It's so bright," she commented. Her words felt hollow, but she could think of nothing else to say.

"This part of the tunnel is well lit by Yorien's Hand," Brant explained. "Let us leave the unused torches here for the return trip."

"In all creation, there is nothing that takes my breath away more than this place," Kiernan's voice was barely a whisper, but his words were yet loud enough to be heard.

Kamarie squinted at him. "You make it sound as if you've been here before."

"Yes," Kiernan replied. "Many times."

"What?" Brant turned to the minstrel, dumbfounded. "How many times?"

"This is my sixth visit, I believe," Kiernan surprised them all with his willingness to answer Brant's question. Kamarie stared at him. It was so out of character for Kiernan to give information freely and devoid of riddles.

Brant opened and closed his mouth several times, his brow furrowed. At length he gave his head a small shake. "I don't even know where to begin," he growled. "What possible reason could you have for coming here six times?"

Kiernan's mouth quirked up on one side. "Six High Kings," he replied, then he shivered slightly. When he spoke again, it was not in hushed tones. "Come, the end of your quest is near."

He moved away, beginning the trek across the hall with long, sure strides. Kamarie watched him, mystified. His words gave her a chill, and she rubbed her arms briskly.

Hope was fresh in her heart and it grew with each step towards the end of their journey. She could tell there was a lightness to the others as well. Yet the fear of failure was far more acute now that their goal was within their grasp. The hall grew brighter and brighter the farther they continued. The ceiling sloped up, or perhaps it was the floor that sloped down— Kamarie could not have said for sure—she glanced up once and instantly regretted it; the brilliance made her dizzy. Reflected light bounced off the walls in a dazzling display and Kamarie noticed scattered diamonds glistening in the floor.

"It's like we're walking above the sky at night," she murmured.

They were halfway across the hall when the path began to grow narrow, leading up to a bridge across a deep, yawning chasm. As they approached the bridge, the chill brought on by Kiernan's words earlier returned. Kamarie hung back, loath to set foot on the bridge.

Why did I come on this journey? She forced herself to continue, following Kiernan, and asking herself the question she had been avoiding. Here they were, nearly to their goal, and she was compelled to admit to herself that she had added no value to the quest. She had only endangered her friends along the way. Kiernan had discovered the portal. Brant, Oraeyn, and the dragons had fought off the whyvrens. Ina had given them the key to the secret tunnel. Even Leila, trapped by the enemy for days, had given them more useful information and insight than anything Kamarie had been able to contribute. She had done nothing helpful. Her thoughts strayed to Oraeyn's arguments against her coming and her shoulders slumped.

"I shouldn't have come," she whispered.

Even as she spoke, she felt a presence behind her and whirled, searching for the source of her discomfort. A moment later, bursting into the cavern from the tunnel's exit, three creatures came racing across the floor.

"Brant!" Kamarie shouted.

"Dracors!" Kiernan's voice rang out.

Brant and Oraeyn rushed back to Kamarie, their swords drawn as they stepped in front of her. They stood their ground as the dracors reached them and halted. They were lizard-like in appearance, and a foot taller than a grown man. Their eyes were filled with hatred; saliva dripped from their mouths, soiling the beautiful floor beneath their wickedly sharp claws. The creatures crouched and roared, the sound reverberating off of the walls. Kamarie clapped her hands over her ears and cried out.

"Kamarie?" Oraeyn asked, though he did not turn. All of his attention was fixed on the three dracors.

"I'm all right," Kamarie felt shaky. She pressed the palm of her hand to her temple. "Their voices... they... it hurts my head, but there are words... not words, um, pictures? I can't explain it."

"Just back away," Oraeyn replied. "We'll hold them."

The dracors prowled forward, their claws clicking on the

ground. They roared again and shook their heads, their blunt noses raised, testing the air.

Kamarie reached out and tapped Oraeyn's shoulder. "I don't think they can see. The light blinds them."

"How do you know?" Oraeyn hissed.

"It's in their voices, when they call out. They don't want to be here. They're afraid of something..."

"Well, I'm afraid of them," Oraeyn's voice rose a bit, and the dracors swung their heads towards him.

Brant raised a hand. "Kamarie," he whispered. "Do you think you can communicate with them? They're not were-folk, just animals. Usually nocturnal. I've heard of them, but I've never seen one before."

"I..." Kamarie hesitated, her mind racing. "I don't..."

"You seem to understand them," Brant continued in a hushed tone. "I know you have not explored your mother's side of your heritage. I know it frightens you. But it is part of you. Leila can speak with beasts. Dylanna is the best shape-shifter I've ever encountered. Calyssia's power to protect was legendary. Your grandfather was one of the greatest wizards of history and if Dylanna is right, your mother could have exceeded his power. It is time to discover your own."

Kamarie's face grew pale as Brant spoke. She drew her upper lip between her teeth, her eyebrows furrowing in consternation. The dracors roared again and headed towards the company.

"Very well," Kamarie stepped up to stand next to Oraeyn. "You are right."

She held up a hand and concentrated on radiating calm, composure. She took a deep breath and tried to relax.

"You don't want to be here," her voice trembled. The dracors snarled, advancing another step. Kamarie tried to summon a vision of her aunt when she was talking to her animals. She straightened, looking directly at the creatures and hiding her fear of them. "You don't want to be here," her voice grew firm, commanding. "This isn't a place for you. Brightness. It hurts. It pains. You are of the night, the cool. You wish to sleep. The thing that drives you, it is not your master. Go. Go now. Sleep now. Hunt later."

The lead dracor swayed slightly.

Kamarie took a deep breath. "This place is not good for you. There is no food here. No dark. You are exposed, vulnerable, leave now, find trees, dark. There will you be safe." The words flowed from her mouth in a strange, clipped pattern. They were not her words, but they felt natural nonetheless.

The lead dracor made a whimpering sound and then hissed at his companions and they turned and fled back the way they had come.

Oraeyn turned to Kamarie, a jubilant light in his eyes. "That was..."

A rumble like a volcano about to erupt shook the floor. A horrifying scream reverberated around the tunnel and a whirling rush of wind howled past their faces. Into the tunnel flew the largest bird they had ever seen. Its feathers were blacker than the obsidian beneath their feet, but tipped with shining argent tones. As it descended to the floor of the tunnel it snapped its beak and screamed again, sounding angry.

"'Black death rides on silver wings,'" Kamarie quoted a piece of the prophecy. Cold horror clutched her stomach as a massive being stepped off the back of the werehawk. Her chest tightened, making it difficult to breathe.

The creature was a foot taller than Brant. His body was encased in obsidian armor. The dull onyx hue of the armor swallowed any light that sought to touch him. The breastplate was adorned with an etched crest: two crossed swords with a star hanging suspended above them. The man, if man he was, wore a helm formed in the likeness of a wolf's maw, which concealed everything about his face.

"Ghrendourak."

Kamarie was not sure who whispered the name, perhaps it was torn from her own throat, though she did not know if she had the breath left to utter even a single syllable. In the same way the light was being sucked into the creature's armor, Kamarie felt that her breath was being stolen away as well.

Ghrendourak stood still for a moment, and the world stilled.

Then he drew his sword. The great blade shrieked triumphantly as it came out of the sheath, eager to leap into its owner's hands and wreak destruction. The sword was a twisted and ugly thing, jagged and ill-formed, but deadly nonetheless.

Brant and Oraeyn drew their own swords as they stepped in front of Kamarie. Belatedly, she began to tug her sword from its sheath, but her fingers felt numb and clumsy. She scowled, angry at herself for being so afraid. Clenching her fingers around the hilt of her sword, Kamarie tugged it from its sheath only to find herself being inexplicably swept backwards. She looked up and blinked in confusion as she realized that Kiernan Kane had come forward and was now standing in front of Ghrendourak, blocking the enemy's path.

Evil laughter screeched painfully from Ghrendourak's throat as he gazed down at the minstrel. "Ah, my old adversary. I should have known you would be here, guiding those deluded enough to think they can defeat me."

The minstrel made no reply; he stood before Ghrendourak cloaked in calm. Kiernan suddenly appeared to be a completely different creature. He did not flinch or cower, but stood with straight back and head held high. There was defiance etched in every line of his stance. The mandolin strapped to his back was strangely incongruous attached to this man brandishing a sword with such a firm and steady hand.

Ghrendourak's voice became a snarl, "You are old, *Minstrel*, and weak. You cannot stop me this time! Stand aside!"

With a swift movement of his arm Ghrendourak attacked; the jagged blade hissed as it arced through the air towards the minstrel. Kiernan's own sword swept upwards to meet Ghrendourak's blade. There was a loud *crack* and a shower of sparks as the minstrel's sword halted the enemy's blade. Kamarie blinked in disbelief and stared: Kiernan's sword was glowing a pure white. The light poured out of the blade and twined around Ghrendourak's sword, swallowing its darkness and wending towards his hand.

"*RUN!*"

Kamarie turned and fled across the bridge she had been so

hesitant to navigate a moment before. Behind her, she could hear Brant and Oraeyn, their footsteps keeping time with her own. Together they raced across the chasm, leaving the minstrel to face Ghrendourak alone. The werehawk screeched angrily. They were halfway across the bridge when Kamarie felt the wind from its wings just before it attacked. She ducked and stabbed upwards with her sword. Resistance nearly tore the hilt from her hands as the blade connected with something solid. The creature screamed and wheeled away, giving Kamarie, Oraeyn, and Brant the chance to ready themselves for the next attack. The great bird dove again, talons outstretched. Kamarie swept her arm and felt her sword bite into the werehawk's belly. Scaly feathers rustled and warm blood poured from the wound. Quicker than thought, the werehawk banked and attacked again, plunging into their midst and striking at them with its wings and beak. Brant's sword flashed in the light and the creature hissed as the blade connected with one of its wings. It whirled, the other wing coming close to knocking Kamarie over. She avoided colliding with the sharp feathers only to find herself slipping in the creature's blood. She fell to the ground, dangerously close to the sharp talons. The bird caught sight of her and attacked, its head darting towards the princess.

Time slowed. Kamarie felt no fear as her training took hold. She waited, appearing helpless as the striking beak plunged down. At the last instant, she flicked her blade up between herself and the werehawk. The creature was unprepared for such a sudden attack from its seemingly defeated prey, and was unable to change direction swiftly enough to save itself. It dove forward, impaling itself on Kamarie's blade. A great, gurgling shriek emanated from its open beak and then the werehawk's eyes turned glassy as it fell limply to the ground.

Kamarie had no way of defending herself as the great beast toppled towards her. She could not even raise her arms to shield her face. But then someone grabbed her roughly by the shoulders and yanked her out of the way. She just had the presence of mind to keep a tight grip on the hilt of her sword, pulling it from the werehawk's corpse as it fell, crashing through the delicate railing of the bridge and plummeting into the chasm.

Kamarie turned and saw that it was Brant who had pulled her to safety and she gave a wide-eyed shake of her head.

"Thank you," she said.

Brant opened his mouth to reply, but the ringing of metal on metal drew their attention to the end of the bridge they had come from; a brief look showed Kiernan still battling Ghrendourak. The minstrel was holding his own, but Kamarie worried he could not last much longer. Ghrendourak was a powerful warrior, and Kiernan Kane was just a minstrel.

They raced the rest of the way across the bridge, heading ever towards the shining beacon on the other side of the cavern.

"There!" Oraeyn gasped.

Ahead, resting on a stone plinth, Yorien's Hand lit the great hall. Its effulgence was beyond dazzling. Kamarie held up a hand, shielding her face. In all her days to come, she never could describe what the star was like, or what she experienced in its presence. Waves of heat washed over her, mixed with blasts of frigid, icy air. Colors danced in her vision, blinding her, and yet she believed in that moment that she saw more clearly than ever before. The world filled with music that emanated from the depths of the star, and yet all was silence.

"Yorien's Hand," Brant's voice was reverent. "The greatest gift our world has ever received."

They were still a fair distance from the plinth upon which the star rested, but it drew them in, beckoning them to come bask in its radiance and embrace its impossibilities. Behind them, the battle between Ghrendourak and Kiernan Kane raged. A noise like thunder rumbled down the hallway and the whole tunnel shook with its force. With a mighty cracking sound like mountains being rent asunder the marble floor split open right beneath Kamarie's feet. Rocks and pebbles rained down from above. Kamarie screamed, flailing her arms wildly. For a heart-stopping moment she felt she would regain her balance, but then the hall trembled again and her foot slipped. With a terrified shriek, she tumbled down into the abyss that yawned hungrily beneath her.

Leila urged Hawkspin into a gallop, and together they plunged into the fray. Rearing and whirling, the horse lashed out with its hooves as Leila commanded a hurricane to sweep away her enemies. Power filled her, consumed her, and poured through her. Seheowks gnashed their teeth and screamed in terror as the windstorm of Leila's wrath lifted them up and hurled them back into the sea.

A whyvren landed heavily on the ground before Leila, spewing darkness at her. Hawkspin reared up, hooves pawing at the air, as a glimmering shaft of light like a spear appeared in Leila's hand. She flung the spear at the whyvren's center and the creature burst into a million tiny motes of dust, dissipating swiftly like morning mist.

Anger at the pain this enemy had caused roared through her veins and she let it loose in a javelin of flame, pushing the monsters back, ever back. They recoiled and fled from her, scattering like frightened beetles that scurry to the edges of a room when the drapes are pulled back to let in the light of day.

Power coursing through her, Leila urged Hawkspin towards the center of the gap. Her cloak streamed out behind her, flapping as she raced into the enemy, one hand raised in defiance of all the sorrow and darkness that this foe had caused. As she rode through their ranks, the aethalons raised a cry.

"The Wizardess! The Wizardess!"

Leila did not hear them. All she knew was the joy of being restored to herself. She continued to fight, beating back the creatures of shadow. More and more of them began to focus on this new threat, but nothing could withstand the fury of the wizardess unshackled.

Reacting without thought, Oraeyn leaped after the princess and caught Kamarie's wrist. Her weight threw him off balance and he was pulled to the floor. The world spun crazily out of control and turned upside down as Oraeyn felt himself falling and sliding towards the fissure. He scrabbled frantically at the tunnel floor with his free hand. Just as he reached the edge, his fingers found purchase and their descent was halted. Kamarie dangled above the chasm, her wrist clutched in his grasp. She stared up at him in fright. From a distance, Oraeyn heard his name being called.

"Oraeyn! Oraeyn!" Brant's voice pulled him back out of his panic. "Oraeyn! You must finish the quest, you must take the star! You hold the golden blade, you must... Oraeyn..." there was anguish in Brant's voice.

Oraeyn twisted to look at the warrior. Another wide fissure had opened between himself and Brant, cutting him off from them. There was no way for Brant to reach them, no help for Kamarie without Oraeyn. The young king gazed across the cavern into Brant's eyes and saw his own doubts reflected there, his own worry and helplessness. And yet, there was a sternness there as well, a determination that Oraeyn could not muster.

The earthquake had not blocked either his or Brant's path to the star. But fractures in the floor threatened to split open if too much stress was applied to them. Tears blurred Oraeyn's vision as he gazed down at Kamarie. Her beautiful face stared up at him. He could tell from the intensity of her gaze that she had guessed what had happened.

"My love," he choked on the words.

"Oraeyn..." Kamarie's voice trembled, but there was a strength in it, as well. "Oraeyn, please..."

Oraeyn's heart throbbed and ached as it was ripped apart. In a flash, his nightmare returned. In his mind's eye, he watched in horror as the dream Kamarie fell away from him once more, tumbling down into the abyss, heard his own voice reverberate in his ears in a scream of agony. With an effort, he pushed the dream away and stared down into the real face of the one he loved, memorizing her face, and he realized that he had no choice. His throat felt tight, and it took all his strength just to form the words he had to say.

"Kamarie, my love, I am so sorry... I have no choice," he whispered, his voice breaking. "I—I never had any choice."

Kamarie's face twisted in dread. He could see the muscles in her throat contracting as she swallowed. But when she spoke, her voice was calm, "I understand. I love you."

"Are you ready?"

"Yes."

Oraeyn gritted his teeth. Strengthening his grip on her wrist he gave a tremendous heave. Groaning with the effort, muscles straining, Oraeyn lifted Kamarie out of the chasm and set her on solid ground. She stared at him in shocked disbelief for the span of a breath, and then she collapsed into his arms. He pulled her close to him and held her while she shook with frightened sobs.

In that moment, the ground trembled again and the floor split open once more. Oraeyn held Kamarie tightly to his chest as more dust from above fell around them. When the earthquake stopped, Oraeyn peered around in dismay. The tremor had cracked the earth open in several places, and it had left a wide, unbridgeable gap between him and Yorien's Hand.

"Oraeyn!" Brant's shout made Oraeyn turn. The ground around Brant was untouched by the earthquake, he could still reach the star, but there was no way for Oraeyn to reach Brant. He and Kamarie were stranded on a thin peninsula, with nowhere to turn except back the way that they had come.

"I can't get across!" Oraeyn shouted. He felt a cold and overwhelming despair clawing wildly within him as he realized the cost of Kamarie's life. His breath came fast as his mind raced.

He stared at Brant in the flickering light of the unattainable star. The warrior nodded once, approval for Oraeyn's choice gleaming on his face in defiance of all they had come through, all they had suffered. And as Oraeyn watched, his aspect changed. He was still Brant, the familiar face and stature, but there was also something more, a presence that the light of the star revealed. Authority and strength rested on Brant like a second skin. The golden glow of the star reached out to encase him and a radiant crown of dazzling light adorned his head. In that moment, Oraeyn saw Brant as he was meant to be, as he had always been meant to be. In a flash of insight, Oraeyn realized

his true role in the quest they had undertaken; for the first time
in weeks he knew exactly what to do.

"Brant!" he unbuckled his sword belt and wrapped it around
the scabbard of the Fang Blade. Then he flung it across the gap
between them. "Catch!"

Reacting instinctively, the warrior reached up and caught the
blade by the hilt. He stared at Oraeyn in confusion. He drew the
sword from its sheath and the blade began to glow. The glow
flamed into a blaze of luminous gold, brighter than it had ever
shone in Oraeyn's hands.

"I can't reach the star, Brant," Oraeyn shouted, and the
absolute rightness of his words welled up within him along with
an overwhelming peace. "I was never meant to."

As he held the blade, Brant's mind lit with the same
understanding that had enveloped Oraeyn. The warrior's jaw
hardened with resolve as he held Oraeyn's gaze across the chasm,
then he turned and faced the glowing orb. Abandoning his own
sword and sheathing the Fang Blade he walked steadily and
carefully towards Yorien's Hand. All thought and emotion
ceased; he was consumed by the enormity of the task at hand,
the task he had failed once before.

As he approached the star, thought and feeling returned in a
painful rush of awareness. Heat from the star raged, burning his
skin. Freezing air encased him, and he shivered in its icy blast.
Brant peeked at his hands, half expecting them to be covered
with blisters. He was surprised to see that they appeared
untouched by the heat or the cold.

Brant edged towards the plinth until he was standing before
it. Cautiously, he reached his hands out to the star. As he touched
its edges images of his life rushed towards him in a dizzying
cascade of pain and sorrow. Faces of loved ones flashed by him.
Remembering the ordeal he had endured the first time, Brant
jerked away. Breathing heavily, he paused. When he had stood
here before, he had been but a boy, hungry for adventure, for
glory, for the thrill of a conquest. Now he was a man, and he
only wished to serve as best he could to protect as many as he
could. All hesitation gone, Brant reached out and grasped the

star with both hands. There was a flash of white light, and then everything stopped.

From where they had been standing and watching, Kamarie and Oraeyn clung to each other in terror, wondering if they had been struck blind. A weak tremor rippled through the cavern, far less violent than the previous quakes. Then, for the space of several heartbeats all was still. As they clung to each other, Kamarie and Oraeyn began to notice a hazy glow emanating from the spot where they had last seen Brant. The glow grew brighter until they could make out the figure of a man holding a sword.

Oraeyn felt a jolt of shock as Brant became fully visible, his body filled with light. He strode towards them with confident strides across a floor that was once more a solid whole. The cracks and crevices caused by the earthquakes had sealed up like they had never existed.

"How is that possible?" Oraeyn's voice burst from his lips in the sudden silence.

"It's not over yet," Brant said, not stopping as he passed them. "Follow me."

Together, as they had begun, the three of them raced back across the bridge. At the end of the bridge, several large boulders lay on the floor where they had fallen from the ceiling. The three companions crouched behind the largest of these.

Kiernan was still holding his own against Ghrendourak, and Oraeyn felt admiration as he watched the minstrel fight. Kiernan only defended, he did not attack. His every movement was graceful, poised, and—it was obvious after just a moment of observation—designed to prevent his opponent from reaching the bridge.

"Stay here," Brant said firmly. Then he stepped out from behind the boulder and strode towards Kiernan. "Ghrendourak!" he boomed; authority rang in his voice.

Ghrendourak paused for a moment, his sword halted in the midst of its arc towards the minstrel. He swung his head around to look at Brant. There was hesitation in his movements even as he responded to Brant's challenge. He looked back at the minstrel and a strangled sound came from deep within the helm.

"What mockery is this, Minstrel?"

Kiernan's lips twitched. He turned and his gaze found Oraeyn and Kamarie. He winked at them, grin widening.

"Your time is done, Ghrendourak," Kiernan said.

Ghrendourak laughed, an evil sound that echoed gratingly off the walls. "What? This is not the one whose dreams I visited! You have made a mistake, Minstrel, and it shall be your last!" He took a single, menacing step towards Brant. "You are not the one who can stand against me. Haven't you heard the prophecy? *Only two can stand before him. Only one can hope to fell him.* You see? You are nothing to me." His words were confident, but his voice wavered, and lacked conviction. "I have defeated my greatest threat already: he is either dead, or he has not been able to finish his quest. All that stands between me and the throne is my old enemy here," Ghrendourak gestured towards Kiernan Kane, "and he is soon defeated."

Brant's voice was steady, "You are wrong."

But Ghrendourak had stopped listening. Turning his back on Brant once more, his attention was focused solely on Kiernan Kane. "Yours is the time that has come to an end, *Minstrel.*" His words ended in a snarl of hate, and the twisted, ugly blade swung with deadly speed.

Faster than thought, Brant drew the Fang Blade and leaped between Kiernan and Ghrendourak. The sword hummed with power as it sliced through the air and halted the blow. The Fang Blade rang out with a mighty crash as it met the enemy's sword solidly and stopped its descent. That sound as the two great blades collided was one Oraeyn knew he would never forget, no matter how long he lived.

With a cry of rage that carried a hint of pain, Ghrendourak stumbled away, for the first time seeming vulnerable. He stared at Brant in disbelief and growled deep in his throat. With ominous steps he advanced. The warrior stood calmly waiting for his opponent. There was no fear on Brant's face, only peace. As Oraeyn watched, he saw that there was a glow surrounding Brant in the same way that eerie darkness surrounded Ghrendourak. At first he thought it was because Brant was holding the Fang Blade, but then he realized that the light was coming from Brant himself. It began deep within him and radiated outwards. The closer Ghrendourak came, the more Brant's appearance shone like the face of the Dragon's Eye, until he blazed as bright as Ghrendourak's darkness. Without a sound, Ghrendourak struck.

Oraeyn could not follow all the moves. Time stood still; he seemed to see in slow motion, and yet the battle raged faster than he could follow. Later, when asked, he said only that it had been a whirlwind of swords and a thunder of metal clashing against metal. He tried to watch, but the brilliant light pouring from Brant had been too bright for him to see much at all, while the murk that flowed from Ghrendourak made it impossible to see anything. That was never something Oraeyn could explain well, in all his years after. Kamarie found similar difficulty, later, putting the experience into adequate words. All either of them could ever say to anyone's satisfaction was that watching Brant fight had been like staring into the molten center of a volcano or the mesmerizing flashes of lightning: hypnotic and beautiful, but deadly.

Brant sidestepped and thrust and parried, his movements graceful and fluid. The swords rang as they clashed together. Light continued to pour from Brant, filling the air as he struck and retreated. Ghrendourak blocked each of Brant's attacks, but his power appeared to be fading with every movement.

At long last, in a blur of motion nobody could follow, Brant drove the Fang Blade through Ghrendourak's defenses. The ancient enemy roared in defiant despair as the light of the blade grew brighter and brighter until all Ghrendourak's darkness was swallowed. And then the enemy was no more. He neither vanished nor evaporated nor burned, he simply ceased to be. There was a rush of wind, a great howl, and then silence.

Brant stood triumphant for a moment, radiant and untouchable. Then he dropped to the ground and lay there like a dead man. Oraeyn and Kamarie rushed out from behind the boulder to his side, but Kiernan Kane reached him first. The minstrel looked up at them, his expression reassuring.

"Give him a moment; he will revive."

Brant gasped and convulsed and the others helped him sit up.

"Hold on," Kamarie said firmly, her voice resembling the same no-nonsense tone that Dylanna often used. "If you get up too quickly, you will only collapse again." Her words sounded so normal in the aftermath of the battle that they made Oraeyn laugh out loud.

TWENTY-SEVEN

"Well, we just saved the world," Oraeyn broke the triumphant, weary silence as they gathered around Brant, who was still sitting on the cavern floor.

"And the world has a new High King," Kiernan added.

Brant's expression turned pensive and startled. "I hadn't quite thought about it that way, yet."

"I'm glad it's you," Oraeyn said earnestly.

Kamarie squeezed Oraeyn's hand. "Me too."

"I'm not sure I'm the right choice," Brant replied, closing his eyes in a sudden wave of dizziness. The world spun around him, taunting him. Prophecies and rhymes gathered around, shouting their words at him.

"But you were chosen," Kiernan replied, his voice quelling the flood of thoughts. "It was not a mistake."

The dizziness abated and Brant stood with a weary groan. He unbuckled his sword belt and extended the bundle containing the Fang Blade to Oraeyn. "Either way, I should return this to its rightful owner."

Oraeyn shook his head. "No, you keep it."

Brant frowned, not understanding Oraeyn's reluctance. "But it's yours. It was forged in Aom-igh, for Aom-igh. It should stay with her king." Brant held the sword out and shook it slightly, mild exasperation creeping into his tone. "Here."

"No," Oraeyn's held his hands out, rejecting the proffered blade. "It is yours. The prophecy was about you. It was always about you. I was only ever supposed to hold the sword, not use it. To tell you the truth, I'm relieved, I never felt that it belonged to me anyway. But if you need another reason, then accept it as a gift: my token of fealty to the new High King."

Brant lowered his arm. "You're sure?"

"Completely. More sure than I've ever been. The Fang Blade belongs to you. I wouldn't have it any other way."

"Thank you." Brant met and held Oraeyn's gaze, and more passed between them than words could express. "Well then," Brant said, eventually, "we should get moving."

"Are you sure you're ready?" Kamarie asked.

"I'm fine," Brant assured her. "I just needed a short rest. Come on, it's time we left this place."

Together, they began the first steps of the long journey home.

Daylight penetrated the thick clouds, and the were-folk that did not vanish in its light fled from the battlefield with all the speed they possessed. Pain lanced through Justan's body, causing his vision to waver and blur, but he forced himself to watch as the glow of the Dragon's Eye swept over the castle, down into the valleys, and then out across the sea. It shone with a radiance brighter than ever before, at least, to Justan's memory.

The battle was over. They had held the enemy off long enough, and King Oraeyn had succeeded.

From where he lay, Justan was unable to see much of the battlefield. The area around him was littered with the bodies of those who were dead or dying. At the retreat of the were-folk, the unicorns ventured out onto the field searching through the bodies for those who might still live, hoping to save as many as they could. He could see their equine forms picking their way towards him. He felt a surge of triumph at lasting long enough to see the enemy banished. Justan knew that grief would come soon, and tears for those who had given their lives this day, but for now he could not help but allow a slight smile to creep across his lips in the healing light of dawn.

He was gravely injured and did not have the strength to raise himself from where he had fallen. But he could no longer feel the pain. It had passed with the arrival of the light. He was content to let go and drift away. If he died here, he died well, having accomplished what he set out to do. For now, that was good enough.

The war was over. King Jemson watched in fascination as the rays of light drove the creatures into retreat. Victory came without herald. Light spread out over the land in a burst of glory, as if day and night had been held in an intense struggle for supremacy and day had won. Daylight overwhelmed every last vestige of night in its brilliance and those who had fought back the were-folk rejoiced in its welcome effulgence.

Even in the midst of celebration over their triumph, sorrow and grief had their place as well. The cost of victory was dear. Stephran, and many others, had not survived the battle.

Devrin found the body of his Chief of Staff, pierced by many arrows and surrounded by his fallen foes. With Shentallyia's help he carried his advisor and friend back to the camp and gently laid his body amongst the others. Then he returned to Jemson's side, his shoulders and head bowed with the weight of loss.

The dead were counted and the numbers of their fallen overwhelmed Jemson. The battle had taken a terrible toll. As the aethalons searched through the bodies and recognized their fallen comrades and brothers-in-arms, they would call out the name of the man and a wail would permeate the air. The sound was not loud, but it carried eerily across the battlefield, memorializing those who had fallen.

It was good to mourn now, Jemson reflected. Too often and in too many places, grief was not properly observed. He had witnessed his father eaten alive from the inside out by it, leading to tragedy for so many others. But that was not typically the way of the aethalons.

There would be a traditional burial here later. The names of the fallen would be read and the families or warrior-brethren, would place memorial stones upon the field for every fallen aethalon. Their true-names would be whispered as the stones were placed, and then the living would depart. The stones were a memorial, but they were also a symbol that the mourning period was over, a reminder that just as those left alive could not carry the stones forever, neither should they carry their grief.

"A heavy day," Devrin said, coming up behind him.

Jemson turned and looked at his commander. Earlier, Devrin and Shentallyia had flown after the enemy to ensure that the retreat was not a trick. They were just now returned. Jemson nodded at Devrin's words, his face grave.

"The were-folk are truly gone," Devrin reported.

"That is good news."

Devrin nodded, his expression vacant.

"I am sorry about Stephran. He was your friend?"

"Yes."

"It is a hard loss. He was a good warrior."

"And a good man. He will be missed on the Border Patrol... I had thought to make him a member of the King's Helm, but now..."

"He would have been a good choice."

Devrin gave a long, slow sigh and gave his head a tiny shake, as if still trying to grasp the reality of their situation. "The enemy is well and truly gone."

"Then King Oraeyn must have succeeded and Ghrendourak is defeated."

"A great victory."

Jemson shook his head. "There is no victory for us on this day. We stood our ground against a great evil, and a great price was exacted. But this is not victory, it is simply what was required on this day."

Devrin winced. The Dragon's Eye blazed overhead; together they basked in its warmth. As they stood together on the battlefield, sorrowful and weary, yet grateful to be alive and witnessing the start of a new day, Jemson wondered where his uncle was standing on this morning. He knew the quest to find the Hand of Yorien and defeat Ghrendourak had succeeded, but he did not know how that success had come about. His place was here in Llycaelon, he accepted that, but he could not help but wish he had been there to see the end of that auspicious quest.

Justan awoke to familiar surroundings and a splitting headache. He was lying on a bunk in the barracks, a blanket drawn up to his chin. All was still; soft light filtered in through the window. He sat up. Soft snores, punctuated by quiet groans drew his attention to the other bunks in the long room. Each held a slumbering form, and pallets had been arranged on the floor for even more wounded and weary soldiers. He put a hand to his head, gingerly touching the bandage wound around it. His other wounds had been dressed and, though he felt sore and dizzy, it was apparent that he would survive. After a moment, the dizziness abated a little, and he felt ready to stand. Moving with great care, he rose and tottered over to the window. It was nighttime.

He remembered the light breaking through the clouds and flooding the battlefield with a brilliant luster. He remembered thinking he was going to die.

"Rena," he whispered.

Every step was excruciating, but Justan made his slow way across the palace grounds and up the stairs to the room where Rena was sleeping. He lifted the latch and pushed the door open.

Rena lay on the bed within, her expression serene. Justan stared at her for a long moment, drinking in the sight of her. Kessella was sitting at the bedside. She half-rose, turning as she did so, when the door swung open.

Justan felt a wave of gratitude sweep over him at the sight of the ancient unicorn.

"Thank you," he rasped, "for staying with her."

Kessella's eyes were large and mournful as she met Justan's

gaze. Then she gave the tiniest shake of her head.

There were no words. None needed to be said. Justan's head throbbed with renewed intensity and his vision narrowed and dimmed.

Kessella crossed the room and placed a steadying hand on his arm. She looked into his face with a questioning look, and Justan took a shaky breath and waved a hand.

"I, um, thank you, I..." he faltered, unable to speak another word, unable to think another word as his world collapsed.

The woman nodded, then slipped out the door, leaving Justan alone with his grief.

He stood in the doorway long after Kessella was gone. With halting, trembling steps he crossed the room and sat in the chair that was already pulled up to the bedside.

"You did it," he whispered, his voice hoarse and filled with pain. "The shield provided what we needed in order to give King Oraeyn time." He paused, then lifted her hand in his own. "It's done," he could barely force the words past the lump in his throat. "You can come back now." Tears wound their way down his face and he pressed his lips to the lifeless hand of the woman he loved. "Please," he whispered.

A hollowness filled his chest as he bowed his head, shoulders shaking with sobs of grief and loss.

Kiernan strummed an idle, cheerful tune on his mandolin as the companions reached the end of the tunnel and emerged once more into the palace of the High Kings. The long passage felt much shorter on the return trip, and though they were weary to their very bones, the companions talked and laughed along the way. There was a lightness to their hearts that had been absent for many days.

As they exited the tunnel, Oraeyn gasped in wonder. The walls of the palace were whole and strong. The roof was freshly timbered. Veins of gold outlined the windows and adorned oaken trim in intricate, decorative filigrees. Chandeliers high above them glittered with diamonds, casting rainbows on the walls. Tapestries of velvet and silk, woven with threads of every color imaginable, hung from massive wrought iron rods. The floor was carpeted with thick, soft rugs and the windows gleamed in the light of day.

The four companions wandered through the palace in amazement until they came to the front doors. Brant pulled them open, and they stared out at a true courtyard, with a garden in full bloom. The hedges were neatly trimmed, and every flower had burst open, even the ones not in season. The gates were adorned with gold plating and the painting on the doors was fresh and new. But as they gazed about the garden the greatest wonder of all was seeing Yole, in human form, limping up the garden path towards them.

Oraeyn gave a shout of joy and raced to the boy's side.

"Yole!"

He put an arm around the lad and helped him sit down on a nearby bench. "I never thought to see you again."

Yole managed a wan smile. "You very nearly never did."

Kamarie knelt down and peeled back Yole's pant-leg, revealing a deep, red gash. She set down her pack and pulled out clean cloth and began wrapping it around the wound.

"What happened after we left?" Oraeyn asked. "Where is Thorayenak?"

Yole's mouth twisted, his face crumpling in heavy sorrow. "After he urged the rest of you to run, Thorayenak and I returned to battle with the whyvrens. We held them at bay as long as we could, but they wounded me and... they killed Thorayenak. They must have believed I was dead as well, for as soon as we had both fallen, they raced away in the direction you had gone. I tried to follow, fearing that they would catch you, but I could not find any trace of your path. I wandered for a long time with no notion of where I was, lost and confused. Then, yesterday morning, the clouds parted and daylight shone through the trees. I found the path once more and made my way to the palace. I had no way of finding you, but I knew you had come this way, and had not yet returned. I have been waiting since then. But what happened to you?"

Yole listened as they related the story of their journey down the tunnel. When they reached the part about Kamarie falling, Oraeyn took over the story-telling and explained how he had made the decision to save her first. Then he described the second earthquake and how he had found himself cut off from his goal. Yole was curious about how he had discovered the answer to the final riddle. Oraeyn could not explain it himself, except to say that he had felt what he was supposed to do through the sword.

Yole nodded his head, his expression filled with grief and wisdom. "It was good for you to trust the sword. It has the magic of dragons buried within. It knew its true place and owner. You were its bearer for many reasons, most of which we will probably never know. But it knew when the time came that it had served you long enough and must now serve another to fulfill a different purpose." Yole stopped speaking and then his face turned bright red. "I sounded like my teachers just then."

They related to him the battle between Brant and Ghrendourak, and at length the stories had been exhausted.

Yole let out a weary breath. "Others must be told of this. The word must be spread that a High King sits on the throne at Emnolae once more."

"In good time," Brant agreed. "But there are other things that need finishing first. We must discover what has happened in our absence before we can turn to celebration. It was always our assumption that defeating Ghrendourak was the key to victory, but I would like to see with my own eyes that the invasions have ceased before I turn my thoughts to what it means to be High King."

"I cannot carry you all by myself," Yole's words held an ocean of loss. "I will see if I can contact any of my brethren and request their aid."

"Thank you," Brant replied. "We would be much obliged."

TWENTY-EIGHT

Kamarie stood with her father just outside the garden gates as soft music filled the twilight air around Ardura Palace. It had been three months since Ghrendourak's defeat. There had been much sorrow in the months since the battle, and endless days of back-breaking work as the people of Tellurae Aquaous worked to rebuild their lands. Much of what had followed their victory on Emnolae still seemed to her like it had passed in a blur. The somber flight home. The memorial services to honor the heroes, both those who had fallen in battle, and the ones who had survived. The solemn task of beginning to rebuild what had been destroyed by the enemy. But now there was time for a moment of joy.

A pair of fireflies flitted past and Kamarie's gaze followed them, a fluttery feeling of her own matching their flight. Arnaud smiled down at her and lightly brushed the end of her nose with a gentle finger. She laughed at the familiar gesture and then leaned forward impulsively to embrace him.

"How do I look?" she asked, nervously raising a hand to her hair and patting the flowers that had been braided into a crown. She pulled her fingers away, internally reminding herself that playing with them would just cause the arrangement to loosen, and also refrained from fiddling with the pearls worked into the long white skirt of her dress.

"You are beautiful," Arnaud said. His voice brimmed with a type of love and affirmation that only a father can truly express.

Kamarie beamed up at him and threw her arms around his neck, burying her face in his shoulder and breathing in the familiar scent of wool and lumber and freshly mown hay. Even when he was king, Arnaud had managed to carry with him the aroma of commonplace things, and now that he had his own farm, the scents of his daily life seemed less incongruous.

Kamarie let out a deep breath as she pulled away. "Don't let me trip."

"Never." The music intensified and Arnaud offered his arm. "Are you ready?"

Kamarie took the proffered arm, the fluttering of butterflies within her stomach growing stronger. "Absolutely."

They walked through the gate into a garden of vibrant color. The night was clear and cool. Lanterns hung along the path, swaying in the gentle breeze and casting their ethereal glow over the small gathering. As she glided on her father's arm past rows of familiar and beloved faces, Kamarie's focus was wholly fixed on the man waiting for her at the end of the garden.

He looked so handsome, standing next to Brant, watching her come towards him. His boots were polished to a fine sheen, and the soft green of his shirt reminded her of the forest canopy. His hair was slightly tousled, though, as if he had run his hands through it. Kamarie felt a little relieved to see this sign of nervousness. It made her feel better about fiddling with the flowers in her hair.

When they reached the end of the garden path, Oraeyn stepped forward to take Kamarie's arm. Arnaud kissed her cheek and then turned to sit beside Zara. Kamarie held Oraeyn's hands and gazed into his eyes. The love she saw there washed through her in an overwhelming flood, calming the fluttering of her stomach. Then he winked, and she bit back a giggle.

"In the sight of Cruithaor Elchiyl and before their family and friends, Oraeyn and Kamarie have come today to pledge their hearts, hands, and lives to one another," Brant spoke the traditional words. He nodded to Yole, who came forward with a length of golden cord.

Fingers intertwined, Oraeyn and Kamarie held their arms up as Yole looped the cord loosely around their wrists.

"Now you are bound together with a tie not easy to break," Brant said. "Grow in wisdom and love that your marriage may be ever strong, that your love may last in this life and beyond. Will you speak the words of that pledge together now?"

"My beloved, my friend, my wife," Oraeyn said, tones of love pouring from his lips with every word. "I pledge my heart to you, now and forevermore. Where you are, there I will be. I will love you and care for you until the end of our days. The path you walk, I shall walk with you."

A lump rose in Kamarie's throat and she felt all her emotions welling up in an attempt to tumble out together. She cleared her throat and Oraeyn squeezed her fingers gently, reassuringly.

"My beloved, my friend, my husband," Kamarie's voice was soft and overflowing with love. "I pledge my heart to you, now and forevermore. Where you are, there I will be. I will love you and care for you until the end of our days. The path you walk, I shall walk with you."

Brant nodded once more, and Yole removed the golden cord from their wrists. Brant handed Oraeyn a ring. Oraeyn turned to Kamarie, holding her hand up and slipping the small circlet— crafted in an intricate pattern designed to look as though bands of silver had been woven together—onto her finger.

"I take you, my heart, at Toreth's rise and at the setting of the stars, to love and to honor through all that may come in all our lives."

"It is completed," Brant said. Then he grinned. "Oraeyn, you may kiss your wife."

It wasn't a huge wedding, but the celebration lasted long into the night. Oraeyn danced with his bride as Kiernan played several pieces of music he had written specifically for the occasion which he presented as humbly as he knew how. Friends and family offered their congratulations and said words of blessing and peace to them, but Oraeyn did not notice any of it. Kamarie was the epicenter of his entire being, and he could spare no thought for anyone or anything else.

She was radiant with her long hair flowing down her back in loose waves, lavender flowers braided into a crown around her head; her entire being sparkled with starlight and laughter and love. She thanked their guests graciously, with a poise and elegance that Oraeyn envied and adored.

As he spun her around the garden, the perfume of night blooming flowers wafted on the barest breeze. He pulled her close.

"I love you," he whispered in her ear. "I love you, Kamarie."

She sighed and leaned her head against his shoulder. "I love you, too."

CHAPTER
TWENTY-NINE

A full six months after Oraeyn and Kamarie's wedding, the people of Tellurae Aquaous gathered on Emnolae to witness an historic event. Brant knelt on the dais in the massive throne room of the Hall of the Great Kings as Kiernan raised a crown above his head and spoke the solemn words. The room was filled with a captive audience, and many more stood outside the great doors, listening and craning to catch a glimpse of the new High King. He wrapped his fingers around the hilt of the Fang Blade and fought down the rise of panic welling within him.

I never wanted this, the thought reverberated throughout his mind. *I did not seek this out.*

And yet, as Kiernan Kane lowered the circlet of gold onto his head, Brant felt a renewal of purpose fill his soul. It was hard to admit that he had been floundering for the past few years, searching for a new direction. But it was true. Guiding and mentoring Oraeyn and Jemson as they took their thrones had given him meaning, but both young men were more than ready to stand on their own. Brant knew in his heart that his advice was no longer vital to either of their kingdoms. They may not know it or believe it yet, but he did. It was time for him to distance himself as a mentor so they could stand on their own as kings.

Brant rose and turned to face the audience, his people. A cheer greeted him and he raised a grateful hand in response, his gaze seeking out one face more dear to him than the others. He found Dylanna, and he shrugged at her slightly, questioning. She suppressed a small smile and nodded her approval and Brant's heart filled with an emotion he had denied for far too long.

"Friends," he began, "I want to thank you for making the long journey to witness this event. As a token of my thanks, I would like to invite you to join us for a celebratory feast."

The crowd dispersed, following stewards and hosts to the largest of the ballrooms, where tables were set and waiting. Brant was concerned that they would not all fit, and yet the room managed to accommodate every guest, and still have plenty of room for dancing.

Brant had not been keen on the idea of a formal coronation or celebration, but Dylanna had convinced him that it was necessary.

"The people need to celebrate," she had reminded him gently. "In the ruins that are the wake of Ghrendourak's march, everyone is aware that the only victory we can claim is that of survival. Even Kiernan Kane keeps muttering dolefully about how the true enemy hasn't been defeated, but is biding his time until he rises again. Truly, I've never seen him in such a foul mood. I don't know if he is even aware that others can hear him, or how it affects their morale. A celebration is needed, and you are all we have. Besides, it will be a good reminder that there is now a king on the High King's throne. And it will also be a good time for the kings you now serve to pay the homage due your new position."

Brant had muttered beneath his breath, sounding every bit as sour and pessimistic as the minstrel, but eventually he agreed that Dylanna was right and made no further complaints.

He stood now at the head of the room, greeting people as they came to meet him, speaking a word or two with each of his guests. He took in the array of colorful garments, the happy faces, and the way the bright candlelight chased away the shade of grief haunting each face and was forced to admit Dylanna's wisdom, but then, she had always understood people better than he.

At long last, the line of people dwindled and Brant felt himself relax as he finished speaking to the last guest. His stomach was rumbling. Brant took a half step towards the nearest table, everything looked delicious.

"Your Majesty," a new voice made him pause. He had been so sure the line of guests had come to an end. He gave a little sigh and turned to stare directly into a most welcome face.

He relaxed. "Dylanna."

"I brought you a plate of food. You could have excused yourself to go eat, you know. The guests would have waited."

"I didn't want to make them wait. I serve them, now. I wanted them to feel that I was available from the start."

"Your humility is your strength, but an attitude like that will bring you to your knees in exhaustion in under a month," Dylanna's lips quirked to the side. "You are going to need a good staff around you that will protect you from yourself."

"You sound as if you have some people in mind." Brant took the proffered plate of food and took a bite of a delicacy he did not recognize. It was delicious. He took a moment to just enjoy the flavor.

"A few," Dylanna admitted.

"Whoever cooked this," he said as he took another bite. "I want them on staff."

Dylanna shook her head, chuckling. "That can be arranged."

Brant cocked his head to the side, a thoughtful expression on his face. "Want to help me find a good staff for this place? I think the palace will take care of itself to some extent, but it's kind of big for just me."

"You are planning on living here, then?"

Brant nodded. "I didn't want to, at first, but there's a connection between me and the palace. And it's been getting stronger. I think it has something to do with Yorien's Hand. I'm sure I'll spend the rest of my life trying to figure out what exactly Yorien's Hand is, and how holding its power is going to affect me."

"I see." Dylanna turned her head and stared across the room of people engaged in laughter, conversation, and dancing. She turned back, a bright smile on her face, but there was a hint of sorrow in her expression. "Of course, I'd be happy to help you find a staff."

Brant finished chewing his last bite of food, swallowed, and handed the plate to an accommodating server. Then he reached for Dylanna's hand, taking it in his own.

"That is good to hear," he said, earnestly. "You are a dear friend, Dylanna."

She made a small sound in her throat that resembled a whimper, but she smiled thinly at him. She opened her mouth to reply, but Brant put a finger to his lips.

He knelt down, and a hush spread across the room as his movement attracted the attention of the guests. "But you're also so much more than a friend. I'm not one for grand gestures, Dylanna. You know me enough to know that I don't show my heart very often. However, you are very dear to me, and you are worth a little embarrassment and a grand gesture. I love you, Dylanna. Will you marry me?"

Dylanna gave a soft gasp and covered her mouth with the fingers of her free hand. Then she knelt down and threw her arms around his neck.

"Yes," she gasped, laughing and crying all at once.

The guests broke into wild applause and cheering and Brant rose, lifting Dylanna with him and then leaning forward to kiss her. She beamed at him and he offered her his arm.

"Care to dance?"

"Well, it's about time," Kamarie said to Oraeyn as Brant led Dylanna out onto the dance floor.

He smiled down at her and pulled her close before spinning her around. Music filled the room. Thousands of candles hung above them, held aloft in diamond chandeliers. Outside, the glittering stars had crept down from the heavens to peer in at the windows in honor of the new High King. The ballroom was filled with kings and queens from every land, as well as noblemen, merchants, shepherds, and farmers.

The women wore silk and satin gowns, which rustled when they moved. Entertainers were at the front of the room playing music together, and myth-folk in human form could be glimpsed throughout the gathering, if one knew how to spot them. There were many people from Llycaelon and Aom-igh, but those faces Oraeyn was most familiar with were lost in the sea of guests, for neither Oraeyn nor Kamarie had seen anybody they knew more than once.

He studied Brant as he danced with Dylanna. He had never seen the man looking so relaxed or happy. The Fang Blade hung at his side, gleaming with unparalleled brilliance in the ceremonial crystal sheath that had been designed for it by the dragons as a coronation present. His clothing was well-made, but as unadorned as the simple gold circlet on his head.

"True power doesn't need to be flaunted, it speaks for itself," Brant had once told Oraeyn, and he embodied that statement now as he stood before the crowd that had gathered to acknowledge him as their new High King.

Looking at Brant now, Oraeyn realized that the man had been right. Every move Brant made spoke paragraphs. There was nothing flashy or pretentious about his appearance. It was just something about his mien: the way he carried himself, a tilt of his head, the way he held his shoulders, his stance, the graceful but authoritative way he strode across the room. He was authority and justice, strong and valiant, every inch a king. When Oraeyn looked at him, there was no question about who Brant was or whether or not he was the right person to claim the throne. He simply *was* the High King. This was the man who would bring worlds together, the man under whom peace would reign.

The celebration lasted long into the night. It was nearly dawn when Oraeyn, Kamarie, Dylanna, Yole, and Brant stole away to a cozy den where they could relax and just enjoy a few moments of peace together. They sat and stared up through the tall windows, watching the glimmering stars and basking in the welcome peace after all the noise of celebration.

"It's never going to be the same again, is it?" Oraeyn asked. "No more adventures."

Brant put a reassuring hand on Oraeyn's shoulder. "There will always be adventures in life, Oraeyn. You and Kamarie have recently begun a brand new chapter of life. I promise, your adventures have only just begun."

Oraeyn pulled Kamarie close and kissed her temple. "That's true."

Yole stretched. "There will be more adventures for us," he said confidently through a great yawn, "I can feel it."

The others laughed, and then after a while they fell silent again, enjoying the quiet company of friends. As the Toreth began to approach its zenith, Oraeyn noticed that Brant and Dylanna were sneaking glances at each other, but trying to be inconspicuous about it. He understood their desire to be alone for a little while, so he sighed and rose.

"Well, it has been a long day, a long several months, really," he announced, "and I, for one, am ready for bed."

He took Kamarie's hand, and she stood with him. There were hugs all around, and then Yole agreed that it was past time to be asleep and he rose as well. Brant smiled at Oraeyn gratefully.

"Goodnight my friends. I wish you a restful night. I will see you in the morning to say farewell before you return to Aom-igh. However, I'm not quite tired yet. I think I will go walk through the garden for a bit." He looked to Dylanna. "Would you care to join me?"

Dylanna flushed. "I think I would," she said. "I am not all that tired yet either."

Kamarie looked around. "Where *is* Kiernan? Shouldn't he be here with us?"

"Do you remember him leaving the celebration?" Oraeyn asked.

"No," Yole said. "I remember him playing with the

musicians for a while, though. He really is as good as he claims, you know."

"That he is," Brant agreed, chuckling softly. "It's maddening. But I'm starting to appreciate it." He rose and offered his arm to Dylanna. "Since you asked, Kiernan left quite some time ago. He told me he was needed elsewhere." Brant gave a small shake of his head. "I will never understand him, but I am starting to get used to him."

Kamarie watched fondly as Dylanna threaded her arm through Brant's and the two exited the room, heads close together as they conversed in soft tones. Then she yawned and Oraeyn suggested they retire to bed. Kamarie agreed. They had a long journey ahead of them come morning, but at the end of it all home awaited them. Oraeyn found that his heart was eager to return home. He cast a look back towards the gardens where Brant and Dylanna's forms were mere silhouettes against the star-sprinkled sky. It was good that the world had a High King to aid in the aftermath of the ruin Ghrendourak and his armies had wrought. But Oraeyn also found that he was a little apprehensive about the future, knowing that Brant would no longer be there for him in quite the same capacity as mentor and teacher. He would need to stand on his own, now. He gazed at Kamarie and amended his thoughts. He did not stand alone. As Yole had said and Brant had intimated, the best adventures were yet to come.

EPILOGUE

Mandolin strapped to his back, Kiernan Kane stood outside the Hall of the High Kings. Quietly, he watched through the tall windows as the lights were extinguished, one by one. At long last, the castle slumbered and the only light that remained was the cool, silvery light of the Toreth. Humming to himself the minstrel turned and faced the road before him. He did not know where this path would take him, but he knew where he was going. He might not know the exact words of the story ahead, but he knew his role within it. He was indeed a wanderer, a teller of stories, a troubadour, but mostly he was, as ever, the Minstrel. His humming increased and then he began to sing softly,

> *"When what could be*
> *Might have been*
> *We stop to think*
> *Then think again.*
>
> *Awaking from the dream-world*
> *Once more*
> *Methinks I've traveled*
> *This road before…"*

Ghrendourak was defeated, and the ease with which that

defeat had occurred was quite telling. The Ancient Enemy had shown his hand—his chains were breaking, and he would soon be free to roam the world once more. Kiernan needed to prepare. The pieces in the game had been chosen and placed. Now all that remained was to wait for the first move.

For now, Kiernan would wander for a while, and during his wanderings he would find them: the ones who needed his stories and songs. They might be people who had despaired so long that they had forgotten how to be merry: he would teach them how to laugh. He would seek out those who needed to remember sorrow and find a way to bring a tear to their eyes. Perhaps there were those who had forgotten compassion; he would teach them kindness. And for those who knew only fear, or who had forgotten their own nobility, Kiernan would remind them of courage and teach them justice and truth.

And when the battle began, he would return from his wanderings and take up his place amongst the people he had come to love best. He had wandered many long years. But despite the countless faces stored in his memory, these were the ones who touched his heart. They were dearest to him of any others he had come to know in all his travels. It was at their sides he would stand when the Enemy arose for the final time.

"And thus, it ends," the words fell from his lips with ringing finality. "The final pieces have been chosen, the final game is begun."

Deep beneath the Nameless Isles, the imprisoned one shook in his chains. Staring down at the Karradoc board before him, he gnashed his teeth in frustration.

"You knew all along, didn't you?" he growled. "You knew the boy with the golden blade was not the one of whom the prophecy spoke. Well played, brother. Well played. But the time for misdirection has now passed. Your pieces are chosen. Let the game begin!"

Maniacal laughter bubbled up within him and echoed around him. His host had been defeated, but he had expected no less. It was not this battle that mattered, but the war, and he was closer than ever to victory. Cracks and fissures spiderwebbed across the cobalt walls of his prison, and his chains weakened as he called his power back to himself from the empty shell of his defeated host. He had not exerted himself in this battle. Instead, he had held back, allowing a faint trickle of his power to manifest within Ghrendourak, just enough to fool his enemy.

Soon, soon he would be able to break free of this prison and take a form for himself, and not just any form, but his own, true shape, and then how the world would tremble before him. The little mortal creatures would bow to him and serve him as he had always known they should. He would take his birthright, the right that had been denied him for far too long. And then, at long last, the glory for which he had been created would be within his grasp, and he would never relinquish it. Never. And none would challenge him ever again.

"And as for my brother," he allowed himself to revel in the pleasure of his fantasy for a long moment, "my ancient enemy shall occupy this exact prison for the rest of eternity. But first, I will make him pay dearly for his betrayal. I will have him see everything he loves crushed and broken beneath my feet, and then I shall banish him here to dwell in his defeat, in his failure, for all time. Let him bask in his supposed victory for now," he whispered into the emptiness surrounding him. "The end of all he holds dear is coming. Soon...."

GLOSSARY

Aethelon (ay-ETH-eh-lahn): The name for warriors of Llycaelon

Aetoli (AY-eh-TOLL-ee): The most elite rank of Aethalon

Aom-igh (AY-ome-EYE): A small country to the west of Llycaelon

Arnaud (ar-NAWD): Former king of Aom-igh. Kamarie's father

Artair (are-TARE): A Great King who first pulled the fabled sword from the stone

Ayollan (AY-ōl-ăn): Capital city of Aom-igh

Brant (BRANT): Youngest son of the royal family of Llycaelon

Caethyr Gap (KAY-eth-er Gap): A hole in the wall of Llycaelon's defenses on the north-western border

Calla (CAH-luh): Young Rambler girl, friend from Brant's past

Calyssia (cuh-LEE-see-ah): A wizardess, first daughter of Scelwhyn

Change-Term: Autumn

Chareel (shar-EEL): A constellation

Colas (KOH-lahs): A middle-aged man who lives on Emnolae

Cold-Term: Winter

Cruithaor Elchiyl (KREW-thay-ore ell-KEEL): The Creator

Delmar (DELL-mar): Captain of the "Silver Hydra"

Devrin (DEV-rin): An aethalon assigned to the Border Patrol near the Caethyr Gap

Dracor (DRAY-kor): One of the many kinds of werefolk, like shadowy wingless dragons

Dragon's Eye, The: The sun

Dru (DREW): A thief and friend from Brant's past

Dylanna (dĭ-LAHN-ah): A wizardess, daughter of Scelwhyn

Efoin-Ebedd (EH-foyn—EB-ehd): Country to the east of Llycaelon

Emnolae (EMM-no-lay): A country to the south of Llycaelon

Etharae Ocean (ETH-air-ay): Ocean between Llycaelon and Emnolae

Garen (GAIR-ehn): Last student of Scelwhyn, knight of Aom-igh, Kamarie's instructor and mentor

Ghrendourak (gren-DOOR-ak): The creature being used by the Ancient Enemy in an attempt to rule the world and break free from his prison

Hydra (HI-druh): Sea serpents that often attack unwary ships

Ina (EEN-uh): A blind woman who has the gift of sight

Kallayohm (kǎ-LAY-ōme): A country to the southeast of Llycaelon

Kamarie Lynelle (kuh-MARR-ee lih-NELL): Princess of Aom-igh

Kane, Kiernan (KANE, KEE-YAIR-nen): A wandering minstrel

Kessella (KEH-sell-uh): A powerful unicorn

Khoranaderek (KOR-uh-NAH-dur-ik): A dragon from Llycaelon

Jemson (JEM-sun): Ruler of Llycaelon, Brant's nephew

Justan (JUS-tin): A trusted knight in Oraeyn's kingdom

Leila (lee-Ī-luh): A wizardess, third daughter of Scelwhyn

Llycaelon (lie-KAY-ell-on): The true name of the "Dark Country"

New-Term: Spring

Queen Fiora (fee-YOR-uh): The queen of Llycaelon, mother of Brant

Rena (REE-nuh): Woman from Aom-igh, has the ability to play the magical Dragon Pipes, mother to Kaitryn, wife of Justan

Rhendak (ren-DAK): King of the Dragons

Rhoyan (ROY-ehn): Brant's name when he was a child

Scelwhyn (SELL-win): A wizard

Seamas (SHAW-mus): Jemson's father and Brant's older brother

Seheowks (SEE-owks): Dark creatures of magic, another race of werefolk

Tellurae Aquaous (TELL-yure-eye AH-kway-ose): The world

Toreth (TOR-eth): The moon

Warm-Term: Summer

Whyvrens (WIV-rehns): Another race of werefolk, have deadly stingers, are extremely powerful, and can spray darkness like a web

Yochathain (YAW-kah-thane): Country west of the Nameless Isles

Yorien (YORE-ee-ehn): A constellation

Zara (ZAR-ah): Former queen of Aom-igh, mother of Kamarie

Turn the page to read the prologue of

MINSTREL'S CALL
the final installment of the Minstrel's Song

Coming Soon!

Read on for a sneak preview of the final book in The Minstrel's Song

MINSTREL'S CALL

Coming Soon

It was dawn when my brothers and I awoke for the first time. Brightness assailed my eyes as I stared about, blinking in confusion and curiosity. I was aware of others about me, but my attention was drawn solely to a single *presence* that filled me with joy and awe. I glanced about, exercising my new eyesight. A blinding light slashed across my vision, making it necessary to cover my eyes. I lifted my wings to my face. Astonishment thrilled throughout my being to find that I had wings. I stared for a moment at them, blinking as they shielded me from the incredible brightness that had nearly taken my newfound sight from me. My wings were a deep golden hue, with flecks of red and orange dancing through them. They were filled with moving energy and covered in feathers of flame that danced in dazzling, mesmerizing patterns. When I had overcome the wonder of seeing my wings I found that I could see through them, and now that my wings stood between myself and the source of the great light I could see clearly the one who had awoken me. His face was full of such power, compassion, and wisdom that I quickly covered my feet as a sign of respect with another set of wings. It was then I discovered that I had a total of six wings. As I looked into the face of the one who had awoken me, self-awareness and knowledge of who it was that stood before me filled the core of my being. It was as if I had gone from infant to adult in the blink of an eye.

"My dear one," his voice was beautiful and terrible and I shuddered to think that he was addressing one so lowly as I, "thou shalt be called 'Aloysius' which means 'Guide to mankind and Warrior of the Lord.' This name gives you great honor and places on you a great task if you are willing."

There was a moment of choice, and my heart quailed at the unknown task laid before me. I trembled, but then I looked into his eyes and drew courage, "Yes, Lord. I do accept this task, and

I thank thee for the responsibility." There was bright joy on his face and my spirit soared at his smile.

"The time is not yet, dear one, but it will soon come, when thou shalt leave on thy errand." He spoke gently, but I must confess that I was terrified.

"Leave, my Lord?" I asked timidly.

He nodded silently, but said no more. He turned from me to greet my brothers. The knowledge of the burden I must someday carry weighed heavily on my heart, but it also filled me with a thrill of excitement. There was a strangeness to the way He had spoken, though, some quality in his tone I did not understand and could not place. Little did I comprehend that my Creator had spoken with sadness in his voice, for I was not yet acquainted with sadness. I only knew the joy of His presence and the wonder of praising Him. All too soon would I learn sorrow and anger and pain.

I listened and heard my brothers being named: Malachi the glorious, Stanislaus the steadfast, Gaebreil the strong, Haeronymous the one chosen for glory, and many others; their names were powerful, but a question formed in my mind as the naming continued. I nearly felt impatience as I waited to ask my question. I *did* wait, however, until all had been named and then I cried out in desperation.

"Lord! Tell us *your* name: that we might proclaim your praises better." I do not know what made the words pour from my throat, and I wished that I had held my tongue. I did not know fear, and I did not know shame, but I did wish that I had remained silent. But then he was there, lifting my face and looking kindly into my eyes. There was no rebuke in his face, merely love and joy.

"You were well named, guide of mankind," he beamed, and the glory of his smile nearly blinded me, even through the shield of my fiery wings. "You will serve me well and teach the ones I will create. Your task will be to guide them into knowledge of me. Your question is good, my child, for how can you teach who I am if you do not know my name? I have many names, but in this time and in the place to which I will send you you will call me Cruithaor Elchiyl, Almighty Creator Lord; for that is the name by which I would be recognized."

It was then that my brother Haeronymous began a chant of praise and we all joined in, knowing the words well for they were written on our hearts. I do not remember how long the chant lasted, but the chorus repeated again and again. Each verse was new and beautiful, and as our voices blended together Cruithaor Elchiyl spun amazing things into existence. It was a delight to declare his praises! Joy made my spirit soar into the limitless vastness of the heavens and I felt wondrously complete. I could have remained forever, watching the creativity of Cruithaor Elchiyl, but alas, it was not to be.